More praise for

DUE PREPARATIONS FOR THE PLAGUE

Winner of the Queensland Premier's Literary Award for Fiction
Winner of the Patrick White Award
A finalist for the Adelaide Festival Award
Nominated for the Miles Franklin Award
Nominated for the New South Wales Premier's Literary Award
A *Toronto Globe & Mail* Best Book of 2003

"Hospital is a writer of many gifts; her dark imagination, astute insights into societal interactions and the supple beauty of her prose, provide an irresistible combination. . . . A thought-provoking glimpse of the sociopolitical intricacies of the individuals and organizations that track terrorism."
—*Publishers Weekly*, starred review

"Every now and then a book comes along that's scarily, almost prophetically, in step with the times. . . . [*Due Preparations for the Plague*] is gripping, the prose beautiful, the characters sympathetic and believable."
—*Time Out New York*

"The works and words of Janette Turner Hospital are richly imbued with a highly lyrical and luminous quality . . . compelling, mesmerizing and poetically ethereal."
—Gordon Hauptfleisch, *San Diego Union Tribune*

"Hospital asks us to confront a world where government 'intelligence' has become the ultimate weapon of mass destruction, but she shows us that destruction in the most intimate of terms."
—Bill Ott, *Booklist*, starred review

"Hospital's novel is a contemporary ride into the heart of darkness.

. . . [It] wades through the shadowy currents of a world that usually . . . remains below the water line of our everyday lives."
—Ellen Emry Heltzel, *Times Post Intelligencer*

"Hospital has crafted a novel of fiercely powerful emotions and deeply unsettling implications." —Lawrence Rungren, *Library Journal*

"In elegant and restrained passages, Turner Hospital examines the preparations for death, weaving her meditation out of the way in which the final victims make amends, showing reparation and preparation are inextricably bound together." —Lorna Gibb, *Times Literary Supplement*

"An act of terrorism is the specter that haunts the maddeningly real characters in Janette Turner Hospital's brilliant novel *Due Preparations for the Plague*." —Jim Fusilli, *Boston Globe*

"[*Due Preparations for the Plague*] combines driving story telling with a genuine inquiry into complicity and the reaping of sown seeds."
—Elisabeth Lindner, *Miami Herald*

"By turns a character study and espionage thriller in which Janette Turner Hospital takes her audience on a roller coaster ride that chills the audience with spasms of uncontrolled emotions."
—Harriet Klausner, *Midwest Book Review*

"Compelling." —*Daily News*

"A mesmerizing tale of grief, mystery and revelation."
—Gregory Harris, *BookPage*

"Hospital continually locates, in inhuman events, the unyieldingly human experience." —Megan Harlan, *San Francisco Chronicle*

"An elegant writer . . . brilliantly brutal."

—Rebecca Ascher-Walsh, *Entertainment Weekly*

"Astonishing. . . . [A] literary tour de force. . . . Constantly innovative and authentic, this is a brilliant novel for our disturbing times."

—citation of judges for Queensland Premier's Literary Award

"A novelist of cool intelligence . . . her labyrinthine plot, which shifts breathlessly through time and space . . . owes less to Tom Clancy than to Jorge Luis Borges. . . . At the heart of horror, Turner Hospital finds an unlikely note of loveliness—and salvation of sorts through storytelling."

—*Time*

"A densely layered tale of international terrorism, political intrigue and deceit in the mode of John le Carré, . . . a thriller with existential underpinnings that attends to the big question of the human condition and the nature of evil itself."

—*Sydney Morning Herald*

"Janette Turner Hospital writes so passionately about death, you instinctively know she is in love with life. *Due Preparations for the Plague* carries you on a fast trek through the dark alleys of terror, love, loneliness and living."

—*The West Australian*

"A complex, multi-layered work with a plot that functions beautifully in its own right, but one that is also a mechanism for a profound exploration of the most important questions we ask ourselves."

—*The Age*, Melbourne

"Complex, riveting, timely, and quite brilliant. Turner Hospital's skill in creating the skewed universe of intelligence is so impressive I can't help wondering if she herself, in the course of her research, came under surveillance."

—*New Zealand Herald*

"Janette Turner Hospital's new novel has been getting across-the-board raves the likes of which haven't been seen since Don DeLillo's *Underworld*. . . . The book achieves that rare combination of timeliness and timelessness, all the more impressively by making the two seem one and the same. . . . While it looks without blinking into some of the darkest corners of the human condition, the effect, as in any great work of art, is finally uplifting." —*Montreal Gazette*

"[*Due Preparations for the Plague*'s] mood finds resonance, as well as moments of human grace, in the shadows of global affairs that both the pawns and kings who set them in motion find impossible to control." —Keith Phillips, *The Onion*

"A truly brilliant story . . . rarely does an espionage story seem as eerily prescient as the stunning new novel from Janette Turner Hospital." —Peter Handel, *Pages*

"Janette Turner Hospital deeply understands that the dead are not the only victims of terrorism. As if she were taking us behind today's headlines where public and private intersect, she imagines families—especially the children—whose lives are mutilated by secrets and atrocious events beyond the power of love and loyalty. This is a rich and powerfully imagined novel of chilling timeliness." —Rosellen Brown

"Janette Turner Hospital is a writer of consummate craft and visionary insight. She is always surprising, and seems always to be renewing herself as one of our major writers." —Joyce Carol Oates

"A race though the inner precincts of terror and espionage, *Due Preparations for the Plague* is harrowing and intense and ultimately redemptive." —Richard Rhodes

By the same author

The Ivory Swing

The Tiger in the Tiger Pit

Borderline

Dislocations

Charades

Isobars

The Last Magician

Collected Stories

Oyster

DUE PREPARATIONS FOR THE PLAGUE

DUE PREPARATIONS FOR THE PLAGUE

Janette Turner Hospital

W. W. NORTON & COMPANY • NEW YORK • LONDON

The author wishes to express her thanks to Lieutenant Colonel (Ret.) M. G. McKeown for information on biochemical warfare and on the use of gas masks and protective clothing. Any misinterpretation or misunderstanding of this material is entirely the author's responsibility.

Printed in the United States of America
First published as a Norton paperback 2004

Manufacturing by The Haddon Craftsmen, Inc.
Production manager: Amanda Morrison

Library of Congress Cataloging-in-Publication Data

Hospital, Janette Turner, 1942–
Due preparations for the plague / by Janette Turner Hospital.—1st ed.
p. cm.
ISBN 0-393-05764-X (hardcover)
1. Child witnesses—Fiction. 2. Victims of terrorism—Fiction. 3. Hijacking of aircraft—Fiction. 4. Murder victims' families—Fiction. I. Title.
PR9619.3.H674D84 2003
823'.914—dc21 2002156598
ISBN 0-393-32573-3 pbk.

W. W. Norton & Company, Inc.
500 Fifth Avenue, New York, N.Y. 10110
www.wwnorton.com

W. W. Norton & Company Ltd.
Castle House, 75/76 Wells Street, London W1T 3QT

1 2 3 4 5 6 7 8 9 0

CONTENTS

BOOK I . . . . .OLD MOLE 3

BOOK II . . . . .FOG 47

BOOK III . . . . . .CODE NAME: BLACK DEATH 101

BOOK IV . . . . .VANISHING POINTS 169

BOOK V . . . . . . .JOURNAL OF S: ENCRYPTED 221

BOOK VI .IN THE MARSH 275

BOOK VII . . . . .THE DECAMERON TAPE 303

BOOK VIII .AFTERMATH 365

I have often asked myself what I mean by preparations for the plague . . . and I think that preparations for the plague are preparations for death. But what is it to make preparations for death? or what preparations are proper to be made for death?

—DANIEL DEFOE, **DUE PREPARATIONS FOR THE PLAGUE** (1722)

To state quite simply what we learn in a time of pestilence: that there are more things to admire in men than to despise.

–ALBERT CAMUS, **THE PLAGUE**

DUE PREPARATIONS FOR THE PLAGUE

Book I

OLD MOLE

Hamlet (to the ghost of his father):
Well said, old mole! cans't work in the earth so fast?

—HAMLET, ACT I, SCENE V

Nobody chooses his parents,
but everyone invents them.

—ADAM PHILLIPS

1.

Brightness falls from the air, and so do the words, which rush him. They swoop like starlings from the radio hooked to his belt, though before *brightness,* before *Queens have died young and fair,* the broadcast was blurred murmur, bits of music, bits of talk, voices heard but not listened to. Now the phrases flock about Lowell and he bats at them, distressed. *Dust hath closed Helen's eye, I am sick, I must die*—but no, Lowell thinks, I must not—*Lord, have mercy on us,* and yes, Lowell prays, Lord have mercy, because in spite of the fact that the reader has a mellow voice, a soothing and expensive poetry-reading voice, an unmistakably National Public Radio voice, what Lowell can hear is his own father in shadow duet, word for word and line for line, and then suddenly, with a sharp change of tone, *Forty thousand feet,* he hears, *severed fuselage . . . the fatal plunge. . . .*

Shocked, he almost loses his balance on the ladder. *Death,* he hears, and it is plummeting at him, no question, *final cure of all diseases.* The news commentator says these words. (Does he really say them? Is it possible?) The paint can, mad rudder, swings wild and a length of eavestrough comes away in Lowell's hand. He throws himself forward across the steeply pitched roof and lies sprawled there. The tiles beat against his heart like frightened birds.

Oblivion has taken to offering herself this way, quick and shameless. She tries it once or twice a week. She sickens him because he is not immune to her whorish charms. He can feel the ladder with his feet and if he puts his weight on the top rung, he thinks the whole contraption of self-erected scaffolding will stay firm. Probably. Perhaps. The brush is still in his right hand, the can of Milky Way White (high gloss, oil-based, exterior finish) in his left. There is a comet's tail of spilled cream across the cedar shakes and he will have to climb down for the turpentine.

Later, he thinks, looking below. He feels queasy. Anniversaries of the airline disaster are a very bad time. Every year, every September, this sort of thing happens, even though every year, as September approaches, he believes he has put it all behind him, he believes he has laid the ghosts, he believes he will feel nothing more than a dull, almost pleasurable sort of pain, like a toothache. And then: *Shazam*, he is a wreck again.

Have the words really come from his radio? Or from the messy attic of his mind? He supposes he could check, call the station, order a cassette, replay the show, and if they really had been spoken, what would that prove? A convergence of inner and outer worlds? Thoughts and fears escape, Lowell thinks. When the pressure inside the head builds too high, thoughts fly the coop and speak themselves back at us through other people's mouths. He dips his brush in the can and paints a long wide stripe on the fascia board. From two stories down, through the window, he can hear the phone ring. The house is not his, but even so he fears it will be that girl again, that young woman, the one who will not let sleeping dogs lie. He knows this is irrational. He knows there is no possible way she could reach him here. Even so, whenever he hears a telephone, he trembles. He fears it will be that young woman. Samantha. That is her name. He never returns her calls.

"There are too many unanswered questions concerning the deaths," she says on his answering machine, but he will not listen. "We are gathering data," she says, because of course Lowell is not the only one to turn manic at anniversary time. "If you are interested, I have extensive information on the hijacking and on the death of your mother."

Lowell erases her messages.

"We have new information," the voice of Samantha says, said, yesterday, last week, the week before, "we have just received startling new information from a woman in Paris," whom Lowell erases from the machine immediately and entirely, though less successfully, less entirely, from his memory and from his sleep, a certain Françoise of the seventh arrondissement in Paris who had intended to be on that flight, *the fateful flight,* that hovers blackly whenever Lowell thinks of it—and even when he does not—like a vulture above his head.

"She has unexpected ties to your father," Samantha says, the voice of Samantha says, speaking of Lowell Hawthorne's father, "which I think will be of interest to you. Of *considerable* interest, I think you will find—"

Lowell cuts off her call.

What people will believe and what they will hope for and what they will do within a thirty-day radius of the anniversary of the hijacking is utterly unpredictable. This is a dangerous time. This is a time when clinical depression is epidemic and the death rate peaks, both for survivors and for relatives of the deceased. Lowell knows about this. "We have information, but we *need* information, we need it desperately," the voice of Samantha cajoles, "so I'm begging you—" Sometimes she cannot speak for sobbing. Sometimes Lowell pulls the jack from the wall.

"This woman in Paris—Françoise—she says she has an avoidance instinct for anything to do with the flight," Samantha tells Lowell's answering machine. "But it's also a magnet. You know that, I know that, we both know that only too well. Which is why she happened on our website. And which is why, eventually, she couldn't resist making contact—" *Erase, erase.* "She thinks your father knew about Flight 64." *Erase.* "Why are you so afraid to speak to me?" *Erase.*

"Listen," Samantha pleads directly into his ear. "You've got to listen. Françoise believes she is your half-sister—"

"I have no siblings, half or otherwise," he says, and hangs up.

"What can be worse than not knowing?" Samantha's voice asks in a rush, anticipating digital cutoff. "The deaths could have been prevented. What can be worse than that?"

The explanation might be worse, Lowell thinks.

Everywhere, his father shrugs, brightness falls from the air. Dust hath closed Helen's eye, his father reminds, and death is merely the final cure of every ill.

But it is after a death, Lowell knows, that riddles and slow torments begin.

2.

In the week of the thirteenth anniversary of his mother's death—four days before the actual date—Lowell cries out in his sleep. There is a lightning flash or an explosion—he does not know what it is—some terrible intrusive slash of sound, white at the center with red capillaries rivering out. It thump-thumps at his eardrums and skin. Pain razors him, and he knows his heart is going to pop like a balloon.

"What is it, what is it, Daddy?" His daughter, barefoot and frightened, appears in the bedroom doorway and he sits bolt upright and holds the pillow like a shield. *Weapon,* his reflexes urge, but as he gropes for the lamp, he sees Amy's eyes and remembers that the children are with him this weekend.

Amy, he says, but a strange sound comes out.

"Daddy, Daddy." Amy is shivering. "Why did you scream?" She pulls at her hair, a nervous habit, and little hanks of it come away in her hand. She always has trouble sleeping at her father's place because her father often talks unintelligibly in sleep, pleading with someone. His sheets smell of wet animal.

The pain, he tries to explain. He lurches around the room, arms outstretched. He thumps on his chest.

"Daddy, Daddy!" she quavers, throwing herself at him, hugging his thighs.

"No," Lowell moans.

Wailing sounds, plaintive as the call of loons in fog, float through the room, and there is Jason, flannelette blanket balled into his mouth, stumbling over his pajama bottoms. Amy runs to him and holds his little face against her chest. "Jason's scared," she says bravely. And then, with an edge of anger: "You're frightening him, Daddy."

Their father turns and fixes them with his eyes. "Did you hear it?"

"Y-y-yes," Jason blubbers, sniffling, wetting his PJs. Amy can feel a trickle of warm pee at the soles of her feet.

"We heard you scream, Daddy."

Lowell is shaking. He bends down and hugs the children to himself. "Poor little fellas," he says. He takes deep slow breaths. "Daddy had a bad dream, that's all. I didn't mean to scare you, pun'kins."

"Daddy?"

"It's sleepy time. Let's go."

He changes Jason's pajamas and tucks the children in and kisses them and sits on the edge of his son's bed. By the greenish glow of the night-light, he croons lullabies and pats his little boy's behind until he hears deep even breathing.

"Daddy?" Amy whispers, as he is tiptoeing out.

"What is it, sweetheart?"

"What did you dream about?"

"I can't remember," he says, and he really can't. He can remember bright light, the electric sense of danger. Tree? Tree struck by lightning? Something to do with a tree and shattered glass. Pieces of metal. A great vulture overhead, as always. He can remember bloodied hands, pulsing heart, *thump-thump, thump-thump*. He can remember not being able to breathe.

"Where do bad dreams go?" Amy wants to know.

"They go down the garbage disposer," Lowell says, "and they get smashed up into little pieces and then they get washed into the Charles

River and carried out into Boston Harbor and they go miles and miles away into the ocean and they never come back."

"Mine come back," she says.

"Oh baby." He sits on her bed and cradles her in his arms. "What do you have bad dreams about?"

"There's one dream," she says, and he can feel her shy away from the telling.

What rotten luck, he thinks, for Amy and Jason to have him, Lowell Hawthorne, for a father, since clearly someone, something, is a jealous keeper of the curse, *visiting the iniquity of the fathers upon the children, even unto the third and fourth generation.* . . . He wishes he had a spell to break the spell.

"Look," he says, snapping his fingers and then blowing on them as though scattering dandelion puffs. "It's gone now, your bad dream. And mine too."

But she is very solemn. "You were driving away," she says. "In my dream. You were driving away in your pickup."

"Did I have my ladders on top?" He has to make this bright and tangibly detailed, slapstick, something light as air. He mimes the sway of the ladders as he drives.

"Yes, and all your paint cans and stuff. And the baby-sitter hasn't come and Jason and me are running and running because we want to get in the pickup with you and you won't stop and you keep shouting that Mommy will come."

"Sweetheart," he says.

"But she doesn't. And we wait and wait, but she never comes, and we are all by ourselves and it gets dark."

"Oh, Amy, baby." He cups her face in his hands. "I will never drive away and leave you, never ever. And you know that Mommy and Daddy would nevernevernever—"

The phone rings and both of them jump. Amy will not let go of her father. She clings to him as he shambles down the hall.

"Yes?" he says. "What? Who is this?

"Yes, this is Lowell Hawthorne.

. . .

"Yes, that . . .

. . .

"Yes.

. . .

"Yes, it is."

Amy feels the muscles in his arm flinch and go still as he listens. He hangs up.

"Daddy?"

He remains leaning against the wall, and Amy, who comes to just above his waist, holds on to him so tightly that she can feel the button on his pajama jacket like a cookie cutter against her cheek. The pain reassures her. She wants to wear his sign. She can smell the wet animal smell again, mixed in with the smell of paint and paint thinner which can never be completely scrubbed off.

"Who was it, Daddy?"

He does not hear, or at any rate does not answer, but scoops her up and carries her back to bed.

"Daddy, who was it?"

"It was nothing," he says. "Nothing to worry your little head over."

"Daddy, if you don't tell me, my dream will come back."

That is the trouble with a curse, Lowell thinks: no eject button. You're stuck with it. Around and around and around forever and ever amen.

"It was a hospital," he says. "In Washington, D.C. Your Grandpa Hawthorne died." *Massive heart attack at the wheel . . . dead on arrival . . . fortunately no other cars on the road . . .*

"How did he die, Daddy?"

"His car crashed into a tree."

Lowell can hear the sound of impact, the flying glass. He remembers that in his dream he could not breathe.

3.

Lowell thinks that his losses may have become simple at last. He thinks they may have become simple and respectable and therefore manageable. He thinks he will be able to speak of them almost lightly. *My mother died in that airline disaster of '87 when I was sixteen years old,* he will be able to say, *and the effect on my father was devastating. Our lives were never the same.*

He tries out a version of this first with Amy and Jason three days after his father's death, the day before he flies down for the funeral in Washington. His ex-wife has agreed to his pleas for an extra visit, "but try not to upset them," she warns, when she drops the children off. "I mean it, Lowell."

"I won't," he promises, and indeed, he has no intention of discussing dark matters, but Amy has her grandfather's wrecked vehicle very much on her mind. From the window of her father's apartment, she watches cars pass. "Which ones will crash into a tree?" she wants to know.

"None of them," Lowell reassures her. "Your grandpa's car crash," he explains, "wasn't an ordinary . . . it was a different sort of thing. It's not the first time in our family, pun'kin. I've never told you how your grandma died, but she was in a terrible accident too, and that affected Grandpa, you see."

"I don't like cars," Amy says. Her lips quiver. She hangs on to the sleeve of her father's sweater with one hand. "Did Grandma's car hit a tree too?"

"No. No, no, oh no, sweetheart, that was something totally different. Grandma was on a plane and the plane was hijacked."

"What's *hijacked?*"

"Some bad men with machine guns wouldn't let her plane fly back to New York."

Huge-eyed, Amy digests this information. "Where did it go?" she asks.

"Well, it went to other places where it wasn't supposed to go, and then it landed in Germany and all the children got off the plane, because nobody, not even bad men, wants children to get hurt."

"Did Grandma get off the plane?"

"No," he says. "The plane took off again, and then it landed somewhere else and then it blew up and everyone was killed."

Amy begins to cry. "But maybe Grandma wasn't on it then," Lowell adds hurriedly, appalled with himself. "Maybe the bad men let her get off somewhere else first, because they said they did that. They took ten hostages off the plane before they— That's what they said on TV. So maybe your grandma—"

Amy is sobbing convulsively, gasping for air. "I want Mommy," she says.

"Yes," Lowell says, panicky, "right. I'll drive you back to Mommy's place now, okay?"

"I don't want to go in your pickup," Amy sobs. She seems to be choking. A thin stream of bile trickles over her chin, and when Lowell wipes her mouth with a tissue, she throws up over his hand. "I want . . . Mommy . . . to come . . . and get us."

"I'll call her, I'm calling her now," Lowell promises. Amy's eye sockets look dark and bruised, and there is a bluish tinge to her lips. He holds her while he dials her mother's number.

Rowena, his former wife, is exasperated. "I was afraid of this," she says. "I'll be right there." In his driveway, she says despairingly, "For God's sake, Lowell. As if their nightmares weren't vivid enough. You have to tell them about planes blowing up."

"Oh God." Lowell rakes his fingers through his hair. He knows he is incurably inept.

"They already have counseling once a week," Rowena says. "Jason's been wetting the bed ever since you moved out."

"That wasn't my choice," Lowell reminds her.

"Especially when you are *flying* down for the funeral," she says. "When they know you'll be on a plane."

"Rowena, couldn't you come too? Couldn't we bring them? Don't you think that might—"

"Out of the question," Rowena says. She says it quietly, more in disbelief than in anger. "Lowell, are you completely blind? Every time they're with you, Amy runs a fever afterwards, and Jason wets the bed."

Lowell, stricken with remorse, leans in the back window to kiss his children goodbye, but they flinch away from him slightly before submitting. He feels the pain of this like a razor blade in his heart. He is never sure which might inflict greater damage: not spending enough time with his children, or spending time with them. He is highly infectious with doom. "I'm sorry, Rowena." It is his own desolate experience that there is nothing anyone can do. Nothing will shelter children from life. The young, the fragile, the vulnerable, all are at catastrophic risk. "I guess I thought, you know, if I told them about the hijacking, it might explain why their grandfather—"

"Call them when you get there," Rowena says crossly. "And call them when you get back. Otherwise they will worry themselves sick."

"Yes," he promises.

"Oh, Lowell," she says, not without tenderness. "You're such a mess."

He thinks of telling her that things might begin to improve. It could be different now.

"And you won't do anything about it," she says. "You're *stuck,* and you don't even try to get *unstuck.*"

You don't even try. The injustice of this is so monumental that Lowell can think of nothing to say.

Rowena turns the key in the ignition. "And for heaven's sake," she says in parting, "when you get back, get a new muffler on your pickup. The noise scares them."

At Logan Airport, he leaves the pickup in the long-term lot. He checks in for the Boston-Washington shuttle, leisurely, because there is time to kill, *time to kill,* and then he looks at his boarding pass and sees the word *terminal* and a panic-bird big as a bald eagle picks him up in its talons and carries him off, jerking him along corridors and up and down elevators and into restrooms and out again and into the shuttle that weaves between parking lots and then back again until it drops him abruptly and unceremoniously and he finds himself sequestered in the middle nook of a bank of Bell telephones, a cozy and semi-private and semi-safe spot. He needs to talk to his children again, he must speak with them, but when he gets Rowena's answering machine, he hangs up without saying a word. Instead, he talks to a waitress in Starbucks. "Flying down for my father's funeral," he explains. "He died violently, just like my mother. I think I've always been waiting for it. Other shoe to fall, you know?"

Later, circling high above Boston, he tells the passenger seated next to him in the plane. He tells a cab driver in D.C. and he tells the manager of the funeral home. He edits and fine-tunes as he goes.

"The explosion devastated him," he says. "It was the second time my father had been widowed."

"Sixteen years old?" The passenger next to him, a woman, touches his wrist. "It's a terrible age to lose your mother."

"He lived under a curse," Lowell says.

"Shock takes people funny ways," the D.C. taxi driver says. "Takes a long time to wear off too. You just go ahead and get it off your chest."

He eases into the Beltway traffic. "I get a lot of funeral business." He looks at Lowell in the rearview mirror. "Arlington," he explains. "That where yours is?"

"Yes," Lowell says.

He has several evening hours to kill, *hours to kill,* and he moves like the Ancient Mariner from this bar to that. He drinks beer, only beer, and only Sam Adams. "It's a kind of a statement," he tells the bartender. "A reaction against the cocktail parties I had to endure. My father tried to keep me in those social circles, and I won't touch spirits or wine." After two schooners of Sam Adams, he leans toward the guy on the next barstool.

"My father gave the impression," Lowell says, "of a man soldered to doom."

His listener grunts and glances momentarily sideways, then returns to the TV screen. "Yankees gonna win," he tells Lowell gloomily. "You a Yankee fan?"

"No," Lowell says.

"Good."

"My father knew in his bones he was doomed," Lowell explains. "He accepted it, he didn't think he had any choice, but he took it like a man. He made a vow he'd give no sign. At any rate, that was my theory when I was sixteen years old, and I still hold to it." He orders another drink for himself and for the ball-game watcher. "Of course, it cost him," he says.

He shakes his head sadly.

"Manager oughta change pitchers," his neighbor complains.

Lowell says, "He should have changed games, but he was stubborn."

"At times," he tells someone else in a different tavern at the dangerous end of M Street, "you would have thought he was a robot. You would have thought some kingpin was pushing buttons on his remote. I mean, even the way he moved. He had this strange jerky—I don't know, as though his clockwork was jammed."

Lowell's clockwork moves smoothly on amber juice.

"Hey, listen, pal." A black bartender, big as a house, bends toward him. "Don't want to be nosy, it's your funeral. But don't you think you've had a few too many?"

"I asked him once," Lowell says, as though earnestly refuting the bartender's claim, "is it the Mafia or something? Because it wasn't just the Soviets, you know. They kept tabs on all sorts, the Mafia, the Klan, the neo-Nazis, the crazy Unabomber types, you name it. And you and me, we'd be a lot more worried about a Mafia contract than the Soviets, right?"

"Listen, pal," the bartender says, "I don't think you fully understand where you are. What part of town, I mean. I think you got the wrong joint."

"I got the feeling something dangerous was yanking his strings," Lowell explains earnestly. He leans back, straining against fierce bonds. "It was like there was this hidden force dragging him one way, but he dug in his heels and kept on going in the other. Or tried to." Lowell's body jerks itself around, fish on a line. "It was probably only me who noticed," he says. "Maybe I imagined it. He got kind of distant after the plane exploded. Even more so, I mean. Couldn't reach him. Work gobbled him up."

The bartender rolls his eyes.

"Depressed?" Lowell asks, on the bartender's behalf. "You think so? Good question, when you think of the way my mother . . . But he never had any patience with stuff like that. No excuses, no whining. He couldn't stand wimps who let personal matters . . . the therapy junkies spilling their guts, you know the type. Common as dirt in this neck of the woods, I bet. I bet you hear a few sob stories. Confessions a dime a dozen around here, I'll bet. And now it's all over," he says. He looks around the bar and pronounces solemnly and drunkenly, "My father, Mather Lowell Hawthorne, died on September ninth in the year 2000, just four days short of the thirteenth anniversary of the death of my mother."

"R.I.P.," the bartender says. "Go home and sleep it off, pal. You've had enough."

"For which death, he seemed to hold himself responsible," Lowell announces. "Against all logic."

He lifts his glass.

"You celebrating?" the bartender asks.

Lowell watches the light move through his beer.

Mather Hawthorne was already dead, the coroner has explained to him, at the point of impact with a shagbark hickory. Lowell closes his eyes and imagines the scattershot of nuts, kettledrummers of death. Although the wreckage of the car is absolute, and although Lowell's stepmother (his father's young third wife) was barely able to identify the body, the mortuary certificate indicates, *Death due to natural causes: heart attack.*

"Fortunately," Lowell explains in an all-night hamburger joint, "the accident happened in the small hours of the morning and there were no other cars on the road. My father was only sixty-seven."

Lowell can imagine himself repeating all this, casually, from time to time, and after several drinks, to strangers at parties and in bars.

4.

At the cemetery, Lowell feels strangely lightened. He wonders if the sense of freedom, the sense of a lifelong congestion clearing, might be what other people call happiness. He wonders if he might be able to begin to be as other people are. Now officially orphaned, he feels for the first time in his life not-lonely. Rain is falling lightly, which seems appropriate. An old self is being washed away. Lowell feels clean and new. He is barely able to restrain himself from a gregarious impulse to tug at the sleeve of one of the other pallbearers, a total stranger in an officer's uniform, some former colleague of his father's no doubt, and say: *I was an only child. For many years, I tried with all my heart and soul to please my father, but I was a disappointment to him.*

He manages not to splash confession on the pallbearer's sleeve, but he does nod at his stepmother and smile. She is small and pale and looks, Lowell thinks, rather striking dressed in grief. Is she beautiful? He supposes so; his father always had an eye for women; but since this thought evokes the memory of Lowell's own mother, he shies away from it. Even so, his stepmother or the occasion or something else makes him smile again. His smile goes on too long. Elizabeth, his stepmother, raises an eyebrow in surprise and stares at him.

Words, intoned, drift between and obscure Lowell's view.

. . . exceptional service to his country . . . Mather Lowell Hawthorne, guardian of our most precious . . . unsung work, and invisible, but essential to the preservation of liberty and justice for all.

Mather Lowell Hawthorne's widow is not much older than her stepson, who now, on impulse, pulls a gardenia from the wreath that she has placed on his father's coffin and hands it to her. Some of the mourners exchange glances. Elizabeth begins to cry then, soundlessly. Her hair, rain-wet, clings to her cheeks, and Lowell wonders if perhaps they may begin to become not-lonely together.

Forasmuch as it hath pleased Almighty God of His great mercy to take unto Himself the soul of Mather Lowell Hawthorne, we therefore commit his body to the ground; earth to earth, ashes to ashes, dust to dust; in sure and certain hope . . .

"I hardly knew my father, really," Lowell tells Elizabeth later, hours later, over drinks in a quiet lounge. "I worshiped him when I was little. He wasn't often home, but when he was, he used to sit on my bed and tell me stories. Strange stories to tell a child, I suppose, but I was greedy for them. I hung on his every word: Greek gods and goddesses, the *Iliad* and the *Odyssey*. My favorite was Odysseus tied to the mast, trying to hurl himself into the sea while the sirens sang."

"How old were you?"

"Four. Five."

"Must have given you strange dreams," Elizabeth says.

"I still have mermaid fantasies. I get a humming in my ears whenever I see a woman with wet hair."

"Sometimes," Elizabeth says, lowering her eyes and studying the stem of her glass, "in the middle of the night, I would find him reading Homer in his study. He said it calmed him."

"That was always his first love. But he won prizes in math and science too, and that's where he went."

"He claimed all he ever really wanted to be was a classics professor."

"Sometimes I believed that," Lowell says. "But mostly I didn't. What made him take the direction he finally did, I've never understood."

"They needed linguists," she says. "In Intelligence. That's what he told me. Especially ones with scientific training as well. An old friend from his prep school recruited him, he said."

"He used to have me reciting Homer in Greek at dinner parties when I was six," Lowell says. "Like a little parrot. His personal performing dwarf. Still, he was less strange to me then than later."

"It was like living in parallel universes, he said. All the time. Simultaneously." Elizabeth sighs and turns the stem of her wineglass in her fingers, clockwise, three revolutions. "I was never sure which one he was in when he was with me."

"He was always somewhere else. Even when he was with us, he wasn't with us. I never really knew him at all."

"I didn't either," she says.

"I wanted so much to please him, but he kept on raising the bar. I could never measure up. So of course I chose to measure down. Easier to get his attention."

"I had the same problem," she says. "I could never measure up either."

"That's not true." Lowell stares at her. "You were the ideal Washington hostess, he told me. Everything my mother wasn't, he said."

"I tried," she says. "I was sad when you stopped accepting our invitations."

"Not your fault," he assures her.

"You and I never got a chance to know each other."

"No. Well. Nothing to do with you."

"So why?"

"Well, he just made me too nervous. I always felt like I was twelve years old again, not measuring up. And then, Rowena . . . I mean, my own marriage falling apart. I didn't want one of his third-degrees."

"Your father was sad too. When you stopped coming, I mean."

"That's a laugh. My father couldn't stand sadness. My mother was sad for years, and it irritated him. It irritated him to have me around."

"I think you're wrong," she says. "I think he missed you. He was very proud of you."

"Oh no, believe me, he was embarrassed by me. He sent me to his own boarding school—"

"Yes, I know."

"—but I blew it. Loser in a school for winners. My father's name was on all the honor boards, Mather Lowell Hawthorne, gold medal in this, gold medal in that, Latin, Greek, math, physics, athletics, glee club, drama club. Awful. Like a millstone around my neck. Most expensive private school in Massachusetts, and I could always see him thinking *sow's ear* when he looked at me."

"He kept a photograph of you on the bedroom dresser."

"He did?"

"You're wearing your school blazer and holding a silver cup."

"Oh yeah. That. Cross-country run. Only prize I ever won. Yeah, I'm good at running. Running away's my specialty. But there you are. The way my father calls it, you win or you lose. He was a winner, I was a loser. Like my mother."

"You seem to me very like your father," she says. "Sharp-minded and courtly and sad."

"*Courtly!* Me?" Lowell laughs. He looks curiously at his reflection in the dark plate glass behind the bar.

"He could be so gentle," she says. "It's not true that he never showed his feelings. He was always sad. Always haunted."

"He *was* haunted," Lowell agrees. "My mother did that. You know she left him for another man before the . . . I never forgave her. They were both on that plane."

"No, I didn't know," she says. "You mean they went down together, your mother and her—?"

"Not *down*. You know the details. The hijacking, the explosion."

"Hijacking?" she says, leaning forward, avid. "I *don't* know details. I hardly know anything. He'd never— He just said she died in an airline disaster."

Lowell is stunned. "September '87," he says. "Paris to New York, the nerve-gas hijackers—"

"Oh my God. That hijacking."

"Air France Si— I can't say it. I'm superstitious about the number."

"No survivors." Elizabeth presses her hand against her lips. "Isn't that right?"

"Except for the children."

"Oh, the children, that's right, I remember now. I remember seeing those poor little children on TV."

"I can't believe you didn't know."

"No. Nothing. He'd never say a word about the past. I've always been curious."

"Look," he says uneasily. "It isn't something I can talk about."

"No, of course not. I'm sorry." She plays with her wineglass, puddling spilled wine with her finger. She draws an *S* in the liquid on the low table. "Was the man's name Sirocco? The man your mother left him for?"

Lowell frowns. "It was Levinstein. Violinist."

"Who was Sirocco?"

"I have no idea."

"He was tormented by Sirocco," she says. "He used to cry out in his sleep."

"My father?"

"He never mentioned Sirocco to you?"

"Doesn't ring any bells. Mafia, maybe? They gathered intelligence on all sorts."

"What exactly was Mather's role?" she wants to know.

"I never exactly knew. Not precisely. Gathering information and misinformation and deciding which was which, I suppose. He was a spook, and then after the hijacking, when he stopped junketing all over the planet, he *trained* spooks. That's all I know. Maybe he still did other stuff too, I really don't know. He used to say someone has to do the dirty work to keep the country safe. I never got much more detail than that."

"Nor did I," she says.

"When I was little, he was always flying off to talk to 'contacts.' He'd never tell us where, but I'd pick up clues, you know. He'd bring back presents and say *Got it in a bazaar in Cairo*, or *The wives of the camel-men in Afghanistan make these.* Stuff like that."

"We never traveled anywhere by plane. He wouldn't let me fly alone either."

"Planes spooked him after '87. Plus I think, you know, he was pushed into semi-retirement. I think they were afraid he was losing it. Kept him in Washington."

"There used to be a car and a driver," she says. "Every day. And then suddenly, no more official limo, and he had to use his own car. Mostly he shut himself up in his study with his computer and his books."

"They put him out to pasture," Lowell says. "Short life span in Intelligence, he always said that."

"It gnawed at him," she says. "It wasn't just the nightmares. Sometimes he would disappear all night. Just driving around the city, I think."

Lowell stares at her.

"I could tell from the mileage," she says. "I'd check the odometer. He could put in fifty, sixty miles in a night."

"I told you he was a stranger to me. I knew the mailman better."

"There was no one I could ask about it," she says. "Everything's classified, or else that was his excuse."

"*Ask me no questions and I'll tell you no lies,*" Lowell says. "I know the routine."

"He said if I mentioned anything to anyone, our lives were in danger. I never knew whether to believe him or not."

"I never knew either," Lowell says. "This calling out in his sleep . . . did he do that often?"

"Toward the end, every night. Arguing with Sirocco. Shouting at him. Or with Salamander. That name mean anything?"

"Not to me."

"They stalked him. They terrified him. Especially Sirocco."

"I guess I suspected he was losing it. But he kept such a tight hold on himself."

From the pocket of her black suit jacket, she takes the gardenia that Lowell gave her at the graveside and holds it in the palm of her hand. The edges of the petals have turned brown. She reaches for Lowell's hand and opens it and places the gardenia in it. "And now we have both lost Mather," she says. "Permanently."

At that point, he is able to cry; well, not cry, exactly, not cry in any luxurious or extravagant or consolatory or even noticeable way, but he does become aware of functioning tear ducts, of a physical sense of swollenness, of overflow which moves him profoundly. The fact of grief moves him, as of some precious thing long mislaid. He is overcome by this reentry into the experience of emotion per se, and he thinks of it as an atmosphere emanating from Elizabeth. She drives him back to the airport and he wears dark glasses and stares out the window all the way.

"You could stay the night, Lowell," she offers.

He turns then, but does not remove his dark glasses. They sit for some time, not speaking, on the fifth level of the airport parking garage. When she turns the key in the ignition, as though agreement has been reached, he says, "Thank you, Elizabeth, but I can't. Rowena says Amy and Jason will panic if I don't get back tomorrow, and I know she's right. The kids . . . you know, I have a bad effect on them, but they need to see me. They need to know I'm okay. I promised I'd take them to the Public Garden tomorrow."

"You will need to go through your father's things," she says, "and decide what you want. Give me a call when you're ready. You can stay at the house."

"All right," he promises. "And anytime you're in Boston . . . "

But weeks pass, and they do not make contact with each other again, and then Dr. Reuben calls Lowell.

5.

One month after the funeral, Lowell receives a letter of sorts and certain documents in his father's handwriting. Dr. Reuben delivers the package, and the circumstances are strange. "I've just flown up from Washington," Dr. Reuben says. "Your father wanted me to do this personally."

Lowell tries to put a face to the voice on the telephone. "Do I know you?"

"No, you don't, and I'm afraid I don't know Boston. We need to meet somewhere central and very public. Where do you suggest?"

"I don't understand," Lowell says later. They are walking side by side in the Public Garden. Lowell marvels at the shine on Dr. Reuben's black leather shoes. His own sneakers are badly scuffed.

"I was your father's psychiatrist," Dr. Reuben explains.

"I see. I didn't know he— I never thought he had any time for that sort of thing." Lowell is mesmerized by the flash of black leather alongside his own paint-spattered joggers. He and his father's psychiatrist are out of step. His sneakers do a quick-step, skip-step, to bring themselves into alignment, but Dr. Reuben stops abruptly—startled or perhaps affronted by the maneuver—and looks back over his shoulder. When they move forward again, they are still not in step.

"Precautions had to be taken," Dr. Reuben says. He seems to be embarrassed, and is seized by a fit of coughing as though the words are too peppery in his mouth. His eyes water. "At least," he says, "your father believed so." He gives way to another short paroxysm of coughing and then laughs in a self-deprecating way. "Your father was very convincing. You know what I'm talking about."

"I'm not sure," Lowell says.

"To tell you the truth, I can't tell if all this is necessary, or if I've been swept up into his condition." Dr. Reuben looks sideways at Lowell, waiting.

"His heart condition? Congestive heart failure, they said—"

"No," Dr. Reuben says. "I mean paranoia."

Lowell thinks: This is a trap. My father has arranged for this. He's paid someone to keep tabs and report on me. He's keeping postmortem files.

"He believed he was to be murdered," Dr. Reuben says. "Does that surprise you?"

"What?" Lowell says.

"Murder wasn't his word for it. Eliminated, he said. I actually tried to get hold of the police report, you know, to see if brake lines were cut, anything like that. But just as he always said, the police reports were classified. Still, I think suicide is equally likely."

"He had a heart attack at the wheel," Lowell says. "There was a medical report."

"Hmm. Maybe. I was unable to see a copy of that report."

Lowell frowns. "Well, I saw it." Then he thinks about it. "Maybe I didn't. I guess they told me and it didn't occur . . . It was classified too?"

"Classified."

"Did you know it was the anniversary—?"

"Of course. That's why I believe it was suicide. I'll tell you what I think. I think he made the arrangements I'm about to discuss with you, and then his conscience was clear. It was the thing he had to do, and then he could eliminate himself. But either way, it's . . . well, really, I'm ethically bound. There are only two sacrosanct relationships, aren't there? Priests and shrinks. He might have been mad, or he might have been right. I'm supposed to be the one who can tell." There is something plaintive about the laugh this time.

He made arrangements, Lowell thinks wearily. Surprise, surprise. So there will be conditions. There will be expectations. And still Lowell will not measure up.

For a month, one calm month, he has been almost at peace.

"This is not a situation I have ever encountered before," Dr. Reuben says. In the Public Garden, the trees are turning red and gold. "And even now I can't swear that I haven't been infected with his . . . condition. I mean, I can observe myself becoming paranoid, which is an interesting and curious thing for a psychiatrist to observe in himself. Do you see that man staring at us?"

"Where?"

"The man on the bench over there."

"The one reading the newspaper?"

"He's staring at us."

"He's watching that little kid on the tricycle."

"Maybe," Dr. Reuben says. "But you see what I mean? Now that he's gone, I've started to think like your father. Just the same, it seems better to err on the side of caution. And I made your father a promise. I did make him a promise. And I could tell that once I had made that promise, something shifted within him. His conscience was clear. Or as clear as past events would ever permit. Let's sit here for a while."

From a bench beside the pond, they watch the swan boats with their cargo of tourists rock gently in one another's wakes. Willows trail in the water. Families throw crumbs to the ducks. "You will make of his message what you will," Dr. Reuben says. "Even I haven't seen the tapes or the journal, you understand."

"You've got something to give me from him."

"Indirectly. I have a key to give you. I will leave it on this bench and I want you to put your hand over it, very casually, and stay like that for a full ten minutes after I walk away." He gives another embarrassed laugh. "I am quoting your father's directions verbatim. If nothing else, he had a finely developed sense of the dramatic."

Lowell thinks about this. A phrase comes back to him suddenly, falling out of a willow tree: *the necessary rituals of risk.*

Where are you going, Daddy?

I can't tell you that, son, but I'll bring back a present. One for Mommy and one for you.

When will you be back?

I can't tell you that, Lowell.

For show-and-tell, we have to share if our daddy is on a trip and we have to show pictures.

I'm sorry, Lowell, but I can't tell you where I'm going.

What will I say in show-and-tell? Will I say that my daddy is not allowed to tell where he's going?

No, no, you mustn't say that I can't say.

What will I say?

You could tell them that your daddy's on a business trip to Hawaii.

You're going to Hawaii?

No, I'm not going to Hawaii, but that's what you can say in show-and-tell.

I can tell them a lie?

Sometimes, when you have to look after the whole country, a lie is not really a lie. These are the necessary rituals of risk, Lowell. Do you understand? If you say anything, you could put lives in danger.

It was a catechism that Lowell often rehearsed to himself. *I must never never say that I'm not allowed to say.*

"This key?" Lowell asks. This damned key to a Pandora's box of secrets that he has no wish to know.

"It's the key to a locker at Logan Airport," Dr. Reuben says. "International terminal. Locker B-64."

Lowell chokes.

"Are you all right?"

"That was the flight number," Lowell says.

"Air France 64, yes. You can see a great deal of planning went into this. Don't drive or take a taxi, take the subway. I'm quoting your father again."

"And I must never never say why I'm not allowed to say."

"Excuse me?"

"His rules," Lowell says. "The necessary rituals of risk."

"He felt hunted. I can tell you that. He was a man in mortal agony. That might make it easier to forgive him. Planning this gave him a little peace at the end."

"So what is in the locker?"

"I don't know precisely. A journal, I believe. And some papers, possibly classified ones. And some videotapes—I don't know of what—but the tapes are of crucial importance. *Crucial,* your father said. I haven't seen any of this material. I didn't put it there. Your father put it there and gave me the key, and made me promise to hand-deliver the key to you."

"When did he put it there?"

"I don't know exactly. But recently, obviously."

"My father was in Boston recently?"

"Yes. He saw you, he said."

Lowell feels an oceanic surge of rage and grief. "He was good at watching. It was the thing he did best."

"He himself always felt watched."

"He was a control freak," Lowell says. "A spook. A puppeteer. I don't know why I thought the grave would stop him."

"He was a tormented man," Dr. Reuben says. "I think the key will tell you everything you need to know."

Lowell sighs. "The key is to lock me in for life. I'm shackled to him."

"You have a lot of anger locked inside you."

Lowell laughs. "Oh shit. Wow. That's clever. People pay you for that?"

"The key is under my hand on the bench now."

"What if I throw the key away?"

"That, of course, would be up to you. But I would advise against it."

"Sacred last will and testament. Honor thy father."

"No. I would advise against it for much more pragmatic reasons. Because a message sent from beyond the grave, but thrown away unread, is going to haunt you. If you're in an unstable state already, and I sense that you are . . . well, I know that you are. I know a great deal about you, naturally, because your father . . . Anyway, that sort of reactive impulsivity could be the coup de grâce, it could drive you over the edge. I'm going to put my hand back in my pocket now and I'm leaving. Please put your own hand over the key. There should be no need for further contact between us, but can I recommend strongly that you seek professional help?" He takes six steps and returns. "I would also request, however, that if you seek professional help, as you certainly should, you never mention my name."

He walks away and does not look back.

Lowell places his hand over the key and sits watching the swan boats until the light fades.

6.

Locker B-64 has taken up ghostly residence in Lowell's bedroom. Sometimes, in dreams, he is inside it, banging on the door for the key holder to let him out. Sometimes, mathematically and malevolently, the walls of his room shift subtly, they pleat and grid themselves, and a steep honeycombed arrangement of locked boxes forms a canyon around his bed. Steel cubes, serried ranks of them, skyscraper upward, each with its own keyhole and small system of vents, while he, Lowell, falls downward, faster and faster, down and down, clutching at handles that come away in his fingers and never getting below or beyond the endless doors. He falls down through basements, through underground library stacks, through caves that are ten stories deep and hold camouflaged tanks and burning planes, he falls, he continues to fall, but he can never get to the bottom of the riddle of Locker B.

In sleep, many times, he has parked his car near Union Square Station in Somerville, taken the Red Line, and then the Blue, and finally the free shuttle bus. When the driver asks, "Terminal?"—usually speaking without moving his lips—Lowell always says, "Yes. It would seem so. That's the crux of the Locker B riddle, isn't it?" and the driver always laughs: "That was terminal, all right, yes sir, and where would you like to be blown up?"

Lowell has also made the trip awake, and by day. He sits facing the bank of steel lockers in the international terminal and stares at Number B-64. Inside the pocket of jacket or of jeans, his fingers play with the key, dextrous games, sinister games, increasingly complicated games. He passes the key over and under his fingers and back again, a woven password. At first he goes once a week, on Sundays, then on Saturdays too, except on those weekends when the children are with him. In the Amy-and-Jason weeks, he goes on Wednesdays instead, then on Wednesdays and Thursdays, and finally every day.

"Where are we going, Daddy?" Amy asks.

"To the airport," he says. He has not taken the children before, but Monday is too far away. "You can watch the planes taking off and landing."

On the flight observation deck, he leaves Amy with strict instructions. "You stay here with Jason, okay, till I come back? I have to go do something. I won't be long."

"We want to come with you."

"No, you can't. I have to see a man about a painting job. I won't be very long, and I'll come back here for you, okay?"

"How long will you be gone?"

"Ten minutes," he says. "Fifteen at the most. You stay right here with Jason and watch the planes."

But when he rises from his vigil before Locker B-64, he sees them watching him, half hiding behind a water fountain. He knows himself to be the guilty party.

"Amy," he says reproachfully, "what did I tell you?"

"Jason was crying," she says. "Didn't the man come?"

"What man?"

"The man you had to see about the painting job."

"Oh," he says. "No. He didn't show up."

"Why were you staring at the lockers, Daddy?"

He says slowly, "I left something in one of them, but I've lost the key."

Amy watches his hand, hidden under denim, clenching and unclenching itself. "Maybe it's in your pocket," she suggests.

"What do you know?" he laughs. "Little Miss Magic. You're right. Here it is after all, down in the lining. There's a little hole and it's almost . . . You want to open the locker for me?"

"Okay."

He has to lift her. Her lips are parted; the tip of her tongue draws tiny arcs of concentration as she inserts the key into the lock and turns. She tips herself back to open the door. "It's a bag," she says. "Is it yours, Daddy?"

"Yes," he says. "Well, no. But I'm looking after it for someone."

"For the man who didn't come?"

"Right." He pulls out a blue sports tote with a Nike logo on the side. The bag is surprisingly heavy. "Amy," he says. "Wait here with Jason. I have to go to the bathroom."

"Jason wants to go with you," Amy tells him.

"Daddy, I come with you," Jason echoes in his two-year-old lisp.

Lowell kisses the top of Jason's head. "Daddy's in a big hurry," he says. "You stay with Amy, okay? I'll be back in a minute."

Jason wails loudly. "Come with you," he insists.

"No," Lowell calls over his shoulder, running. "Daddy's in a big, big hurry. Wait there."

He intends to lock himself into a stall, but there are too many people present and this makes him nervous, though he does not wish to draw attention to himself by leaving without taking a leak. He is afraid to set the bag down. Indecisive, he moves into a space between a businessman and some drifter who reeks of gin. He stands with the bag between his legs, feet close together, and unzips.

No one pays him the slightest attention and he picks up the blue tote and leaves.

"Daddy, Daddy!" he hears Amy call, and he turns. The children are running after him, breathless. Jason is crying. Dear God, Lowell thinks. What is happening to me? He sweeps Jason up with his right arm. He holds the blue tote in his left. "You didn't think I'd forgotten you, did you?" he asks, smothering Jason with kisses. "Silly Jason. Okay, let's go home now. First the shuttle bus, then the subway, then home. Who remembers where the shuttle stop is?"

"I do," Amy says.

"Okay, Captain. I'll follow you."

Why the international terminal? a voice buzzes inside his head. He tries to picture his father on the shuttle up from New York, the elegantly dressed professional man. He cannot visualize his father with a blue sports tote. Had it been inside something else? Did his father disappear into a men's bathroom at the domestic terminal, change into jeans and baseball cap, and carry the blue tote to the lockers at international? Is there some suggestion that Lowell will be required to embark on a journey after he sees the contents of the bag? Or is this purely memento mori for the flight that never reached its intended destination, the flight from which Lowell's mother never disembarked? Unless she was one of the hostages. Unless there *were* hostages, ten hostages, as the hijackers claimed.

The hostage hoax, the State Department said, *is the final ruse of a handful of desperate terrorists. . . .*

Lowell remembers that. He remembers watching the news when that statement was made.

There is no evidence, the president told the nation in September 1987, *of any survivors of Air France Flight 64, apart from the children who were disembarked in Germany. The final landing was somewhere in Iraq where the plane was blown up. Although Iraq has not permitted the Red Cross . . . nevertheless our Intelligence sources have confirmed . . .*

Lowell finds himself pausing at an arrivals monitor, scanning for flights due in from Paris.

"Daddy." Amy tugs at his sleeve. "Come *on*."

"Just a second, Amy." Air France seems to have changed its numbering system. He sees AF 002, AF 006 . . . but of course flight AF 64 was going to New York, not Boston.

"Hey." Someone bumps into him. "People been coming through yet?"

"What?" Lowell says. The man who has collided with him is disheveled and out of breath. He points to the monitor.

"Flight from Frankfurt. It's landed. People through yet?"

"I don't know," Lowell says.

"What flight you waiting for?"

"I'm not. I'm just . . ." *Why is he interrogating me?* "Look." Lowell points to the large automatic doors of frosted glass. "There are people just coming through now." But he cannot resist looking back over his shoulder as he leaves the terminal, and the man waiting for the flight from Frankfurt is not moving toward the glass doors, but is still watching Lowell. This means nothing, of course.

Though it *could* mean something.

It might mean something.

Lowell decides he will not go direct to the subway with the children, in case he is being watched. "Here's our bus," he tells Amy, and they get on the free shuttle that moves between the terminals and they get off again at terminal C.

"This isn't our stop," Amy says. "The subway is two more stops."

"Jason's hungry," Lowell says. "Want some french fries, Jason? Want a Coke?"

"French fries!" Jason grins. "Yummy yum."

"Yummy yum yum," Lowell chants. "Want some french fries, Amy?"

"Okay," she says, wary.

There are numerous fast-food stands, none of them appealing, but he buys fries and Cokes for the children, a coffee for himself. He sets the blue bag on the floor and keeps it tightly between his feet, though an inordinate number of people seem to knock it in passing. He tries to imagine his father, with a sports tote between his ankles, having coffee from a Styrofoam cup. He cannot visualize this.

"Okay, kids," he says. "Let's go."

They take the shuttle to the MBTA stop, then the Blue Line to State. They change to the Green Line, change again at Park Street, take the Red Line to Union Square.

Lowell's car, a slightly battered pickup with a steel hold-all across the back, is where he left it in the parking lot. He unlocks the steel coffer. Nothing missing. He puts the sports tote inside, turns the key in the padlock, changes his mind, unlocks it, takes the tote with him into the cab. "Footrest," he says. "Pillow for your feet."

"What's inside the bag, Daddy?" asks Amy, clicking her seat belt shut.

"Just stuff. Can you do up Jason's belt?"

He could take one quick look, he thinks, and then, if necessary, if he deems it necessary, he could toss the blue container and its contents into a Dumpster. He sits there, his hand on the ignition key, thinking. The owner of the car in the next parking space arrives and the door of his white Nissan taps the side of Lowell's car. Is it deliberate? The Nissan driver wears a plaid shirt and has a bald patch. Lowell waits for him to leave, analyzing the plaid: vertical stripes and horizontal, green, black, gray, a thin vertical red line.

"Daddy," Amy says. She is pulling at her hair.

"Right." He starts the car. "Amy, sweetheart, don't do that to your hair."

The soundtrack of *Babe* comes softly through the bedroom wall.

"Excuse me," the little pig is saying to the sheep in his gravelly-sweet voice, "but would you ladies mind . . . ?" And then Jason's high-pitched laughter, and Amy's voice-over in her big-sister tone: "He thinks he's a dog." This must be the fourth time this weekend, but the children never tire of the video of the little pig that could.

Outside, from the Somerville night, come the sounds of horns, brakes applied almost too late, fights, shouts, the bells of St. Anne's on the hill. Lowell has the glazed look of a man masturbating in the cinema. He stares at the wall. His hand, inside the blue sports tote, itemizes three objects, angular, bulky, hard-edged: two thick ring binders and something unstable and irregularly shaped in a drawstring bag that could have been, that was once, a pillowcase. Lowell pulls out the pillowcase bag and stares at it. Rows of knights, with lances poised and pennants on their helmets, gallop toward each other in the lists: this was his own pillow until he was six years old and started school. At the mere touch of the worn cotton, he can smell his bedroom, feel the weight of his father sitting on the end of the bed, smell his mother's perfume as she bends over to kiss him good night. *Once upon a time,* his father begins. *Once upon a time, in the springtime of the world, when Persephone, the beautiful daughter of Zeus and Demeter, was gathering flowers with her maidens in the field, she was kidnapped and carried off by Hades, king of the Underworld. . . .*

Lowell examines the pillowcase.

Attached to the drawstring at its neck is a luggage tag, crudely lettered in black felt marker. He recognizes his father's handwriting.

AF 64
Operation Black Death
Bunker Tapes & Decameron Tape

Broadside. Blunt weapon, Lowell thinks, with a sense of having absorbed the explosion of Air France 64 in the gut. He bends forward over the sports bag and the zipper jams and the tapes refuse to be crammed back in, slithering around in their fabric casing—how many? how many are there? five? six?—clacketing, plasticking, live inside the pillowcase, miles of nylon ribbon, they are videocassettes, he can tell that through the cloth, but confessions? obscene revelations? death scenes? what? The pillowcase is damp and clammy to the touch now, revolting. He shoves the whole toxic blue bundle under his bed and paces the room. He counts slowly to ten, forward and back, breathing deep. His heartbeat is fast and erratic. Through the wall, he hears climactic music from *Babe,* the film nearly done. Supper, he thinks. They'll want supper. I can't take them out. I can't leave the bag in the house. Pasta, he decides.

He has spaghetti, he has a jar of Ragú sauce somewhere at the back of the fridge.

How can he leave the room with the bag unguarded?

He lies on the floor and pulls the wretched thing out from under the bed. Its limbs sprawl, its heavy end lolls like a broken neck, the drawstring bag containing the tapes juts from the slit. He pulls at the stuck zipper and gets the bag open again. His hands feel bloodied. He pushes the ungainly pillowcase properly inside the sports tote and takes note of the two other items, ring binders, both black, both barely able to contain the thick wad of pages inside them. He takes one out and opens it.

It is labeled, on the first page, *Report Dossier: Classified*. He flips through the pages. Almost all are typed, but there are often just one or two paragraphs to a page. In the bottom right-hand corner of each page is a brief notation—*report filed*—in his father's handwriting. At the top of each page is a date. He reads one at random:

> February 19, 1977:
>
> Re Air France 139 (Tel Aviv to Paris) hijacked to Uganda, June 27, 1976: Nimrod confirms that Sirocco was involved; confirms sighting Sirocco in Entebbe on June 30. Nimrod believed Sirocco killed on July 4 in Israel's rescue operation, but subsequently received reliable evidence that Sirocco involved in shipment of arms from Libya to IRA (November '76). Believes Sirocco is Saudi, but possibly Iraqi or Algerian. Holds four passports that we know of: Saudi Arabia, Iraq, Algeria, Pakistan, at least one of these presumably legitimate. Fluent in Arabic, Urdu, English, and French. Holds forged *carte de séjour* for France. Was

a trainer in Mujahadeen camps in Pakistan and Afghanistan in early '70s. Has also recently been identified in newsclip of Dal Khalsa separatist Sikh demonstrations in Amritsar in late '76. Highly proficient in explosives and chemical warfare. A brilliant mercenary but not a fundamentalist zealot, Nimrod believes. Believes Sirocco could be bought, but advises caution. Sirocco is dangerously loose cannon. Advises meeting between Sirocco and Salamander.
Action taken: Information passed up chain of command.

And on the next page:

March 16, 1977

Directive received from highest level: Sirocco known to be dangerous and untrustworthy, but use of rogue agent warranted, given present situation; necessary ritual of risk; need for accurate information on terrorist cells in Middle East and re training facilities on Pakistani/Afghanistan border outweighs other concerns.
Action taken: Nimrod to approach Sirocco, arrange meeting with Salamander.

And on the next page, in his father's handwriting, a brief note:

March 19, 1977

Meeting arranged. Probable site of first meeting: Peshawar.

Lowell grasps a half-inch wad of pages and turns.

November 4, 1981

Received Sirocco's report on Sadat assassination. Islamic fundamentalist affair. Actual agent not previously on our records, but known links with 10 people on our files, all trained in Afghanistan, 3 now in this country. Sirocco willing to recruit assassins for Begin or Arafat if desired; suggests chaos in Middle

> East would provide rationale for "protectorate monitoring" of oil cartels, which he recommends, but demands control of own oil company. Salamander directed to supply funding and arms for Afghanistan project.

Lowell flips through pages and more pages, and Sirocco leaks through the volume like spilled black motor oil. So does Salamander.

He was tormented by Sirocco, Elizabeth said.

Nightmares, she said. *Toward the end, every night. Arguing with Sirocco. Or with Salamander. They stalked him. They terrified him. Especially Sirocco.*

Lowell closes the ring binder nervously and puts it back in the bag. He opens the cover of the second volume and reads on the title page, *Journal of S: Encrypted.* He riffles through pages. All are written in some sort of code, in vertical columns of Greek letters and numbers, unintelligible. He pushes the journal back into the blue bag and zips it shut. He pushes it under the bed. He wishes he had not opened the locker. He wishes he had thrown away the key.

"Daddy!" Amy calls.

"Coming." He almost stumbles over the children at the door. "Guess what we're having for supper," he says brightly.

"Macaroni and cheese."

"Wrong." He puts a large pot of water on the stove. "But close. Okay, who's going to get the spaghetti for me?"

"Me," Jason calls, excited. "Me, me, me."

"And who's going to get the spaghetti sauce?"

"I'll get it," Amy says. There is reproach in her voice.

"Don't you like spaghetti?"

"It's okay."

But she does like to be the one who holds the colander and the one who dispenses Parmesan from the Kraft shaker.

"Okay," Lowell says. "Enjoy. I'll be back in a minute. I have to make a phone call."

In the hallway, he takes a small black address book from his pocket and looks up a name. He dials his stepmother's Washington number and waits. If he gets her answering machine, he thinks, he will not leave a message but will simply eat supper with the children, then take them to Blockbuster, then watch another movie with them (yes, he will stay with them in the room), and then they will all go to sleep, *to sleep, perchance to dream,* and therefore no, he thinks he will avoid sleep for a night or ten, but if Elizabeth does not answer, he will surely have to pace, he will surely have to do violent push-ups on the living room carpet, he will surely have to take the children to the gym at the Y.

"Elizabeth," he says. "Thank God. This is Lowell."

"Oh, Lowell. Hi."

"Are you all right?"

"I suppose so, more or less. I can't seem to . . . I feel strange, mostly. Strange things have been happening."

"Strange how?"

"Oh, just . . . it's nothing, really. How are your children?"

"Fine. They're fine. Well, Rowena thinks I'm a health hazard for them right now, and she's right, of course. Jason wets his bed all the time."

"Oh dear, I'm so sorry. And you? How about you?"

"At this moment, very shaky," he says. "Actually, at this moment, I feel as though . . ."

"Lowell?"

". . . set up for something." Yes, that was it. "One of his pawns again. He hasn't stopped."

"What's happened?"

"You asked me about Sirocco, remember? And Salamander? I've found out who they are. Should've realized. They're code names for secret agents." He can hear an intake of breath. "Elizabeth?" He hears a click and then her line goes dead. He dials back immediately and gets her answering machine.

Now he wishes more urgently than ever to be back at yesterday.

He half expects the blue Nike bag to have vanished, but it is there, under the bed. He stashes it inside a plaid pillowcase and hides the whole thing at the back of his linen closet with another pillow in front of it, and in front of that he places a small stack of folded towels.

His phone rings and he stumbles to reach it before Amy does.

"Lowell?" Elizabeth's voice trembles. "I'm calling from the pay phone at the gas station near me. A few days ago, two men came to the house. They said they were from Security, and when I asked what kind of security, which agency, they said national. They said they just had a few questions to ask, but they were here for hours. It was grueling. It was like Mather was a suspect in some crime and that made me a suspect too, or an accomplice or something. I mean, they didn't say that, but that's how it felt. I'm probably being paranoid, but I think my phone might be tapped. That's why I didn't want you to, you know, say any more. I'll try to call back later, but don't call me, okay?"

"Elizabeth," he says. But she has already hung up.

Amy is pulling at her hair. "I want to call Mommy," she says.

The phone rings again and Lowell leaps at it. "Lowell?" a woman's voice says. "This is Samantha. Can we talk about the hijacking?"

Lowell hangs up. "Don't answer that," he says to Amy when it rings again.

"Look, just hear me out, okay?" Samantha says to his answering machine. Lowell closes his eyes. He believes he could sleep standing up. Exhaustion, he thinks, is about running out of energy to resist. "I was *on* Air France 64, which gives me some sort of right, okay? I was six years old and both my parents were killed. This is just so you'll understand why I'm obsessive about it. Okay?"

She seems to be waiting for him to pick up, but he simply stares at the blinking light on his machine.

"Thanks for not cutting me off," she says. "I've been burying myself in Freedom of Information applications, anything and everything declassified, which is precious little, needless to say. . . ." She takes a deep breath. "I'm certain that American Intelligence had information before it hap—" The digital timer chops her off midword, but Lowell already knows that Samantha is not easily deterred. She calls again. "We were disposable pawns for a sting operation, but now we're chickens coming home to roost. Just think about it, okay, because you probably hold clues that you don't even know you hold."

Lowell pushes the erase button on his machine.

Amy says, "I want to call Mommy."

"Yes," Lowell says. "Okay. Perhaps that's best."

While Amy talks to her mother, Lowell sits on the sofa, Jason in his arms, and stares at the wall.

Book II

FOG

Fear death? To feel the fog in my throat,
the mist in my face. . . .

—ROBERT BROWNING

1.

SALAMANDER

I spy.

With my manifold eye.

This is Salamander's morning canticle.

He leans in close to the bathroom mirror and his words come back lush, fully orchestrated, thick with toothpaste and shower fog. He squints and sees galaxies: bright floating points, moons, multiple planetary rings. He has the eyes of a fly or a god. The things that he knows, weighty matters of life and death—not natural death, or swift death—orbit his consciousness, but he must not speak of them.

This is the way Samantha imagines him. She has constructed him, like a trick question, from undeleted half lines in documents. Morning exhausts him, she imagines. His eyes, in the bathroom mirror, would be bloodshot. Dreams, dispersing though still opaque, would cloud the room. He would not recall the dreams, though they would leave a layer of unease that he would scrub at under the shower and slough off.

In the trade, and to those who do research in previously classified files, he is known as Salamander, or S, and that—for the time being, and to Samantha's chagrin—will have to suffice.

Salamander: a mythical creature having the power to endure fire without harm; an elemental being inhabiting flames in the theory of Paracelsus; any of numerous amphibians superficially resembling lizards but scaleless and covered with a soft moist skin and breathing by gills in the larval stage.

He is all of the above, Samantha believes, closing the dictionary. She imagines him in front of his bathroom mirror. He would watch himself without blinking as reptiles do.

Unobtrusive, soft as a snake, he slithers under and around many lives. Around Samantha's life. Around Lowell's. Around yours. Around mine. We deposit data ceaselessly. He gathers it: phone conversations, e-mails, airline tickets, credit card purchases, income and taxation information, websites visited, buying habits, tastes and eccentricities. He has photographs: from banks, retail stores, elevators, public bathrooms, pedestrian crossings, parking lots, airports.

Those whom he chooses to observe are known to him intimately.

Their nerve systems are digitally mapped.

As flies to wanton boys are the chosen to Salamander.

When it pleases him, he nudges them in this direction or that, according to his game plan. He makes up the rules as he goes.

Samantha is one of his subjects. In the beginning, this was inadvertent, but then he became obsessed with her and she with him.

She deposits data. He gorges on it.

She studies the patterns of his gorging, and posits him.

She posits him because her own existence requires it. Her own existence? From day to day, it feels to her an uncertain thing, without stable landmarks or fixed signs. Some days, when she watches children playing in the park, she can feel the ground giving way. You have no idea, she wants to tell the children. The swings, the sandbox: they are all illusions. You have no idea how unreliable things are, or how suddenly the sky can turn to fire. The playground dips and sways in front of her. In fog everything shifts with the light, everything floats.

On other days, in her classes at Georgetown University, she looks around the seminar table at fellow students and thinks: We live on different planets.

She is nineteen years old, majoring in American history and government, but how could she even begin to translate her life, her inner life, so that it would be intelligible to her peers? They take safety for granted, she knows, and they are certain that two and two always make four, but this could change. She thinks of it this way: that we are composed of a frail string of learned sequences (we recognize our own face in a mirror, we know our own name, we can put on our shoes without thinking, we know how to make love, and we know what to do—more or less—when we feel acute physical pain), and these pieces which make up the puzzle of the self are held together by the glue of memory. Certain solvents can dissolve this glue: a stroke, catastrophic events. Then we are forced to become scavengers of our own past, searching, finding, relearning, reassembling the self.

Samantha tracks different threads of light, painstakingly, one by one, and she follows their beams into the haze. Here and there, little by little, events can be catalogued and flagged, and eventually she hopes she will be able to recalculate the unknown quantities of herself and of Salamander who made and unmade her. She constructs him from the traces he leaves in other lives. She puts him together like a jigsaw puzzle in order to explain what happened in September 1987 and how it happened and why.

She is mapping her way out of fog.

Look at Samantha: here she is, the day the world changed, on the border between *Before* and *After*, in fading color on Kodak paper. She is six years old. She is wearing a blue woolen coat with a darker blue velvet collar and a cotton dress (it is white, prinked with forget-me-nots, and has a smocked bodice and puffed sleeves; it is visible through her unbuttoned coat). She is also wearing white lace-edged socks and black patent-leather shoes. The sign above her head says *PORTE 12* because this photograph was taken at Charles de Gaulle Airport in September 1987. Framed by the doorway to the boarding tunnel, she is turning back to wave. Her left hand clutches the hand of a young man, not a good-looking man, not particularly, but a man whose skin barely seems to contain him. Even in the photograph, an aura of intensity comes off him. The man is her father, Jonathan Raleigh. A one-armed teddy bear, once Samantha's but given to her baby brother weeks earlier, dangles from her right hand, and when she waves, the teddy bear swoops about like a flag. She is laughing, and there is a dimple just to one side of her mouth. She can feel the fire passing from her father's hand to her own. There are high mad notes in the pressure of his fingers, messages she is picking up but cannot translate. Her father is also laughing and waving. Beside him, a woman, perhaps weary, her smile slightly tense, holds baby Matthew up to the view of those who have come to see the family off.

"Your mother made your coat," Samantha's aunt tells her.

"She did?"

"She made all your clothes. She was that kind of mother."

That kind of mother. Samantha saves this phrase. She saves every fragment, every splinter of information.

"The bodice of your dress was hand-smocked," her aunt says. "These days, you have to go to a museum to see that sort of thing."

"I still have the dress," Samantha says.

"Your mother was not afraid of being old-fashioned."

Sometimes at night, when Samantha cannot sleep, she takes the dress out of its tissue paper and holds it against her cheek, but it keeps its secrets. "It's torn," she tells her aunt. "There's a rip in the skirt."

"Yes. I remember."

"From the hem right up to the smocking on the bodice. But it's not torn in the photograph."

"No."

"It must have caught on something when they put us on the escape hatch."

"Or later, perhaps," her aunt says.

"I can't remember tearing it."

"We couldn't get that coat off you, you even wanted to sleep in it."

"I must have taken it off, though," Samantha says. "Eventually. My mother must have talked me into it." She studies the woman in the photograph—her mother, Rosalie Hamilton Raleigh—with a magnifying glass. Her mother is not much more than a girl, really, twenty-six years old, at the time of the photograph. "It must have been in the overhead locker." Samantha thinks she can remember her father putting the coat there. Sometimes she can remember. It all depends on which way she tells the story to herself. "Perhaps during the first landing," she says.

"Morocco," her aunt says.

"We didn't know where we were."

"Morocco. Every landing is imprinted on my brain, up to the final one in Iraq. They kept showing us maps and flight paths on TV."

For some reason, this makes Samantha feel giddy. The room tilts. She closes her eyes and grips the arm of the sofa because a curving hall of mirrors seems to be sloping away from her and at the far end, very tiny, she can almost see her mother with a baby in her arms.

"It was horrible," her aunt says. "Just watching and watching, completely helpless. It was horrible."

"Was it?" Samantha cannot keep an edge of anger from her voice, and something else too, a low buzz of excitement which her aunt detects and which Samantha will not let go. Like a terrier, she works at her aunt's growing agitation. "Was it, Lou?" she needles. She never says *Aunt Lou,* only Lou. She watches her aunt the way a cat watches: tense, ready to pounce.

"Sam," her aunt says. She sounds very tired. "I am not trying to compete. It goes without saying that it was far, far more horrible on the plane."

But it is the different angle of vision that excites and disturbs Samantha. If she could see the little girl in the blue coat in someone else's frame, if she could study her, would the puzzle solve itself? "Tell me about watching us on TV."

Lou clenches her interlocked fingers and the knuckles give off soft cracking sounds that make Samantha wince. Lou's hands turn the color of sunburn. Then she lifts her elbows like wings and her fingers stretch and pull at each other, her hands involved in a tug-of-war. Neither hand lets go. Her elbows droop at her side. "Sometimes, especially during the Morocco landing, the camera would zoom in close," Lou says in a low voice, "and you could see someone's face through a window."

"It was very hot," Samantha says. She undoes several buttons at the neck of her cotton dress. "People were fainting from the heat, I remember that." She remembers, across the aisle, a tiny woman with gray hair. *I have a granddaughter who's just your size,* the little gray-haired woman told Samantha. That was before anything unusual had happened. The woman was wearing a black dress. Later, when the plane was on the ground again, when it grew hotter and hotter, Samantha remembers that the gray-haired woman reached over and tugged at her sleeve. *Water,* the woman said, *water, water,* although she did not make any sound. It was the shape of the words that Samantha heard. "My teddy's thirsty too," Samantha told her, and the tiny woman opened her mouth and then she went soft and slithered down to the floor like a towel falling into a pool and Samantha's mother said, *Heat prostration, and Sam, if you don't take off your coat,* and she took it off then, she thinks, and maybe her father put it up in the overhead locker or maybe Sam kicked it under the seat. Wherever it was, the coat remained on the plane. It did not slide down the escape hatch with Sam.

More than thirteen years later, the lost coat still gnaws at her days and her nights. It has eaten her. In dreams, she looks under the seat and she opens the overhead locker, but her coat has gone, and a salamander with sluglike skin and a smell of blocked drainpipe slithers out. Its eyes are bloodshot. How much do you know? its eyes ask.

I know more than you think, Samantha tells the bloodshot eyes, and what I don't know yet, I'll find out.

"For days, I never turned the TV off," her aunt says.

"You've never told me this before."

"You've never wanted to talk about it."

"Now I do," Samantha says. "Tell me about watching us on TV."

"I didn't sleep. I ate in front of the set. But I never saw you. I never saw any of you; at least, not while you were on the plane. When the children were being off-loaded, I watched for you like a hawk. You were almost last. I was afraid you weren't going to get off."

"I didn't want to. They had to push me."

"The camera got you in close-up at the top of the chute. I'll never forget your eyes." Lou touches her niece's cheek and then throws her arms around Sam and hugs her tightly. "I'd been so afraid," she says. "I burst into tears when I saw you. I couldn't stop."

Samantha disengages herself and moves away. "It was so hot on the plane. It was so hot. We couldn't breathe." She feels feverish. "Do you have something cold? Iced tea or something?" She fans herself with one of her aunt's magazines. The paper feels damp. "Don't you have air-conditioning?"

Her aunt is startled. *In October?* she does not say. "I've got the heat set low, Sam, because we're supposed to be conserving energy, but I can turn it right off, if you like. The mayor will thank me. In Manhattan, there's always risk of outages."

Samantha feels faint from the heat, but when Lou lowers the thermostat, she starts to shiver. "Can you turn it up again?" she asks. She can hear a baby crying fretfully. "Doesn't that get on your nerves?" she asks. "Is it from next door?"

"I can't hear anything," Lou says.

"It sounds like Matthew." On the plane, her baby brother's crying went on and on and on. Her mother crooned to him and put her lips against his burning cheeks, but he wouldn't stop. "He had a heat rash," Samantha says. "He'd drunk all his formula and they wouldn't give us any—"

"Don't," her aunt says. "Samantha, please don't."

Don't worry, there's a blind curve just ahead, Samantha could have told her. She cannot finish any of her stories, they are full of holes. As for the connecting tissue: she cannot tell if she remembers the thing itself, or the newsreel clips, or the events as she has pored over them in previously classified documents, obtained through much diligence and cunning on her part. A lot of the past comes back at her in print, with lines and half lines and whole paragraphs blocked out.

> *Approximate time frame known XXXXXXXXXXXX anticipated strike at major airport XXXXXXXXXX Paris or London XXXXXXXXXXXX XXXXX flight bound for New York City, passengers Americans and Jews XXXXXXXXXXXXXXXXXXXXXXXXXX XXXXXXXXXXXXX codes broken, connections engineered XXXXXXXXXXXXXXX sting operation, code name Black Death, controlled damage XXXXXXXXXXXXXXXXX XXXXXXX Salamander in charge of operations XXXXXXXXXXXXXXX XXXXXXXXXXXXXXXXXXXX*

That is where she met Salamander. In a document. It was a case of obsession at first sight.

But Salamander's number is unlisted.

Your call cannot go through as dialed, the recordings say. Please check your information and try again. This is the answering service, a voice advises. Please leave a message and we will get back to you. That is not our department, people say. That person is no longer with us. That happened before our time. All matters falling within the purview of national security are beyond the scope of our . . . We have no records, we are unable to confirm, we cannot release that information, we cannot be answerable for acts of God, acts of terrorism, acts of double agents, acts of rogue elements of foreign powers, acts of war.

Rogue agent, she reads in other documents, following Salamander's trail.

> *Salamander to negotiate with Sirocco XXXXXXXXXXXX arrangements for payment to be made in XXXXXXXXXXXX Sirocco dangerous and unreliable but usable XXXXXXXXXXXXXXXXX loose cannon, Salamander warns, but as rogue agents go, we can use for Black Death XXXXXXXXXX*

backstairs contacts in the palaces and has usable information on the princes that not even XXXXXXXXXXXXXXX

Sometimes people Samantha is talking to thin out into block capitals and blacked-out spaces before her eyes. At other times, images with torn edges, scraps of them, flicker without warning across the screen of her mind: butt of machine gun, severed arm, child on inflatable slide, gas masks (bug-eyed), breathing snouts. She slaps at them feverishly, she brushes them away, but they dart and sting. Her dream-films are always jump-cut. They do not add up. When she and Jacob—with whom she first collided at the bottom of an airplane chute, with whom she huddled on a camp cot in Germany—when she and Jacob find someone, when they track down some new link, they treat the pieces like chips from a precious mosaic—from Byzantium say, or Pompeii or Ravenna—from some lost world, fabulous and perhaps impossible to reconstruct. Samantha searches for fragments of cobalt, hunting for the child in the forget-me-not outfit, but the blue notes always disappear. She and Jacob piece together faces but their edges are never sharp and they drift into fog. The task gives them vertigo.

They are inside us, Jacob tells her. We could find them if we concentrated long enough. The brain is a massive retrieval system, he insists, a mainframe of electronic impulses. Everything is there, he assures her, if we could nudge the right nerve ends. He rakes his fingers through his hair and across his skull. He clasps hanks of his curls and pulls as though pulling will give relief. I have a crowd in my head, he says.

"I can't put my baby brother's face back together," Sam tells her aunt. "I've tried. I can feel him in my arms. I have certain kinds of physical memory that are quite intense, but not a visual one. I can remember the weight of him, and the sound of his crying, and the fever coming off him, and the way his skin felt bumpy like a plastic bubble-sheet used for packing, but when I look, he doesn't have a face."

Her aunt straightens a photograph in the album. "Please don't do this, Sam."

"Believe me," Sam tells her, "I'm working on improving the ending. We're all working on it. Jacob's migraines are getting so bad, the medication can't help him any more."

"Who is Jacob?"

"Jacob Levinstein. He's one of us."

"One of . . . ?" Lou's eyes widen. She closes the photo album. She seems distressed. She seems angry. She moves away from Sam as though Sam might be infectious. "I would have thought," Lou says in a strained voice, "that contact . . . that it would exacerbate . . ." She hugs the album to her chest. "I read somewhere," she says reproachfully, "that survivors of the *Titanic* avoided each other. Reporters tried to arrange reunions, but survivors resisted. I found that easy to understand."

It *is* easy to understand, Samantha thinks, especially for the survivors, especially for the children of Air France 64, but the kind of intense connection that her lot shares—physical proximity is irrelevant—is not something Sam is likely to discuss. "We don't care to be circus acts for the media," she tells her aunt. "But we tend to link up. There's a website now, and we find each other. We need to do it, the same way that war vets do."

"A *website*." Lou paces from one window to another, the photo album pressed against her chest like a shield. "This is amazing to me, Samantha. Of course I can see . . . when I think about it, I can see how necessary, how inevitable . . ."

"It's just that there are things I don't know," Samantha pleads, "and they drive me . . ." *You have to be extremely careful,* Jacob warns, *about what you reveal*. "The gaps keep me awake sometimes," she says. "That's all. Well, they keep me awake a lot, actually. I hoped you might fill in some blanks."

Lou's hand is shaking. Lou is Samantha's mother's sister and Sam knows everything and nothing about her.

"For me, Samantha . . ." Lou says, but her sentence peters out.

"Can I see the photograph again?"

"This is hard for me."

Samantha pulls the photograph album from her aunt's hands.

"It's not what I was expecting," Lou says in a low voice. "When you called. After such a long time."

"What were you expecting?"

Lou turns away and makes a dismissive gesture which Sam translates as: *That's of no consequence now*. She leaves the room so abruptly, she trips on the rug and almost falls into the hall. Sam hears her locking herself in the bathroom. She decides to wait.

There is turbulent history between Lou and Sam. There is something more complex and more volatile than aunt and niece, and how could it not be so? When Lou came to collect Sam from the warehouse of camp cots and frightened children in Germany, Sam kicked her simply because she was Lou. She was not Sam's mother. This is not something that Sam has ever let her aunt forget, not in principals' offices nor counselors' rooms, not in police stations, and not when teachers came to call. "Lou is my legal guardian," Samantha would say, sulky. She would roll her eyes. "But she thinks she's my mother." Her aunt's tolerance has been without limit. It is as though her aunt has worn Sam's labels as penance: runaway, disturbed child, troubled teen.

Ten minutes pass, fifteen, and then Sam knocks on the bathroom door. "Lou?" she says. "Are you all right in there?"

Silence.

"Lou?"

"I'll just be a minute," Lou says, though her voice sounds strange.

In the living room, she speaks quite calmly again. "Would you like more tea?"

"I have to relive it all the time," Samantha says, defensive.

"I know that, Sam. Whereas I try not to. I try to stay back here in the photo album, before it happened." The muscles in Lou's shoulders and back are taut. "Two different ways of coping, that's all."

"You have more *before* than I have," Sam accuses.

Lou breathes slowly. Samantha can see her counting silently to keep her agitation in check. "Sam, don't you think this is pointless? You've already won the gold medal for suffering—I'll sign a certificate if you like—and I'm not even a runner-up. Nothing we do will change the past, will it?"

"I would just like to *have* a past."

Samantha's aunt presses her fingertips against her brows, the way Jacob does when his migraines come. She pushes hard at the edge of her skull. She presses the pads of her thumbs against her temples. She speaks so quietly, Sam has to lean forward to hear. "I'm sorry, Sam, I don't know what more I can tell you. I can't do it. I can't give you what you want."

"Won't, you mean."

"The truth is, I don't see you for six months at a time, I miss you, I feel so happy when you call to say you'll come by, and then it takes me weeks to recover when you do."

"Okay, then I won't visit anymore."

"I think that would be best," Lou says, and Samantha feels a small lurch of panic.

"Fine," she says bitterly. "I'll head for the escape hatch, then."

"Sam, Sam."

Even Sam is embarrassed by herself, though she does feel queasy. She can see the dark nothing below the hatch, before she was pushed from the plane. "I'm sorry. That was cheap. I didn't mean—"

"Of course you didn't, of course you didn't. I'll try, Sam. What exactly did you want to know this time?"

"What were we all doing in Paris? I've never known that."

"You never let me talk about it."

"Now I'm letting you. Why were we there?"

"You were there because I was," Lou sighs. "Officially I was studying French painting."

"We were there because you were. All these years and you never once said."

"You always storm out before I get to that." Lou goes to her shelves and takes down books on the Louvre and the Musée d'Orsay, large heavy tomes of colored plates. "I was twenty-four. When you're twenty-four, you think living in Paris will be the most glamorous thing you'll ever do. You think you'll be in seventh heaven, and in fact you live in some miserable little studio apartment in the thirteenth arrondissement where it's cheap, and you have to share it with someone you don't much like, and you're so lonely you'd take the next plane home except your pride and your scholarship won't let you." She stares for a long time at Manet's *White Peonies with Secateurs*. "My roommate was a French girl and we didn't like each other much. She was moody and strange and she despised Americans."

"Why?"

"She had an American father, she said. I guess she didn't think much of him, but he wasn't around, so she took it out on me."

"And that's why you were miserable."

"Françoise didn't help, but it wasn't her fault." Lou traces Manet's secateurs with a fingertip. Only the black blades are visible; the handles are outside the frame. "I was depressed when I went and I got into one of those—"

"Depressed."

"—downward spirals . . ."

"Why were you depressed?"

Lou studies Sam without speaking for some time, and her melancholy eyes irritate her niece. "I'd really gone away to get over someone," she says.

"Oh. A broken heart." Sam gives the statement a sardonic edge.

"Yes."

In the page of text opposite the peonies, Samantha manages to read: *Manet's "Olympia" caused a tremendous scandal in 1865 because of its subversive reinterpretation of the past and its almost satirical echo of Titian's*— Her aunt turns the page. There is a double spread of *Olympia*, the center fold passing through the creamy thighs of the woman lounging on satin sheets. "When you're desperate," Lou says, "you do things that you—"

"I know about desperate."

"I suppose you do, Sam." But Lou is lost in the desolation of thirteen years ago in Paris.

"So what did you do?" Sam demands.

Lou turns away and presses her forehead against Manet's brushstrokes, but Samantha does not relent. "What did you do?" she prods.

"I gave in and called my big sister."

Big sister. A rush of excitement seizes Samantha: a new angle; another puzzle piece; something that might jar a two-dimensional image into life.

"You were close." Samantha keeps her voice neutral. "You and my mother."

"Of course we were. We used to be so close that you couldn't have put—"

"*Used to be*."

"Before you came along. Before she got married."

"You resented me." Samantha pounces on an undernote and will not let go. "You resented my father and me."

"Nothing's that simple, Sam." Lou studies her niece, deciding what to tell. " I needed to see you again so badly—"

"Me?" Samantha says, startled.

"All of you, I mean. When your mother had Matthew, I went into a tailspin. I can't explain. I just had to— Rosalie and you, and the new baby, and Jonathan, before you all dis—" Lou's hand flies to her mouth. "It had been so long."

"You were going to say *disappeared*." Samantha is watching Lou closely, riveted. She does not believe in chance or coincidence. Every thread, in her experience, leads into the knot.

"I was going to say: *disappeared into terminal respectability*. You wouldn't understand."

A word comes back to Samantha from nowhere. *Disreputable. Your sister is so disreputable*.

"Were you disreputable, Lou?"

Lou gives her niece a strange look. "What made you say that?"

"My father said it. Grandma and Grandpa used to say it."

Lou looks as though Samantha has struck her. She stretches her fingers out flat and covers Olympia with them. Her veins crisscross the backs of her hands like string. She picks up the photo album and turns the pages. She stops. She points to a photograph. Sam's mother and

Sam's aunt, her father between them—a happy threesome—are ankle-deep in white sand. All three are in swimsuits. Sam's mother wears a one-piece suit, demure; her aunt is in a bikini and has a flower in her hair. Her father, in the middle, has his arms around them both. "The good sister and the disreputable sister on the beach at Isle of Palms, South Carolina," Sam's aunt says in a sardonic tone. "The summer after my high school graduation. Rosalie and Jonathan were engaged already. Look, you can see her ring in the photograph. And I was supposed to be getting ready for the College of Charleston in the fall, but I ran away to New York instead."

She points to another photograph. Lou must be about eighteen, Rosalie twenty. They are standing in front of a church. "Someone else's wedding," Lou says. "Later that same summer." In the photograph, Lou has bright red bad-girl lips and wears an off-the-shoulder dress. Her eyes are outlined in kohl. Sam's mother looks sweet and shy. "The disreputable one," Sam's aunt says, tapping her own image on the head. "And you're in the photograph too, though nobody knows it yet, not even your mother. Did you know your parents had to get married sooner than planned?"

Samantha closes her eyes for a moment, the better to rehear the pinprick of malice.

"I figured it out," she says. "So what? Is that a big deal?"

"It was, back then. In Charleston, South Carolina, believe me, that sort of thing was still a very big deal. At least, in the best families it was. When she found out about the pregnancy, your grandmother was distraught. She was actually hospitalized with 'nervous prostration.' "

"Is that why I was born in New York?"

"Yes. And that's why your mother had to give up her Charleston wedding, which broke your grandmother's heart. That's why your parents were married in a registry office in Manhattan, and why they moved to Atlanta immediately afterwards, and why I stayed in New York."

"Hurricane Sam, that's me," Samantha jokes, to hide her disturbance. "Cause of wholesale evacuation of Charleston"—and perhaps, she has always irrationally feared, of her parents' deaths.

"That's pretty much the way it was," her aunt says. "Certainly as far as our parents—your grandparents—were concerned."

Samantha studies the three people in the photograph, her mother Rosalie and her aunt Lou and her own invisible self.

"Who's this?" she asks, pointing to a photograph of her aunt and another woman in front of the Tour Eiffel. The woman is frowning.

"That's Françoise. The one I shared the apartment with."

"She looks pretty glum."

"I put up with her because I only had to pay a pittance for rent. She paid most of it, and she paid all utilities. Of course there was a downside. Sometimes her boyfriend would show up and I'd have to find somewhere else for the night."

"Françoise," Samantha says. "That's a funny coincidence. There's a Françoise who just contacted me through the website, the Flight 64 website. She lives in Paris."

"It's a very common name."

"Did I meet her? Your roommate? Did we visit your apartment?"

"No, you stayed in a hotel."

"Would she have known—*your* Françoise—that you had relatives on the flight?"

"It was her TV set that I was glued to for days, but then I moved out anyway to collect you in Germany."

"And then we flew back to Charleston," Sam says.

"You remember that?"

Sam remembers verandas, porch swings, jasmine. She remembers planes that exploded every night. She remembers tantrums. She remembers throwing things at her grandparents and at her aunt. "I remember we didn't last long in Charleston."

"No."

"And then you and Grandma Hamilton had a big fight, and you brought me here to New York."

"Yes," Lou says sadly.

"You should have known it would never work," Samantha says.

She remembers years of shuttling between her aunt Lou in New York and her grandparents in Charleston, fighting with all of them, always moody, always in trouble at school, until her grandparents paid for a boarding school in Vermont, which seemed to them an institution both sufficiently distinguished and sufficiently far away, and there Samantha discovered American history and American government, and then she discovered obsession. She became obsessed with the politics of hijacked planes and with the capacity of press and public for quick forgetting, and with the quiet erasure of events from government records. She decided that Washington, D.C., was where she needed to be, and she applied to Georgetown University and was accepted.

Samantha holds the magnifying glass again to the shot of the family boarding the plane. "Why is my father watching you like that?"

"I had the camera," her aunt says.

"Why is my mother watching my father like that? She's worried about something. What is she worried about?"

"Your mother never liked traveling much," her aunt says.

Samantha jumps up and walks out to Lou's kitchen and looks in her fridge and rummages there as though a different possible past is hidden somewhere behind the milk carton. Her head is deep inside the white-enameled cold. "If she hadn't begged them to come to Paris, we would never have been on that flight," Samantha says in a low voice to the back wall of the refrigerator, trying out the words. They bounce back from a tub of butter. She shuts the fridge door. She goes back into the living room and picks up the photo album and puts it down and goes out to the kitchen again. She goes to the sink. She turns on the cold tap, then the hot. She lets both of them run full blast. She watches her life running down the drain.

Her aunt follows and puts her hands on Samantha's shoulders. Samantha has a sudden violent wish to push Lou's hands into the Cuisinart and turn it on. "Grandma Hamilton calls you the black sheep of the family," she says, wanting to draw blood. "You slept around." The tap water is plunging ferociously down the drain. "There would even have been a baby, Grandma says, if the family hadn't taken care of the matter."

Sam can see the sudden pain in Lou's eyes, but nevertheless the eyes rest on her niece's face, calm and assessing, disappointed perhaps. *Is she embarrassed for me?* Sam asks herself. This makes her furious. She puts her head under the rush of water and hears chance. It roars like Niagara. She can see the fog, angry-colored, that hangs over Porte 12, between her aunt's camera and herself. There is something about the camera that sends rockets of anger scudding under the surface of Sam's skin. This anger beats in and out like a bass drum in her ears and it signals war, but the truth is, she does not really understand why she is so furiously angry with her aunt and the awkwardness of being in the wrong makes her angrier.

"Let it go, Sam," Lou says. "Let them be. Let them rest in peace."

"I can't," Samantha says.

She wants to show the world photographs that don't exist. Look at this, she wants to say: my mother's eyes. These are my mother's eyes at the moment when Matthew finally stopped crying altogether. And here is something else, she wants to say: here are the eyes of the children all around me, some time later (days later, airports later, negotiations, ultimatums, deadlines later) when we huddled together watching TV—we were crowded on makeshift cots in some vast room, I think it was a high school gym, I know it was somewhere in Germany—forty pairs of eyes, opened wide, unblinking, watching the fate of their parents on one small screen. The plane, before it turned into an underwater sun, before it branched into red and orange coral, seemed to swim in blue haze like a fish. We knew we had been dropped like tiny eggs from its belly, we were vague about when. *Pow, pow*, one little boy said, pointing his fingers at the screen. No one cried then. All the eyes were so dry, they prickled. There was an eerie silence in the room.

Here is a photograph, Samantha wants to say to the world. Here is a photograph, never taken, which I would like you to see: the eyes of forty frightened children as they step off the lip of an abyss.

2.

CHIEN BLEU

Onstage, back in Washington, D.C., Samantha blazes with light and looks into the dark. Chien Bleu is murkily lit. This is a basement dive, thick with perfume and blues and jazz and the hot scent of illicit assignations. Chien Bleu caters to the lower levels, so to speak, but the baseness is exclusive. Inside the Washington Beltway, all sex is costly and the Chien Bleu's cover price is high. Tables are so close that the waiters must pass between them sideways, trays held aloft. Couple by couple, even one by one, clients sift in past the bouncers. No standees are allowed. In the heat of the overhead spotlight, Samantha dabs at her forehead—she has tissues tucked into her bra—but she can feel her makeup melting on her face. She waits for the sax backstage to well up and flow over the din of conversation and she rides the wave.

"Hi," she says huskily, floating herself out on an arpeggio. The soft curl of attention washes back toward her.

"I can't sing," she tells them, almost touching the mike with her lips. "I'm the entr'acte between musical sets." She makes this sound like a proposition, low and sultry.

She takes a clasp out of her hair and lets it cascade around her shoulders. She unbuttons the cuffs on her long white sleeves. (She is dressed like a schoolteacher or a librarian: prim white blouse with high collar, a plain gray skirt which is ankle-length and severe.) She gives a quick tug to each sleeve, and as each pulls away from the arm hole, she discards it, tossing it into the crowd. "Ahh," she says languidly. "That feels better." There is a thin scatter of laughter as men reach for the floating sleeves and then a heightened attentiveness that even in the dark she can feel. She unbuttons her blouse very slowly. From backstage, a riff of cool jazz rises like mist. "No, I don't sing," she says. "I'm the stand-up comic."

In one quick move, she steps out of blouse and skirt. Underneath, she is wearing a filthy sleeveless undershirt and gray flannel long johns from a Salvation Army bin. "I'm a bag lady," she says. "I live a few intersections from the Capitol. You know that crossover point where the property taxes plummet and there's a kind of sea change in the type of human being you see? Someone offered me twenty bucks to strip while the trumpeter pours the spit out of his horn. Throw in a meal and a bed, I told them, and it's a deal. So here I am.

"Now the question is," she murmurs into the mike, stepping down off the stage and feeling her way between the tables, "the question is: whose bed is it going to be? Who's going to be the lucky man?" She taps this man and that on the shoulder. "Not you, not you, not you," she says. There is laughter at each table as she passes. "I'm rather particular," she says, "about the men whose bed I'll crawl into. I'm partial to the smell of power. Well, it's the local aphrodisiac in this town, isn't it? Can't get up without it."

As faces loom out of the candlelight, Samantha sniffs at them with elaborate show. Sometimes she sees one of her professors from Georgetown U, but not often. It's more a hangout for congressmen, senators, lobbyists, publicists, Pentagon brass, the whole Capitol Hill tribe. "This man," she says, tapping him on the shoulder, and suddenly the spot swings toward them and highlights a well-known face, "this man has more government secrets tucked into his jockey shorts than you have bees in your honeysuckle. But we've got our little secrets here too." And the spot moves slightly to bathe in white light the pillowy-lipped young woman at his side. She is expensively dressed—perhaps *wrapped* is a better word—in something clingy and silver. "Tinfoil," Samantha announces, crumpling a little of the cloth in her hand. The metallic sound of foil comes from the speakers. People laugh. "Luckily for our patrons," Samantha says, "we don't allow cameras in here. If we did, they might have to pay dearly for their pleasures." The spot lingers on the bare shoulders of the young woman and pans along the slit that runs from the hem of her skirt to thigh-high. "Anyway . . ." Samantha pauses dramatically, and the spot turns back to the senator's face. "I'm sure he's paid enough for her already." Much laughter, as the spot and Samantha move on.

She weaves between tables, she moves between dark and light. Each stretch of dark is immense. She slides her foot forward on the tiled floor and feels for the void. It can open up anywhere with no more than a second's warning. Sometimes she has to steady herself by catching hold of a chair back or someone's shoulder. She believes that Salamander may be present. He is her compass and her magnetic North Pole. She will find him. She believes she will know him by his smell. She has fantasies of causing Salamander pain, and when he is screaming, she will make him lead her to Sirocco, because Sirocco may have been the one who lit the fuse. But both of them *knew,* both of them *planned,* and the knowing is not something that Sam will forgive. "Halloween was a week ago," she says, "but it's always Halloween here, isn't it? The place is always full of spooks. Trick or treat, that's the question. Who's the spook of the week?

"Not you, not you, not you," she says, tapping shoulders as she passes by. "When the lights go out in Washington, the powerful play musical secrets and musical beds. Did you hear the one about the guy in Intelligence who made his own lie and went to bed with it? Gave birth to an international incident but the CIA and the NSA pressured him to put it up for adoption. It grew up to be a full-sized war and then—because this is the way things go these days—it went looking for its birth father. There were blood tests, DNA, the whole works. Everything pointed to someone high up in Intelligence, who denied all on the grounds that he never fucked with the lie of the land. Turned out he was a double agent so they tripled him and packed him off to Pakistan and arranged for another double agent to accidentally on purpose bump him off."

This is the way it goes. Samantha loves the nervousness of the laughter. She gets high on it. "Who's going to make the honor roll tonight?" she croons. She likes to tantalize. The spotlight roams and picks out faces here and there. "All sinners together, isn't this cozy?" she asks. "All in the same boat. It's like being crammed into the same hijacked plane.

"You know," she confides, "I only go to bed with men powerful enough to have code names. I went to bed once with a man whose code name was Goliath, but he was too much of a Philistine for my taste. Another time, I had sex with Arctic Fox, but it left me cold. And then there was Salamander, whoosh, what a slitherer, what a fire-cracker, comes like a rocket. I had to turn the hose on him, but it didn't douse his flame for one second. That guy is burning, burning, burning, first cousin to a desert wind. Keep your fire extinguisher handy when Salamander's around because he knows about explosions before they come, and he knows where the hot sirocco blows.

"Did you hear the one about the former head of the CIA who made a deal with bin Laden? 'Look,' he says to bin Laden, 'it's the year 2000, and we know you've got a millennial itch. You need global publicity and global sympathy. We need to nail your ass. Neither of us can make a move, because we know everything you plan to do before you do it, and you know every countermove we plan to take. We're both stalemated. So here's a proposal. How about we bankroll a movie, *Getting Osama,* with a look-alike actor? In the movie, your cave stronghold is infiltrated by Bruce Willis and Harrison Ford. Your guys catch them. Our guys survive barbaric Islamic persuasion. They get their hands cut off, then their ears. They don't talk. They escape and blow your compound and the entire Taliban army to smithereens. In the movie, only your little son survives the blast, and Harrison Ford gives him his pack of baseball cards and takes him back to California. When your son asks Sammy Sosa for his autograph, there's not a dry eye in the house. Your little boy becomes an icon like Elian Gonzalez. Think of the public relations coup. As far as global opinion is concerned, depending on political allegiance, of course, you die a tragic hero or you got what was coming to you. Either way, the violence ends, the famine ends, the suffering ends, and the whole world loves your little son.'

" 'What's the catch?' bin Laden wants to know.

" 'The catch is, we film on location in Afghanistan.' "

And so it goes, and so it goes.

Even by candlelight, there are men who murmur comments into handheld dictaphones. But stand-up comics are like jesters in the court of medieval kings. They can take liberties. They can get away with murder, so to speak. They can make fools of those who walk in the corridors of power, and the powerful love them for it. The powerful court them. They offer proposals and enticements. They seek occasions to compile a photographic dossier in case the need for future blackmail should arise.

"My dear," a silver-haired gentleman says, stroking Samantha's thigh. "What a wickedly delicious mind you have. May I buy you a drink?"

> *(Will you walk into my parlor? says the spider to the fly.*
> *There's a microphone behind me and a hidden camera eye.)*

"You may buy me anything you please," Samantha murmurs, making sheep's eyes and sitting on his lap.

"Excuse me," some clumsy lout says, lurching against her. She is doused in ice cubes and scotch, and the drunken bungler catches hold of her wrist.

"Sam," he says, low and intense, "are you out of you mind?"

"Jacob," she murmurs, her lips against his ear, "mind your own damn business."

"I'm minding it," he whispers.

"You are sabotaging *weeks* of preparation."

"I'm saving your skin. I'll meet you out on the street in fifteen minutes. Be there."

Samantha shakes her head in a gesture of incredulity. "Can you believe this?" she says to the silver-haired gentleman, brushing scotch from her bag-lady shirt. "I'm soaked. I'll have to go change."

3.

PHOENIX ONE, PHOENIX TWO

"You're sailing way too close to the wind, Sam. It's stupid and it's dangerous."

"Part of the fallout, isn't it? We're all addicted to risk."

"Is that so?" Jacob lines up cardboard drink coasters, three round ones on his left, two diamond-shaped ones on his right. He moves a round one from the left side to the right and places it between the two diamonds. He frowns, considering this equation, then moves it back. The tavern they are in is small and dimly lit, which suits them. Ironically, they seem to need confined spaces.

"It's well known," Samantha says flippantly. She is at pains to be flippant with Jacob, to stop herself sliding into him. Sometimes their edges match so exactly that a waiter will bring them only one drink. Nutrient fusion, Jacob calls it. No; ego confusion, Sam insists. Phoenix One and Phoenix Two are the names they are known by in their circle—sometimes for particular kinds of communication, sometimes for a grim private joke—but they are Siamesed from the same charcoal pit, two barbecued peas in a pod. Their circle is small and exclusive. The members call themselves the Phoenix Club, and they mostly make contact via the Web.

"Risk addiction's a commonplace for our lot," Samantha says. "For all survivors. Earthquake survivors, rape survivors, whatever. There's a special section in bookstores now: survival lit. Articles all over the place. You must have read some."

"Not my cup of tea."

"Well, I'm telling you, whether you want to know about it or not, risk addiction's part of the syndrome. There's statistical evidence, conferences, papers, proceedings, God knows what. Interesting to speculate on the reasons, don't you think? And if you want to know why I'm babbling on like this, it's because that disapproving look of yours upsets me."

"There are certain kinds of risk that you don't have the right to take."

"Why not?"

"Because they put all of us in greater jeopardy, that's why."

"We're all in perpetual jeopardy anyway. Don't we take that as a given?"

"That's why we have a certain understanding."

"Right," Samantha snaps. "We understand that all of us manage in whatever way we can and we don't sit in judgment on each other. I don't judge, you don't judge, he doesn't judge, we don't judge—"

"But we do keep an eye out for each other. That's part of the deal." He touches Samantha's cheek. "You're manic," he says uneasily. "What are you on?"

"On getting somewhere. On the trail getting hot. On nailing down answers."

"Sam, Sam. There aren't any answers. Or none that will make the slightest difference."

"It's amazing what I'm learning from next-of-kin. It's amazing what the website brings in."

"You're burning yourself up."

"I'm on fire," she acknowledges, "but I'm learning plenty. I'm doing this for the future. I'm doing this for the historical record. As well as for my thesis in American history, don't forget. It's like a map coming into focus."

"The Phoenix Club's one thing. We need each other. It helps, keeping contact, it helps us all. But you're casting your net too wide. You're drawing dangerous attention."

"I *need* to draw fire. I know exactly what I'm doing and I'm careful."

"You're reckless." He clenches his hands together. He leans across the table, his forearms over the lineup of coasters. He looks like a gambler shielding a spread of cards. "We need each other to survive, Sam. We need each other too much. If something happened to you—"

"It won't."

"If something did—"

"What can happen to someone who's indifferent to what happens?"

"Enough."

"We're immune to harm, Jacob, or we wouldn't be here. You can't snuff a phoenix out."

"Unfortunately, you can." He pulls at his fingers and the knuckles make an ominous sound. He looks more ravaged than usual. "I went to see Cassie yesterday."

"Ah," Samantha says uneasily. "How is she?"

"Getting worse, I think."

"So that's what all this is about."

"Not only that."

Jacob blinks, slowly and heavily. He makes Samantha think of an owl and the thought trips a nervous tic in her hand. Her thumb, of its own free will, does a little series of calisthenics. "You had that look on your face," she says, "when the news broke—"

"Why are you whispering? I can't hear you."

"You were sitting on the cot across from me. In Germany. When we watched the plane go up. That's how you looked."

"Stop it, Sam."

She hasn't meant to go there, but all roads lead back to the airstrip on the TV screen.

Jacob turns a coaster around and around in his hands.

The cots and the blankets smell musty to Samantha. They must have been pulled out of storage in a damp basement. This must have been hurriedly done. There is a boy next to Samantha sucking a blanket, there is another boy across from her, an older boy whose eyelids droop and who plays with the lid of a screwtop jar. Samantha does not yet know that his name is Jacob. He turns the lid around and around. *We interrupt this program to bring you a news alert. . . .*

Samantha takes the coaster roughly from Jacob's hands. "You're making me edgy."

"You should be edgy. You're drawing fire, Sam. You know what's going to happen? Someone will get nervous and clamp down on access to documents again, but that won't be the worst of it."

"What will be the worst of it?"

"More of us will start meeting up with accidents."

"More of us? What do you mean?"

"Stick to finishing your degree at Georgetown," he says. "Stop this crazy moonlighting stuff. As a stand-up comic, you're not funny."

"Students have to moonlight to survive, and this pays better than waiting tables. What did you mean, *more of us*?"

"More dead phoenixes. Chien Bleu is not a good way to go. I have an ominous feeling about it." He turns to signal for the waiter. When he turns, his shirtsleeve rides up on his arm. The cuffs are unbuttoned and turned back, pale blue cotton against his faint tan, and the tracks on his forearm look to Sam like the footprints of the beast.

"Oh, Jacob." She catches hold of his wrist in blind panic. "What are you doing?"

"It's no more dangerous than what you're doing," he says. He pulls his wrist away and buttons his cuffs. "And a lot less stupid."

"How can you say that?" When she closes her eyes, she feels the nothing under the table. Her sense of balance goes. "You're right," she concedes. "We're not safe."

Jacob leans over the table and takes both her hands in his. "Look at me, Sam."

"How's that going to help me when you're covered in needle tracks?"

"So governments do shady things when national security's at stake. They make mistakes. Is this news to anyone?"

"Oh, forgive me. I thought accountability for shady activity, even in wartime, was one of the pillars of our democracy. I thought I remembered learning that in high school. Silly me. I thought a secret service accountable to no one was Nazi Germany and evil-Soviet-empire stuff."

"Oh for God's sake, get down out of your pulpit," Jacob says. "Governments make mistakes and they cover them up and they do not appreciate exposure. We stand a better chance of making it if we take that as the starting point."

"Oh, right," Samantha says bitterly. "I can see where that starting point is getting you."

"It's been a bad week," he concedes. "And it'll get worse if you don't put on the brakes."

"You said that before. More of us will have accidents, you said. What did you mean, *more of us*?"

"We lost another one."

She stares at him.

"Another phoenix. We lost him in August, but I just found out about it."

"Wait," Samantha says. It is not as though they are not used to bad news, but due preparations must be made. "Wait. I have to—I'll just . . ."

She goes to the bathroom and locks the door. Her hands are shaking. She starts counting backward from one hundred. She counts down through ritual layers, down through the Cenozoic and the Mesozoic and the Paleozoic and the Precambrian. Under the Precambrian is the time before the plane disappeared in a ball of fire, and there's a space there, a space that Samantha can think her way into if she counts backward far enough. In that space, everyone is still alive. She imagines it with chandeliers and a dance floor. Her mother is in a strapless dress of pale blue silk, her father kisses her mother on the neck. The dancers move in slow motion, the future casts no shadow at all, and there is music. Samantha can wind it in like a ribbon from the violin of Jacob's father, Avi Levinstein, who plays with his whole body; and Jacob, he says, bending over his instrument and his bow, Jacob, I am so happy that you and Samantha . . . and Samantha, he says, I have pleasure to present to you some of our friends on this flight, and the inventory unscrolls itself, a gold-leaf list of the gifted, the flamboyant, the intense, the cellist Izak Goldberg and his wife Victoria, bel canto soprano, and Cassie, their daughter; Yasmina Shankara, the Bombay movie star, and Agit, her son; and so on and so forth until Samantha turns to Jacob and asks: Does your father know *everyone*? and she watches the patterns that people make with the swirls of their lives, brushing one another in passing, sometimes knowing it, sometimes not. She can see everyone who was on the plane. She holds them that way in her mind.

When she gets back to the table, Jacob has his head down. His hair brushes a small jigger of mustard. "Hey," Samantha says. "You asleep?"

"We lost Agit."

Samantha holds herself still.

"Agit Shankara," he says. "We lost him August eighth, exactly a month before the anniversary of the hijacking."

"No." Samantha has a sudden memory of huddling on a cot with Agit in Germany. They were watching children's cartoons until the interruption came. They had to share a blanket, and Agit had one corner balled up into his mouth though his quiet little sobs still leaked out. *We interrupt this program for the latest bulletin. . . .* When they saw the plane, Agit turned quiet. He took the blanket out of his mouth and wiped his nose with it and then put it back in his mouth. Samantha hit him. That's dirty, she told him.

"Agit drew attention to himself," Jacob says.

"How did he draw attention?"

"He published a book of short stories. Not here. In India. But just the same."

"Stories?"

"A collection called *Flight into the Dark.*"

"No one in government circles or Intelligence pays any attention to fiction."

"It was published in June. He sent me a copy in July and I haven't heard from him since. He stopped answering e-mails."

"Is that all?" Samantha asks, euphoric with relief. "He's gone into withdrawal. I've done that, you've done that. It's nothing."

"It's not nothing. I found out what happened."

"I don't want to know."

"I'm not going to tell you."

"How'd you find out?"

"On-line, from the *Indian Express*. Just a filler item. Took me hours of scrolling to find it. *Son of beautiful former movie icon Yasmina Shankara who perished in the tragic hijacking,* et cetera. "

"That makes six of us." Samantha wraps her arms around herself. She feels cold.

"This affects us," Jacob says.

"Yes. What happened to him?"

"You don't want to know."

"I know I don't. But tell me." Samantha leans across the table and takes hold of the lapels of Jacob's jacket. His jacket is worn at the edges. He looks scruffy, Jacob. He is an assistant professor of mathematics and looks like it. In mathematics, he says, unknown quantities can be calculated. Answers are morally neutral and can be nailed down. Chance can be predicted and fractally expressed.

"Tell me what happened to Agit," Samantha insists.

"He threw himself under a train, the newspaper said. Hundreds of people saw him. At the central railway station in Bombay."

"Threw himself? Or was pushed?"

"That's the question, isn't it?"

They don't know which ending they'd prefer. What kind of operation, they ask themselves, goes on wiping out survivors and witnesses so many years after the event? They hold each other, Jacob and Samantha.

"You're shivering," she whispers.

"I'm cold."

"But you're burning," she says. "You've got a fever."

"Come home with me."

"All right."

In Jacob's apartment, they lie for a long time, side by side, staring up at his bedroom ceiling. Jacob has painted it black, and has added to it in phosphorescent white and with absolute accuracy, the star map of the northern September sky. "I could see Polaris through my window," he says. "That first landing."

"Morocco."

"Wasn't Egypt first? Then Morocco."

"It was Morocco. According to my aunt."

"Wherever. I could see Polaris the whole time. And I knew that everything would go on. Because Polaris was there when Jericho fell, and when Troy fell, and when Rome fell, and when Hitler fell. I knew everything would go on."

"And here we are," Samantha says. "Going on. Two phoenixes."

"The random chosen," he says.

"But still the chosen."

"Except that doesn't mean anything. Or if it does, we'll never know what it means."

"This means something," Samantha says, turning to him, and they bite and moan, ravenous, and then they sleep. They dream.

"I dream everyone," Samantha tells Jacob. "I know them so well now, I dream their dreams."

4.

PHOENIX THREE

The abandoned boathouse where the local members of the Phoenix Club meet is sparsely furnished. Samantha and Jacob find it beautiful. Sometimes they sit in the rowboat and sometimes they climb the ladder and sit on the weathered boards of the loft where gulls nest. The gulls fly off across Chesapeake Bay with shrieks and a great hullabaloo of wings and outrage that they do not let go. Patrolling in pairs, they wheel past the gable window and the open A of the roofline where the boat winch used to be. They hurl imprecations. They fix Jacob and Samantha and Cassie with their black beady eyes, but the members of the Phoenix Club are used to being watched. How to live under and around surveillance is something they know about. They settle into the rotting piles of fishnets. Ropes and wooden floats and one anchor hang from the rafters. There are abandoned oars lying about, smooth as soapstone, lovely to the touch, mapped with the wood grain's sinewy curves.

Cassie buckles herself into a life vest, though all of these are moldy and torn and have discharges of flotation stuffing poking from seams. Cassie's vest is Day-Glo orange, faded now, and crusted in a latticework of salt which smells of boating disasters averted. Cassie finds the smell comforting. The three of them laze there, cradled in fishnet heaps, listening to the soft slap of water against the pylons below. Sometimes they spend hours like this without speaking. No one disturbs them, because this is the unfashionable part of the bay, an unstable landscape of salt marsh and mudflats that even most fishermen avoid.

They chose the place for its isolation, but also because they like enclosed spaces. They like to have water nearby. Fire could touch them here, but they would hear it coming across the salt marsh and due preparations could be made. Intruders could reach them, but the gulls would give warning, and they would descend into the boat and glide away, soundlessly, through the tall brown stubble of the marsh, a labyrinth for which few know the code. For those not intimate with tides and rushes, boating is dangerous. The narrow channels change shape and direction by the hour. The members of the Phoenix Club are safe here. Cassie knows this intuitively. Jacob found the boathouse, and they bring Cassie from time to time because it is the only other place besides her room in the psychiatric hospital where she is calm. Hunched into themselves in the loft, they can close their eyes and enter that state they call *Before*.

"When Papa has the boat . . ." Cassie says. The others turn to her and wait, but she usually finishes her sentences internally, or perhaps she forgets where they were going.

"Cass?" Samantha prompts, but she is far from them, absorbed by marsh birds.

"I think her parents had a cottage on the bay somewhere," Jacob says. "She used to spend summers here."

"How do you know?"

"I remember visiting once, when I was small. I don't remember where, of course, but my father's agent told me it was somewhere around the bay. He was agent for Cassie's parents too, for the string quartet and for her mother's concert performances."

Cassie says suddenly, "My mother has a beautiful voice."

Jacob leans over to take Cass's hand and he holds it between his own and strokes her arm. "Yes," he says. "Your mother did have a lovely voice. An extraordinary voice." He has recordings of Cass's mother singing Renaissance and troubadour songs, accompanied by Cass's father on cello, and by his own father on violin. He has newspaper clippings. He has the memories of relatives and family friends. Nevertheless, his eyes quicken—Samantha can see it—because there is a chance, slim, unpredictable, that he might pick up a new chip for the mosaic. Cass is twenty-seven: three years older than Jacob, who is five years older than Sam. Cassie has—when it is not completely fogged in—more memory of Before.

But Cass's memory comes in single thin beams of light that touch on an image for a second or two and then extinguish themselves. She watches Jacob stroking her arm with an air of abstracted curiosity. She begins to hum, a sound that comes from low in her throat and gets stronger though the melody is in a plaintive minor key. Samantha recognizes the song from Jacob's recordings. Jacob blinks in his heavy-lidded, owllike way. He begins to hum in harmony with Cass. Samantha closes her eyes and lets the duet float around her, and Victoria and Izak Goldberg and Avi Levinstein—she knows them from photographs and newsreel clips and from the jacket of an old LP—rise from it like wraiths.

There is a long long silence when the humming ends, and then Jacob says, "They did make such good music together." But his voice is uneven. He is as skittish as Cass when it comes to connecting one bead of the past to another.

Cass says, "Papa said, don't hurt the cello, but the man with the mask smashed it with his . . . what do you call it, Jacob?"

"Kalashnikov."

"Kalashnikov. It's a funny word." Cass begins to keen on a high note and to rock back and forth.

"Oh shit," Samantha murmurs. "What triggered this?" She remembers the smashing of the cello. She remembers how it seemed to happen in slow motion, how it seemed to float like a kite before it fell to the runway, and then Cassie screamed and spread her arms and flew after it, and catapulted down the chute headfirst.

"Cass," Jacob says. He strokes her hair. "I'm so sorry, Cass."

"I saw photographs," Cass says. "When we were in Paris. Your father had no clothes on, Jacob. And Lowell's mother had no clothes. The man with the photographs told Papa he was a detective and he would give Papa money if Papa could tell him things. But Papa tore up the photographs and the man said, *You will regret that.*"

Samantha stares at Jacob. "What is that about?" she wants to know.

"It wasn't my mother on that flight," Jacob says curtly. "My father was with another woman."

"Why have you never told me?"

"Why should I have to? I try not to remember." The worst thing he has to live with, he thinks, is that his father was in love and he resented it. He resented his father's happiness. He felt left out. "I was upset. After takeoff, I wouldn't sit with them."

"*Lowell's* mother," Sam repeats in astonishment. "You wouldn't sit with your father and Lowell's mother?"

Jacob starts combing his skull with his fingers, a tic Samantha recognizes: first sign of one of his migraines coming on.

"Your father and Lowell's mother," Cass says. "In a photograph. With no clothes on. Papa tore it up but I saw."

"Cass," Samantha says gently. "Do you know Lowell? How do you know Lowell?" But Cass's mind is off with the birds in the marsh.

"Her name was Isabella Hawthorne," Jacob says. "I know she was leaving a husband and son. I know nothing else about her and never wanted to."

Samantha can feel heat rising, she can feel the low thrilling hum of new data coming in from new directions, which means new curves can be plotted on the graph. "This is so strange," she says. She knows the airline's passenger manifest by heart: *Isabella Hawthorne. Next of kin: Lowell Hawthorne, son.* "It's strange because I tracked down the son a few weeks ago. I've tracked down Lowell Hawthorne, but he won't return calls."

Jacob stares at her. "Don't touch this, Sam." He begins massaging the front of his skull at a frantic pace. "Oh God," he moans. "Have you got something I can tie over my . . . ? I need to block out the light." He rocks his head against one of the beams.

"This might work." She takes off the linen jacket she is wearing and folds it, once, twice, a thick bandage. She puts it over Jacob's eyes and uses the sleeves to tie it behind his head. "Does that help?"

"Mmm," he moans. "Thanks. Can you drive us?"

"Yes, of course," she says. "Jacob? Do you think if you met with Lowell Hawthorne, it would help?"

He pulls the jacket from his eyes and stares at her in anguish, his left eye horribly bloodshot. "No," he says. "I don't think it would help. The repercussions of what you're doing terrify me, Sam." With a groan, he re-covers his eyes. "You might as well post a sign on the Internet: *I'm going after classified secrets. I'm stirring up trouble. Come and get me.*"

"But they can tell us things, all the next-of-kin can. There are things they don't know they know."

"I know more than I want to know already. I'm in agony, Sam."

"It's unresolved grief, you know it is. Just listen to me, Jacob. It's weird how many links and cross-connections there were between passengers, and between the families of passengers. It defies statistical odds. It has to mean something."

"I don't want to know what it means," Jacob says. "Sam, Sam." He is rocking his head in pain. "I need my medication. I'm begging."

"Sorry," she says. "Oh God, sorry. Let me help Cass down first, and we'll go."

5.

LOWELL

Even before Lowell speaks, Samantha has an intuition that the phone call will be momentous, but that is because she is already in a state of febrile and heightened alert. She hears the under- and overtones when people talk. She imagines an aura of electro-magnetic feelers extending invisibly from her skin and waving about her like angel hair, like the sustenance system of certain sea creatures on tropical reefs: as water rakes through their unseen silken mesh traps, all that is needed stays. Information is falling toward her. It adheres.

"Samantha?" Lowell says, and she recognizes his voice instantly. She has heard it often enough on his answering machine. She has scripted future conversations they will have.

An avalanche starts with a pebble. Samantha thinks of the random searchlight of Cassie's lucidity as setting scree tumbling, loose drifts of it that pull scattered data along in their train. They gather density and speed. Clusters of detail roll over each other and cling. They generate force and the force intensifies. Disparate pieces of information cohere, connections pick up momentum, new facts are exposed. Samantha has a premonition that critical mass has been reached, that the accumulation of data has hooked up isolated circuits, that currents are fizzing around the elaborate latticework and traplines of her research, sparks jumping gaps, missing information being sucked into the black hole of her intense need to know.

"Um . . . it's Lowell," he says.

Samantha holds her breath.

"This isn't easy," he says.

"I know." She can barely speak, and an inner catechism warns: *Don't breathe. Don't frighten him off.* "Not for any of us. It's like picking a scab."

"Yes," he says. "Yes, that's what it's like." That is exactly what it is like, he thinks. As soon as he starts to think about the hijacking, fresh bleeding begins.

It is strange how a silence can suck at two people and how it can vibrate between them and how much information can be sent and received through the mere sound of air moving in and out of lungs. And because something is already understood between the two of them, that the *thing itself*—the blown-up plane, the horrible deaths—is beyond comprehension and beyond language, because of this, they do not feel any awkwardness in a prolonged silence.

Samantha waits.

"In my case," Lowell says, "the death was . . . the death itself . . . the death of my mother was not the major thing." His breath, turning labored, is loud in Samantha's ear. "Look," he says. "I don't think I can manage this, after all. I don't think I can talk about it."

Samantha listens to the plosive beat, rapid and uneven, of air entering and leaving his lungs. She risks saying, "Is that because of Avi Levinstein?"

Lowell makes a small violent sound—he is hyperventilating—and Samantha is afraid he will hang up.

"How do you know about Levinstein?" he asks at last.

"I know his son. I only just learned that the woman Avi Levinstein took with him to Paris was your mother, so I know this must be a painful—"

Lowell hangs up. A week passes and then he calls again.

"You have no idea how angry I was," he tells Sam without preamble.

"I wanted both of them to die." His voice is faint, and Samantha has to strain to hear. "To make a wish like that and have it come true. Do you see what that makes me?"

Samantha says nothing.

"Do you understand what that makes me?" he persists.

"I understand what you *fear* it makes you. But it was natural for you to be angry—" She can almost hear Lowell twisting in the fires of his own savage guilt. "Look," she says, "I don't know if this might help, or if you'll want to do this. And I'm not at all sure he'll want to do it either. But I know Jacob Levinstein well. He's a phoenix. I mean, he's one of us, the children who survived. We have an Internet club. We call ourselves phoenixes because we rose up out of the ashes, so to speak. Jacob's the son of Avi—"

Lowell makes a strangled sound, somewhere between laughter and pain. "Are you crazy?"

"He feels pretty much the same way as you do, I think. It might clear the air for both of you if you—"

"I didn't call to talk about my mother."

Samantha suddenly wonders if Lowell's mother was one of those who caressed her as she passed, when the hijackers were pushing the children along the aisles, when the children were being herded, prodded with rifles, when the rough hands of gunmen slapped them, when the gunmen stuffed rags into sobbing mouths. Samantha finds herself wondering which hands might have belonged to Lowell's mother, because hands had come from everywhere as the children passed, hands stroking them, touching, giving blessing, sending messages that she bears in her body still.

"I'm really calling," Lowell says more calmly, "because you said you had information about my father—"

"It may not be the kind of information that you want."

"I'm sure it won't be," Lowell says. "But you said there was a woman in Paris who knew my father, who claims to be—you said I have a half-sister."

"I think so, yes."

"Is she claiming this, or are you?"

"She is. But she claims she has proof. You didn't know about her?"

"No. And I don't believe her, but I'm curious."

"I'll understand if you're not ready for this," Samantha says, but *Please,* she is thinking, please stay on the line, please give me something, another crumb, two crumbs, I can wait for the trail.

"My father's first wife died," Lowell says. "And they never had children. My mother was his second wife and I was an only child." He pauses, assessing possible evidence, pro and con. "But he *was* stationed in Paris for several years," he concedes. "During his first marriage."

"He had an affair with a Frenchwoman. I've semi-confirmed this from declassified documents. The CIA kept files on a woman who worked at the American Embassy because they considered her a security risk. She had a daughter by an American, a diplomat or an agent, it isn't clear which. Françoise claims that was your father. She says she has photographs to prove it. You can make contact with her through our website if you want."

"I have to think about it."

"She seems to know a lot about your father. She says he's in Intelligence."

"He was."

"Was?"

"He died in a car crash two months ago. September."

"Oh," Samantha says. She feels winded. She can feel a red-hot trail fizzle out. "What date?"

"Two days before the anniversary," he says. "So you don't know everything."

"There's way too much I don't know."

"You hadn't been hounding my father the way you hounded me?"

"I apologize for hounding you. I guess I was obnoxious. I'm sorry."

"Well, not obnoxious," he says. "But relentless, yes."

"I'm sorry. I get like that every September."

"Yeah," he says, softening. "I freak out too. Every year."

"I'm obsessive-compulsive about it, I guess. About anything to do with the hijacking."

"I am too, but in the opposite way. Compulsive avoidance. But if you're, you know, so obsessive, how come you *didn't* hound my father?"

"I only just found out about him, from Françoise. People like your father aren't listed in the telephone book."

"How'd you find out about me?"

"The passenger list's always been available. Each passenger listed one next-of-kin with the airline for notification. Your mother listed you."

"Yes, I suppose she would. How'd you find this Françoise?"

"I didn't. She contacted me. On the website for Flight 64."

"I avoid anything like that," Lowell says.

"So. Do you want to meet me and talk?"

"I'm not sure. Where's this area code? D.C., isn't it? Is that where you live?"

"Yes. But I could come up to Boston for a weekend. Or we could pick somewhere in between, like New York."

"Maybe," he says. "I'm not sure. I have to be careful."

"Why? What do you mean?"

"Nothing," Lowell says nervously. "I don't mean anything."

A hole-in-the-wall café in Penn Station is not where Samantha would have picked, but Lowell insists. He has a soft-sided overnight bag with him and he keeps it on his lap. He looks around.

"Are you expecting someone?" Sam asks.

"What? No. No, no. Just checking the joint. It's like lead in paint."

"Lead in paint?"

"Old paint. Before they banned lead? Once you know about it, you see it everywhere. I've had medical problems," he says. "Even walls become dangerous, know what I mean?"

"Uh-huh," she says doubtfully, trying to follow.

"I paint houses," he explains. "Lot of old houses in Boston, peeling paint. I have to strip them. Lead levels are up in my blood."

"Uh-huh. I don't know much about—"

"Heart problems. Nervous system. I get tested every month. You live with it." Eyes darting, he checks each stream of New York commuters spilling into the concourse at Penn. "You get to expect danger. Could come from any direction."

"Got you," she says. "But, ah, it's not lead poisoning you're checking for here."

"No." Their eyes meet for a moment, then skitter away.

"Message received," she breathes. She suddenly wants to call Jacob. She wants to check in with him, make sure he is okay. "I could order us a bottle," she says to Lowell. "I need a drink, don't you? But I wouldn't trust the house wine here. Sweetened cleaning fluid."

Lowell blinks at her. "Wine? No, not my poison. Whatever's on tap," he tells the waiter.

"Your father was in Intelligence." Sam's voice has dropped to a whisper.

Lowell says warily, "If you were hoping for information about that, I don't have any."

"Your half-sister thinks—"

"This Françoise—"

"Yes. She thinks your father—her father—knew about Flight 64. In advance, I mean."

Lowell is holding his overnight bag tightly against his chest. He feels the skin of the bag incessantly with his fingers as though checking that its internal organs are still there. He prods at something, and reassures himself about its outline, a rectangular one. A book, Samantha thinks; or perhaps a box. One of Lowell's feet against the leg of the bistro table is making the metal rattle against the floor.

"You're not surprised," Sam whispers, watching him closely. "You knew that your father knew."

Lowell lurches and the table tips and Sam grabs for her wine. An amber wave sloshes over the edge of Lowell's beer glass. "What? I *am* surprised," he whispers fiercely. "Of course I'm surprised. Why wouldn't I be surprised? Besides, the statement's ridiculous. Flights to the U.S. are always at risk, all the time. My father knew that, the way all of us know it, only he was more aware of it than most. Naturally."

"This was quite specific, Françoise claims. There was a tip-off about Flight 64."

The bistro table is rattling so noisily that both Lowell and Sam lean forward on the marble top, dampening the racket with their weight. Sam can feel the tremor reaching her fingertips. When Lowell speaks, she can feel the puff of air from his lips. "There are scores of tip-offs every week," he says. "Most of them hoaxes."

"But not this one. The French police had Charles de Gaulle on high security alert, except the passengers weren't told. Françoise thinks your father knew. She thinks his information was quite precise."

Why? Lowell's lips form the question, though no sound comes out. He is beginning to hyperventilate.

"She had a ticket for Flight 64, but she never got on the plane because—"

Lowell laughs in a nervous high-pitched way. "I bet this is about blackmail," he says.

Sam presses her own foot down on Lowell's, to stop the trembling. "That doesn't seem to be her motivation," she says. "She's got something heavy on her conscience, is my impression. She wants to set something right. She wants to make contact with you."

Lowell recoils. "You didn't tell her how to reach me?"

His eyes constantly monitor the Penn Station throng. Sometimes he twists his chair to carry out sentry duty from a new angle. From time to time, he partially unzips his overnight bag and reaches in to feel the contents, checking.

"What's in your bag?" Samantha asks in a low voice.

"Nothing," he says. "My things. How much information did you give her?"

"I didn't give her anything, but she can easily find it herself."

"Great," Lowell says. "That's just great. Wait. Where are you going?"

"I have to make a phone call," Samantha says. Her own panic reflex is high. In a pay phone booth, she dials Jacob's office number, then tries him at home. Both times, she gets his answering machine.

"Jacob," she says. Her voice wavers. "It's Sam. Just wanted to know you're okay. Don't get upset, but I'm meeting with Lowell, you know, the son of the woman . . . We're in a fast-food joint at Penn Station, and he knows more than he's letting on. I'll call back later, okay? I just want you to know where I am."

At the table, Lowell has his backpack pinned between his knees. He is holding his beer glass with both hands. "There are Civil War junkies," he says, "and *Titanic* junkies, and Elvis-sighting junkies." He gulps down his beer. "I can tell you're a hijack junkie. Someone who collects every harebrained rumor from loonies on the Web—"

Samantha bridles. "I may be a junkie, but I'm rigorous. I read declassified documents, I read the airline reports, I read newspaper archives, I contact survivors and families. I'm doing this for a senior thesis in American history. Everything has to be documented."

"So what have you documented?"

"Nothing much yet," she concedes. "But I'm working on it. And I think the odds are that you do have a half-sister even though Françoise may not be her real name."

"Okay, so maybe I have a half-sister. And okay, maybe she had a ticket for the same flight—is that confirmed?"

"Not yet. But it will be. I've applied for a research grant to go to Paris for my spring semester. I want to meet with Françoise. I want to see her ticket. She says she's still got it."

"Air tickets are easy to forge. She's just a name on the Web. Some people get high on that. They make up names, they cruise websites—"

"I know that. That's why I want to go to Paris. I want to meet her, check her ID, check her birth certificate, date of birth, check her driver's—"

"I bet this is about the will," Lowell says. "My father's will. Fishy that she suddenly pops up now, the way scores of women claimed to be Anastasia, the czar's daughter—"

"Maybe. But she made contact in August, before your father died."

"Maybe she knew what was coming," Lowell says.

They stare at each other.

"I'll tell you something else that's creepy," Samantha whispers. "My mother was on that flight, right? My mother's sister was living in Paris and sharing an apartment with a woman named Françoise. I know, I know, it's a common name. It gives me a strange little buzz, just the same. That's another reason why I want to go to Paris. My aunt has a photograph of *her* Françoise."

"Thirteen years," Lowell says. "People change."

"We can ask Françoise who her roommate was in '87. If she names my aunt—"

"It might mean she's as good at ferreting out information as you are. Professional con men—or con women—are brilliant at that sort of thing."

"I know. I know that might be all it means. On the other hand, it might mean that your half-sister shared an apartment with my aunt."

"And what would that prove?" Lowell asks.

"I don't know what it would prove, but it would be very creepy."

"Have you ever heard of Sirocco?" Lowell whispers, leaning close.

"Yes." Samantha watches him intently. "I've met him in declassified documents. Not too often. Probably only when the declassifying inspector missed blacking him out."

"What do you know about him?"

"He had something to do with the hijacking. I think he was the chief hatchet man. The 'rogue agent,' as they say."

"The foreigner who actually does the dirty work," Lowell says.

"I think so."

"Saudi," Lowell says.

"I think so. Or possibly Egyptian. So you've been filing Freedom of Information applications too."

"No." Lowell reaches for the bag on the floor between his feet and lifts it back onto his lap. He keeps the soft handles twisted around his wrist. "I have a different source of . . . I happened on inside information accidentally."

Samantha leans across the table toward him. "What about Salamander?" she asks. "Do you have anything on him?"

"He's American."

"I know he is. He's the one I want to find. He's the prime mover."

"I think my father knew who Salamander was," Lowell says. "I think he knew who Sirocco was. I think my father died because he knew."

"What is in your bag?"

"Better you don't know."

"Your father," Samantha says carefully, "that August and September. Is there anything you can remember that might shed light . . . ?"

Lowell groans. "If you knew how much I've tried to forget."

And then he starts to explain the too much that he remembers too well.

Lowell remembers bad dreams and wet sheets and his mother there, holding him. He remembers giants with eyes of green fire. He remembers clanking monsters made of cans, like the Tin Man grown huge as an elephant. The giants shook his father like a toy, they sliced him in two. "Daddy, Daddy!" Lowell would scream, and his mother was always there, holding him, rocking him, crooning.

"Daddy's away, baby," she would murmur. "But Mommy's here."

He remembers the sweet smell of her skin and her hair, the smell of talcum and of Parisian perfume. She would turn on the light and read a story, and then she would sing in the dark.

He remembers two birthday parties when his father was home: his fourth birthday and his seventh. He remembers the three happy faces in the glow of the candles on his cake. He remembers the bedtime stories his father told. He remembers Odysseus tied to the mast, and Theseus and the Minotaur, and Atalanta and the golden apples, and

Leda and the swan. He remembers his first day at school: how lonely his mother looked, standing there. He can feel it still, like an oceanic grief that drowns, that swamps, that pulls at him, that takes his air, the way her sad smile washes over him, and he vows he will devote each day of his life to making her happy. It is the thing he most passionately desires. He remembers the day she sat at the kitchen table, not moving, and said, "Are you ready for school, Lowell? Your lunch box is in the fridge," and he remembers how the flatness of her voice frightened him because it was late afternoon and he had stayed to play baseball after class. He remembers how he had gone outside and searched for the most perfect flower in the garden to give to her. He remembers how he prayed that the flower would make her smile, and he remembers how she looked at it vaguely—it was a white rose, heavily fragrant—as though not knowing what it was, and how she then frowned and looked at it steadily and how her eyes filled with tears. He remembers how she pressed her lips together and how she could not speak for some time, and how she then said to him, "Dearest Lowell, what a gift you are. What a gift. You are all I have," and how he had the sensation of being sucked into a funnel that went down into the center of the earth where blackness and nothingness were.

Lowell remembers his father saying, "Your mother doesn't have the resources, Lowell, to cope with my frequent absences," his father saying it gravely and kindly, "or with the requirements of my position, the requirements of silence and secrecy, which demand a special kind . . . ," his father explaining, "I married too young the first time, Lowell, and then I was lonely when my first wife died, and I made another mistake, but you've made up for that. I'm counting on you. I'm counting on you to look after your mother, you know what I mean.

"I'm counting on you," his father said, "to be strong like Achilles, and to carry on the Hawthorne tradition at school. It's all the more important, Lowell. . . .

"Your mother," his father said, he remembers his father saying, "is in a state of low-grade nervous depression, Lowell. It's not her fault, not really, but I'm counting on you to keep an eye . . ." He remembers all the textures of sadness, his father's sadness, his mother's, and his own, and he remembers the absences, the loneliness, the sound of his mother crying at night. Lowell remembers, remembers, his head in his hands. Lowell remembers too much, and the silences between his revelations grow long.

"Was she?" Samantha prompts at last. "Your mother? Was she clinically depressed?"

"I suppose so. I suppose I was too, when I think back. It's not that she wasn't functional. She did all the right things. Whenever my father was home, there were dinner parties and receptions and soirees and little chamber music groups. It was all a glittering whirl, and my mother hosted all that. But there was . . ." Everywhere he turned, their lives were overcast with sadness and it almost choked Lowell, it made the house bleak. "There was always this fog," he says. "I couldn't shift it." It exhausted him.

And then one day, suddenly, he was angry instead of sad, and that was easier. That was so much easier. He went off to boarding school, and he dreaded coming home. He would accept invitations to other homes, he'd even stay at school for long weekends. It was so much simpler not being home. Not having to note his father's absence or see his mother's sad smile.

And then, one spring break, he ran out of options and he had to go home. His father was there for once and his parents hosted a reception for a string quartet. . . .

Lowell *felt* the chemistry, he felt it the first time his mother and Avi Levinstein looked at each other, and it broke his heart. All his life's energy, all his little-boy prayers, all his wishbone wishes at Christmas and Thanksgiving dinners, had gone into trying to shift that black cloud of sadness from her shoulders, and Avi Levinstein walked in and did it by looking at her.

"I hated Levinstein. And I could never forgive my mother."

The more alive, the more beautiful she became, the more angry Lowell grew. She told him she was leaving in May. "Lowell," she said, radiant, "I'm in love."

"You want a gold star for that?" he said rudely. He had just turned sixteen.

"Oh, Lowell," she said. "Please be happy for me," and he remembers that she told him that his father was a good man, a dear man, such a dear man, and how she did not want to hurt his father or make him unhappy, but Lowell surely knew, he surely understood that between them, between his father and his mother, things had not been working out very well, Lowell must have known that. And he remembers that she told him that *they*—that his mother and Levinstein—were going to Paris for a while, and that his father was filing for divorce and she would not contest, she would consent to being the guilty party, she would grant his father that, but that after the divorce she and Avi Levinstein would return to New York and would get married. "But for the time being, we will stay in Paris," he remembers her saying with wings on her voice. "Will you come and visit us in Paris? Please, Lowell. It is something I would like very much."

"I turned around and walked away," Lowell says. "I refused to kiss her goodbye. That was in May. May 1987. I never saw her again."

Four months later, she called from Paris to say they were flying home. The fall term had just begun and Lowell took the call in the hallway of his boarding-school dorm, a bleak brown tunnel with no light at either end. His mother sounded rapturously happy. She gave Lowell her flight number and date of arrival, and Lowell hung up on her. He dialed Washington and left a message on his father's answering machine. He said only, "They are coming back."

Two days later, he took another call in the same hallway. "How are you, Lowell?"

"I'm fine, Dad."

"I have handled my life very badly," his father said.

Lowell said awkwardly, "No, you haven't, Dad."

"Don't make my mistakes, Lowell," his father said. He sounded agitated. Then he said, "Would you do something for me?"

"Sure," Lowell said.

"It's very important," his father said. "It's very, *very* important, Lowell."

"Sure, Dad."

"I want you to call you mother and tell her not to come back. Not yet. Not at this particular . . . It's a very bad time for me. Tell her it's a very bad time."

Lowell said doubtfully, "I don't think she's going to pay much attention, Dad."

"She *has* to," his father said. "You have to make her pay attention, Lowell. Tell her to wait another month. This is very important, Lowell."

"Okay, Dad. I'll try."

Lowell called his mother's hotel in Paris to leave a message, and was disconcerted to be connected with her direct. "Dad's very upset," he said icily. "He doesn't want you to come back. He wants you to wait another month."

After a small silence, she asked him, "What do you want, Lowell?"

"I want you to stop hurting Dad."

"All right," she said. "I'll do that, Lowell. Tell your father I'll change our flights. We won't come back till October."

Lowell called his father's office immediately. "Your father's out of the country," the secretary said, "but he checks for messages every day. What would you like me to tell him?"

"Tell him she agreed," Lowell said. "She won't come back till October. He'll know what that means."

The secretary repeated the message. "*She agreed. Won't come back till October.* I'll let him know."

"Where is he?" Lowell asked.

"You know I'm not supposed to tell you that," the secretary said. "But I did book his flight to Paris."

"Do you know where he's staying? Do you have a number?"

"They never let us know that," the secretary said. "You know that, Lowell. For all I know, he might have flown on to Moscow or Timbuktu.

I never know where they're calling in from, they have a code. But he'll get your message," she promised.

Not until days after the hijacking did Lowell receive the note scribbled down by someone else in his dorm. *Your mother called and wants you to call her back. Says she can't change the flight because ** (sorry, couldn't catch name)** because someone-or-other has concert scheduled.*

Lowell could never bring himself to show this note to his father. He was too shocked, too stunned, when he saw Mather next. His father seemed to have aged twenty years in a single week. *Gaunt*, Lowell thought. His father was the very embodiment of the word. There was a swatch of white hair at his temples. His face seemed to have shrunk back against the skull, the cheeks sunken beneath the bones.

"You said she agreed." His father's voice broke. Almost, Lowell sensed, his father was going to hug him. His father swayed, then steadied himself and extended his right hand.

Lowell shook it. "Dad," he said.

"Son."

"*I would rather be a serf in the house of some landless man,*" his father said, "*than king of all these dead men*. Do you recognize that, Lowell?"

"The *Odyssey*," Lowell said.

"This is a dreadful thing," his father said. "A dreadful thing."

"Yes," Lowell said.

"*Bear, O my heart; thou hast borne a yet harder thing*. You said your mother agreed to wait till October."

"She did," Lowell said. He felt as ill as his father looked. He was vertiginous with guilt. "She did agree. I just don't understand what happened."

"I tried," his father said. "I did what I could."

It was the only time Lowell ever saw his father weep.

Book III

CODE NAME: BLACK DEATH

There have been as many plagues as wars in history; yet always plagues and wars take people equally by surprise.

—ALBERT CAMUS, THE PLAGUE

Death has only given every one of us a jog on the Elbow, or a pull by the sleeve as he passed by, as it were, to bid us get ready against next time he comes this Way.

—DANIEL DEFOE, A JOURNAL OF THE PLAGUE YEAR

[AUTHOR'S NOTE: In the week of 12–19 September 1665, in the city of London, 7,165 persons died of the plague, the worst single week of the epidemic called the Black Death. Daniel Defoe was five years old. All his life, he remained obsessively afraid that the plague would return.]

1.

CODE NAME: TOCADE

The policeman studies Tristan's passport. "You are Monsieur Charron?"

"Yes."

"Tristan Charron?"

"Yes."

"Your ticket and boarding pass, please."

Tristan takes his travel wallet from the pocket inside his jacket and the two gendarmes ask him to step aside. They study his ticket closely: *Air France, vol 64. Paris (CDG) à New York (JFK). 8 Septembre, 1987. Embarquement: Porte 12.* Their eyes move from his passport to his face and back again. Evidently, his identity does not convince. They leaf through pages, studying stamps and dates. "You travel very much," they say, "Monsieur Charron." There is something odd about their tone, something odd about the innuendo with which they seem to invest his name. Mock deference, he decides. But why? He has been stopped at random in the airport concourse, seemingly at random. He has thought of demanding to know on what grounds—after all, he is in Paris, not Prague—but he knows that this tactic, when deployed with the French gendarmerie, will not be helpful.

He cranes his head in order to see the Silk Route shop, he sees someone spinning the wheel of scarves, he sees a little girl in a blue coat with a woman who, for a moment, looks vaguely familiar to him, though he cannot remember why, he sees several men looking for last-minute presents for wives and girlfriends, but Génie—or the woman who looks like Génie—is no longer visible.

She has a gift for disappearing, a genius for it.

When she resurfaces in dreams or in memory, she is always leaving the little hotel on rue de Birague and crossing the Place des Vosges, which is why, when he saw her there two days ago, he did not trust his senses. The fourth arrondissement is permanently imbued with her presence, and so he thought he had magicked her up, particularly since he is still disoriented and jumpy. He has just returned from Prague where a manuscript hidden in his suitcase was found. The manuscript was confiscated. The writer of the manuscript, a novelist, is now in prison. Tristan himself was detained for a night and interrogated, but then released. Nevertheless, he is still shaken, and high-anxiety levels spawn fantasies. He knows this. He knows how shining messengers can appear and point to a doorway. DELIVERANCE, the doorway is marked.

Hence, when a vision of Génie appears as soon as he is safely back in Paris, he knows better than to follow phantom temptation. Even so, watching her cross the Place des Vosges, he restrains himself with great difficulty.

Instead, in the afterglow of his vision of her, he dropped into the tiny office out of which he runs Editions du Double. He tried to check galleys, he worked on drafts of new press announcements, he gave his assistant a list of bookstores to call. His assistant handed him a week's worth of messages—faxes and telephone memos—but he stuffed them into his briefcase without looking at them. His ability to concentrate was poor. He needed sleep. In Prague, he had spent the entire night harshly illuminated, looking into a sunspot from which questions had streamed like electrons. He had to go home and sleep. He dreamed he was back in the interrogation cell and Génie appeared like a patch of shade on the sun. Follow me, she said, vanishing.

He woke the next morning feeling light-headed. He shaved and went to his office and worked for several hours. He left for a midmorning espresso in Place des Vosges and saw Génie again (or saw her double.) This time, he followed discreetly, but in the crowded Métro station of Bastille, he lost her. That was yesterday.

Today he saw her for the third time.

"We must ask you to step aside," the policemen say, "into this room."

They ask questions, he answers. Is Interpol involved in this? he wonders. Is this coincidence, or is this about Prague? He tries to watch the concourse through a slender glass panel. The police are waiting for an answer. "Monsieur?" they prompt.

"There must be an explanation," he says, pondering the triple apparition of Génie. Perhaps, given the oddities of time and space, given surreal linkages that have been scientifically vouched for, perhaps molecules of past events continue to coalesce around their original points of occurrence, although in some other dimension. He believes a trick of the light or the memory can reassemble them.

"You seem very agitated, monsieur. Something distracts you?"

It was the way she walked, that was what caught his eye, that strange lopsided gait, the way she could never quite keep to a path or straight line, the way she veered left. It's a political compulsion, she used to joke, though she was embarrassed by seeing everything on the slant. It's your genius for going astray, he always countered, *ton génie pour t'égarer*. On her passport, an Australian one, she is Genevieve Teague, but he has always called her Génie. She can materialize like smoke from a dream. He can rub a memory and there she is. So now, three days in a row, three times in the same place: he has to admit this is improbable, though even so he has postponed returning his passport to the locked safe in his room. The passport has remained in his vest pocket ever since Prague in case he sees her again, in case he needs suddenly to take a taxi to the airport and shadow her to London or Rome or Timbuktu.

His third sighting has been less than—what?—three hours ago (if he were to measure time in the normal dimension): he saw her crossing the Place des Vosges pulling behind her a small carry-on suitcase with wheels. In the stone arcade on the southern side, near the Victor Hugo museum, she stopped to listen to a black musician playing jazz. A small crowd had gathered. Tristan watched from behind a stone pillar. The man was playing Duke Ellington's "Caravan" on tenor sax. Tristan found this coincidence so extraordinary—his first gift to her had been a Duke Ellington cassette, her first to him had been Thelonious Monk, and "Caravan" had been on both tapes—that the music seemed to him proof positive his grasp on reality had slipped. He saw Génie step forward and drop coins in the sax player's hat, and then he followed her down the rue de Birague, past the little hotel, two stars, at Number 12, where they first made love. She paused there. Or was this something his own wishful thinking made her apparition do? He saw her enter the bistro on the corner of rue Saint Antoine. He hovered behind a fruit and vegetable barrow and watched as a waiter brought an espresso. Just as he was working up the courage to cross the street and sit at the vacant table next to hers, someone took a photograph. Probably, to the tourist, the scene seemed quintessentially French—interior of a bistro in the Marais—but Tristan had the uneasy and no doubt illogical sense that the intention was to keep a record of the woman who looked like Génie. Apparently the woman thought so too. She slid a twenty-franc note under her saucer and left abruptly. Tristan followed her to Place de la Bastille. When she descended into the Métro and then up into the street again at Place de l'Opéra, he was a discreet shadow. He watched covertly as she boarded the Roissybus. He hailed a cab.

"Airport," he said, agitated. "Can you stay close to the bus?"

A flashbulb popped. A tourist leaned in close to the rear window. There was a video camera in the tourist's hand and it spoke with a soft clicking whir.

The cab driver laughed. "Is it a movie?"

Was it? Tristan wondered. He felt dizzy. He had an uneasy sense of *déjà vu*. But whose movie was it?

"You're not at risk of becoming a star," he said irritably. His hands were sweating. He needed to know whether he was hallucinating or not. Simply that. His heartbeat had gone erratic. He felt light-headed, he felt something like a clamp above his ribs. "My heart," he said, clutching at his chest in alarm. "*Cas d'urgence*. Don't lose the bus."

The driver laughed again. "*Vraiment une affaire de cœur, monsieur? Ou de queue?*" Either way, the cab driver promised—truly a matter of the heart, or one of lust—he was the right man for the occasion. He drove through every red light. He reached the Air France terminal as the Roissybus was spilling travelers and luggage like swill.

"She is there, monsieur?" he asked.

Tristan could not see her. Then he could. But was it Génie?

From some angles, Tristan felt quite certain; from others, less so. She had changed her hairstyle. She was thinner. Five years had passed since he had seen her—since they lived together; since she vanished—yet often during those years, especially in the beginning, he would think he saw her. He would follow a woman through crowded streets, and then . . . *Excuse me,* he would say, but the woman never resembled Génie at all, not up close, and he would feel worse than a fool. Pathetic, he would think. I'm pathetic. He did not want to make a public clown of himself at the airport.

He tipped the cab driver lavishly and then hovered near the Air France desk watching as the woman who looked like Génie checked in. She did not check her bag. When she moved off to study the big departures/arrivals board, he tried to stay discreetly close but mishap derailed him. Fifty Japanese tourists surged like floodwaters rising. Tristan was awash. He was trapped. The tourists gazed up at the monitor. *Aah, aah, aah,* they sang in little high-pitched riffs as the numerals blinked and changed. The tourists all wore matching red shoulder bags and each bag bore the logo of the rising sun. Tristan found himself face-to-face with a woman wearing white gloves. She was dressed in a bright red suit with a rising-sun pin in her lapel and she held a sign high above her head with her white-gloved hands. FUJI TRAVEL, it said in Japanese characters and in English. WE FOLLOW THE RISING SUN. Her dawn-seekers pressed close in a jostling circle.

"Excuse me, excuse me," Tristan said.

"You should not be with us," the woman reproved. "You do not have a Fuji bag."

"I'm not with you," Tristan assured her, fighting free. But he had lost sight of the woman who looked like Génie.

He felt foolish. All he had with him was his briefcase. He bought himself an espresso, sat on a high stool at a coffee counter in the upper concourse, and began going through the week's messages. He ignored the phone memos—anyone important would call back, he figured—and turned to the faxes. When he got to the third item, the demitasse in his hand lurched violently and a cord of black coffee rose like a question mark. It quivered in the air for a second, then made a dark asterisk on the fax.

Tristan, the fax read. *Arriving Friday. Same return flight as you. Génie.* He noted the date and time of reception. When the fax arrived, he was in Prague. He was in a cell in Prague, dreaming of Génie. *Same return flight as you.* What on earth did she mean?

He looked at the next fax: from his printer in Singapore. He thumbed quickly through several more: from his distributor, from a magazine running an article on one of his authors, from a translator, and then . . .

The fax had reached his office that very morning.

Tristan, he read. *Sorry you did not show up for the rendez-vous at our hotel, no. 12, rue de Birague. Am flying back to New York on September 8, AF 64, which leaves at 1600 hours. If you can make it to CDG in time, we could have a drink for old times' sake.*

The message was unsigned, but Tristan knew what he knew.

Who else but Génie could use the hotel on rue de Birague as code?

He looked at his watch: ten minutes past noon. Why would she come to the airport so early? Why would she come here four hours before her flight? He shoved everything back into his briefcase and ran to the Air France desk, bumping into people, slipping on squashed *pommes frites,* being frowned at and rerouted by someone in uniform. A red sea of shoulder bags parted, and he passed through unscathed.

There were, he discovered, only five seats left on Flight 64 to New York. "*Grâce à Dieu*," he said fervently and bought a ticket. How many bags was he checking? None. "*Je n'ai pas de bagages.* I have nothing but my briefcase," he said.

"Only a briefcase, monsieur?" The ticket girl laughed and shook her head. "*C'est étonnant!* " she said. "You are not the first. These days people travel around the world with almost nothing. I do not understand at all. The Australians especially." She shook her head. "I do not understand these Australians. I ask myself if they spin clothes out of air."

"You have someone else on this flight who travels light?"

"There was a woman with an Australian passport and nothing more than a carry-on. For me," the girl said—she made a fetching little *moue* with her lips—"for a French woman, this is not possible. *Chez nous, la mode compte trop, n'est-ce pas?*"

Tristan smiled.

"I say to her: 'Not one baggage *à enregistrer*, madame? Not one single baggage when you have traveled so far from Australia?' And she tells me that she is living now in New York. '*Quand même,*' I tell her, '*c'est pas normal.*' '*Cas d'urgence,*' she explains to me. She does have a suitcase, but she has left it at the hotel, because she has decided to leave suddenly. She says that in the suitcase there is *rien d'important. Exactement ça, monsieur. Rien d'important.* Can you imagine?"

Now he knew for sure. How is it possible, Génie, he once asked, to lose a *suitcase*?

She said: If it doesn't hold anything that matters, how can you call that a loss?

But how is it possible, he persisted, to travel as much as you do with so little?

How is it possible to live, she had countered, with so much stuff that you can't pick up and move on like *that*? She'd snapped her fingers. Besides, she laughed, I'm a genie, right? When you live in a lamp, there's not much room.

Now that he had a ticket for her flight, he did not want to wait until boarding time to find her, but at Charles de Gaulle Airport, overclotted, perpetually under construction and expansion but chronically short of space, you could lose your own shadow, he thought irritably.

"The Australian woman," he asked the ticket girl. "Did you see where she went? I'm going to Australia on business soon, and I'd like to ask her advice."

"She went that way, monsieur." The ticket girl pointed to the escalator going down to the underground concourse. *"Bonne chance, monsieur."*

He searched every bar and bistro and bookshop in that subterranean limbo without seeing her. Though the flight was not for hours, he concluded she must have gone back up to the check-in level, must have gone through security already. He was on the up escalator, his field of vision extended, when he caught a glimpse of her, below, still on the underground level. She was at the limit of the concourse, at the point where it sucked itself into a long tunnel that led to the domestic terminals. He felt suddenly weightless and free. He believed, for a moment, he could fly. He ran back down the up escalator.

Weaving between the fast-food tables, he lurched against a man who was holding a baby in his arms. A little girl in a blue coat screamed. He swerved to avoid a man with bucket and mop. He could still see Génie. She was examining the scarves on a turnstile at a Silk Route boutique.

That was when he was stopped and taken into a small room.

"It should not be a difficult question, monsieur."

"What?" He blinks at the policeman. "Uh . . ." He waits for a prompt, but his interrogator offers no help. "I'm sorry. What did you ask?"

"We are very interested in the reason for so much travel."

"So much . . . ?" He plays the sentence back to himself and finds he knows the answer. "My work. My work requires a lot of travel."

"You have just returned from Prague."

"Yes."

"Why?"

"On business. There was a literary festival. I'm a publisher."

"And before Prague, Germany."

"Yes."

"Why?"

"The Frankfurt Book Fair is next month. I had to make arrangements in advance for our display. As I told you, I'm a publisher."

"Ah yes. So your papers claim. We have not heard of this publishing house."

"No. I would be surprised if you had." Monsieur Charron makes an effort not to give offense. "I don't imagine that the kind of book I publish would interest you."

"What kind of book is that, Monsieur Charron?"

"Not the kind you can buy at airports." He avoids direct comment on the reading habits of the gendarmerie. "Highbrow," he says, with a rueful apologetic shrug.

"Ah yes, of course. Literature." The policeman makes the word sound lascivious and faintly *louche*.

"*Belles lettres*. Yes."

"And this festival in Prague. Why does that interest you?"

"I publish several East European writers in translation."

"Ah yes, of course. You meet with the translators."

"No. I meet with the writers. The translators all live here in Paris."

"They have close ties, of course, with Eastern Europe?"

"The translators? I suppose. I know nothing about their personal lives. They freelance for all the publishers, big and small."

"And you are small."

"Very small."

"But distinguished, naturally."

Monsieur Charron raises his eyebrows, but says nothing.

"And yet, in spite of this smallness, there is always money."

Tristan frowns. "You seem to have heard of me after all, gentlemen."

"We are making an assumption," one of the gendarmes says, "because of so much travel."

"Like all small literary houses, I survive on smoke and mirrors and cultural grants."

"Grants from foreign governments."

"When I'm lucky. Also grants from our own Ministry of Culture."

"To visit Prague these days, monsieur, one must either have close contacts with the Communists or with the dissidents, who have close ties to certain dissident groups in France. Your books, monsieur"—and there is definitely a provocative innuendo, an edge of contempt—"your very literary books, they all have political topics."

"Not usually, no. Or not in any ordinary sense. I publish fiction."

"Oh, of course, fiction. And Algeria. Why Algeria?"

"I have a couple of Algerian writers. They live in Paris."

"Algerians in Paris have a violent record, monsieur."

"A handful of Algerian extremists do. None of them writers, as far as I've heard."

"They have many sympathizers, monsieur. So what is the reason for your visit to Algeria?"

Tristan raises his eyebrows. "I'm not going to Algeria."

"Ostensibly not, monsieur, as we see from your ticket. Though one of your Algerian writers, the woman, who was originally scheduled for this flight, appears to have been in some confusion about its destination. She has since canceled her reservation, but we intercepted a communication of hers."

Tristan stares at them. "I don't know what this is about," he says. "I have met the writer herself only once. We discussed Camus."

"You are aware that she has ties to the extremists?"

"No. I find it hard to believe. In any case, I don't concern myself with the politics of the books I publish. She wrote a fine novel."

"About a little Arab boy who grew up in the eighteenth arrondissement."

"I must compliment you, gentlemen," Tristan says dryly. "You are very well read."

"In the novel, the Algerian is sent to a French prison where he causes a riot."

"It is about his sexuality," Tristan says. "Not his politics."

"Ah yes. His violent sexuality. And your earlier visits to Algiers?"

"I've never been to Algeria."

"And Morocco?"

"Morocco? The last time I was in Morocco I was a child on summer vacation with my parents."

"I'm afraid we must ask you to come with us, monsieur."

"But I don't understand. What is this about? My Algerian writer?" It seems to Tristan, now that he looks around, that there are many more police than usual at the airport. "What's going on?" he asks.

"Precautions, monsieur. Standard precautions." He is required to accompany the gendarmes for quite some distance down the long tunnel that leads to parking, and then down another level in an elevator, and then along a corridor that turns several times and seems to be without end. In the small interrogation room, the policemen lock the door. "We note, Monsieur Charron, that you have purchased your ticket to fly to New York only within the last hour. Why is that?"

Will I tell them the truth? he wonders. Will I say: Because of a woman. Because yesterday I saw a woman I had not seen for five years. Because today, and yesterday, and the day before that, I saw a woman in the Place des Vosges . . . no; I *think* I saw a woman I once knew intimately. But the night before that, I was roughed up in Prague and so it is possible—and he tries to imagine himself admitting it—it is possible that I have summoned her up out of loss and desire.

He is not about to mention what happened in Prague.

Will he say: I bought a ticket because I just received a secret message from this woman. I have no idea how it reached me, but I am ludicrously superstitious (it comes from my Catalan grandmother, and I seem unable to cure myself, even though I would die of intellectual shame if the proclivity were made known in the publishing precincts of the boulevard St. Germain); because I am superstitious, and three times is a sign.

He frowns. How do they know he has just bought his ticket? The airlines report last-minute purchases? But if so, how could they learn so much about him so quickly? They were watching the ticket desks for him? Because of his Algerian writer? Because of Prague? Because of the manuscripts from Eastern Europe which he has published under pseudonymous names? Minimal research would tell them that publishers—in certain circumstances, for their own protection, by design—know few details about the personal lives of their writers. So they have been following him, then, but for how long? He recalls the click of the camera in Place de l'Opéra.

"We are waiting for an explanation, Monsieur Charron."

"I was not aware," he says angrily, ill-advisedly, "that French citizens have to give a reason for travel."

"In exceptional circumstances, monsieur, French citizens are answerable to the law."

"And how do I come to be an exceptional circumstance?" Monsieur Charron demands.

"We are not at liberty to disclose, monsieur, the particular details of the exceptional circumstances. But we advise you to give us the reason for this very sudden decision to fly to New York."

"So soon," the second policeman says, "after you met with certain writers in Frankfurt and Prague."

"And so quickly after your Algerian writer canceled her reservation," the first one reminds, "for this flight."

"I know nothing about that," Tristan says.

"So what is your reason for choosing this flight, monsieur?"

"No reason," he says. "A whim."

"Ah." They exchange a significant look. They inspect his passport again. "A whim. As in your name."

"That's right," he says, amused. "*Une tocade.*"

"Tristan Tocade Charron. A curious name, monsieur."

"Is it? Tocade is my mother's family name."

"We have reason to know, monsieur, that this is a code name."

Monsieur Charron stares at them. "What?" He waits for a laugh, and when no one laughs, he begins to expect the gendarmes to levitate. He begins to expect the small table in the room to float. He begins to think Génie will rise out of somebody's pocket like cigarette smoke. He begins to think he should get up and walk out of this dream. He stands.

"Please sit down, monsieur."

He laughs uneasily. "Is this some kind of a joke?"

"You have been involved with a woman who works in Intelligence."

"I have?" Tristan Charron laughs again. "You mean my Algerian writer."

"No, monsieur. You know who we mean."

They watch him impassively, waiting. The strangeness of the last twenty minutes now strikes him as ominous. A woman who works in Intelligence? Not Génie, surely? Certainly it cannot be Génie. The idea is ludicrous. But then again, what would be a more perfect cover than teaching English as a second language, on call around the world as it were, her clients often politicians, corporate leaders, the children of presidents? And is that what she really does? Is that a financial backup for the travel writing, or vice versa? Is the travel writing simply a hobby, an amusing sideline, as she has claimed? Or is it a complicated mask, this endless updating of information for some wildly successful publisher of guides for the footloose? He has considerable professional admiration for the *Wandering Earthling* series, a global success story from a shoestring operation, and an Australian one at that, of all the unlikely . . .

When he thinks about it, there has been a lot of talk, a lot of speculation in the publishing industry. How could this dark horse have come so far so fast? Who is bankrolling the series?

He tries to imagine Génie as the Wandering Earthling gathering data of an altogether different sort. He tries to imagine her as the bearer of messages from one government leader to another, messages transferred in coded grammar exercises in an English-as-Second-Language class. It does not seem probable. *The rain in the Ukraine falls mainly on the hijacked plane. Do you think the weather is propitious? I do not think so, we do not think so, they do not think the weather is propitious*. Tristan does not think any of this is likely.

The Génie he knows, or knew, could go astray between the Pont Louis Philippe and the Pont Marie. She could get lost in the Métro for twenty minutes between getting off the train and finding her way up to the street. She could be waylaid by children in a courtyard, or by an old man walking home with a baguette. "What could you possibly talk about for so long?" he would ask, exasperated. "To total strangers!"

"Imagine," Génie would say. "All his life, that old man has been a *randonneur.* Just last year, he hiked for three days in the Pyrenees. He's eighty! And he gave me the name of a farmhouse where hikers can stay."

The idea of Génie gathering information that would matter to anyone other than a low-budget traveler is absurd. Then again, why had she disappeared?

Well, he knew the answer to that.

She disappeared because he had given a stupid ultimatum. I cannot live with a travel writer, he had said. I cannot live with a woman who is so often *not* in my bed. When you are gone, I wonder who you are sleeping with at night. I cannot sleep. It is intolerable, it torments me. It is not normal for a woman to live like that. He had been violent with jealousy. He had thrown things across the room.

You make me feel caged, she had said. You are right, she said. So much distrust is intolerable.

Either you stop being a travel writer, he shouted, or you leave.

And she had left. She had vanished without a trace.

But she left because he had been stupid, not for espionage. Surely not? No. Not Génie. Then who?

"You know who we mean, monsieur," the policeman repeats. "You know very well."

Does he? Nothing is making sense. Nothing much has been making any sense at all since Prague.

He suddenly remembers Françoise, whom he still bumps into from time to time. Long ago—well, a decade ago, when they were both students at the Sorbonne—it had often seemed to him that they were followed. A jealous former boyfriend, he assumed. A single moment comes back now with a force that winds him. They are in a bistro on the rue Clovis, behind the Panthéon, and Françoise has provocatively raised her skirt. She slides two fingers under the top of her stocking. Her suspender makes a small snapping sound against her skin. She does this demurely. She wears stockings and suspenders solely because he has asked her to, but she makes it clear that the request irritates her, and so she punishes him, teasing him in public. Under the bistro table, he slides his hand up her stockinged thigh. And then there is the soft pop of a flashbulb. But when he turns, all he can see is a bland-faced American tourist with a camera.

"Someone took a photograph," he tells Françoise, angry.

"That's what tourists do," she says.

"No. This was different." There have been other times and they come back to him. "Someone is following us," he says.

"That's ridiculous." Paranoia or jealousy on his part, Françoise implies. But then, later, sometime during the two years of their not-very-satisfactory relationship, she lets slip that her father has connections with the American Embassy. "Papa had it brought in for me in a diplomatic pouch," is what she says of a butter-soft leather briefcase he admires. "It's from Bangkok." She is afraid of her father. She waves Tristan's questions aside. "He's American," she says. "He was stationed here in the late fifties. He took up with my mother then, but he always played fast and loose with her. He comes and goes."

Tristan asks sharply, "He's a diplomat? Or CIA?"

"He does research for the American government, or the military, or something. He travels. I don't know. I pay no attention to his life. We have no time for him, my mother and I."

"But he pays for your apartment," Tristan says. It is small and elegant, in the seventh arrondissement, near Les Invalides, and though they meet there from time to time for assignations, he has never stayed the night.

"Who told you that?" She is annoyed with him, and alarmed.

"You did."

She lights a cigarette and inhales. Her fingers tremble slightly. "He's a control freak," she says. "He pays because he thinks he will know where I am. Which is why I don't often stay there. I let my friends use it." She inhales hungrily. He sometimes thinks she must live on smoke and wine.

He asks quietly, "And where do you stay when you are not in your apartment near Les Invalides and not with me?"

She busies herself with stubbing out her cigarette, but then lights another immediately. "I stay with my mother," she says. "Or with various friends."

"I see."

It is her elusiveness and her intensity which attract Tristan. Her possessiveness flatters him. Her jealousy at first excites him but then irritates him.

"I can't stand not knowing where you are," she tells him. "I saw what that did to my mother. My father was never around, but he always wanted my mother to be waiting when he showed up," she says. "Just waiting for him. He always wanted to know where she was. He would call her twice a week and if she wasn't there . . . ! It drove her crazy after a while.

"She said he needed her because she would do things that his American wife would not do. There is no spice in American sex, he told her. With American women, there is only baby-food sex. No flavor, no danger, no risk.

"Then leave your American wife, my mother told him.

"And he told her: American women are for marrying and daytime, Frenchwomen are for the night. You are my danger. You could be used against me for blackmail. That is what excites me, and that is why I need to know where you are."

"Now you see me, my mother told him, and now you don't. You won't know where danger is coming from.

"She wouldn't sleep with him again, she wouldn't see him, but she knew he always had other women. He always kept his dangers on the side."

Back then, a decade ago, Tristan had a sense of her father in some shadowy but powerful role. The knowledge had made him uneasy. After that, especially in the apartment near Les Invalides, he found it increasingly difficult to rise to the carnal occasion. A flashbulb would go off in his mind. He felt watched.

He has not the slightest idea what Françoise does with her life these days. When they meet by chance, he is perfunctory and anxious to get away. He finds himself imagining her father's watchdogs hovering around her, keeping tabs on her and on him. The last time was maybe three months ago and she was with some woman—her roommate, she said; an American student on exchange—and she'd introduced them, and then she'd asked—

Two images unexpectedly coalesce in his mind and match exactly, and light comes off them. He'd seen Génie at the Silk Route boutique, he'd seen a child in a blue coat with a woman who looked vaguely familiar . . . that woman was the American student who'd been with Françoise.

Did that mean something?

How could that mean anything?

And then there was another bizarre meeting, how far back? Ages ago, seven years ago, the first time Génie had invited him to her place in the thirteenth arrondissement, before they both moved to his apartment in the fourth. They had pushed through the great wooden door off Avenue des Gobelins, crossed the courtyard, and pressed the timer switch in the dark stairwell of *escalier A*. Before they reached the second floor, the light went out, and two people, descending, almost collided with them.

"Tristan!" came the voice of a woman from out of the dark.

He squinted at her in the half-light. "Françoise."

"You two know each other?" Génie asked.

What a weird coincidence, he had thought then. With the whole of Paris to choose from, two women whom I know intimately live in the same building. Off the same staircase. It bothered him. Someone pushed the light button again and he stared at Françoise and her friend. Her sexual tastes, he concluded, had changed since her days at the Sorbonne. She preferred bookish types then, intellectuals. This boyfriend had a street-smart swagger and macho style. He was Egyptian, perhaps? Algerian? He threw Tristan an insolent smile that Tristan translated as: *If you touch her, I kill*. And then the boyfriend spoke to Génie. "*Ton ami?*" he asked, and Tristan turned in outrage, ready to strike, because of the intimate pronoun. What impudence.

Génie put her hand on his arm. "Ignore him," she murmured. "Don't give him what he wants."

"Why did he use *tu*?" Tristan demanded. His jealousy often flared up like a rash. He knew his possessiveness bothered Génie, and sometimes amused her, but he could do nothing about it. "Why was he intimate with you?" He had to know.

"Because he could tell it would annoy you," Génie said.

The policemen are watching Tristan intently. He becomes aware that he has clenched both hands into fists. "I have been involved with many women, monsieur," he says lightly, relaxing his hands. "They are all a mystery to me. When it comes to spying and interrogation, any one of them could put Torquemada to shame."

One of the gendarmes gives a short sharp laugh. The other remains expressionless. "Why would a publisher fly to New York when he will meet with American colleagues at Frankfurt next month? Why would he do this?"

Tristan shrugs. "I told you. A whim."

"*Une tocade.*"

"Yes."

"The same flight as your Algerian writer who canceled. The same flight as the writer from Belgrade."

"What? Which writer from Belgrade?"

"The one you met in Prague."

Tristan puckers his brows. "I met several writers from Belgrade. Which one do you mean?"

"Which ones did you meet with, monsieur?"

"You will have to give me a legal reason," Monsieur Charron says carefully, "for why I am required to answer that. The physical safety of those writers could be at stake."

"Physical safety is an issue which concerns us very greatly, monsieur, especially on a flight which includes a Jewish writer from Belgrade, a Jewish string quartet, and a group of Israelis traveling to a conference on Yiddish literature. A very interesting and unusual flight for a publisher who claims to have no politics."

"You're joking." Tristan stares from one face to the other. "You're not joking?" He marvels at this.

"Of course, you will claim you are going to the conference in Yiddish literature."

"In fact, I knew nothing about it," he says. "Though it certainly interests me. I'd like to have details."

"No doubt, monsieur. No doubt you would. But you will have to give us a more honest answer for why you suddenly decided on this flight."

Monsieur Charron makes a *moue* with his lips and turns up the palms of his hands. Three can play cat and mouse, he thinks, and truth is always the best defense, especially since they will not believe it. "For the oldest reason of all," he says. "I am a Frenchman. I saw a woman. *J'ai une tocade pour elle*." I'm crazy about her. Still.

"Thank you, monsieur. The Australian travel writer, the woman whose code name is Geneva. We know this. It is a point in your favor that you acknowledge the connection."

"Code name? She has a code name?" Tristan asks, dumbfounded.

"One more thing, Monsieur Charron. You are no doubt aware that the woman Françoise Galette, with whom you had a former association, also canceled her reservation for this flight."

"What?" Tristan feels dazed.

"Several hours ago," they tell him. "By telephone. She canceled her flight."

"I don't believe this. This doesn't make any sense."

"Clearly *someone,* monsieur, has the key to these riddles. You may go now."

Tristan is startled. The sudden dismissal seems to him even stranger than the interview.

As he leaves, flanked by his interrogators, three people emerge from the small room next door: two uniformed men and a woman.

"Génie," Tristan says, stumbling, and one of the gendarmes lifts a restraining hand.

The woman stares at him, disbelieving. "Tristan!"

"*C'est vraiment toi,*" he says. "*Je t'ai vraiment vue.*" It really is you. I really saw you. He reaches out to touch her, and she lifts her hand to meet his. Their fingertips brush. His tongue feels thick and clumsy in his mouth. "*Comment vas-tu?*"

"*C'est toi,* Tristan," she says sadly, as though some interminable inner argument has been resolved. "I might have known."

2.

CODE NAME: GENEVA

So now Tristan appears, in custody, flanked by men in uniform, after three days of making appointments and not keeping them. Genevieve has never been certain if he lives by the rules of disorder or by a design so labyrinthine that even he, perhaps, has forgotten the way out. To how many codes has he lost the key? She herself has a habit of losing things: countries, suitcases, people dear to her. She thinks of herself as carrying a virus of bereavement. She thinks it is in her genes. She thinks that she must have been born with it since she began losing people so early: first her parents, then the vagabond uncle who carted her round on his photo shoots. *Me and your dad*, he used to tell her, *me and your dad, we never could stand to gather moss. It's in the Teague blood cells, Gen. We've got restless blood. Our hearts don't pump if they have to stay in one place.* Inconsiderately, he swooped into a crevasse with his Leica. He was on assignment with a mountain-climbing team when this happened, and Génie was in school in Australia. She remembers the way the headmistress beckoned from the classroom door. She remembers the way the other girls looked at her, then looked at each other. In boarding schools, news travels by the twitch of an eyebrow. She remembers that she knew instantly, before the headmistress spoke. She knows that any door can open into nothing. She is loss-prone. The defect is like malaria: lurking about in the blood, dormant sometimes, flaring up without warning.

She has cultivated the habit of leaving before she is left—this is her security system—but sometimes in the middle of a night the erratic beat of her heart will wake her. She will be alone in a room somewhere, it could be anywhere, she cannot usually remember which country, not at first. She hears nothing but the crazy syncopated riffs of her heart which sings Billie Holiday songs. *In my sol-i-tude* . . . If she were to disappear, who would notice?

Perhaps the *Wandering Earthling* would print a two-line obituary. *Over a year since traveling freelance writer Genevieve Teague . . . missing, presumed killed in an accident . . . no known family . . . her detailed itineraries will be sorely . . .*

And if Tristan—scavenging publisher, voracious reader of books—were to come across this brief item?

She likes to think he would be briefly stricken. She likes to think he would regret the last argument, the last ultimatum. She likes to think he would remember that they once promised each other in writing, half seriously, half in jest, that even if both had moved on to other lovers, they would still come back like lightning, *comme une traînée de poudre,* if urgently summoned.

"In fifty years, if you call me, if you say: I am in danger at the end of the world," Tristan had written extravagantly on a card that came with three dozen roses, "*pouff! En un clin d'œil,* in an eye blink, I am there."

Génie had sent back a bottle of vintage wine with a lampshade affixed, a handwritten note taped to the shade. "Simply say *I am in extremis* while rubbing the lamp, and abracadabra: Génie appears."

The memory of this exchange comforts her on desolate nights and on those nights when the phone rings in dreams but is always dead by the time her hand finds it. Faxes from Europe also arrive in dreams, as well as in the small hours of night, and once upon a sleepless predawn in the August of 1987 she hears the high hum of her machine and watches a fax uncurl itself like a tongue.

Dear Génie: I am in extremis. Will you come? Love, Tristan.
P.S. Please reply by fax to number above.

This is the way it happens: a certain name, a certain phrase, a face in a crowd—minute, unpredictable things—and she can feel grief in her finger joints, armpits, groin. It breaks out like a fever. It swells and throbs, a contagion of loss. So she tries not to miss anyone. She tries not to get close to anyone she might come to miss. She works long hours, she stays on the road, she keeps moving, and moving on, she keeps changing one unlisted phone number for another, she does her best to be unreachable and to gather no moss.

But two lines had slipped through this obstacle course.

She managed to wait a whole hour, then she sent a reply.

Dear Tristan: Of course I will come. Evidently, from fax number, you must still be in Paris. Same address? Can I have a week to make necessary arrangements and find a cheap flight, or is it too urgent? Love, Genevieve.
P.S. How on earth did you track down my number?

For a week she checked her fax machine compulsively, every few hours. There were no further messages from Tristan. She called his apartment in Paris. That is to say, she called a number that was once, and perhaps was still, the number of his apartment, of their old apartment, in the fourth arrondissement. An answering machine spoke to her. A woman's voice announced in brisk French: *You have reached Jean-Luc and Sylvie. We are not available at present to take . . .* Genevieve hung up.

She called his publishing house. The receptionist had never heard of Monsieur Charron. She had only been there a few months, the receptionist explained. She put Genevieve through to one of the editors. Tristan Charron had not been with them for several years, the editor explained. He had his own small publishing house now, she could not remember the name, but he was doing quite well. He was specializing in translations, she thought she remembered; in introducing non-French writers into France. She had seen favorable articles in *Livres-Hebdo,* in *Le Nouvel Observateur,* in other trade magazines. Probably Agence France could locate him.

Genevieve checked her fax folder to read Tristan's message again. Already, on the shiny thermal paper, it was fading. She put on a track suit and went running. She ran for five miles, until the stitch in her side grew sharp and filled every cranny of thought. She showered and wrapped herself in a towel and called half a dozen acquaintances and arranged a dinner party. Not until the day after the party did she fax a query to Agence France, and not until two days after that did she receive the address and phone number of a small publishing house: Editions du Double. When she called, an assistant answered. Monsieur Charron was at a festival in Prague, he explained, but if madame would like to leave a message . . . "Just tell him that Génie called," she said, "and that—" But then she changed her mind and declined to leave any word.

Prague? Then how could he have faxed her from Paris?

The next morning another message arrived.

Dear Génie: Can you be here next Friday? Take a night flight; you'll get in before the traffic and I'll meet you at eleven hundred hours precisely in the bookstore of the Hôtel de Sully. Do not enter from rue St Antoine. Go through Place des Vosges, the south-west corner, into the courtyard-garden in the rear. The bookstore is on the main floor. It will be crowded with tourists, and therefore safe. Communication is not easy, nor is meeting. If I'm late, wait for me. If you can stay 3 days, we can fly back to New York together. I have meetings set up. I'll be flying on September 8, Air France 64. Try to book the same flight.
Love, Tristan.

Where the sender's number was usually displayed, there was nothing but a string of zeros. She tried sending a reply to the same number as last time, but the fax would not go through. She called the small publishing house and left a message. "Tell him Génie called. Say I'm coming." She made reservations and faxed Editions du Double.

Tristan: Arriving Friday. Same return flight as you. Génie.

She had arrived in Paris, as requested, on Friday morning, three days ago. She had taken the Roissybus from Charles de Gaulle Airport to Place de l'Opéra, then the Métro to Bastille. She had walked to Place des Vosges and waited in the bookshop of Hôtel de Sully. She had browsed. She had skimmed a facsimile edition of the sketches of Viollet le Duc for the restoration of Notre Dame. She had pondered his design for the delicate wooden spire between the towers, and for the pulpit. She read his notebook entries on the restoration of the Sainte Chapelle. She read of the speed with which that exquisite little church had been built, she read of its progress all the way from idea in the mind of Louis IX to filigreed spires and rose window and glowing glass, all achieved in the space of three years, the entire Gothic jewel box completed by 1248.

It can hardly be imagined, Viollet Le Duc wrote, *how this work, so astonishing in the multiplicity and variety of its details, the purity of its execution, and the beauty of its materials, could have been accomplished in so short a time.*

It can hardly be imagined, Genevieve thought, that such an urgent request for a meeting, with instructions so precise as to time and place, could remain so nebulous, so uncertain of fulfillment, after so long a time. She browsed more art books. She read more than she really cared to know about architectural detail in the Musée Carnavalet, Madame de Sévigné's town house just a stone's throw from where Genevieve now stood. She could have dazzled a soirée with the ideas of its designer, Pierre Lescot, and with the social gossip of 1550. After one hour, she left the bookstore through the rear exit. She sat, perplexed and anxious and irritated, on the low stone wall beneath a spreading chestnut in the Sully garden. A youthful employee from the bookstore came out after her.

"Madame," he said. "You left this behind."

"I didn't buy anything," she said. "It must have been someone else."

"I saw you put it down."

"You are mistaken," Genevieve said.

"Then you may have it anyway, madame," the young clerk said graciously, "because I saw how much you loved this book, and how can I find the person who actually left it?"

He set the book beside her on the wall. It was a small monograph, lavishly illustrated, many plates in full color, on the subject of the stained glass in the Sainte Chapelle. A piece of notepaper was inserted as a bookmark at the rose window page. On the paper, a message was typed:

Difficulties. Will explain. Tomorrow, same place, same time.

Yesterday and again today: same place, same time, same routine more or less (*Excuse me, madame, you dropped something. . .*), slightly different note on the second day, and on the third: *May need to meet at airport*. Did this have anything to do with Tristan? The notes were unaddressed and unsigned.

And the faxes? She began to wonder if yearning, tamped down, swept out of sight, had summoned them up. If they were real, on the other hand, anyone could have sent them. But why? And who, other than Tristan himself, could possibly know that an urgent message, phrased in a certain way and bearing his name, would bring her immediately to Paris? Well, she supposed, his old girlfriend Françoise would know, but Françoise would have ceased to care years ago, and would have no possible way of locating Genevieve.

And if Tristan himself did send them? Suppose he was watching from somewhere, trying to reach her, begging her to wait? What possible reason could there be? *In extremis*: What did that mean? What kind of crisis was he in?

She sometimes wondered if he had a completely separate underground life, or indeed several other lives. There had been occasions when the thought came to her that he might work in Intelligence, presumably for the French government, though once he had said something that made her think his relationship with the American government was unusual. If it weren't so complicated getting a green card for you, she had said, we could live in New York. It wouldn't be so complicated, he said. I could call in my chips. What do you mean? she asked, and he said, Nothing. I'm joking. An old girlfriend of mine used to claim her father could get Carlos the Jackal a green card if she wanted him to. Which old girlfriend? she had asked. Do you mean Françoise? And he had looked startled. I forgot you knew her, he said.

At other times, Genevieve had thought that he might have ties with some shadowy organization on the wrong (but not disreputable) side of the law, some kind of classy white-collar dubious borderline thing: the smuggling of art, perhaps. Or something more noble: the smuggling of manuscripts out of totalitarian countries. This thought had crossed her mind whenever she herself took on another assignment for Caritas, ferrying private letters out of regions where the postal service was closely monitored or where war interfered with it unduly. Mothers wrote to sons and daughters who had gotten away; husbands in the democratic West sent secret letters back through iron and bamboo curtains to wives and children; sweethearts separated by the horrible accidents of history sent burning promises back and forth. She never told anyone, not even Tristan, that she worked for Caritas. She thought of the work as personal and compassionate, not political, but too many small and ordinary lives behind too many dangerous barriers depended on secrecy. It was quite possible, after all, that Tristan was doing the same sort of thing.

She also pondered his possible clandestine activities on those occasions—they sometimes seemed to her oddly frequent—when street photographers had taken photographs, not of Tristan and Genevieve solely, nor even centrally, but of street scenes, courtyards, sidewalk cafés, with Tristan and Genevieve in the frame. Probably this sort of thing happened constantly in Paris, a city where tourists outnumbered residents in summer, though it seemed to her to happen more frequently when she was with Tristan. And there was always an aura of the clandestine: she never knew if the reasons were rational or not.

On the second day, after Tristan failed to appear, she made contact with Caritas and a meeting was arranged in the tropical greenhouse of the Jardin des Plantes. The Caritas woman handed her a copy of *Le Monde*. Between the obituaries and the sporting triumphs of *les bleus*, letters on thin onionskin paper were interleafed. Génie could detect no difference in texture between the paper of the letters and the pages of *Le Monde*.

In the courtyard of the Sully, third day, she felt a chill. Still no Tristan. A note that said: *May need to meet at airport.*

Airports are Génie's natural turf, and she has a gift for making people disappear. She feels pain in her finger joints and in the soft creases of her arms. If she does not keep moving, her joints will stiffen and swell. She wanders to Place de la Bastille. By instinct, she walks the length of boulevard Henri IV to the Ile St. Louis and strolls along the Quai d'Anjou. She has a sense of being followed. She turns quickly and for an instant she thinks she sees Tristan in the shadowy curve of a bridge, but when she goes back there is only an old man with a newspaper, asleep.

She continues along the Quai d'Anjou. Venerable trees dip their crowns toward the Seine and she is half hypnotized by reflections (theirs and hers). She pauses at a cast-iron mooring ring in the wall by the Pont Marie. She runs her fingers around it, then touches it lightly with her forehead, leaning there, almost like someone at prayer.

She checks out of her hotel on Ile St. Louis and leaves her suitcase with the concierge for later. She decides, however, to take the wheeled carry-on with her because she plans to buy books, and books make her shoulder bag too heavy. She browses the bookstores and *bouqinistes* along the Seine. She buys with reckless delight. She decides to return to the Place des Vosges *just in case.* In the terrace café near Hôtel de Sully, she will sit over lunch with an early edition of Chrétien de Troyes and a glass of wine.

She drags the little case down the rue de Birague and through the arched colonnade of Place des Vosges, and that is when the past, conjured up so intensely, breaks into song. She can hear "Caravan" on a tenor sax. She stops to listen. The young black musician must be American; the style is pure New Orleans. She is standing under the stone arcades, but what she is seeing is the moon through the window of the apartment she and Tristan once shared, and the nights when they would sit in the dark with wine and figs and a platter of Rosette de Lyon. They would listen to Duke Ellington.

Surely Tristan is close by. She can sense him. She turns and studies the Place until she feels foolish. She nods at the musician and drops a few francs in his hat and leaves through the stone arcade. At Number 12, rue de Birague, she pauses, and then she sits for a time in the bistro at the corner of rue St. Antoine.

She wants to be gone. *May need to meet at airport.* Maybe Tristan will be there, maybe not. Either way, what is the point of hanging around? Flight 64 does not leave for hours yet, but she has her return ticket in her purse.

A passing tourist takes a photograph through the bistro door: of the scatter of small tables, of men with newspapers and espresso, of couples in love, of Genevieve. A pigeon lands on one of the bistro tables and pecks at a torn sachet of sugar. Something prickles along the back of Genevieve's neck. She senses danger.

The instinct, bred of much living and traveling alone, is so powerful that she decides not to return to her hotel for the suitcase since everything of consequence—and this includes a toothbrush and a change of underwear as well as the Caritas letters—is either in the large shoulder bag that she never sets down or in the carry-on. She decides to take the Roissybus. At the airport, she will sit over a cup of coffee and prepare her classes for next week.

At Charles de Gaulle, she has a sense of being followed. She moves in a weather of anxiety. She no longer expects to see Tristan. She walks for miles, it seems like miles, along one of the underground tunnels. She cannot keep still. She walks all the way to one of the domestic terminals and back and then slides into a bistro booth.

She sips coffee and makes notes for the coming classes at NYU, three total-immersion weeks with South Korean businessmen. The men are to be flown in by a U.S. corporation. Some of them will come bearing letters that have passed from hand to hand, along secret and dangerous routes, from citizens of North Korea to relatives in other parts of the world. No one is willing to consign these precious letters to regular postal services, certainly not in North Korea, but not in the United States either, no matter what assurances are given. Genevieve will send the letters farther along their way and will give others in return. The letters are on onionskin paper, and the South Koreans will hide them in various ingenious ways—sometimes sandwiched between two book pages, glued together—in order to pass them on, via certain bribable conduits at the border, into North Korea. Genevieve, finding it difficult to concentrate, prepares her lessons for the forthcoming week.

Still hours to boarding time.

She watches a family at the next table: a mother with a fretful baby, a little girl in a blue coat, the father deep in conversation with some younger woman who has apparently come to see them off. Genevieve feels an ache like a bruise at her wrists. She wants to reach for the baby and for the little girl clambering all over her father. Absentmindedly, the father sets the girl down. "Put your paper cup in the garbage," he tells her, pointing.

The little girl contemplates her paper cup. Passing Genevieve's table, she says solemnly, "We're going home. In New York we have to change planes, and then we're going to Atlanta."

"We must be on the same flight," Genevieve says. "What's your name?"

"Samantha," the little girl says. "What's yours?"

"I'm Genevieve."

"Sam," her father says. "Stop bothering the lady. We're going through security now. Come on."

Genevieve feels restless. She does not know how long she walks or where she is walking. She stops to caress silk scarves in a small boutique. When she is asked to step aside by two men in uniform, her first thought is: So. Someone knows about the letters. She knows the Caritas offices in Paris have been raided. She wonders if Caritas is considered subversive by the French government or, more likely, by some right-wing group, by one of the ultra-nationalist vigilante cells.

She also wonders if she is about to be approached as a potential courier of something rather more dangerous than the letters.

Her second thought is: Does this have anything to do with Tristan? Or is it Tristan who is monitoring me?

And then he materializes from the thought. "Tristan," she says, sadly. "I might have known." He was always guarded, she thinks. Always. "Four keepers with weapons, Tristan," she says flippantly, gesturing at his armed escort and her own. "Don't you think that's a bit excessive?"

"Génie." He lifts one hand to her cheek and their fingers brush. A tic pulls at her mouth. She turns slightly away, but he leans forward impulsively and kisses her full on the lips. "I heard someone playing 'Caravan' in the Place des Vosges," he murmurs, too low for the policemen to hear, "and I saw you there, but I didn't trust my own ears and eyes."

She stares at him. "Is this *your* game, Tristan, or theirs?"

"You must come with us, madame," a policeman says.

"Are you stalking me, Tristan?"

"What?"

She says significantly, "I'm writing a piece on the stained glass in the Sainte Chapelle." She watches his face. "For the *Wandering Earthling,*" she says.

"Madame."

She turns to the policeman and makes a coquettish gesture, very Gallic. "An old flame, monsieur." She makes a rueful *moue* with her lips. "Two minutes, after all these years?"

"Two minutes, madame."

"You stopped at Number 12, rue de Birague," Tristan says. "I watched you."

"You watched me." She keeps her voice neutral.

"I followed you." He smiles wryly. "But you're very good at disappearing. Why are you here?"

"You should know."

"I mean, what brought you to Paris?"

Whose code are we using? she wonders. For whose benefit? Who is translating?

"Madame," the policeman says. "I must insist."

"Off to the *conciergerie,*" she says lightly.

"What do you mean?" Tristan wants to know. "What's happening?"

She pauses and turns back to look at him. Is he innocent? Is he simply a consummate actor? She feels an immeasurable sadness.

"I have no idea what's going on," he says. "Do you?"

3.

CODE NAME: S

Genevieve thinks of the letters in her carry-on baggage, some of them interleafed between the pages of *Le Monde,* others hidden between the pages of books. They are family letters containing news of a grandfather's death and a cousin's wedding. Another is full of a yearning sadness being passed to a husband in Ohio from a wife who is still inside Iran, a village wife, a wife who sends news of growing sons whenever she can. Genevieve's Caritas contact in New York had told her: it's short notice, but if you're going to Paris, we have letters to get into Algeria, and one to Iran. And our contact in Paris can give you others in return. Genevieve imagines the fantastic arabesques of the routes these letters have traveled, tracing them across the curved forehead of the French policeman—he has such bushy brows—and over his right ear and down the arm that is searching her capacious shoulder bag and the carry-on case. If he finds the letters, then a handful of families used to expecting the worst will go on as usual, waiting, waiting, waiting for word, living on a memory of hope and on the raw nub of energy that comes from the sheer refusal to give up. Genevieve does not think she has anything to be afraid of beyond frustration and delay. There is nothing seditious in what she does, except perhaps for the fact that somewhere along the line, at those points where forbidden borders are crossed, bribery and collusion are involved. Presumably. But that is not her affair. She knows nothing about how that part is done.

"You are Australian, mademoiselle."

Genevieve smiles.

"The Australians are troublemakers," he says. "They have made terrorist attacks on French ships in the South Pacific."

"With due respect, monsieur," Genevieve says, "the Australians were unarmed and on inflatable boats, and the French ships carried nuclear warheads." She knows this is not a wise answer. She knows it would be better to keep silent, but keeping discreetly silent has never been to the taste of Australians in general, or of Genevieve in particular. "And was it not French officers," she asks politely, "who were tried and convicted of blowing up a Greenpeace vessel and killing civilians?"

"You are a member of Greenpeace, mademoiselle?"

"No, I'm not. But to kill nonviolent protestors—"

"Politics interest you, it seems."

"No more than average, I think."

"You travel a great deal."

"I'm a travel writer and I teach English as a second language at institutes around the world. I spend most of my life on the road."

"Yet you stayed in Paris for two years."

Genevieve combs her fingers through her hair. The gesture is one of studied composure, though her fingers are trembling a little because this suggestion of close surveillance disturbs her. Then she remembers the *carte de séjour* and her passport stamp. Naturally they know she has lived here. This is routine security stuff. "Not quite two years," she says. "And I still moved about, I still had travel assignments. But yes."

"Why was that?"

"Why did I continue to travel?"

"Why did you live in France?"

She says simply, "I was in love with a Frenchman."

"Ah yes. The publisher. The one who works in Intelligence with a little trafficking on the side."

A nerve flutters near Genevieve's right eye. "That's what writers and publishers do," she says flippantly. "They work in intelligence and traffic in ideas." She is afraid a twitching at the corner of her mouth will become visible. Her right foot taps out, of its own volition, a soft kettledrum roll.

"That is not the kind of Intelligence we mean, mademoiselle."

Genevieve is following the movement of the gendarme's hand within her shoulder bag. He pulls out *Le Monde* without unfolding it; he does not notice that it is yesterday's paper. He pulls out books one by one and fans the pages with one hand. A sound resembling the regular thump of a bass drum is beating in Genevieve's ears and getting faster. One by one, the books are put back, *Le Monde* is put back, the makeup case and travel toiletries are put back, the underwear is held up for examination, the predictable smirk is exchanged, her bra and panties are returned to the bag, and the tab is snapped shut.

"Your lover is involved in espionage," the policeman says.

So, Genevieve thinks. It is confirmed.

Nevertheless, she raises startled eyebrows. "For the French government, monsieur?"

The policeman frowns. "We know you came to Paris to see your lover."

"My former lover," she corrects. "But we haven't been in touch with each other for years. I don't even have his address. It was a big surprise to bump into him just now." She speaks passionately, wrapped in the luxury of truth.

"Why do you use the code name of Geneva?"

"I don't know what you mean."

"We must ask you, mademoiselle, to wait here until boarding time," the policeman says.

"What is the problem?" she asks.

"We are not at liberty to tell you, mademoiselle. Someone will return to escort you to your gate at the appropriate time."

They lock the door when they leave.

Waiting time has no boundary.

When she hears the lock click, Genevieve floats free of the small room, eight feet by nine, and finds herself in the bookstore near the Place de la Bastille again, six years? seven? nearly eight years back. The store has more used books than new. It is as full of junk as of unexpected treasures and she loves to do this—*chiner,* the French say—to poke about for literary finds, rare first editions, oddities. She is browsing through the journal of a nineteenth century traveler in Australia—a French traveler—and suddenly laughs out loud.

> In the homestead of a cattle farmer—he calls himself a pastoralist (*un grand agriculteur*) and owns 100,000 hectares, a wealthy man—I was given what I can only call a *slab* of beef (*un vrai pavé de bœuf*) that would more fittingly have been a main course in hell. I do not know if it is the heat and drought that have destroyed the capacity for taste in this country, or whether the ancestors of these pastoralists—being English, and therefore at a disadvantage in matters of taste, and being, furthermore, from the lowest levels of English society (many having arrived in chains)—have passed on a congenital incapacity for gustatory discrimination. The meat had been thrown into an open fire and left until charred. I suggested to my host that if the meat were to be steeped in red wine and herbs for twenty-four hours, and then braised with garlic and morels, it would be greatly improved. He replied: "We could throw in half a dozen frogs, if you like," a response which astonished and mystified me. No, I replied. I would not like. That is a very strange idea. One should not mix white meat with dark.

"*C'est tellement drôle, ce livre?*" a male voice asks, and she swivels to see a man reading over her shoulder.

"To me it is," she says. "To an Australian. Hilarious."

She shows him the book.

"You are Australian? I have never met an Australian."

"We are extremely rare," she tells him solemnly. "Like unicorns. We eat kangaroos and drink wine made from eucalyptus leaves. It tastes like cleaning fluid."

"I have been told so," he says, and she laughs again. "You are making fun of me," he protests.

"I'm told the French have no sense of humor whatsoever. They are incapable of laughing at themselves."

"This is what the English mistakenly believe," he says gravely, "because *les doubles sens* in French are too intricate for English speakers to understand. The French have *beaucoup d'esprit.*"

"So I have been told," she says. "By many French people. The English have jokes, but the French have wit and linguistic finesse."

"Wit and finesse, yes. Your French is very good."

"You're being kind. But I'm improving. I've been living in Paris for two months."

"*Vraiment?* You are not a tourist? Why are you living here?"

"I teach English to French businessmen for Berlitz. But I'm also a travel writer. That's why other travel writers interest me, especially the history of travel writing."

"My own interests," he says, "are biography and fiction."

"Travel writing's both."

"*Comment?*" he says, startled.

"Travel writing reveals more about the observer than the place observed. In that sense, it's autobiography, don't you think? A book like this . . . it makes me ask myself how many blind spots and how much ignorance I'm exposing every time I write. You know, twenty years from now, when a Frenchman picks up my articles on Paris in some bookstore and kills himself laughing . . . ?"

"A travel writer and a philosopher," he says, amused. "This is a great coincidence. I am a publisher."

"Imagine," she says dryly. "A writer and a publisher in a bookstore, both checking out other people's books. What a surprise."

This time, it is he who laughs. "*Touché*. For someone who is English, you have *beaucoup d'esprit*."

"Monsieur," she says, with mock outrage. "You must never tell an Australian she is English. It offends us to the core of our being."

"*Vraiment?* It is like calling a Corsican French?"

"Very similar, I would think."

"*Mademoiselle l'Australienne, enchanté*," he says, taking her hand and bowing over it, mock formal. "*Je me présente: Tristan Charron, éditeur*."

"Tristan! What a name for a publisher. You're not going to believe this, but I'm Genevieve."

"*C'est génial*." He has not let go of her hand and Genevieve marvels that so much sensation, none of it to be trusted, can pass between epidermal layers. "*Et aussi un peu provocant, n'est-ce pas?*"

"A mismatch, I'd say"—politely, she pulls her hand free—"since both were victims of grand passion, but not for each other."

"*Comment?*"

"Tristan and Genevieve, as handed down to us by Chrétien de Troyes. Both doomed. Both victims of passion."

"*Victims!*" He is shocked. "Why are the English terrified of passion? Victims? *Au contraire*. They were gifted for love, Tristan and Genevieve. Great love was their destiny."

"In *literature*. Love's usually on a grander scale there."

"There is a Brasserie Camelot," he says, "not far from here. *Vraiment*. We could debate this subject."

"Camelot ended in ruins," she parries. She thinks his eyes, and the way he uses them—*Frenchmen are so good at this, so practiced*—give an unfair edge. "And the thunderbolt of passion wrecked Tristan's life, so take warning." She is aware of disconcerting physical reactions in her body: movements of blood, engorgements, liquefactions. She imagines running her tongue over Tristan's lips. She imagines the taste of him. She is mesmerized by a smudge of birthmark beneath one eye. "This meeting is full of risky omens," she says flippantly, "but at least you're not Lancelot, thank God." The comment pops up like a champagne cork and mortifies her. She busies herself with book spines, runs her finger over titles, pulls out a volume and fans through it. She sees nothing, puts it back, and pulls out another.

"In literature," he says, "as your Shakespeare has stated so well, the world is well lost for love."

"Yes, in literature. Madness comes off quite well there too."

"*Ça, c'est l'amour*. Divine madness. Tristan drank the love potion and was divinely insanely happy. Love was his destiny."

"And he and Iseult lived tragically ever after. Are Frenchmen always this—"

"Yes," he says. "We are."

She says nervously, too brightly, "Well, if we could find an edition of Chrétien de Troyes in this bookstore, that would spell destiny no doubt, and a pot of gold at the next *coup de foudre*."

"Every good bookstore in Paris has at least one edition of Chrétien de Troyes," he assures her, "and I will certainly find it," which he does.

"Impressive. Do you always get what you want?"

"Yes," he says. "I do. It is one of my rules. Listen." He flips to the tragic romance of Sir Lancelot du Lac, reads a little in Old French, then translates freely into modern French and broken English and *franglais*. "He is *tout à fait comblé* by the golden hairs of Genevieve, he is *prostré*, he has *chair de poule*—how do you say . . . ?"

She splutters with laughter. "Goose bumps."

"Yes. He is sick with passion."

"You see? That's ridiculous. Sick with passion over hairs in a comb. Can you imagine any man—"

"Yes," he says. "The French can imagine that without difficulty. *L'amour est le destin*."

"Ah, the Mack truck of destiny." She makes an extravagant Sarah Bernhardt gesture, hand over heart. "If you're marked, you can't get out of its way."

"Macktruck?" he says, puzzled.

"Um . . . lorry; juggernaut . . . *camion,* that's it. *Le grand camion.* . . . No. That won't work in French. Um . . . *le poids lourd du Destin.*"

"*C'est vrai,*" he says. "One must celebrate as one surrenders. *Voulez-vous une coupe de champagne?*"

"What persistence." She laughs. "Okay, you win."

And so it begins, from bookstore to brasserie to more bookstores and cafés, a flirtatious friendship between two people who read a lot and argue a lot, and then Tristan invites her to a small publishing party, *un cocktail* for the launch of a book, and in the middle of the crush of reviewers and writers and hangers-on, hemmed in by gossip, noise, champagne, fizzing currents of sexual invitation, she senses something, she puts a hand to her cheek, she feels heat, she feels a magnetic pull. From across the room, Tristan is looking at her and has been looking for who knows how long, and she experiences vertigo, she reaches out for something to hold on to, and it is Tristan who takes the flute of champagne from her hand and drinks it. "That is a dangerous thing to do," she says unsteadily, because she is suddenly without edges or definition, and they seem to be down by the Seine near the Pont Marie and she can feel the impress of a mooring ring against her back and then Tristan is carrying her up the stairs of a small hotel on the rue de Birague and they are falling into bed, and then someone is banging on the door and the policeman is saying: "Your flight is boarding now, mademoiselle. You may proceed to Gate 12."

Genevieve supposes the policeman has escorted her, since here she is at Gate 12 with no recollection of the passage from waiting room to the boarding area. The words of the policemen go around like a stuck record in her head (*your lover works in Intelligence . . . trafficking . . . espionage*) and the little doubts of seven years, all the misgivings, all the mysterious silences and absences that did not quite add up, all the evasions, all the sudden appearances of photographers, all of them coalesce into something towering and menacing, with a gargoyle face.

She stares through the plate-glass window at the plane, seeing nothing.

"Génie," Tristan says, tapping her on the shoulder.

She startles. "Oh, Tristan, it's you. I thought it would be the police again." She can scarcely bear to look at him. "Well, I suppose it is."

"*Tu blagues!*"

"No, I'm not joking. Although this seems to be *someone's* idea of a joke. Why are you here?"

"I'm flying to New York," he says.

"Why?"

"Because you are. Because you sent me a fax to say you were coming, but I didn't get it till a few hours ago." Their eyes meet at last, warily, and then steadily and intensely. "I've been following you for three days." He puts his hand up to touch her cheek and she covers it with her own. "I bought a ticket for this flight as soon as I read your fax." He reaches for her other hand, and they stand there, like two children, fingers entwined.

"Why didn't you meet me in the Hôtel de Sully?"

"In the Sully?"

"In the bookshop."

"What do you mean?"

"You asked me to meet you there."

"Wait," he says. "This is too confusing. Let's back up a bit. Why are you in Paris?"

"Because you asked me to come."

"You can hear my wishes?"

"You didn't fax me?"

"Fax you? How could I fax you?"

"*In extremis,* the fax said. Please come at once. Signed, Tristan."

"I never even know which country you're in. You vanished. No forwarding address, no phone number. That was so cruel, Génie, so *unnecessary*—"

"Swear to me that you didn't fax me."

"I swear by this"—on instinct, reckless, he kisses her, a long, hungry, tongue-in-mouth kiss—"that I did not fax you." He kisses her again. "If I did have your number, I would fax you and phone you every day."

Her head is against his chest. She comes just to his shoulder. "Tristan," she says, looking up at him. "Please don't lie to me. For God's sake, give me that. Don't lie to me."

"I swear by every time we made love that I'm not lying."

"The police claim you're involved in espionage, and trafficking on the side."

"*What?* Trafficking! That's bullshit." He laughs. "Trafficking in manuscripts, they mean. I got caught in Prague last week trying to smuggle a manuscript out. I guess the cops here must have informers in Prague."

"And espionage?"

"Only if that's what meeting Czech writers is. And I didn't fax you."

"Then who did? Who knows us well enough to know I'd drop everything and fly to Paris? I mean, if you said it that way: *I'm in extremis*."

"No one does."

"Someone does. Someone who knew us when we lived together. Françoise, for example?"

He frowns. "She probably saw that card you sent with the lamp. She used to go through my pockets." He opens his wallet and pulls out a grubby and dog-eared scrap of parchment. Génie reads her own faded handwriting: *Simply say I am in extremis while rubbing the lamp, and abracadabra: Génie appears.* "See?" Tristan says. "Still got it. Carry it with me like a talisman." He grins at her. "Rubbed it in the prison cell in Prague, and look what's happened."

"Françoise used to go through your pockets?"

"Yes, but we haven't had contact for years."

Over the address system, rows fifty and higher are summoned for boarding.

"What's your seat number?" Tristan asks.

"11A."

"Mine's 29B. I know the flight's almost full. When I bought my ticket there were hardly any seats left, and those would have gone to the standbys. But maybe we can change places with someone."

"After takeoff, maybe."

"Excuse me," a young woman with a camera says, nudging them aside. "I wonder if you'd mind moving . . . ?" The young woman presses the shutter once, twice, recording for history the family about to board the plane: a father, a mother with a baby, a little girl with a teddy bear. The child, who is wearing a blue coat with a blue velvet collar, waves to Genevieve and Genevieve waves back. "Hi, Samantha."

"You know them?" Tristan asks sharply.

"I don't know them. I saw them in the coffee shop."

"The woman with the camera," Tristan says. "I've seen her before. I think she lives with Françoise. Shares her apartment, I mean."

Genevieve's eyebrows lift. "So you do stay in touch with Françoise?"

"No. God, no. I bumped into her a few weeks ago, and she was with that American woman."

"You bump into each other often?"

"No. Hardly ever." He frowns. "But Françoise . . ." He shakes his head. "I don't know. She never wanted to let go. I'm sure she moved into that apartment on Avenue des Gobelins because you were in the same building. It's the kind of thing she would do."

"Could she have kept track of me?"

"You used to give her the key to your apartment."

"To water the plants, yes, when I was traveling, but that's centuries ago." She thinks about it. "She could have found the *Wandering Earthling*'s address—"

"They won't give out any information on their writers," Tristan says. "I tried that myself. No luck."

"But you tried?"

"What do you think? I went crazy."

"You'd given me very clear marching orders."

"You had to know I didn't mean it. Not literally."

"I'm not the type who sits around waiting to be dismissed."

"I nearly went berserk."

"I was pretty miserable myself."

"If you'd called . . . if you'd sent a postcard, even . . ."

"I had to protect myself."

"That was so wrong, what you did. You should never have left."

"I've spent a lot of time wishing I hadn't. But you tried to clip my wings, Tristan, and I can't . . . I just can't . . . Clip them? What am I saying? You tried to cut them off."

"I know, I know, I was stupid, *con et fou à la fois.* But I've learned my lesson." He puts his hand on his heart. "I swear to God. Couldn't we start over?"

"Perhaps we could."

Five minutes later, when their rows are called, they are still hand in hand. The stewardess who checks their boarding passes is flustered. "We're way behind schedule," she explains, "because of all the extra security."

"What's the reason?"

"They never tell us anything. Usually turns out to be some crank bomb threat, but we don't want them taking chances, do we? At least this way, you may miss a connection, but you know you're safe."

At Row 11, Génie kisses him. "After takeoff," she says, "I'll sweet-talk my neighbor into switching."

But the man who arrives to occupy 11B does not look promising.

He arrives late, after almost everyone else has boarded.

"Hi," Genevieve says. "Were you held up for interrogation too?" He ignores her so completely that she supposes he is deaf. He has no carry-on luggage at all. He concentrates on buckling his seat belt, his left arm across the armrest, invading her space. He is a short, stocky man with tanned skin, a shock of dark hair in his eyes, a good-looking man. A hum of intensity—of concentration, of impatience, of nervousness perhaps, or maybe anger—comes off him. He looks vaguely familiar, and Genevieve wonders if he might be a football player, one of the Algerian *bleus*, or from the Marseilles team, perhaps? She thinks she must have seen him on television or in the newspaper.

She tries again. "Did they make you check your hand baggage in?" And then he looks at her. Fully. Intently. She could almost say he attacks her with his eyes, his expression cold to the point of hostility. Genevieve flinches. He waits, saying nothing, and she wonders if his rudeness has been intentional, or if he simply does not understand.

"Vous avez dû enregistrer votre baggage à main?" she tries. He does smile then, but in a way that makes Genevieve's heart lurch like an elevator whose cable has been sliced through. The smile is macho, backlit with an innuendo of violence. He is Egyptian, perhaps? Algerian? Saudi? About forty, she thinks. He holds her gaze for seconds too long, and then suddenly the sense of threat vanishes and he is charming, full of warmth and remorse. He touches Genevieve's arm. "Forgive me," he says, in excellent English. His accent is British. "I've been preoccupied. My taxi was caught in a traffic jam and I thought I would miss the flight."

"Did you go to school in England?" she asks, curious.

He laughs. "England. Riyadh. Paris. New York. I'm a nomad, like you."

She is startled. "Like me? What makes you say that?"

"Just guessing. But I'm highly intuitive. You speak English, but your French is very good. Therefore you travel."

"Very perceptive. I'm a travel writer. And I lived in Paris for a couple of years."

He says, "So did I. For quite a few years."

"Where do you live now?"

"Oh, here and there."

"What do you do?"

"Import, export. I represent my clients' interests in foreign countries."

"I'm Genevieve, by the way."

"Mohammad."

Perhaps she has seen him in the business pages. "Would I have seen your picture in a newspaper?"

"Possibly." A smile plays about his lips. He is pleased to be recognized; no, it is more than that, she decides. He is both amused and delighted by the fact. He gives the impression of enjoying a private joke. "I've been on TV," he says.

"I thought so. I knew I'd seen you somewhere."

They lapse into magazines and silence during takeoff and for twenty minutes thereafter, but when the flight attendants distribute pretzels and drinks, she ventures, "Could I ask a favor?"

Again, momentarily, his smile and his eyes—*basilisk,* that is the word, she thinks—cause a stab of uneasiness, but the coldness is fleeting, he is charming, he is solicitous, he touches her wrist, and she doubts her own earlier perception. She feels confused.

"Yes?" he says.

"I have a friend sitting farther back. We haven't seen each other for years and we were wondering—"

They are interrupted by the flight attendant and when Mohammad passes her the Bloody Mary she has ordered, his sleeve rides up on his forearm and she sees the S tattooed on his wrist. A fugitive memory alights, quivers, vanishes again, hovers half seen on the other side of a filmy curtain, and extinguishes itself. She has seen that tattoo before. She *knows* it, though no context presents itself. The sensation is maddening. The sensation has the smell of slept-in sheets and of dreams going out with the tide. It is like trying to hold onto the skein of a sleep in which crucial revelations have occurred. One wakes into the awareness, the *certainty*, of momentous truths just unfolded, but what? But what are they? They seep into morning and no amount of clutching at the bedding will make them stay.

"Your friend?" Mohammad prompts. "Whom you haven't seen for years?" But he speaks in French. *Ton ami? Que tu n'as pas vu depuis des lustres?*

Ton ami . . . And then it hits her.

It hits her like the comet that punched St. Paul on the road to

Damascus. She is winded and blinded by it. It is not just the rudeness of a total stranger addressing her as *tu. Ton ami* . . . the random conjunction of the words themselves and the impertinence strikes white light on the splinters of recall, she sees the holograph whole, the floating past, the half-light, the turn in the stair. . . .

Tristan, Mohammad, a dark stairwell.

On Avenue des Gobelins, in the thirteenth district, Tristan is visiting for the night. It is early in their relationship, the first wintry months of 1980, before she has moved into Tristan's apartment in the fourth; sometimes they sleep at her place, sometimes at his. The timed light in her stairwell, as always, blinks out before they reach the second landing. There is a shadowy buffeting as residents from higher floors descend. *Bonjour, Genevieve. Bonjour, Françoise,* and she notes that Françoise is with the intermittent boyfriend who comes and goes. The boyfriend is never introduced, he rarely speaks, she has never seen him clearly in the dark, but as usual, he contrives to brush against Genevieve *en passant*. He turns back to look at her. He always does this. He is the kind of man who undresses every woman with his eyes and she has the impression that Françoise, whom she scarcely knows, is made unhappy by him and is frightened of him too. He makes a lewd gesture with left arm and fist, though the lewdness is mitigated by a wink that implies: *This is all just a joke.* He has an S tattooed on his left wrist. "*Tristan!*" Françoise says in the dark stairwell. Tristan turns and someone pushes the button for the light and he says, astonished, "*Françoise!*"

"You know each other?" Genevieve asks, surprised.

"It's been a while," Françoise says. "*Tu vas bien, Tristan?*"

"*Ça va,*" he says. "*Et toi?*"

"*Ça va.*"

The boyfriend is looking back up the stairwell, winking. "*Ton ami?*" he says to Genevieve with a smirk.

Tristan stiffens, offended at the liberty taken, a thuggish stranger using the intimate form of address.

"Let it go," Genevieve whispers. "It's done to provoke."

Your friend? the boyfriend mouths again, in French, behind Tristan's back. He makes a throat-slitting gesture with index finger across his own neck. Genevieve stares at him.

"How do you know Françoise?" she asks Tristan later.

"An old girlfriend." Tristan is shaking his head in disbelief. "In the same building as you, *c'est incroyable*! How long has she been here?"

"A few months."

"What a strange coincidence."

"Her boyfriend's strange."

"There's something a bit strange about Françoise. She's . . . she doesn't like to let go. She always made me feel *watched*. How well do you know her?"

"Only slightly. We say hello in the stairwell every day. She waters my plants when I'm away and I feed her cat when she is. I'm glad the boyfriend's not around much. He gives me the creeps."

"A real thug, but I'm relieved she's found someone else." When he first left her, Tristan says, she used to call in the middle of the night, threatening suicide.

"What did you do?"

"What could I do? A few times I went to her, and made love again, until she calmed down. Then I got a new phone number, unlisted."

"Your friend," Mohammad, in seat 11B, is saying in English.

"What?"

"You wanted to ask me something because of your friend." Mohammad unfastens his seat belt and leans forward. He is relaxing, pulling off his shoes, watching her, never blinking or wavering in his gaze. She senses menace and the feeling is intense. He is smiling again, waiting for her answer. He remembers her, she realizes. He knows who she is, and that fact is at the core of the menace. He does not yet realize that she too has a context now, that she has identified him, but perhaps he would not care. Perhaps that would be part of the sinister joke, whatever it is. He mock-punches her shoulder with his fist and the tattooed S pauses at the tip of her nose. She knows he is ridiculing her.

She asks stupidly, "What does the S stand for?"

"It stands for Sirocco," he says, smiling. "The wind off the Sahara. Sandstorms. The hot wind that burns where it blows," and there is an announcement then that due to turbulence passengers must not leave their seats, and a roaring begins in Gevevieve's ears that lasts throughout the serving of the meal and then at last the seat belt sign goes off and she stands and says "Excuse me," and everything revs up to dizzying speed for whole seconds and then slows down because Mohammad, code name Sirocco, reaches into his shoe and something flashes, something silver and thin as a blade of grass, and it pricks at her throat. He lifts her as a rough lover might and pulls her into the aisle. She feels a paper cut on her neck, feels wetness there. She has the sense of being choreographed. She is part of a slow-motion pas-de-deux that is moving forward down the plane as strange figures float out of the first-class section, men in masks with snouts, men with the heads of pigs, men with machine guns in their hands, and there is screaming and madness and clawing hands and then blackness as Genevieve falls.

4.

CODE NAME: BLACK DEATH

Tristan can hear, in the pitch-dark, the violent fumble of hands.

Don't, he begs silently, but the woman is frantic, as well as clumsy, and goes on tearing at her gas mask. He assumes a woman; they seem to have lower thresholds of panic. He will have to act quickly. He can hear the muffled rip of the Velcro fastener, her collar beginning to give way. She fights to escape the way a drowning person claws at water. Then she will emerge from her grotesque headpiece and rise up, transfigured, into death.

Seat 27D, he calculates. Two rows in front of him. Isn't that the East Indian family, that whole row? So, the mother, then. Or possibly the tiny elderly one, the grandmother, who was wearing a white sari, not that anyone can see a thing in the dark. It is night and the air-conditioning and all electrical systems have failed, though the fog of heat and body sweat is not the worst of it.

Don't, he begs, willing the message down the aisle.

Think of your children, for God's sake.

Think of all of us.

There is a lull then, a brief lull, as though the Indian woman hears his thought and is checked in her frenzy. Is that such a crazy idea? It seems to Tristan that everyone's edges have dissolved, that they have begun to think and act as one multicelled being. They seem to hear one another's thoughts, or rather to sense them, to receive them whole in some direct intuitive way, the way a swarm of bees or a herd of cattle thinks. And certainly everyone subscribes to this cardinal rule: that it is unacceptable to give way to hysteria because they are all part of one fragile organism now, at unbearable risk. Nevertheless, their swarm-brain knows only too well the seduction of giving way: a few brief minutes of agony and it will be done. Giving way is as totally understandable and forgivable as it is inadmissible.

Tristan shapes these thoughts into a projectile and aims them at Seat 27D. Think of the contagion, he calls silently. He imagines his words, as hard and speedy as a small rock, striking the woman on the edge of her gas mask. He imagines the impact: the way her neck will snap and go limp. For the greater good, he wants to let her know.

He reasons with her. Think of your children, he pleads.

Somewhere, he begs her to remember, somewhere, almost certainly, your children are watching us on a TV screen. See, the world's journalists are telling them, there is the plane, that dull silver gleam in the dark, at the outer edge of the airstrip, just beyond the halo of light. We cannot get closer, the journalists are explaining, without risking the precipitation of some rash act. The hijackers cannot be counted on to behave rationally or logically or with any recognizable human compassion, the newscaster is saying. They are extremists. They are psychopaths. They are ideologically mad.

And there, on some stranger's sofa, Tristan reminds her, or on a camp stretcher in some church hall, your children are huddled, watching. A counselor has been assigned to them. A second cousin on your uncle's side is being flown from Bombay. Your children suck the woolen corners of blankets donated by a local church, and they watch the screen, shivering and wide-eyed. They are too ashamed to mention their underwear, which is hotly wet and ammoniac from their fear. Mommy and Daddy are still inside, their wide eyes say, with those Pigmen who made us fly down the slide. Your youngest begins to sob noisily. "The Pigman touched me," she screams, and a counselor holds her.

Think of your children, Tristan pleads. They have been through horrors. They are watching more unfold on TV. Do not inflict this on them: the sight of your body tossed from the plane.

Tristan sends his argument, passionate, intense, synapse to synapse, and he has a direct connection, he is sure of it, but to his dismay, the sounds of fumbling and tearing recommence. They escalate. He can feel then, in his agitated need, the transformation of his own body into rock. He can feel his hard edges. He pivots on the mass of himself. The Indian woman is only two rows in front of him. He readies himself as projectile. He will smash her head against the seat.

But it is too late. Already the panic is rising and twisting up above 27D like a water spout, like a king tide, like a tsunami, and it is swelling and thrumming and curling along its upper edge and sloshing over the middle block of seats and up the aisle toward the rear of the plane. In the dark, Tristan closes his eyes. He has just enough time, before the rogue wave swamps him, to ask himself with real curiosity: Why is that necessary, closing the eyes, when nothing is all that any of us can see?

He hangs tightly to the spar of this question.

He hears people going under on all sides. He feels the pull of the rip tide and is himself tempted to rip off his mask.

At such times, the choice is stark: survival or peace.

At such times, no one has any illusions that survival will be other than trial by horror; and yet most choose it.

Tristan clings to the spar of his question.

It is instinctive, he realizes, to close the eyes. Dark or not, behind the eyelids, we focus better and we hear more acutely. It is instinctive, Tristan sees—*think of somewhere else, quickly, quickly*—yes, it is instinctive to close the eyes, the way it was on the beach that time, the first time, his ocean debut, and he hunches up again, bracing his small body, being barely thirteen and on the wrong side of his growth spurt, with the wave hanging over him like a vast implacable wall. Terror. He sees the fluted green frown beetling above, utterly indifferent. You are nothing, boy, nothing, it says, bored. He prostrates himself before Wave, the annihilator, the God of Smash. He sees the foaming white of its eyes. I will pound you to shell grit, it hisses, a frothy creaming shussing sweep of sound that enters his lungs. He pukes ribbons of sea salt.

His brother Pierre keeps shouting: Like this, like this, keep your eyes open. You have to watch over your shoulder, watch for it, see? Like this. And curl yourself up in its armpit, give yourself to it, like this, so that you are the wave.

And he does, because he knows he has crossed over, he is beyond help and recovery, he is sea, he is salt water, he is force. He is oceanic ferocity itself. And then he is on the hard wet sand and Pierre is thumping him on the back. You see? You see? Pierre laughs, and Tristan laughs too, a moment of pure and thrilling joy, and he tugs at his older brother's hand and drags him back into the waves.

Again, again! Tristan is breathless on the wild Moroccan coast. . . .

Morocco.

Might they not be in Morocco at this moment? he asks himself, shaken, pressing his hands hard against the arms of the airline seat because the panic has passed over him and he has not succumbed. Might they not be on the tarmac at Rabat? or perhaps Tangier? Yes, it is more than probable, or perhaps Morocco was only the first landing and perhaps they are somewhere else, well, it could be anywhere, there have been too many night landings and night takeoffs to keep track, too many even before the gas masks were issued, but isn't it likely that they are flying in small circles because who is going to let the hijackers land? So this means perhaps that they are farther afield, in space more sympathetic to the hijackers: Libya? Syria? Iraq? He knows he has all the necessary clues.

He believes he could plot the course of Air France 64, which departed from Paris on time but has never reached its scheduled destination of New York. (Or has it? No. It is impossible, he thinks, that they could be on the ground in New York. And yet . . . ? He cannot be sure of anything. He knows he is in a severe state of sensory disorientation.) There are a myriad details crammed into the grab bag of his mind. What he needs is time and calm to sift them through. He needs to unpack them one by one, he needs to classify and sort: the fragments of language heard at two airstrips; the stifling heat of the first two landings, presumably in North Africa somewhere; the smell of an occasional current of fresh air: for example, when the children were off-loaded, which must have been Europe since the dreadful heat had gone. The off-loading could have been at Marseilles, he believes; he is sure he could smell salt air, though it might have been the north Italian coast. Or even, he supposes, somewhere with industrial smells, salt works, phosphate works close by. Frankfurt, perhaps? The security at Frankfurt is known to be poor. It is a city known to harbor terrorist cells. Yes, he thinks, it might have been Frankfurt where the children were disembarked.

The Pigmen (they look like pigs in their space suits and gas masks; they look like ape pigs, alien pigs; sci-fi pigface-people) speak both French and some other language which he supposes is Arabic. When they bark orders in English over the PA system, for the most part their speech is broken and difficult to understand, though one of them, clearly the leader, has issued announcements twice and speaks like a newscaster on the BBC. Tristan recognizes the accent. In his eagerness to improve his English, he has been listening regularly to the European broadcasts of the BBC. The other hijackers—the ones who speak English so poorly—are probably *pieds noirs,* he surmises; Algerian Frenchmen, or Muslims with French citizenship, the same old story, in other words; the same old fugue, variations on an overworked theme. He imagines the banner headline: ALGERIAN JIHAD STRIKES AGAIN.

At another landing, there was the smell of rain and something fragrant: Jasmine? Gardenia? Daphne? So, Martinique? Mauritius? Is that possible? Surely too far afield? The Cape Verde Islands, perhaps?

He needs time to fit the pieces together.

Time and calm. These he will have to arrange. He will need, in the lulls between panic waves, between onsets of claustrophobia, to pace himself. He has to shut out altogether the gas, the knowledge of the constant possibility of fire, the impending inferno.

The frenzy of clawing hands all around him is like padded thunder. In another five minutes, he estimates, the Indian woman will have freed herself into a scream, and then the high beam will come out of the dark and touch her like the finger of God. Oh yes, they will all be made to watch, he knows that. They will be forced to witness the whole horror show again: the blistering, the vomiting, the contortions, the last agony. Sarin, he suspects, though the Pigmen have not bothered to designate which toxic gas they have released. The Indian woman will be the third death, only the third, but her dying will be contagious, Tristan fears. There will be a rash of deaths, an epidemic, maybe a dozen, maybe more within the next hour, and then things will settle down for a while.

This can be survived, Tristan tells himself. It is not in the Pigmen's interests to let too many die (though there, he admits to himself, he could be making a crucial error: the error of assuming a correlation between cunning intelligence on the one hand and logical behavior on the other) but the East Indian woman has succeeded now in ripping off her gas mask, and the spotlight swings and focuses on her, and it turns out that she is not after all from the Indian subcontinent, she is not even a woman but a man, tall, solid, white, American probably, of substance probably, someone used to authority, Tristan thinks, a banker, perhaps, or maybe (this is economy class, after all) a construction foreman, someone used to giving orders, because it is outrage, not fear, that suffuses his face in the moments before agony claims him, before he writhes and jackknifes and crumples, and Tristan concentrates, as mass panic and struggle swirl about him, on whether this is or is not Morocco, he devotes himself afresh to the puzzle that he knows he must solve. He has much of the data. Perhaps he has all of it. It is possible, indeed, that with sufficient care and diligence, in a sufficient state of meditative attentiveness, he can recover details that he is not currently aware he knows. Things float up in dreams, and in terror. He understands this. The unconscious casts a wider net than the conscious mind can grasp. What he needs, simultaneously, is purity of focus and slack. He needs to be loose in his mind.

He thinks of Génie, his body turns instinctively to the thought of Génie, but this agitates him violently, because where is she? How will he get to her? How many hours, how many days, since they parted at Row 11? Is she still alive, even—? He feels panic like marsh fire at his nerve ends and forces his thoughts to jump tracks.

He has been trying to devise a system for telling time, a complex logistical problem for which he is grateful. He is grateful for anything that demands obsessive concentration. It passes the time—a thought which gives him sardonic amusement; even language cannot manage without time—and anything which helps to pass the time is no small matter when he is floating loose in nightmare, when he is trapped in a dream in which masked men with machine guns appear but he cannot run, in which the world collapses in on him in slow motion and he knows he will be crushed, he will be pulverized, unless he can run like the wind, but he finds he is running through molasses. His legs are made of something heavier than lead. This terror, he knows, will last until he wakes, but he cannot wake out of this dream. He has to find a way to measure back to when the nightmare began.

He makes marks, like Robinson Crusoe, on a blank white page in his mind.

Day 1. Takeoff. Almost immediate announcement from the pilot that due to expected turbulence, passengers are to remain in their seats until given permission to move.

Interesting, that, Tristan thinks in retrospect. The pilot must be part of it, unless a gun was already being held to his head. But how could machine guns have been brought on board? How could all that have been spirited past security if flight and loading crews were not involved?

We are expecting extreme turbulence. . . . All passengers are to remain in their seats. . . .

But there is no turbulence.

An hour passes. The meal is served; the flight attendants seem nervous and pale; the passengers are forbidden to move about. And then, at last, breaking the rules, Tristan makes his way down to Row 11, but Génie's seat is empty and so is 11B. "Excuse me," he says to the man across the aisle, "do you know where—?" and at that precise moment the hullabaloo breaks out. From the first-class cabin, figures with machine guns appear, Pigmen in gas masks, three in each side aisle, six in all, and Tristan has a gun barrel in his chest and he is being forced back back back down the plane.

On the PA system, in broken English, a voice keeps saying: *This is the Black Death. If you obey exactly, you will not be hurt. This is the Black Death avenging many century of wrong. Obey or you will be shot. Everybody is prisoner of Black Death. Obey or you will be shot. This is return of the plague. Obey or you will be shot. This is Black Death.*

The first shot comes then. The first killing. It is a random one, for show, and the hijackers wave their guns above their heads, triumphant as schoolyard bullies. *Look, Pa! We scared the shit out of them.*

And then time becomes hazy. A landing. Hours in stifling heat. The stewardesses, at gunpoint, distribute water. Babies and children cry incessantly. Someone goes crazy—with thirst? from the hallucination-inducing heat?—and runs down the aisle and is shot. The body is thrown from the plane.

Negotiations are going on. Sometimes shouting can be heard from the cockpit: radio voices coming in, shouted messages going out.

Night falls. Apparently the plane is being refueled. There is a takeoff. There are more flying hours, perhaps three, perhaps four, but no one is allowed to leave his or her seat, not for any reason whatsoever. The plane begins to stink. People pass out. There is another landing. There are more hours that seem to float in heat. Food and water are distributed. Bodies have slumped into aisles and on to the floor. The Pigmen pass through the plane and collect these bodies like garbage. They drag them down the aisles and toss them from the forward door.

There is another takeoff.

Somewhere here, Day 2 has begun. Tristan marks that on the blank page in his mind, but how is he to keep track of time when the plane is in the air? Two hours? he wonders. Three? He might as well be suspended in thick black ink. Then there is another landing: Tristan's body can sense the loss of altitude. He feels the thump when the wheels hit the ground, then bounce, and then hit again. An amateur landing. He wonders what they did to the pilot. He wonders if the pilot, seriously inexpert, is one of the hijacking team.

This is Black Death, the PA system announces. *The plague falls upon the infidel, but Allah, the All-Merciful, spares the children. Obey or you will be shot.*

The children are herded up and off-loaded; mothers with babies in arms are permitted to leave, though not if the babies are dead. Two mothers are sent back to their seats, the bundles in their arms quite still. Many children do not wish to leave their parents, but the men with pig heads and guns pull them roughly from their seats. Passengers reach out to touch and caress as the little ones are pushed down the aisles. When the last of the screams and the sobbing—*Mommy! I want my mommy!*—have been pushed out of the escape hatch, a terrible silence prevails inside the plane.

All that, Tristan thinks, must have happened on Day 2.

Then night falls. A refueling, another takeoff. How many hours of flying? Another landing. They must have landed into Day 3.

The plane stinks. People have vomited. People have wet and fouled themselves. Trips to the bathrooms are permitted now, but are monitored, row by row, and a turn comes around again only three times a day. Bathrooms are blocked up and the stench is so terrible that people back away from their turn. Each time he is escorted from his seat,

Tristan tries to insist on the bathrooms forward but is always forced back. He has not caught so much as a glimpse of Génie.

On the Day 3 landing (the fourth landing, unless he has lost count), supplies of food and water are brought on board, the bathrooms are cleaned; more refueling, another takeoff, a much longer flight, another landing. Somewhere in here, he thinks, Day 4 begins.

On Day 4, more food and water are brought on board. The plane is fumigated, the bathrooms are cleaned again. Supplies of a different kind are brought on: the gas masks arrive at this point, hundreds of them, one for every passenger. So this must be home territory for the terrorists, Tristan decides. Libya? Iraq? Morocco? Or maybe farther south, closer to the equator, because the heat is extreme. Sudan or Uganda? The masks are distributed, and the passengers are ordered to put them on. The effect is grotesque. A number of people vomit into their gas masks and promptly suffocate. Their bodies are removed.

The leader, the one who speaks BBC English, makes an announcement.

"The world has its eyes on this plane," he says. "The world is listening to me as I speak."

Tristan tries to imagine himself into his apartment in Paris, watching himself on TV. There is the long doomed silver Air France cocoon on the screen, indistinct at its edges. He imagines himself reading the message streaming across the base of his set: *Hijacked plane on airstrip in Uganda*. (Or in Egypt, perhaps? Or in Iraq?) Tristan squints. In peripheral vision, he can see the volumes of Proust and Stendhal on his shelves. If he could just see his television set more clearly, he could find out where he is.

"Toxic gas has now been released into the cabin," the leader of the hijackers says to the passengers and to the television audience of the world. "Your masks will protect you. If you remove your mask, you will die very quickly, in great agony.

"We are returning to Paris," the leader explains. "Before landing, canisters of highly volatile, highly flammable gas will be released inside the plane, so that any misguided attempt at sharpshooting, either by airport security or by American special troops, will result in a firestorm. If our demands are met, if the ten prisoners whose names will be given to *Le Monde* are released from French jails, and if these Muslim freedom fighters are permitted to board the aircraft, then all passengers will also be released. We are asking a small thing: ten Muslim freedom fighters for more than four hundred civilians."

There is another takeoff and a long flight.

Tristan tries to measure the hours.

"We are beginning our descent into Charles de Gaulle Airport in Paris," the leader announces, and the words boom like thunder, but the plane circles, and banks, and levels out, and circles again. The voice of the leader over the PA system is sharp with fury. "We are refused permission to land," he announces. "Idiots. Imbeciles. Cretinaceous-moronic-NATO-American snobs!" His words trip over themselves. "You are dogs!" he tells the passengers icily. "Your lives are nothing to your governments. You are dogs, and you will die like dogs."

We are beyond fear, Tristan thinks. We are far beyond fear. Dying like dogs, when we have been living like dogs for days: it barely even touches us.

When the moment comes, he thinks, when the moment presents itself, he will leap snarling at that fake-BBC throat, though for the time being he seems to have misplaced his own ignition key, and the PA system by which his brain gets messages to his body seems to be on the blink. He tells his hand to make a fist and it drifts like seaweed.

This is a very strange dream, he thinks. When I wake, he thinks, what a story this will be.

He thinks the plane is still circling Paris because he believes he can see the loops of the Seine and the towers of Notre Dame, but he knows this might be part of the dream. He feels sleepy. He dreams that oxygen, like a knight in armor, is battering at the walls of his mask. He sees Génie on a cloud at his window. Have you left us, then? he asks her, and he feels the plane plummeting in grief, but he cannot remember what grief feels like, and the plane levels out and flies south.

Tristan knows they are flying south because the sun that he thinks he sees spells Africa. Génie raps on his window. Prepare for landing, she says.

"We have been permitted landing rights for refueling," the leader announces, and they are on the ground in Toulouse, Tristan thinks. Or perhaps they are in Marseilles? He knows he is watching French on the lips of the men at the gasoline pumps. They handle the rubber hoses as snake charmers might, and the sucked-in hollows in their cheeks are making French. Tristan mouths a question from his window and one of the refuelers looks back at him directly and says: Toulouse.

The plane takes off from Toulouse and flies into the fifth night, Tristan thinks, though it could be the sixth. There is a long flight and another landing, perhaps—probably—a return to the point where the gas masks first came on board.

This is where they now are, several hours from Toulouse, very late on the fifth or sixth day, and the Indian woman who has turned out to be an American man has finished dying, and the ripples of panic throughout the plane have played themselves out.

Nothing moves. The passengers are bewitched.

Tristan is light-headed. He believes he can fly.

5.

TRIAGE

Genevieve floats through her fever. When she opens her eyes, the air is strangely cloudy and opaque, as though life must now be seen darkly and through a glass. She closes her eyes again. Her breath smells like the inside of a rubber tube. Her throat hurts, her head hurts, a high kind of pain is singing behind her eyes. When she touches her neck gingerly with the pads of her fingers, she feels a crust of dried blood, and something else, a collar, a cage, what the—? Panic chokes her, and she floats into blackness again.

"Move," someone says, and she stumbles. Her head is inside a jar. "Move! *Bouge! Bouge!*" and other words too, foreign words, something strange is . . . sound is bal*loon*ing and sloooow, sound is clouding her, scarfs her. Surf is everything she hears, though she can see black flecks of words in front of her eyes and the words are long and then longer, like taffy, and they boom and they fade and reverberate, and they bunch up in her ears and inside her head. She is deep in a tunnel, she hears a train. It is night. Is it night? A hand pushes, brutally, and she pitches forward and rolls down stairs.

Blacktop. A parking lot? Where is she?

Why is there a helmet on her head?

A foot kicks her. "Get up." That was the sense of it, but not the words. The words wrap themselves around her like thunder, but they are not in a language she understands. The foot kicks her again. She tries to stand, but her legs will not hold and she slips as softly as a scarf to the ground. She sees boots, soldiers, machine guns, monster men with grotesque masks on their heads. Someone lifts her as though she were a sack and throws her in the back of a jeep.

Horror. Other hands, other bodies. She floats into dark.

She is conscious, she faints, she is conscious again, they are being driven somewhere, she recognizes the hum of tire tread and engine, she feels the jarring bumps in the terrain. They are driving, at high speed, straight to hell.

Arms help her. Someone half lifts, she is propped against another body; an arm comforts. "You all right?" It is the tone she reads. The sound reverberates without shape from inside somebody's head cage. Bodies moan and huddle against each other and hold clumsy hands. She begins to notice things. She is able to distinguish and catalogue the heat, the stink, the suffocation of the thing on her head. Night. Desert. She imagines millions of stars. Another jeep is following. She decides she is watching the movie of her own captivity on late-night TV. Another vehicle is in front, she thinks, because now she can hear the different pitch and high hum of the tire treads. She is conscious of groping and of being groped: there are three other sets of hands in the same stifling space, three other bodies, each with jars on their heads.

And then whiplash.

Screech of brakes.

The sound comes a split second later than the pain in her neck.

Soldiers, butts of machine guns, fragments. . . . The passengers are shoved and herded from the cars and turned to the north and made to watch.

"Pay attention, dogs," barks the leader with the BBC voice.

A hand rips the Velcro collar at Genevieve's neck and her head is free. Air, blessed fresh air, and dear God, isn't that Tristan she sees over there? But she is thumped with the butt of a gun, and to the north, at the edge of the desert sky, like Jupiter rising, a globe of incandescent brightness lifts itself and sends plumes like meteors up to the stars. Brighter and brighter, the ballooning planet turns orange, then blood red, and its effulgence lights up half the sky. There is a boom like the end of the world and the little cluster of people, newly unmasked and huddled beside three military jeeps, can feel wavelets of sound buffeting their feet. The shock waves set the soldiers to dancing. They raise their guns above their heads in salute. They fire into the night. The others—the little knot of ten former passengers—move together like filings to a magnet. They huddle, body against body, furtive hand in furtive hand, and telegraph intimations of dread.

The Jupiter-sun is a fireball now and casts a shadowy light of almost-day where the jeeps are. One of the robot men takes the cage off his head, though in the twilight his face cannot be clearly seen.

"That is the end of Flight 64," he says. "Welcome to Iraq. Welcome to Tikrit Airport." His English is excellent, his accent is that of a British public school. Genevieve closes her eyes and hears the thin descant of the S on his wrist. Pieces of dream come back to her: Tristan, Sirocco, guns and gas masks, children crying, and then she is falling down a black hole.

Where did yesterday go? Where has Genevieve been? Where is Tristan? An ache more painful than the fire in her throat and her head sets in. A hand brushes hers, feels it, takes hold of it. Tristan's hand. She leans against him and they cling to each other, weak with joy.

"Ten for ten," Sirocco says. "That's a fair exchange, and you fortunate few have been handpicked. You have been handpicked by me personally. Take this as a compliment. Whenever they release one of ours, we release one of you. It's that simple and you'd better say your prayers."

One of the hijackers fires a jubilant round at the sky and Sirocco barks at him, three unintelligible words, but the meaning is clear. There is another command, and each prisoner is roughly seized, and manhandled, and tossed about like spit. Someone splits Tristan and Genevieve apart as though prizing a mussel shell open. A gun butt meets the back of Tristan's head, and Genevieve, punched in the stomach, buckles over. "Put on," a soldier orders, but she is unable to stand and he is dressing her, roughly, brutally, pushing arms and legs into padded suit, fastening her in, putting another cage on her head. Canvas boots are Velcroed on her feet.

"You happy ten," Sirocco says, "might stay alive. For the moment, the air you breathe is safe again, but not for long. You will be famous. Whatever happens, your names and your photographs will be in newspapers and on the covers of magazines around the world. We will transmit your passport photographs to CNN. You will achieve immortality.

"And you may yet be inscribed in the Book of Life. You may be saved. That depends on the decisions of your governments. Ten for ten. An eye for an eye, a life for a life."

He speaks slowly and distinctly, but the sound blurs inside Genevieve's cage, and the fire on the horizon flickers along the edges of his words. *You have just been issued protective suits and mitts,* she hears, *and fresh gas masks with fresh filters. Sealed into protected space, after which . . . both sarin and mustard gas . . . if any part of your skin is exposed . . .* He is gesturing now, speaking in mime, and the listeners huddle their padded bodies together and even in the heat, grief steams off them. . . . *in agony, as you already know. If you remove your gas masks, or any part of your protective clothing, you will die.*

One of Sirocco's men fires into the sky and chants something unintelligible. At the end, all join him in a brief incomprehensible refrain.

I will translate for you, Sirocco says to the prisoners. *This is Operation Black Death, the revenge of Suleiman, praise be to Allah the All-Merciful.*

Is it death that brings the sound into focus? Is it possible to believe, Genevieve finds herself thinking, that this is how we will die? Like extras on a movie set? The memory of Tristan's hand in hers, of his body against hers, gives her a mad surge of hope. Which one is he? She looks from one to the other of the padded prisoners and is unable to tell, yet she feels strangely composed. Sirocco's voice is suddenly so crisp and clear inside her head cage that she wonders if sensory deprivation has switched the channels. She believes she is on the telepathic track.

"If the demands of Operation Black Death are met, then the bunker will be unsealed and you will live.

"If our demands are not met, you will rot. Your equipment will protect you for twenty-four hours, and after that: seeping toxicity through the filters, and slow but agonizing death. You may prefer to remove your masks and take the fast exit: ten minutes, then violent vomiting and the shakes, then *finis*."

Static. The telepathic signal is lost. Genevieve's legs are flowing away from her again. There is a word for this, she knows, sinking, going under. There is a word for this, but the word will not come. Beneath the black water, she watches words swimming by: *caritas*, wandering earthling, rue de Birague, Camelot, *le destin, in extremis*, will you come? *c'est l'amour*, it is madness, the hot desert wind, Black Death, the wind that burns as it blows, *Sirocco*, the wind that burns and destroys, Kalashnikov, gas masks, explosion . . .

Triage, that is the word.

Book IV

VANISHING POINTS

It vanished quite slowly, beginning with the end of the tail, and ending with the grin, which remained some time after the rest of it had gone.

—LEWIS CARROLL, ALICE IN WONDERLAND

1.

Lowell is reading *Alice in Wonderland* to his children. Behind them, the tiny lights on the Christmas tree wink randomly. Sometimes they blink in unison, on, off, on, off, sometimes the power flickers along a string like bright dominoes falling. Rowena's father snores gently in an armchair. In the kitchen, Rowena and her mother load the dishwasher and scrape plates and rinse out glasses. A fire crackles in the hearth. A fragrant smell of cider hangs in the room.

"*Alice began to feel very uneasy,*" Lowell reads. "*To be sure, she had not as yet had any dispute with the Queen, but she knew that it might happen any minute, 'and then,' thought she, 'what would become of me? They're dreadfully fond of beheading people here; the great wonder is, that there's any one left alive!'*

"*She was looking about for some way of escape, and wondering whether she could get away without being seen, when she noticed a curious appearance in the air: it puzzled her very much at first, but, after watching it a minute or two, she made it out to be a grin, and she said to herself 'It's the Cheshire Cat: now I shall have somebody to talk to.'*

" *'How are you getting on?' said the Cat—*"

"Daddy," Amy says, "why can't we see dead people?"

Lowell's eyes flick nervously toward the kitchen door. "The

Cheshire Cat's alive," he says. "Did you think she wasn't because she disappears?"

"No," Amy says. She points to the illustrated grin that sits on the branch of a tree. "The Cheshire Cat's *here,* silly. I know she's alive."

"Right," Lowell says, relieved. "*And Alice waited till the eyes appeared, and then nodded. 'It's no use speaking to it,' she thought, 'till its ears have come, or at least one of them.' In another minute the whole head appeared—*"

"But where do *people* go when we can't see them?" Amy asks.

Lowell waits tensely for the woman in the kitchen to scream, *Off with his head!* He waits to be banished to the outer darkness of his studio apartment, far from the warmth of the season and his children. He is on a strict good behavior bond, and he is not about to cause his children to think of death, so he says cleverly, "You'll have to ask Mommy. Why don't you go and ask Mommy?"

"I want to ask *you,*" Amy whispers. "Where did Grandpa *go*?"

Lowell marvels at this. The more we shield them, he thinks, the more curious children become. But nothing will make him say the D word and forfeit his bond. "Grandpa's in heaven," he says.

"Can people in heaven see us? Can Grandpa see us?"

"I'm sure he can," Lowell says. "Yes, I know he can."

He has not, in fact, been able to free himself of the sense of being watched. He has come to feel like Bunyan's pilgrim with his own load of sin strapped to his back, because he cannot go anywhere, he dares not go anywhere, without the fearful contents of Locker B-64 at his side. He has invested in six different bags, by way of disguise, because he has a vague fear that the blue Nike sports tote might be recognizable outside the house. Today, in the spirit of the season, he put everything into a red nylon drawstring bag, and arrived with it slung across his back. He added a collar of fake snow and an iron-on Santa. After he put his presents under the tree, Rowena said, curious, "You've still got boxes in there."

"Presents for the guys," Lowell said, inventing quickly. "That is, for the children of the guys who work for me. Meant to deliver them yesterday and didn't have time, so I'll do it tomorrow."

"I'll stick the bag in the closet, then," Rowena said, and it caused him anxiety just to see her pick it up. It made him dizzy to watch her swing it by the cord. Even now, when everyone is in a state of post-dinner somnolence, he feels an agitated need to go to the closet and part the coats and lean down and reassure himself that the bag is still there. He does not give in to this urge.

"Does Grandpa know you gave us *Alice* for Christmas?" Amy asks.

"Yes," Lowell says. "I think he does. Do you want me to read the chapter about the March Hare now?"

"No. Jason wants the Cheshire Cat," Amy says. "Don't you, Jason?"

Jason, with a mouth full of cupcake, nods eagerly. "Chesha Cat," he says.

Rowena comes into the room and Amy tells her, "The Queen is going to cut off the Cheshire Cat's head."

"But the problem is," Lowell explains, "that the cat's body is invisible, and you can't cut off a head that hasn't got a body attached."

Amy shrieks with laughter, and Jason joins her, and Rowena says, "Maybe they should work off some of that energy outside. You want to take them tobogganing, Lowell?"

Coats, he thinks, gratefully. *Closet.* He will be able to check. Amongst the jumble of the children's boots and parkas, he feels the outlines within the red bag: ring binders, tapes, everything there. He breathes easy.

"You're not going to take your Santa bag tobogganing, are you?" Rowena asks.

"Why not?" he says. "I'm the Santa man, and we're going for a ride in my sleigh."

"Hadn't you better take the presents out, then?"

"Presents? Oh, for the— Yeah, you're right. On second thought, I'd better leave the bag here."

Rowena shakes her head and lifts her eyebrows, but smiles. "Oh, Lowell," she says. She kisses him on the cheek. She finds his eccentricities almost endearing, now that they are getting a divorce. "I think you're calmer these days," she says.

"I am," he agrees. "I am." Even as he tucks the red bag back behind snowboots, he feels he could bask like a cat in the smells of Rowena's kitchen, in the cradle of family, in the sounds that his children make. He feels safer here. He feels that Rowena, and especially Rowena's parents, would not permit anything out of the ordinary to occur. This has always been the secret of Rowena's appeal. She is so *normal*. Menace does not peer through the windows of her house—it would not dare—the way it floats at the third-floor casements of the building where Lowell's apartment is.

Amy and Jason and Lowell slide down the hill on a bright red plastic toboggan, then Lowell and Amy pull Jason back up the slope. They slide down again and again, they roll in the soft white powder, they make snow angels and a snowman with pebble eyes and a stick for a nose. They play till the children begin to feel the cold at fingertips and toes, and Rowena calls them in for hot turkey sandwiches with cranberry sauce.

"I'm so grateful for this, Rowena," Lowell tells her, slightly weepy from too much mulled toddy and an excess of frosty outdoor air. "For a day like this. It's the best Christmas present you could give me."

"It's for the kids, Lowell," she says, embarrassed.

His former mother-in-law says, "It's good to see you two working things out," and Lowell can feel strings of lights popping on at all his nerve ends, he feels sparklers fizzing in his veins and spreading to the tips of his fingers, but then Rowena says, "Now, Mother. Let's not go through all that again," and his hands feel suddenly chilled and he holds them out to the fire.

"Good to have you back in the fold, Lowell," his father-in-law says.

"Good to be back." Lowell glances at Rowena from the corner of his eye, but Rowena is passing out the sandwiches on little plates and they all lounge around the fireplace, informal, and Lowell's father-in-law, his former father-in-law, tells the children about the sleigh rides he used to take as a boy, and then Rowena's mother plays the piano and they all sing "White Christmas" and "Jingle Bells" and "Let It Snow! Let It Snow! Let It Snow!"

When Rowena finally sends Lowell home in the early evening with a large chunk of Saran-wrapped Christmas cake and the Santa sack beside him on the seat, he feels at peace. He feels that all is almost well with the world. He thinks of Christmases far in the past: the presents under the tree, his father watching as Lowell, trembling with excitement, tears at wrapping paper and cellophane bows, his mother with the camera, the bright glare and pop of the flash. An intense sensory memory of the smell of his mother's body, the smell of his father's, of pillowy Christmas hugging, overwhelms him. Instinctively, he reaches for the red bag on the passenger seat and hugs it. He rubs it against one cheek. He decides he will give himself up to his father's last gift. He will sit in the single armchair in his apartment, pour himself a beer, put up his feet, and mark the evening of Christmas Day 2000 by reading his father's journals and watching the tapes.

In his driveway, a sliver of chill pricks the warmth that he has so carefully carried back in the cab of the truck. No one has shoveled the snow, of course, but he notices in the glow from the streetlights that someone has walked down the drive. Probably a child. What kid can resist a deep drift of untrodden snow? There are no lights because the timer on the porch lamp has broken. The other five tenants are away, visiting families both in and out of state, and the small building—there are six apartments, two on each floor—is completely empty and dark.

Lowell notices that the storm door on the porch is swinging loose and blames the paperboy. He notices that the front door is slightly ajar. His senses go on alert. Christmas is break-in time, he knows that: stockpiles of presents, empty houses, deserted streets, the constant cover of festive noise, it's temptation time, the hour of prime crime. He reaches in through the open door and switches on the hall light. "Anyone here?" he calls.

There is no sound.

He puts on the stairwell light.

He slips off his boots and climbs noiselessly, in his socks, to the third floor where he lives. At each landing, in passing, he checks the other apartment doors. All are locked. His own is deadbolted and secure. He unlocks it and switches on the light and locks the door behind him again. He pushes the bolts across at bottom and at top. Inside, everything appears to be as it should. His unwashed cereal bowl is still in the sink. His muscles relax. Perhaps one of the other tenants came back for a gift bought too early and then forgotten. Perhaps, in his haste, he did not properly relock the front door.

Lowell inserts the CD that his in-laws gave him—*An Olde Tyme Christmas Carol Sampler*—into the player, pours a beer, and sinks into his old leather chair. He opens the drawstring bag.

The ring binder labeled *Journal of S: Encrypted* remains impenetrable to Lowell, though it is all handwritten and he recognizes his father's own hand. He studies the pages of numbers and random letters densely arranged. His father loved secrets and codes. He remembers his father telling him about the Rosetta Stone that Napoleon's soldiers had found in the mud of the Nile. The stone was dated from around 200 BC and was clearly a burial marker, and so its three inscriptions were deduced to be identical: one in hieroglyphs, one in demotic Egyptian, and one in Greek. Since two of the inscriptions could be read, here at last was the magic key to the mysteries of the Pharaohs and the secret lore of the Cities of the Dead. Even so, his father told him, it took Champollion, brilliant French linguist and code-breaker, fourteen years to decipher the message of the stones.

"A code-breaker looks for *patterns*, Lowell," his father said.

Is he setting homework for me, Lowell wonders, the way he used to make me learn Homer? What does he want me to do with this, when he knows it's all Greek to me?

Greek to me! He closes his eyes and feels the weight of his father at the end of his bed. The mattress rocks like a small boat when his father moves, and Lowell sways drowsily, happily, on the rise and fall of his father's voice. Lowell is seven, perhaps eight. Lost languages, his father is saying, can weather storms in the ocean of time like Ulysses, in reckless faith. They go astray, they get shipwrecked, they come ashore in strange places, and everyone believes they are lost, but one day they show up again with a cargo so precious that it takes a king's ransom to buy it.

Take the Dead Sea Scrolls, his father says, and Lowell imagines the scrolls unraveling themselves in his room like brocaded toilet paper that is printed with glittering messages from the holds of Ulysses' ships. Nine hundred scrolls, his father says. Think of it; and the coils of parchment rustle and billow out like jeweled sails in Lowell's dreams. The Essenes buried them two thousand years back, his father says, and not until the middle of this century were they found again. Imagine it, Lowell: a whole library from a lost world, much of it in fragments, of course. They were written in ancient Hebrew and Aramaic and Greek by the Essenes in the last century before the Christian Era, and the first century after. Consider the Essenes, Lowell, his father says, consider the means by which they have survived, and Lowell tries to glue together the half-remembered bits and pieces of his father's accounts, the lost fragments of the Essenes: a monastic sect . . . Jewish . . . John the Baptist was one, maybe Jesus was too . . . Essenes the lost link between Judaism and Christianity . . . strict puritan rules . . . called themselves Children of Light.

Probably at the time of the sacking of Jerusalem in the year 70, he remembers his father saying . . . and something about persecution . . . and something about protecting the writings from destruction. He remembers the burying of the scrolls. He remembers the date of rediscovery in the caves at Qumran: 1947.

Think of it, Lowell, he remembers his father saying: a message sent through twenty centuries of time. What does that tell us, Lowell, about the desperation and the faith of the Essenes?

That they did their Greek homework? the seven-year-old Lowell suggests.

His father does not laugh. His father perhaps does not hear. His father answers the catechism himself.

It tells us that the truth will endure, Lowell. Even if you kill the messenger, it tells us, a dangerous message can hide and bide its time until the message can safely be read.

He wants me to hide it, Lowell thinks, until the message can safely be read.

He places *Journal of S: Encrypted* on the floor beside his chair and picks up the *Report Dossier: Classified*. He flips through the pages. These are typed and easy to read. Sometimes there is only one paragraph to a page—sightings of Sirocco, meetings with Sirocco, Salamander and Sirocco to meet in Pakistan, to meet in Egypt, to meet in Paris, to meet in Afghanistan. Sometimes Nimrod's reports are given. Sometimes Nimrod cautions. Sometimes Salamander is to convey to Sirocco in cash . . . Salamander to arrange shipment of . . . Salamander to relay Sirocco's report. . . .

He stops at May 1987, the month when his mother left for Paris.

May 7, 1987

Report from Sirocco: alleged members of cell are extremely discreet. They do not live in proximity, but are scattered through several arrondissements, not the obvious ones. For the most part, they avoid the Arab quarter. Meeting place is Café Maroc in 18th arrondissement, but never more than two cell members meet at a time. Relay system of passing on messages. Cell members very conscious of risk of drawing attention as group. All highly educated and highly trained, all professionals, engineers, computer experts, etc. Two members highly trained in explosives; one knowledgeable about nerve agents; one a hi-tech wizard. Responsible for five explosions on Métro in past year. At present, focused on French targets, but anti-American sentiment runs high.

Report forwarded by Salamander.

May 10, 1987

Response from Command: Essential to disable group. Salamander to propose aid and ammunition for a hijacking with intent to lure entire group into one operation and one confined space.

Sharpshooters to be used.

Allowance for probable loss of one or two hijackers to sharpshooters. Expect yield of 5 or 6 for extended interrogation. Sirocco—"inadvertently"—to escape.

June 12, 1987

Operation Black Death initiated.

Sirocco to train and direct force at ground zero. Plane to be designated and targeted one month in advance (Sirocco has two men on airline maintenance team). Rashid to install video cameras in plane: entire operation can be transmitted and monitored.

Sirocco also to prepare underground interrogation bunker in Iraq where captured hijackers will be held. CIA base in northern Iraq to undertake interrogation. Bunker to be wired, with video camera installed. Transmission via satellite will make direct monitoring from Washington possible.

Salamander to arrange shipments of CW agents, including protective equipment.

July 1, 1987

Nimrod recommends aborting of Operation Black Death. Cites grave doubts re Sirocco. Cites deaths of two of our double agents. Sirocco responsible, Nimrod thinks.

Salamander to discuss with Command.

July 5, 1987

Operation Black Death to proceed, as best hope for elimination of Paris cell.

Nimrod protests; claims risk of death to civilians too high.

Command responds: risk of continued functioning of Paris cell is higher. This group is highly trained in explosives and chemical warfare. Possibility that they are planning to expand target field outside France; possibility of links with existing cells inside USA, therefore serious possibility of terrorist threat in major city such as New York or Los Angeles.

This cell must be eliminated to forestall unacceptable risks. Operation Black Death is best hope.

Nimrod threatens anonymous leak to press if OBD not aborted before too late.

July 18, 1987

Nimrod erased.

Lowell closes the binder uneasily. He has lost both his mellowness and his willingness to read. His Christmas carol CD has circled back to track one and is beginning again and he gets up to change it. He reaches for his *Bing Crosby's Christmas Classics* and then notices that the small tower of CDs—his favorites—is not where he usually keeps it. He looks around the room, puzzled. Ah. There they are, all his CDs, neatly stacked on top of the TV. Odd. He does not recall putting them there.

In the street, a car backfires, and Lowell jumps.

He decides to hide both his father's coded journal and the classified dossier somewhere that will be safe for a century or so, and to put everything else—that is, the collection of tapes—back into the blue Nike bag. Tomorrow morning, he will return the bag to Logan Airport and he will rent a locker and that is where the bag will stay. After all, his father had considered an airport locker safe space.

He goes to his bedroom closet and gropes in the murky undergrowth of shoes. He feels the back wall and leans down toward the corner where he keeps the blue Nike tote. Since September, since he removed all the risky contents into assorted drawstring bags and backpacks of disguise, he has stuffed the original blue Nike with T-shirts, old sneakers, and a towel.

The bag is not there.

Lowell pulls everything out of his closet, dumping item by item on his bed. There is no blue Nike bag. He puts everything back in the closet, puts on all the lights in all the rooms, and checks in every cupboard and behind every door. There is no sign of an intruder and no sign of the bag. He goes to a kitchen drawer and takes out a flashlight, and then he turns all the lights out and draws the blinds. By the shielded glow from the flashlight, he opens the door of the large cupboard that serves as his pantry. At the back of the bottom shelf is a jumbo pack of toilet rolls. He lifts out the toilet rolls, and a small door, once a milk safe, becomes visible. He opens the door to reveal a shallow uninsulated cavity up against the solid exterior brick. Here, in pre-refrigeration days, milk bottles were once kept cool. He puts the *Journal of S: Encrypted* into the cavity. It fits snugly. He closes the milk-safe door and nails it shut. Over the door, he nails a piece of ply that extends several inches beyond all hinges and joins. Then he replaces the jumbo pack of toilet-paper rolls. Don't squeeze the Charmin, squawks a little voice in his head, and in front of the toilet paper he places a heavy one-gallon tub of laundry detergent and a bottle of viscous fluid used for unclogging drains.

In his small back storage room, the paint cans stand in stacked columns. He has to move a few to reach the wall. He unhooks the pegboard where a dozen brushes hang from S hooks, row by row. Behind the pegboard, in the recessed space between two studs, he places the *Report Dossier: Classified.* He hangs the pegboard in front of it and nails it to the studs. He hooks a row of metal S's in the pegboard holes. He hangs his brushes from the S hooks: the nylon brushes for latex paint on top, the horsehair bristles for oil paint and primer below.

The tapes he transfers from the red drawstring bag to a blue nylon backpack. He slips his arms through the straps, wearing the bag in front the way women carry babies against their hearts.

He decides to call Elizabeth, his father's third wife, who believes her phone might be tapped. He will wish her Merry Christmas, very casually, and then he will suggest, also casually, that he is thinking of coming down to D.C., and perhaps she could call him later in the week to arrange dinner or drinks.

He dials her number. After four rings, he gets an operator's voice. *The number you have called is no longer in service. Please check your directory and try again.*

He sits in his armchair in the dark with the backpack over his chest. He falls asleep and dreams of the Cheshire Cat, but the cat is a stuffed one, made of blue calico with a Nike logo on its side. The cat is stuffed in a strangely lumpy way. Something rectangular juts out at its haunches, and its cheeks bulge over square blocky frames. Little by little, the tail and the bulges and the body disappear, until nothing is left but the grin. He wakes with a cry and feels for the backpack and presses it hard against his heart.

2.

Lou is wrapping Christmas presents and tying them with frosted gold ribbons that she loops into shimmering rosettes. She bends the ribbon around her fingers and counts—ten turns, ten petals—then she twists, knots, cuts, and fluffs out the folds. She has six presents, each wrapped in a different-colored foil, each with its starburst of gold. She tucks a Christmas card under each ribbon. The cards are delicate, printed on parchment and embossed with gold leaf. On each card, Lou writes the same thing: *To Samantha: wishing you the perfect Christmas, with all my love.* When she piles the presents under pine boughs, needles brush her skin and the room smells fragrantly of resin and spice.

Mulled wine simmers. Lou dips in a ladle and tastes. More cloves, she decides. Another cinnamon stick. She checks the turkey. Perfection is what she is after: perfect setting, perfect food, the perfect moment. When the perfect moment comes, she will know. She does not expect fanfare, but she does believe she will know. She will tell what needs to be told.

After that, life will be different.

She checks her watch.

She puts on a new CD—*Hodie, Christus natus est,* the choir of King's

College, Cambridge—and pours some eggnog for herself. She stands at her sixth-floor window and looks up Lexington Avenue, studying each taxi that stops. Hooded figures alight or climb in. Very likely Lou knows them, knows some of them at least, but from her sixth-floor vantage point, all identities are cloaked against the snow.

Secrets are corrosive, she thinks.

Her fingertips drum an anxious bass riff on the sill.

The telephone rings.

"Hello?" she says. "Oh, Sam!" A smile transforms her. "I was beginning to worry. Where are you?"

"I'm still in Washington," Samantha says. "I'm still at the airport. Apparently the problem is snowstorms in the Midwest. All the flights are very late coming in. They said we'd board in thirty minutes, so I guess that means about another hour and a half, plus the taxi from La Guardia. I'm sorry, Lou."

Lou leans back against the wall and closes her eyes. "Not to worry," she says, though her anxiety is acute. Lou herself has no fear of flying, but she is deathly afraid for others when they fly. *Wait right there,* she wants to say. *Stay safe. I'll drive down and bring the turkey and trimmings and everything else that we need. I can be there in four hours. I'll bring Christmas.*

If she says this, she will irritate Samantha. *Stop trying to keep me in cotton wool,* Samantha will say edgily. *Stop acting as though I can't take care of myself.*

You're not my mother, Samantha might say. (Samantha has often said this.) *Stop trying to smother me.*

"I'll cover the turkey," Lou says, "so it won't dry out. Everything will keep. Just get here safely."

She adds a shot of brandy to her eggnog. She turns the oven off and wraps the turkey in foil. She turns off the heat beneath the wine. Restless, she studies the street from the window. Snow is falling, and a walk, she thinks, yes, a walk will help pass the time, coat, hat, mittens, scarf, boots, folding and tucking in, pushing loose hair beneath the toque, knotting the scarf, because solitude is less *interminable* when one is brisk and moving through city streets, yes, even when those streets are eerily deserted, because look, there are others out walking, there are friendly dogs who snuffle at the snow on one's boots. She nods and smiles at the passersby who walk singly—all of them—hands in pockets, heads hooded or toqued, faces barely visible within rings of satin or fur or woolen scarf, eyes fiercely insisting they have somewhere to go.

She sits on a park bench—the park is pocket-handkerchief-sized—and watches children at play. Snow amazes them. They scoop it up and throw it like confetti. Snow makes them laugh and dance. On a swing, a child in hooded parka, mittens, and boots is barely swaying as snow gathers on her shoulders and boots. The child extends her little legs and watches with wonder as fragile white palaces rise like smoke. She kicks energetically at air and the snowflaked towers and turrets fall. The child laughs and claps her mittened hands. Snow settles on her nose and on her cheeks.

The child's baby-sitter is talking to a boy—a Christmas cousin? a boyfriend, perhaps?—and the swing is becalmed. The little girl now bucks at it earnestly, trying to generate motion, frowning with exertion, bewildered, not ready to give up. Lou smiles to herself and rises, arms ready to push, but just then the baby-sitter gives the wooden seat an absentminded shove, and goes on talking, and gives another shove, and lets a few arcs take care of themselves, then indifferently reaches out and pushes again. She does not pause in her conversation with the boyfriend. She does not really look, except peripherally, at child or swing.

Lou returns to her bench and watches. The baby-sitter, preoccupied with examining the buckle on the boyfriend's belt, has forgotten the swing again. The child shakes the chains. She is puzzled. She tries sucking them. She begins to wail. "Stop that!" the baby-sitter says irritably. Lou imagines the baby-sitter wandering off with the boyfriend and abandoning the girl on the swing. The child will grow fretful. At first she will cry quietly and then she will sob. Lou will comfort her. She will carry the child to her own apartment and call 911 and then she will tell the little girl fabulous stories till her parents come.

A man sitting at the other end of the bench stares so fixedly that Lou can feel the pressure of his gaze. "Excuse me," he says, when she turns. "Can I ask you something?"

"Sure. I guess so."

"Are you lonely?"

"Excuse me?"

"Lonely. I thought you seemed . . . aren't you?"

"No, not at all," Lou says sharply. "I'm waiting for someone whose flight has been delayed."

"Oh," he says. "Well. I hope he makes it."

Lou lets that one go.

"*I'm* lonely," the man confesses.

"I'm sorry."

"I've got two grandchildren. You got kids?"

"Sort of," Lou says.

"Give my right arm to have my littl'uns visit for Chistmas, but my son's never even sent a photograph. Can you understand that?"

"People do strange things," Lou acknowledges.

"I can't get my mind around it, I just can't. I'm not saying I was the perfect father, far from it. But not even a photograph. What am I supposed to make of that?"

"People are toughest on their relatives, I think," Lou says. "Especially this time of year. I don't understand why."

"Don't even know what state they live in now. My last Christmas card was returned with one of those yellow post-office stickers on the envelope: *Moved. No forwarding address*."

"I'm so sorry."

"Christmas sucks," the man says. "Worst fucking day of the year."

"It can be rough," Lou acknowledges.

"Want to come up to my place for a drink?"

"Oh, I can see my niece's taxi now," Lou says hurriedly, and runs, with indecent relief, around the corner in the wake of a cab. She finds she is trembling. A plane drones high overhead, humming toward La Guardia, and she holds her breath, watching the winking lights along the wing. The plane does not burst into flame. It does not fall from the sky. Lou breathes a sigh of relief and walks fast enough to keep another aircraft balanced on updrafts of air. She walks for an hour, uptown to Central Park and then across to the East River, then back south on First Avenue. As she takes the elevator up to her apartment, she thinks: Sam should have landed by now. She has probably called.

There are, however, no messages on Lou's answering machine.

She puts the turkey back in the oven without removing the foil. She turns the oven to moderate. She pours herself a glass of wine and goes to her desk. At her computer, she brings up the website for Delta and types in the number of Sam's flight.

FLIGHT DELAYED, she reads.

NO FURTHER INFORMATION AVAILABLE AT THIS TIME.

She stares blankly at the screen, seeing nothing, until there is nothingness—quite suddenly—to see, a moment which startles her, the moment when the screen turns empty and densely black and goes into screensaver mode. Blink. Focus. Stardust is coming at Lou, handfuls of it hurled from somewhere deep inside the microchip core, shooting stars, meteors, glowing fragments of comets, the skyrocketing end of the world, the Milky Way pelting her with hailstones. She stares into them, hypnotized.

She sees an airplane at the upper edge of her screen.

Zoom shot. Close-up.

From the forward door, at the top of the emergency hatch, a child appears. The eyes in the face are huge with fear. Behind the child hulks a masked form, shadowy, a machine gun cradled in its arms. The child looks back over her shoulder, reluctant, but a gun butt pushes her, thumps her, so that she spreads her frail little arms and half flies, half skids, half falls down the chute, all cartwheeling limbs. Lou cries out and folds her arms around the desktop monitor. She holds it tightly. She feels a tiny heart beat against her own.

LIFE DELAYED, she types onto the screen.

NO FURTHER INFORMATION AVAILABLE AT THIS TIME.

The lives delayed float like amoebas in limbo. She stares at them until *Stargazer* mode kicks back in.

She moves with asteroids. She is star-stormed. She is flying backwards through time and Françoise is saying, *"Je déteste Noël. C'est le jour le plus dégueulasse de l'année,"* which Lou translates loosely as *Christmas sucks. Worst fucking day of the year.*

"Well, 1987 will be better," Lou proffers, not believing it. "Better than this year. Has to be."

"To be worse," Françoise says, "it is not possible."

Their apartment on Avenue des Gobelins is stark. There are no smells of Christmas, not in the apartment. The air is rank with stale tobacco and misery. An unpleasant odor of cooked fish rises up the stairwell, drifts under the door, settles in their hair. This is the smell of Christmas 1986 in gay Paree.

The telephone rings and Françoise leaps at it. *"Oui?"* she whispers, breathless. *"Bonjour? C'est toi, Tristan?*

"Oh, *je m'excuse . . .*

"*Qui?*" Her face turns blank. "Who?

"It's for you," she says. "From America. Your sister."

Lou's eyebrows lift. "Rosalie? What a lovely surprise."

"Hi," Rosalie says. "Merry Christmas. We miss you, Lou."

"Miss you too."

"Listen, I do have a surprise, a *real* surprise."

"You're all coming over?"

"You're going to be an auntie again."

"I'm going to be . . . ? Oh, that's— Congratulations. That's great, Ros."

"My baby's due in May."

"That's great," Lou says. "That's . . ."

"Here's Sam to wish you Merry Christmas," Rosalie says. "Sam, say Merry Christmas to Lou."

"Merry Christmas, Lou," Sam says, with an adorable five-year-old's lisp.

Lou is unable to speak.

"Lou? You still there? Lou?"

"Merry Christmas, everyone," Lou says.

"Mom and Dad want a turn."

"Hi, Dad," Lou says. "Hi, Mom. I'm doing fine. No, really, it didn't make sense to come home. Paris is incredibly beautiful in December. You should see the lights. It's a Christmas Wonderland, it really is."

Françoise leans over and cuts off the call with her index finger.

Lou stares at her. "What did you do that for?"

"I thought you would prefer."

"I do," Lou says, "now that I think about it. How did you know?"

"If my father calls from America, I want you to do this for me."

"I remember," Lou says gloomily, "one Christmas when I was little, our cat had kittens. I remember my father drowned them in a sack."

"There are other ways," Françoise says. "There are many ways. There is alcohol. There is Mohammad." She dials a number. *"Moi, je suis un grand bleu,"* she says. "You too. You are one big bruise. Mohammad has friends. You want?"

"I'm going for a walk," Lou says.

"Do not walk by the Seine," Françoise warns, but Lou does. She stands on the Pont Neuf and stares at the brown swirling water. When she gets back, hours later, the boyfriend is there.

"Mohammad and I, we are going to Marseilles," Françoise tells her. There is a dangerous glitter in the eyes of Françoise.

"Are you mad?" Lou whispers.

Françoise touches Lou on the arm. "The kittens, they feel nothing," she assures. *"Joyeux Noël, ma chère Lou."*

"Merry Christmas," Lou says.

When Françoise returns three days later, there is a dark bruise under one eye.

On New Year's Eve 1986, Françoise and Lou get drunk together, seriously drunk. By midnight, they are maudlin, and by the early hours of the new year, confessional. They weep drunkenly in one another's arms.

Lou is hurtling through cyberdust and time.

Her hands on the keyboard touch something inadvertently. *Stargazer* quivers and retreats. Lou clicks on a search engine and types in "Air France 64." In one split second, she is offered 842 websites. She chooses *phoenix.com*—"the official website for survivors of Air France 64"—and when the home page appears, she clicks on "chat room for survivors and relatives." She scrolls through messages till she finds one from "Françoise."

I would be interest to make contact, the message reads in imperfect English, *from others who had ticket but did not fly. Françoise.*

Lou clicks on "reply."

Françoise, she writes. *Did you ever live on Avenue des Gobelins? Do you remember a miserable Christmas? Remember New Year's Eve 1986? Are you the one? Hope your New Year's wish came true. Merry Christmas. Lou in America.*

The telephone rings.

"Sam!" Lou says. She holds her right hand tightly over her mouth and holds her breath, then releases it. "You're here at last," she says.

"I'm not," Samantha says. "I'm afraid I'm not. They finally canceled our flight, and doubled us up on another one, but they didn't have quite enough seats. They asked for volunteers, and, um, well, I thought it seemed a bit pointless this late in the day, so I volunteered. I figured you wouldn't mind too much." Sam laughs awkwardly. "I know I've wrecked a few Christmases. I can be a pain in the ass, I know that."

Lou's head is back against the wall, her eyes closed. She does not trust herself to speak.

"Lou? You don't mind, do you? You said it takes weeks to recover when I visit."

"Hey," Lou says lightly. "That was then. You're getting more bearable all the time. I hate to think of you all by yourself in D.C. D'you have any . . . ?"

"Oh yeah, I've got Jacob. Since he doesn't keep Christmas, it's kind of a blue time for him. We'd lined up New Year's, but I'm worried. I've called him from the airport five times today and he isn't answering, so this gives me a chance. I get antsy about him and it's pretty much a phoenix rule that we, you know . . . It's a high priority. We check in on each other. What'll you do?"

"Oh, you know me," Lou says. "Six invitations on the fridge door. I'll toss a coin."

"The party animal of the family," Sam says. "Have yourself a merry little disreputable."

"You too. Merry Christmas, Sam."

Lou replaces the receiver as though she were stacking eggs. She turns off the oven. She siphons off a mug of cold mulled wine and buzzes it in the microwave. She adds a large shot of rum. She goes to the window and watches the lights coming on, up and down Lexington Avenue. Then she checks her telephone directory and calls Social Services of the City of New York.

"I've got a roast turkey and all the trimmings," she says. "And I've got presents. Is there a family somewhere . . . ? Preferably a family with kids?"

She scribbles down details, packs a hamper, descends to the street, and hails a cab.

"You sure?" the driver says, when she gives the address.

"Sure, I'm sure. I've got a Christmas hamper to deliver."

"You're the one paying," he says.

The farther they drive, the more frequently they pass vacant lots full of rubble and the remnants of walls that have been left by a wrecker's ball. Shells of half-demolished brownstones gape at the sky. Windows are boarded up, and groups of young men stand on corners. The cab driver, a middle-aged African-American man, is nervous. Virgil Jefferson, announces a license which is screwed to the Plexiglas divider.

"Mr. Jefferson," Lou says, leaning forward, "maybe we should—"

Sounds that might be firecrackers, or might be gunfire, drown her words. Virgil Jefferson drives grimly and fast. When he stops and pulls hard against the curb, the crunch of broken glass can be *felt*. Virgil Jefferson swivels around and slides the partition open. "Okay, lady, this is the place, but I ain't going to leave you here. No way."

"I realize I was rather naive about the . . . but there's a family in there," Lou says. "With kids and no dinner."

Virgil Jefferson takes a deep breath. "You want to go in?"

"Not exactly," Lou says. "But I will, I think. Yes, I will. I'm glad you'll wait. I appreciate that."

"Look, lady," he says, half angry. "Tell you what. I'll deliver your basket, but I'm going to leave the engine running and the doors locked. You got that?"

"Thanks," she says. "Oh, thank you." She finds she is shaking. "Do you have children?" she asks him when he opens the back door.

"Three," he says curtly. "We already had Christmas dinner, but they're counting on me coming home tonight."

"Here's the hamper, and this is a gift."

"Lock the doors," he says. He leaves the hazard lights blinking. Once he climbs the low porch steps, the darkness gulps him down whole. Not a chink of light comes from the building, though Lou can see, by the dim glow of a lone street lamp, that each window is boarded with thick ply. She hears a rat-a-tat-tat and thinks he must be using a rock against the door.

A cluster of young men, maybe ten of them, is moving toward the car. Lou scrunches low, but keeps her eye on the porch where the cabdriver stands. *Bang, bang, bang,* she hears, knocker against wood, and the door opens three inches, the length of a chain. Someone shines a flashlight out and for a moment she sees the cab driver's face. Words are exchanged. The chain is unhooked, the door opens, an arm reaches out, grabs the basket, and slams the door shut. The driver takes the porch steps in two leaps, stumbles, and sprints to the curb. The young men swarm closer, a multicelled creature with one intent.

"Hey, man!" voices call to the driver. "What's the rush?"

"What you got there, man?"

Virgil Jefferson hurls himself into his seat and locks the door. The engine roars. The car leaps forward, then seems to pause. A thunder of hands drum threat on the roof and fish-faces flatten themselves against the windshield and against the side windows. Bodies drape themselves over hood and trunk like encrustations. Eyes everywhere, staring at Virgil, staring at Lou. Lou presses the back of her hand against her mouth to stop a scream getting through. She can see Virgil's eyes, huge, in the rearview mirror. She can see his hands shaking on the wheel.

The engine roars. The bodies and eyes fall away.

The back of Lou's hand feels wet, and she sees that she has bitten through a vein. There is blood all over the cuff of her blouse and down her sleeve.

Back on Lexington, where the streetlights are as powerful as suns or the eyes of God, the cab stops in front of Lou's building. They sit in the dark without moving.

"It was a kid, a boy," Virgil Jefferson says, staring forward through his windshield. "That came to the door. 'Bout the age of my son."

"Did you see inside?"

"Squatters," he says. "No plumbing. No power. Couldn't see a thing."

"I don't know," Lou says, "how people keep going. I don't know how they do it."

"When you have to, you do what you have to, " Virgil says. He turns around then and slides the partition open. His hands are still trembling. "I'm going home to my wife and kids."

"Yes," she says. "Yes, you must." She is pulling twenty-dollar bills, double the meter plus a lavish tip, from her purse, but Virgil Jefferson will not accept a fare.

"No way," he says. "We both already got our Christmas present, ma'am. We got more than our share."

"Yes," she says. "You're right. We've got nothing to complain about, have we?"

"Nothing," he says. "We already blessed."

"Just the same," she says. "I'll agree to pay no fare on one condition. You have to take these." She passes the bag of five remaining presents, with their shimmering gold rosettes, through the window. "For your wife and children," she says. "Merry Christmas, Mr. Jefferson."

"Something good going to happen to you," Virgil Jefferson promises. "This is your year. I got the gift of reading signs, and I know it."

"Thank you," she says. "I hope you're right."

She feels lighter, less desolate. It is only seven o'clock, but she is ravenous and it occurs to her that she has not really eaten all day. She opens a can of soup and heats another mug of mulled wine in the microwave. She listens to carols from the King's College Choir. This is definitely better, after all, than Christmas '86 on Avenue des Gobelins, she thinks. Paris. It's after midnight there. She wonders how Françoise spent this Christmas. She wonders what happened to Françoise.

She goes to her computer and clicks her way into the chat room for obsessive survivors of the hijacked flight.

Lou in America, she reads. *Oui, c'est moi. I am the one. Incroyable, n'est-ce pas? How it is strange to meet again like this. As you say in America: what goes around, comes around. We have passed Noël 86 in that apartment, toi et moi. Quel Noël affreux, but 87 was after all worse. I remember the secrets of the New Year's Eve. Love sucks. Did you ever find your BB? Do you come ever to Paris? Françoise.*

Lou holds her left thumb against the pulse in her other wrist. Her blood is bucking. She takes deep breaths. She makes the thump of her heartbeat slow down.

Françoise, she types. *I may come to Paris. (I have not been back since then.)*

Re: BB. Yes I did, but I have not told. (Too afraid.)

And you? Did T come back to you? Do you still mourn?

Did you escape from M? Did he stalk you?

You knew my sister was on AF 64, but you never said anything. You never told me you had a ticket too. Why didn't you? Lou in America.

For several days there is no response from Françoise, but on New Year's Eve a message comes:

Lou in America. It is again the night for confessions.

M bought my ticket for the black flight. He knew.

My father said: Do not fly. Your life is in danger. He knew.

My father knew M, M knew my father.

How could I tell you this?

Now you understand why I could not watch the terrible thing on television.

I could not speak to my father again. I could not speak. I hid from my father.

For many years, I had a sickness of the spirit and mind. I have been in a hospital many years. I have talked with therapists. I have talked with priests. Now I have things that must be told for absolution. When do you come to Paris? Françoise.

3.

Sam tells the taxi not to wait. She buzzes Jacob's apartment from the lobby and puts her ear to the intercom. She hears nothing. She buzzes again and a crackle of static comes from the panel in the wall. "Jacob?" she says, her lips close to the metal mesh. "It's Samantha. My flight was canceled. Can I come up?"

Muddled sound comes from the wall.

"Jacob? I hope you can hear me, because I sure can't hear you. It's Sam." A prolonged hum, both high-pitched and raspy, rises from the heavy inner door, and Sam says, "Okay. Thanks. I'm on my way up," pushing at the door with the bottom of a tissue-swathed bottle of wine. In the hallway, she grimaces at the beige steel elevator panels, both closed. The building is old and the elevators excruciatingly slow. According to the lit monitor, one car is down in the basement garage at level 2B and seems to be stuck there. The other is descending slowly through the tenth floor, ninth, eighth, seventh, and there it stops. Impatient, Sam opts for the stairs and takes them two at a time. On the third-floor landing, slightly breathless, she pushes UP. The elevator is still at the seventh floor. Sam runs up another flight of stairs. She pushes UP on the fourth-floor landing. The elevator is moving from sixth floor to fifth to fourth. The doors open and a man, coated and scarved, looks out at nothing. He is attached to a dog on a leash.

"Merry Christmas," Sam says.

"On the contrary." The man appears to be conversing with his dog. He stares straight ahead and Sam thinks he must be blind, though the dog is not a seeing-eye dog. "I would argue," he says, picking up an ongoing thread, "that the need for solitude runs deeper. I would say it is the primary thing." The dog—a small shaggy mutt—trembles and whimpers, barely able to contain a rebuttal.

Sam pushes button 8.

"We're going down," the man explains to the dog, but the elevator rises directly to the eighth without stopping.

"Sorry," Sam says.

"We're going down."

"They're unpredictable."

"Things devolve," the man insists. "All things devolve."

As though the elevator mechanisms are deliberating, as though they are weighing competing rights and claims, the doors quiver for several seconds but fail to move. When they open, the dog bounds into the hallway and the man of necessity follows and looks blankly about. "We are not at street level," he says reproachfully, his eyes sliding at Sam and away. He is not blind, then, she sees. "The problem," he tells the dog, "is one of focus."

Wild barking ensues and changes pitch in an intricate slide: glissando of joy notes; syncopated yaps of confusion; three sharp pips of outrage; then a dying fall through the lower registers of dismay, each full-throated note bouncing and ricocheting and multiplying itself against the walls.

"What the hell is going on?" a voice demands, and 807 opens to the length of a chain. Renaissance music billows out: lutes, viols, shawms, the soft thump of a drum.

"Someone got off at the wrong floor," Sam says, as man and dog retreat behind the elevator doors and the hullabaloo dwindles away from them like a spent rocket. "Jacob, I've got wine and truffles. Let me in."

"Sam?" One-eyed Jacob, peering through three inches of space, blinks slowly. "What are you doing here?" He unhooks the chain, pondering the dimensions of this riddle. "I thought you were going to New York."

"You have a lousy intercom system in this building," she says. "Even worse than your elevators. Who did you think you were letting in?"

"I wasn't planning on letting anyone in."

"Why'd you buzz me, then?"

"I didn't buzz anyone. The call system's been playing up for months. Someone else must have buzzed the door."

"Well, here I am anyway. Happy holidays." She hands him the wine and a gift bag frothing with tissue. "Lots of goodies under there," she says. "Truffles, figs, sugared almonds, a surprise or two. To go with the music." She tosses her snow-dusted coat and scarf across the back of a chair and stands in front of him, waiting, like a child expecting a star on her activities card. "My flight was canceled," she says. "Anyway, I'd rather be with you." She rests her cheek against his chest and locks her arms around him. It always seems to her that she sinks into him, that she has come home to their skin. "The music's glorious," she sighs.

Jacob, who still has the wine in one hand and the gift bag in the other, folds his arms, somewhat awkwardly, across her back. She feels the wine bottle bump against her thigh. She looks up at him and he makes her think suddenly of the man in the elevator. He is looking at the music, at something in the air.

"What's wrong?" she asks quickly.

He looks at her then. "Nothing. Nothing's wrong."

"I *know* when something's the matter," she says. "You can't hide anything from me, Jacob. There's a telepathic connection, I always know. My anxiety level's high as a kite—feel my heart." She takes the wine bottle out of his hand and sets it down, pulls her sweater up, and places the palm of his hand just above her breast. "That's you," she says. "Making it jump and race like that. What's wrong?"

"Nothing's wrong," he insists. "Quite the reverse. I'm very calm. I have finally come to a place of calm." He picks up the bottle of wine and frowns slightly, as though trying to recall what comes next. He goes to the kitchen, Sam following.

"I called you from the airport five times. Where have you been all day?"

"Arlington Cemetery," he says.

"What? Are you kidding me?"

"No. I took Cass." He takes a corkscrew from his drawer and opens the wine.

"Why?"

"We like the company there. We know a lot of dead people. Cass finds it soothing."

"That's so morbid," Sam says. "You were there all day?"

"Not all day. An hour or so."

"Where were you the rest of the time?"

"I was here."

"Why didn't you answer the phone? You didn't even have the answering machine on."

"I've unplugged the phone. I keep it unplugged. I don't need a phone anymore."

The apartment is full of the lush soft sounds of Early Music. The glorious voice of Cass's mother envelopes them, accompanied by the Levinstein String Quartet. Jacob extracts the cork from the corkscrew, but seems uncertain about what to do next. He opens a drawer and closes it again.

"You want me to pour the wine?" Sam prompts.

"Yes," he says relieved. "Good idea."

He returns to his living room and sits cross-legged on a cushion on the floor. He lifts one of his feet and tucks it under the crease of the other knee.

"You look like the Buddha," Sam says.

"Ssh. Listen to what she does with this phrase. It's remarkable. It's quite remarkable. It's musically and mathematically perfect."

Sam waits for the voice of Cass's mother to fade away from its mellow final chord. "Jacob," she says. "Tell me what's wrong."

"Ssh." He changes the disk in the player. "Schubert's String Quintet in C. My father's playing first violin." He closes his eyes and listens raptly.

Very quietly, Sam returns to the kitchen for the glasses of wine. She takes them back to the living room. She sets one down on the coffee table in front of Jacob. She sits opposite, on the sofa, and studies him. In the second movement, the adagio, when the voice of the violin breaks, when the violin weeps, Jacob rises like a sleepwalker and leaves the room. Sam follows. In his bedroom, he opens a closet and takes his father's violin from a shelf. He lays the case on the bed. He takes out the violin.

"Jacob?" Sam murmurs.

He turns to look at her. "What are you doing here?" he says. He could be looking at a total stranger. He cradles the violin in his arms and returns to his cushion on the floor. He holds the violin as though it were an infant in his arms.

The second movement ends. The quiet sob of the violin falls into silence.

Jacob touches a button on his remote and repeats the track.

When the adagio ends for the second time, he presses STOP.

"I've looked after it for him," he says. "I saved it. It wasn't easy. Especially not on the chute. Remember the way they pushed us down? They weren't gentle."

"Jacob," Sam murmurs, stricken. "Where are you going? Where have you gone?"

"I'm safe, Sam. I'm in a safe place. After Agit's death, I knew it was crucial to find one."

"Agit's death," Sam says. "So that's what this is about."

"That was the writing on the wall."

"That was depression and anniversary time coming up. It's the mission of the Phoenix Club to stop any more of those from happening."

"If they could get to Agit because he published a book, if they can reach out and pulls strings in Bombay, it's just a matter of time. One by one, they'll get us all."

"Unless we get to them first," Sam says angrily. "What am I saying? What's *them*? Who's *they*? You're fucking with your own mind, Jacob. Like Agit did. You're making up your own mindgame and losing."

"There's been a game master right from the start. We're pawns on his board."

"Bullshit! You're not the only one who lost Agit. We both lost him, the Phoenix Club lost him, we all lost him. And now you're going off with the fairies too. How's that going to help us? How's that going to keep the rest of us alive and sane?"

"I had to find a safe place," Jacob says.

Sam is furious. She grabs Jacob's hand and pushes up the sleeve of his shirt. "Fuck!" she says. "*Fuck* you!" A road map of needle tracks graphs his forearm. All the tracks lead to the same dead end. "Why don't you just jump under a train like Agit did?"

"You think he jumped?"

"If he was pushed, he should have fought back. We have to fight. Don't you dare quit on me, don't you dare."

Jacob returns to his bedroom and takes the bow from the violin case. "Listen," he says. He tucks the violin under his chin and plays. "I couldn't do it for a long time," he says. "I couldn't play it. But it's where I belong."

He plays Schubert, the String Quintet, the second movement. He is not a maestro like his father, but he does play well.

"You have to find a safe place too, Sam. The key is being invisible, you understand?"

"Never," Sam says.

Jacob puts down his father's violin. He takes Sam's face between his hands. "We need each other," he says.

"Exactly," Sam says. "Exactly. Don't do this to me."

"You're dangerously naive," Jacob says. "You think you lead a charmed life."

"I don't," Sam says. "I don't think that for a minute. That's why I fight. If I stopped fighting for a minute, I'd go under."

"It's the people who struggle that drown," Jacob says. "They're the ones who go under. You have to stop fighting the current. You have to give yourself to it, go with it. I want you to promise me."

"Okay," Sam says, humoring him. "I promise."

"Listen," he says. "I'll take you somewhere safe."

He tucks the violin under his chin and she sits beside him and strokes his hair as he plays. On Christmas night, they sleep in each other's arms.

4.

Lowell is folding the canvas drop cloths and stacking them neatly in the back of his truck. From habit, he reaches between them for the backpack, and when his hand finds nothing, panic fizzes through his blood and his heart cavorts. Sudden dizziness overwhelms him and he has to lean against the side of his truck. Then it comes to him, with a great lifting of the spirit, that he has taken care of all that. He feels like someone waking from a nightmare. He does not need to worry anymore. The ring binders are safely sealed into his walls. They could stay there for a decade and the only risks would be from insects and damp. As for the backpack and the tapes: they are back where they started, where his own father had deemed them to be perfectly safe, in a locker at Logan Airport. He put them there yesterday and he alone has the key, which he has threaded on a thin gold chain around his neck. He touches the key through his T-shirt and its outline cheers him so much that he whistles as he folds and stacks canvas. *I saw Mommy kissing Santa Claus . . .*

He levers the aluminum extension ladders off the roof rack, balancing them against his gut, lowering them to the ground. They are awkward, but not heavy. He drags them down the drive to the cement-block storage shed that is shared by all tenants. He has his own key for the padlock, and his own section inside. He hangs the ladders on steel hooks high on the wall. He goes back to the truck for his paint cans. In the shed, he pries open a ten-gallon drum of oil primer, tilts it, and pours from its spout to top up a small gallon can.

"Hey, Lowell," Kevin says from the doorway.

"Hey, Kevin. How's things?"

"Great," Kevin says. "Things are great. Great time in Buffalo. Great Christmas. And you?"

"Best Christmas in years. When d'ya get back?"

"Got back this morning, just after you left for work, probably. Met a girl at my brother's Christmas party. Could be the one."

"Go for it, pal. What's her name?"

"Shannon." He smiles when he says it. "Kevin and Shannon McCarthy. I've been trying it out. Has a good sound, don't you think?"

"Sounds meant to be."

Kevin grins. "She's coming east next month, so I was thinking, you know, got to fix the apartment up a bit."

"Hey." Lowell grins. "Serious stuff."

"You better believe it. So I was wondering . . . I mean, that's your thing. I was wondering if we could trade some way. Like, you paint my apartment, I can get you box seats at Fenway Park for a game. I can get 'em from where I work, through my boss."

"You got yourself a deal," Lowell says. "I love to take my kids to Fenway Park. Hey, Rowena might even come."

"Hey. Must have been a really good Christmas."

"Fantastic," Lowell says. "Best ever. Got my fingers crossed."

"Looks like a good year coming up all around," Kevin says. "Going to be the year for the Sox too. I got a good feeling about that."

"I think so," Lowell says. "Great lineup. I think it's going to be a Red Sox year."

"So, d'ya think maybe next weekend we could get a start on my place? Cream, I think. Almond. Whatever they call it."

"Well, I don't know, Kevin. I mean, I hope I'll have the kids this weekend."

"Oh, right. Well, yeah, your kids come first. So, ah, when d'ya think . . . ?"

"How about late on weeknights, instead of weekends?"

"Sure. Sure. No problem. I mean, I can pitch in too. Can't be that much to it."

"Stick a roller in your hand, you can do it."

"Great," Kevin says. "Oh, listen, nearly forgot. The guys came with your sink today."

"Came with my sink?"

"Yeah. The new one. They got it installed."

"Not me. I didn't order a new sink. Must be Darlene."

"It was your apartment," Kevin says. "They showed me the specs. I had to get the master key and let them in."

Lowell can feel foreboding move through his body like heavy blood. "Must be Rowena, then," he says clumsily. His tongue feels wooden in his mouth. "Must be a New Year surprise."

"That must be it," Kevin says. "Well, let me know what night you can start."

"Right. Night, Kevin."

"Night."

Lowell padlocks the shed. He pulls the cover across the back of his pickup and fastens it down. His hands are shaking. The muscles in his legs feel weak, stretched too far. They feel like elastic gone slack. His whole body aches. Dread rises with him up the stairs.

He opens his door and knows instantly. The worst has happened.

White powder floats everywhere like smog. Drywall has been pulled from the studs. The apartment has been stripped and ransacked. He knows without looking, but he looks anyway. His pantry shelves are bare, the milk safe empty. In the storage room, the pegboard lies in fragments on the floor. There is nothing in the space between the studs.

He feels for the chain around his neck. The key to the locker is there.

Very quietly, he closes his front door, pulls off his shoes, and walks downstairs in his socks. On the porch, he slips his feet back into his sneakers. He does not go to his truck. Keeping to shadows, he moves down the street. He is wearing the old paint-spattered running shoes that he uses for interior jobs, and the shoes slip and slide on the snow. He breaks into a run, making for the subway stop in Union Square. He begins to plan his route. He will take the Red Line to Park Street, but he will not take the Blue Line direct to the airport. He will need to be more devious and more cunning. He will need to plan a roundabout route.

5.

On New Year's Eve, Samantha buzzes Jacob's apartment from the lobby. She sets the champagne in its insulated sleeve on the shelf beneath the mailboxes because she anticipates a wait. She pushes buttons randomly and waits for someone, anyone, to let her in. No one responds. Everyone is out. Everyone is partying, she thinks. A couple in evening dress (long velvet gown, tuxedo) emerges from the inner locked door.

"Oh, thank goodness," she says brightly. "A friend in 807's expecting me, but he must be in the shower or have his headphones on. Would you consider . . . ?" She holds up the bottle of champagne. "You can frisk me if you like."

"No problem," the guy laughs. "You look harmless," and he unlocks the inner sanctum and lets her through. The elevator takes her straight to the eighth floor without a stop. She knocks at Jacob's door and rattles the knob.

She waits.

She tears a check out of her checkbook and scribbles *Let me in* on the back. She pushes it through the fine crack beneath the door.

She puts her ear to the lock, but hears nothing.

She takes the elevator back to the ground floor and bangs on the door of the super's apartment. There is no answer. She goes back to the lobby and dials 911.

"My friend's expecting me, but he's not answering the door," she explains to the police. "I'm afraid something's happened to him in there."

"What kind of thing?"

"Well, I'm half afraid he might have taken an overdose, or something like that. He's been depressed."

"Have you called him on the phone?"

"He keeps the phone unplugged," she says. "Because he's, ah, he's been working on a project, he doesn't like interruptions, and . . . as I told you, I think he's been depressed. But he wouldn't . . . not when he's expecting me, and on New Year's Eve. If he were okay, he'd answer the door."

There is a silence at the other end. She has a sense of someone's hand over the receiver, of a conferral going on.

"Officer?"

"You're on our list," the policeman tells her. "We'll get to you, ma'am. Might take a while. I mean, New Year's Eve. A lot of calls, a lot of high priorities. But we'll get there eventually."

And then she waits. And waits.

"Kind of a heavy night, New Year's Eve," two policemen explain nearly an hour later. "We have to prioritize."

When they force the lock and enter Jacob's apartment, there is no sign of him. Nor is there any sign of disorder.

"Well, ma'am," one policeman says awkwardly. He coughs into his hand. "I think you've been stood up for your New Year's date."

"No," Sam says. "It's not like that. He wouldn't do that. Something's happened, I know it has."

"Does he have a car?"

"Yes," she says.

"Does he keep it in the basement garage?"

"Yes."

"Do you know his license number?"

"Yes," she says.

"Let's go, then." But Jacob's car is not in the basement garage.

"We'll let you know," the police promise. "As soon as we hear anything."

"Hello?" Samantha says, starting awake on her sofa and groping for the receiver in the dark. "Have you found him?"

"Samantha? This is Lowell. I'm calling from a pay phone beside—"

"Who?"

"Lowell. Lowell Hawthorne."

"Lowell? Oh, Lowell." She blinks at the sun beyond her window. "What time is it?"

"Time? It's, uh, about eleven, I think. Listen, I'm in a pay phone booth beside the Mass Pike—"

"Eleven. Oh my God. Look, Lowell, I'm sorry, but I'm in the middle of an emergency here. I have to make a call. Sorry."

She cuts Lowell off and calls the police department.

There is no information, she is told.

At midday on New Year's Day, Samantha rouses the superintendent of Jacob's building. The superintendent is hungover, and none too pleased.

"Police have already been here," he tells her irritably. "I don't need this kind of shit."

"Did you see Jacob Levinstein yesterday?" she asks.

"I can't remember if I did or I didn't," he says. "I got a hundred apartments in this building, lady. I don't sit all day and watch who's going out, coming in. Especially not on New Year's Eve."

Samantha fills her car with Renaissance songs. Cass's mother is singing, Jacob's father plays violin. Sam turns the volume up to leave no space for anything else. She drives almost blindly, east of the city and then south around the curve of Chesapeake Bay, oblivious to road signs, sometimes wondering with a start if she has missed her exit, watching for the next signpost but then forgetting to attend to it. Nevertheless, instinct brings her to the stretch of salt marsh and to the small unpaved road that leads to the reed-sucking edge of the bay where the boathouse is. There is no sign of Jacob's car.

Samantha parks and climbs the ladder to the loft.

The heaped fishnets and the orange life vests remain undisturbed.

It is cold. The damp of the wooden roof has whitened to a wafer of frost. Sam puts on a life vest for warmth and drapes one of the nets around her shoulders like a shawl. She huddles into the tangle of knotted rope and stares for hours at seagulls and marsh. The flash of wings and the soft slurp of water against wood pylons mesmerize her. She listens for Jacob's car.

She takes two oars from the rack and drops them carefully, one by one, so that they fall onto the boardwalk edge of the shed below. She climbs back down the ladder and tests the rowboat. She and Jacob and Cass have used it before. It is old and weathered but does not seem to have sprung any leaks. She gets in, unhooks the mooring rope, and pushes herself off with one oar. The mooring rope is crusted with ice and thin wafers of ice float between the reeds. Within a few yards of the boat shed, she enters the labyrinth and has vanished from the view of anyone who might have been watching from the shed. The brittle brown stalks of the marsh weeds, four feet high, close in around her and she peers ahead for the scribbled blue thread of the channel. The channels shift with the tide, sometimes closing behind or ahead of careless boaters. She does not plan to get lost. She rests the oars, lies back in the boat, and looks up at the bleak wintry sky.

Clouds telegraph messages. One looks like a violin, another resembles a row of children hurrying along behind a nurse. She sees towers, high-rise apartment buildings, a map of North Africa. She sees Jacob hunched over a desk. She lifts the oars and rows back to the boat shed, sometimes batting at the canyon of reeds, once ramming an oyster bed and having to push herself off it with an oar.

Twilight already. She drives back into the city and parks and checks her answering machine as soon as she lets herself in the door. Not a single message waits for her. She feels desolation. She cannot concentrate on television, she cannot read. She lies on her bed and closes her eyes and summons up the school gymnasium in Germany in minute detail: the smell of the cots, the smell of the blankets, the ammoniac smell of wet underwear. She recalls the nurses, the slim blondes and the big heavy ones with dark hair. She walks up and down between the cots, concentrating, remembering each row, seeing Agit here, Cass there, Jacob there. She and Jacob sit together on a cot.

The phone rings and she falls off the bed in her haste to reach it.

"Can I speak to Samantha Raleigh, please?" a voice asks, official.

"Speaking," she whispers.

"I'm afraid we have bad news," the voice says.

6.

Samantha is sitting on the floor of her apartment, arms hugged across her stomach, rocking herself back and forth. What does that mean: *identify the body?* She sees pieces of Jacob, disconnected, like a puzzle that must be put together: that impatient little grimace he had, for example, when he was exasperated with her. *You're reckless, Sam. More accidents . . .* His lips float in front of her, grimacing. She remembers the pressure of them, and the taste. She tries to summon up Jacob's face, but all she can remember is his lips.

Car found in Rock Creek Park, the police said. *Hose from exhaust . . . stereo still playing, one of those automatic recycling types, classical music, Schubert or something, the same piece over and over . . .*

She can see the back of his hand as he reaches to adjust the balance of treble and bass. One knuckle is lumpy and swollen. It was broken when he fell down the chute from the plane because he was more concerned with protecting his father's violin. He shielded it with his body as he fell. *I've found a safe place, Sam. It's where I belong.*

The phone rings and she reaches for it in a dazed automatic way.

"Sam," a voice says. "Thank God I've reached you again. Don't cut me off this time."

"What do you want?"

"Something terrible's happened."

"Yes, I know." She frowns, her thinking sluggish. "I have to identify the body."

"Sam?"

"Yes," she says. "Is this the police or the morgue?"

"Sam, this is Lowell."

"Lowell?"

"Lowell Hawthorne."

"Oh, *Lowell*."

"I tried to call you on New Year's Eve, but you—"

"Yes. Sorry I couldn't—"

"I was calling from the Mass Turnpike then. I've been coming south on 87, and now I'm in the Greyhound Terminal in Jersey City. Damn pay phone won't take a card and I've used all my coins, so we have to be quick—"

"Emergency conditions," she says, "so I'm sorry, but I couldn't—"

"*Major* emergency," Lowell says.

Sam is conscious of a small space that outlines her body, a vacuum barrier that sound has to pass through. Lowell speaks, and the words seem to skywrite themselves against the space and Sam reads them slowly and waits for a meaning to drift by. *Sirocco,* he is saying. *Salamander.* Sam knows this means something important, but the meaning is still floating and groping for the words. *The things my father left,* he says.

"Almost no one left now," she says. "Besides me."

"Samantha, I've got one minute left. Can you take down this number and call me back? Got a pencil?"

"No," she says, trying to concentrate.

"Damn it, Samantha, *listen* to me. You started this, you wouldn't leave me alone." His voice is rising, exasperated. "I'm being followed, and you started this, God knows what you've started with that goddamn website, your declassified documents, with all your goddamned calls— I'm in a pay phone. Get a pen or a pencil!" he shouts.

"I'm sorry, I'm in such a— I'm in bad shape, I'm sure I'm not making any sense." Sam tries to think where a pen or a pencil might be. "I think I'm in shock," she says. "I've lost Jacob. I've lost half of myself. I've been *amputated,*" she says, because that's what it feels like.

"Please deposit two dollars," a voice says. "Or recharge your calling card and try again."

The line goes dead.

Shock? Is that the problem? Sam tries to assess her hypothesis. She does seem to be able to go through basic motions. When she hears ringing, she knows to move toward the telephone and she knows to pick up the receiver and speak.

She must find a pencil and paper for when Lowell calls back. Pencil, she thinks. Where? She finds one on her desk and writes on a piece of paper: *Jacob's body. Must identify.* Desire for Jacob's body overwhelms her. She can identify exactly what she wants. She hugs a pillow between her legs and curls herself tightly around it. She keeps the pencil and notepad in her hand.

The phone rings.

Samantha catapults awake and searches for it.

"Yes?" she says. "Have I identified the body?"

"Sam? This is Lowell."

"I've got a pencil."

"Take this number." He dictates ten digits. "Got it?"

"Got it. Where are you?"

"I'm getting closer. Heading south on 95. How fast can you get to a pay phone?"

"Pay phone?" Sam's mind goes blank again. "I don't know."

"Your phone is probably being tapped. Find a pay phone fast and call back this number."

Lowell hangs up. Sam, flustered, thinks: *Pay phone, pay phone.* Mini market, she thinks, around the corner. But that phone isn't private, not at all. She runs downstairs and knocks on the door below. "Doug? Hi. Bit of an emergency. My phone seems to be on the blink and I've got to be— Could I use your phone?"

"No problem. Take the cordless," he says. "Here. Lock yourself in the bathroom and have some privacy."

"Angel," she says.

In the bathroom, she fumbles with the scrap of paper and dials the number Lowell gave her. Lowell answers on the first ring. "Okay," he says. "I'm scared shitless. I figure we've got about five minutes before they put a trace on this phone too."

Sam can hear the terror in his voice, and now she can feel her own terror too, the electric panic of two people who have reason to know that bad will never stop at worse.

"We have to talk," he says, "but we can't do it over the phone. We have to meet. Somewhere safe, though I don't know if anywhere is safe. My apartment was ransacked and the stuff that my father—"

"Stuff that your—"

"I never told you . . . You remember I had a bag with me in New York?"

"You wouldn't let it out of your sight."

"My father sent me classified stuff and it's been stolen. We have to meet somewhere safe."

"I know somewhere safe," Sam tells him—the only safe place left in the world, she thinks—and the boathouse, the abandoned boathouse, is so vivid to her that she can smell the dried salt, smell Cass, smell Jacob, smell a king tide of sorrow that swamps her, and sucks her down. "I do know somewhere quite safe."

"Don't tell me," he says quickly. "Don't say it into anything electronic. I'm being followed, so I'm traveling on Greyhound buses and hitching rides. I have to keep changing routes."

"Is it really that—?"

"I don't know for sure, but I think so. I mean, I might be cracking up, I know that. I also know my house was ransacked, and I do think I'm being followed, and when I can tell you why, you'll understand."

"So how will we—?"

"When I get to D.C., I'll call you from a pay phone and give you the number. Get to another pay phone fast and call me back. I'll tell you where to pick me up. Probably late tonight. Okay?"

"Okay," Sam says. "I have to go and identify—"

"See you later." Lowell hangs up.

In the dark, Sam pulls up to a diner in the dangerous northeastern section of Washington, D.C. A man in a bomber jacket and woolen cap, with a blue backpack slung in front like an Indian papoose, gets into her car. They drive east and then south around the curve of the bay without speaking. Eventually, on the unpaved road that leads to the boathouse, Sam says, "The police found Jacob's body in his car. We used to come here. I don't believe it was suicide, by the way." She turns off the lights and nudges the car as close as she dares. "I mean, I know it could have been. It's possible. But I don't believe he would. Not without making arrangements for the violin."

"Elizabeth's disappeared too," Lowell says. "My father's widow. Not that she knew anything. But someone was afraid she did. Or she was so afraid that someone was afraid that she knew something, she's moved. She's gone away." He holds his backpack as though it were an infant. He cradles it. He strokes it constantly with his hands.

In the boathouse, Sam wraps herself in the fishnets that heap themselves where Jacob used to sit.

". . . Greyhound buses," Lowell is saying, making a nest for himself in the nets. "If you want a crash course on race and class in America, Greyhound bus is the way to go. The last time I traveled Greyhound, I was a student coming home on spring break. And that's the thing. Who uses Greyhound? Students do. American students, and foreign students seeing America on the cheap. Apart from that, it's blacks, Mexicans, the poor, and the desperate." He laughs bitterly. "The plus is, the FBI or the CIA or whoever the hell it is who's after us, they don't go Greyhound. I don't believe those guys have ever set foot in a Greyhound terminal, which is another country, believe me.

Got to be one of the most depressing zones on earth, but at least it's a safe one."

"I wouldn't count on that."

"I do count on it, though, relatively speaking, I mean, because you can *feel* being followed on the back of your neck, and I felt *un*followed on those buses. Of course, I didn't dare go to sleep."

"The boathouse is safe. We've never seen another human being anywhere near."

"I'm exhausted," Lowell says. "I've been on the run two days. Can hardly keep my eyes open."

Sam can smell Jacob on the fishnets and she balls a wad of her jacket sleeve into her mouth. She sleeps. They both sleep. She dreams that Jacob is asking her to get the violin from his apartment and keep it safe and she is trying to untangle it from his clothes. Someone else is in the room giving orders and when she swims up to the surface of Lowell's words, she is tangled up in him and they are both tangled up in the nets and a brackish wind is coming in off the marsh, and gulls, perched in the open gable, swoop off as Sam moves.

Lowell is talking in his sleep.

He sleeps awkwardly, his backpack pushing him out of shape, but when Sam tries to ease it from his shoulders, he cries out and jackknifes up and backhands her across the face.

"Lowell! It's me, it's just me."

He stares wild-eyed, still ready to strike. He is trembling violently.

"We're in the boathouse," Sam says. "We're safe here."

"Oh God, Sam." He takes great gulping breaths, and hugs his knees. "Listen: this blue bag is practically radioactive. My father sent something back from the other side. Some of it's been stolen, and some of it's still in here."

Sam's heartbeat is erratic. "Tell me slowly," she says. "I can't hear properly if you tell me too much at a time. I can't take it in. I get interference or reverberation or something."

"How I got this stuff—" His hands flutter, and the flutter implies:

The explanation won't make any sense. "Too long a story, but I haven't let it out of my sight or out of my reach since it came."

"What's in there?"

"What *was* in the bag was a bunch a videos and two thick ring binders. One of the binders was in some sort of code and I never made any sense of it. My father wanted it hidden, I don't know for how long. Decades, maybe. He wanted me to hide it until it could safely be read. The second one was classified stuff, reports on Salamander and Sirocco, kind of a logbook, I guess, and I read a lot of it."

"Salamander. You've got classified reports on Salamander."

"Did have. Both binders were stolen."

"But *Salamander*!"

"I think my father knew him well. I think my father was killed because he knew who Salamander was. Knew Sirocco too."

"Shit," Sam breathes. "No wonder someone's after this stuff."

"I've still got the videotapes he sent me." He pats the bag that rests in the curve of his body. "I haven't watched them. I haven't had a chance to play them yet."

"What's on them?"

"I have no idea. I've been afraid to find out. I've been afraid for anyone else to see them, and I've been afraid to watch them alone. But I think we have to."

"Yes."

He opens the backpack and pulls out a drawstring bag made from a child's pillowcase. He shows Sam the tag at its neck. **AF 64. Operation Black Death. Bunker Tapes & Decameron Tape.**

"Oh no," Sam says faintly. "I can't watch that."

"We have to. People have been murdered for what's in here."

"I'm not sure I can do it."

"We have to watch before they're stolen or destroyed. But the question is, where? Where can we watch them? You don't have a VCR in the boathouse, I assume."

"The Saltmarsh Motel," Sam says quietly. "It's nowhere. Nobody goes there off season."

"How far?"

"Not far by water. There's an old rowboat below us. We can't do it in the dark, but if we wait until dawn—"

"No," Lowell says. "You can't show up at a motel in the morning, especially not out of season. We'll have to wait till tomorrow afternoon."

"All right. Late afternoon. We'll wait until dusk."

Book V

JOURNAL OF S: ENCRYPTED

And I only am escaped alone to tell thee . . .

—BOOK OF JOB, 1:14

It's to the other man, to Borges, that things happen . . . I live, I let myself live, so that Borges can weave his tales and poems, and those tales and poems are my justification. . . . Little by little, I have been surrendering everything to him, even though I have evidence of his stubborn habit of falsification and exaggeration. . . . Which of us is writing this page I don't know.

—JORGE LUIS BORGES, "**BORGES AND I**"

1.

S for substructure, subterranean, subterfuge.

S for split selves, Siamesed.

It is by the other man, Salamander, that events have been nudged in dreadful directions. I operate from beneath his line of sight, because someone has to do this. Someone has to set the record straight. Someone has to sort through the rubble of words and ideas, and I note, for example, that when Salamander writes "ideas" in his reports, or rather in his handwritten notes for his reports, he writes "ids" for short, a plurality of ids, which is a singular idea when you think about it, and he uses the abbreviation "id" when he is indicating "idea" in the non-plural form, as a solitary fertilized seed. It bears looking into, this habit of his, this exhibitionism, this allusive shorthand that might mean *id*, ideogram, identity, identical, ideologue, or idiot.

I want you to stop this, Dr. Reuben. I want you to stop words from doing this to me, iddying this way and that, uncontrollably. They are driving me mad. I want you to stop them.

I want you to stop Salamander from taking up more and more space while I am becoming—have you noticed?—smaller and smaller, like Alice in Wonderland with the shrinking potion. I want you to stop me from disappearing.

I want you to stop the dreams.

In this dream, the passengers are all walking around in the fire unharmed, and I am the one who is disfigured. My face and my entire body are as folded and pleated and convoluted as a roasted prune. Children point and stare and make forays into the blackened topography of my body. They climb my welts and slide down my scars. I recognize the children and this is what saddens me beyond what I am able to endure, because I was the one who saved them.

These are the children I saved.

I tried to save everyone, but the children, at least, I did save.

At least I did that. It was something.

I spoke to Sirocco directly, I spoke directly into his ear, because we always kept radio contact, he from the plane, and I from a location which of course I cannot disclose, Dr. Reuben, not even to you, though it was not far from here. We kept radio and video contact until almost the end, and when contact was lost . . . well, I do not believe that was Sirocco's doing or his choice.

The most dangerous enemy is the agent you wrongly believe to be on your own side.

While Sirocco and I still had contact, I argued, I negotiated, I made rash and unauthorized offers. I brandished threats and I dangled bribes. This was risky. It is not acceptable, in our line of work, to let personal emotion intrude, and Salamander and I wrestled within ourselves on the matter and I prevailed. I had more substance then. Salamander and I had equal weight. He worked in his sphere, I kept to mine. Operation Black Death was a politically necessary exercise that got out of hand. It was always a gamble, but an intelligent one, and a necessary one, and collateral damage is part of the game. Always. We know that.

Nevertheless.

The official line—Salamander's line—was this: Events set in motion for the best of reasons must play themselves out. They must be allowed to take their course. If you intervene, if you try to throw a wrench in the wheels once the whole idea is in motion, well . . . to put it bluntly: if you get the children out, those children may grow up to destroy you.

That was the way Salamander thought.

But those children are *children,* I protested, and I gave instructions for which no clearance had been received.

Let my children go, I ordered Sirocco, because I did think of them as mine, as my mission; I thought of them as under my care. And from the point where I realized that the children's lives were the only negotiable item, I used the only weapon I had to make Sirocco comply. We have located your own children, I told him.

He had moved them, you see, from Riyadh to Algeria, so that his daughter could attend a French school along with his sons. There will be an accident in this school, I promised him, and many students will be killed. He knew this was something I could arrange. This will come to pass, I promised, if you do not let the children go.

And though Sirocco has a long history of hardening his heart to threat, he did let the children go.

This was a moment of triumph for me, though a short-lived one. In our business, personal hatred of an adversary is a cardinal sin, and we both hated Sirocco, Salamander and I. Our antagonism was passionate, and passion is a major mistake. It clouds judgment.

You will regret this, Salamander predicted.

Possibly, I acknowledged. Probably.

But I went further. I passed up the chain of command a memo detailing all my evidence against Sirocco: the documents, the meeting times, the tapes. Salamander was ordered to hand them over for destruction. It would not be in the interests of national security, he was informed, to pursue. . . .

Salamander, of course, complied.

I, on the other hand, made copies first, so that someday, some year, the truth will be known.

I wear Salamander like a hair shirt. Like an iron lung. But now I want to plead these moments of escape when I defied him. I want to offer them to the children of Flight 64, I want to offer them to my second wife, and to our son L, and to my daughter F, to history, to whatever judges are waiting on the other side of the last abyss. But when I try to explain this to the children in the dream, my words fall from my mouth like hot tar.

Here, where no birds sing, I do not ask for anything unreasonable. My demands are modest, I think, Dr. Reuben, given the price that I have paid. These are my requests:

It is the nights that I wish to avoid. I want you to stop the nights.

On those nights when the torment comes, when nothing else helps, I want continuing access to the basement apartment which is not in my part of the city. Not at all. It is nowhere near the well-groomed tree-shaded streets of Georgetown where I live with E. The building through which one gains access to that dark and desirable basement is quite dissimilar, even violently so, from the graceful town house where I live with my young wife. As you, the ultimate voyeur, inquisitor, lascivious decoder of my journal, as you are very well aware (for remember, I know who you work for, Dr. Reuben. I am always watching you watching, and your reactions are useful and revelatory to me, and are being recorded) . . . as you are aware, I refer to the cramped below-street-level space of the young courtesan, the lovely Anna in leather and chains.

Anna lives in that distant, refreshing, bracingly unsafe northeastern sector of our city. Our lovely city. She lives outside the rings of the satin bus routes and beyond the immaculate white aura of the Capitol, which is not visible from the shabby front porches of her street. She lives on the dark side of the moon. Let me be specific, since I know perfectly well that I am followed and watched (I watch you following me): we are speaking of the derelict rowhouses far out along New York Avenue, sardined between the railway lines and those cavernous potholes where even the purring limousines flowing from and toward the Baltimore-Washington Beltway must, for a harsh moment, touch reality. The lovely Anna, my Nefertiti, is black and croons the blue news of underground, which it is my professional duty to keep beneath sewer caps. We have a contract which both of us understand.

I want Anna to keep that contract.

I want to be inside a different skin. (You could hang up the Salamander one, the burned skin, carefully, like a wedding tuxedo, and someone else could use it secondhand.)

I want you to make that little girl shut up, the one in the blue coat, the one who is bearing down like a vengeful Fury. She does not know, she has no idea, where the fuse she is lighting leads or what dreadful detonations will be sparked. I want you to get the scorch marks off the blue coat.

If you can make that little girl shut up, I will tell everything I know. I will sing like a prisoner on the rack. In any case, I am setting everything down, everything, I swear it; and you alone will hold the code-breaking key.

Is my hour up?

Shall I leave with you the journal of my dreams?

2.

Lecture notes (preliminary): Technology of Modern Warfare and Intelligence Gathering: Introduction

Harvard, Yale, Princeton, MIT, Cal Tech, and all of you, each and every one, Phi Beta Kappa as well. You happy few. You have not only graduated with distinction from our best and brightest institutions, but you have passed through a rigorous vetting system of psychological and security tests. You are clean. You are high-tensile steel. Even so, not all of you will graduate from this course.

You will have noted that there is no standard text. There will be handouts, however, and as you leave the seminar room at the end of this class, please pick up one of these spiral-bound books, to which—please watch as I demonstrate—pages can be added with ease. Ours is a field of knowledge for which new data comes in every month. The chapters of this bible are being written as we speak.

Let us take, for example, an incident that occurred in the Soviet Union in 1979. An accident in Sverdlosk—a leak at the military's microbiology research unit—released anthrax spores into the air.

Result: sixty-eight deaths. What do we learn, what projections can we make from this data?

Think like a terrorist.

Could an anthrax scare occur by malicious planning? Could a small plane—a two-seater, say, trailing GO METS banners—dust anthrax over New York? Could we have anthrax weather? An anthrax mist would be odorless and invisible. It would drift in air currents for great distances before dispersal. Would mass deaths result? What defensive precautions could be taken? Could due preparations be made? On this score, we know too little, though all our evidence does suggest this: only we ourselves, at this point in time, are producing high-octane anthrax of the kind that a terrorist would need, though we are keeping a sharply watchful and deeply nervous eye on Iraq. Later, we will consider in detail all the implications and possible scenarios—offensive and defensive—of bioterrorist anthrax attacks.

So what is our syllabus? You will be expected to know the composition and structure of chemical agents, nerve agents, blister agents, and penetrants. There will be newsreel footage of recent and current deployments. In this field, we learn on the run. We have more data than time to process it. For example: the sarin incident in the Tokyo subway, March 20, 1995, carried out by the Aum Supreme Truth cult. That was rehearsed in outback Australia on a sheep station. It was rehearsed one full year before deployment, and we had evidence, we had satellite photographs: hundreds of acres of sheep carcasses and skeletons. We failed to interpret adequately, we did not make the necessary connections in time, but then Tokyo is not strictly our affair. Within our own borders, I assure you, the Aum Srn Rikyo adherents are being tracked.

There will be lab simulations from time to time.

There will be fieldwork.

We are, if you will pardon the irony of the expression, fortunate in having, at our weekly disposal, a veritable smorgasbord of aggressive operations. Limited spheres of hostility proliferate and the increase in contained war zones is exponential, all of which is ideal for our purposes. You will visit these intimate theaters of belligerence, sometimes literally, and sometimes virtually, by way of our surveillance systems. Both situations will be interactive. The value of information from actual deployments is immense, indeed, it cannot be overstated, since only by such hands-on experiments can we gauge the ripple effect, which is to say, the subsidiary physical and psychological outcomes. Subsidiary physical effects are not restricted to personnel; they may be environmental. A chain reaction in the contextual territory, in turn, devolves into further physical sequences for personnel.

A firestorm, for example.

"All things are on fire," the Buddha said. "The eye is on fire; forms are on fire; impressions received by the eye are on fire."

Siddhārtha Gautama, or the Buddha, as he is generally known, was born in India in the sixth century BC, in the very year that King Nebuchadnezzar died. I like to toy with the fantasy that the Buddha saw in utero the fiery furnace which the Babylonian king had made.

Does it surprise you that this course stretches back to the literatures of the ancients? It should not. Technologies change, but the essence of warfare is, and always has been, psychological. We ignore, therefore, at our peril the artist's insight. It is the artist—it is Homer—who observes and names Achilles' heel. The astute warrior makes use of this information. It was Paris, the great Hector's younger brother, who shot the arrow which slew Achilles through his vulnerable foot.

And who was Paris, that he killed the greatest warrior of all time?

Paris was nothing. Paris was a dreamer, a philanderer, a lover, a coward despised by his own people, the Trojans. Paris was a madman with a stupid cause, the obsessive love of fickle Helen: and it is this, the madness, the cause, which makes him the joker in the pack, the most dangerous figure of all.

We ignore at our peril those who have a cause. No lethal technology will ever exist to stop them. That is why we study the past as well as the future. What, in essence, am I training you for? What is our mission? Our mission is the vigilant observation of, and the *channeling* of, the madness of true believers, and we do this in the interests of global stability for the greater good of all.

It is a high calling.

And so I like to think of the infant Buddha dreaming of those troublesome Jews, those three madmen with a cause, whom Nebuchadnezzar cast in the furnace of biblical lore. Imagine them, Shadrach, Meshach, and Abednego, incandescent. The heat of that furnace, the Book of Daniel tells us, was so great that the men who were stoking the flames were crisped like bacon in their own body fats.

And yet, you will remember, the king's counselors, summoned to report on the rebel deaths, said unto him: "We see men like unto gods, O king, walking in the fire unharmed."

Remember those words, for we too are consumed with a cause.

All that we do has already been dreamed of and foretold. From Sodom and Gomorrah to Nagasaki, we walk with alchemists and gods. We make firestorms from air, and we walk through the fire unharmed. We are Zeus of the thunderbolts, and we are the decontamination and survival experts. We may not yet have learned how to make a heaven on earth—though we strive to keep this planet safe for those who indulge in the idea of heaven—but we are specialists in making that other world spoken of in the Gospel of Mark, a place *where their worm dieth not, and their fire is not quenched.*

This course will train you in both defensive and aggressive postures: in Operation Shadrach and in Operation Nebuchadnezzar; in Operation Redemption and in exercises like Operation Black Death.

The profession to which I have devoted my life, and which you happy few aspire to enter, is as much an art as a science, and more like a highly sophisticated game of chance and skill than either of these. We are chess players who move living pieces on the checkerboard of the world. We are as detached and blameless as gods, but like all creators, we must acknowledge an occupational hazard. Our creatures fascinate us: both those we turn into monsters and those who elude us; especially those who elude us. We become obsessed. We run the risk of envying their lives.

In our profession (*making the world safe for stability,* as we like to say; and sometimes, relishing our own esoteric wit, *making the world safe for moral systems*) it is a given that chaos is all; that order is not only arbitrary but evanescent, and that it is the task of a small strong circle of like-minded people to establish and guard it. Exactly which system of order we sustain—morally and politically speaking—is immaterial. We support the system most likely to stay in place.

Hence our dilemma. I am not speaking here of personal disintegration, or of that futile and panicked attempt to withdraw from the field, though I have lost more friends and colleagues through those two chutes than I care to remember. This is not a field from which one can retire.

Let me repeat that fact, though you already know it or you would not have come this far.

Retirement from this career is not an option. We keep your soul in an escrow account. Take note: of the twenty of you in this room, the crème de la crème who have made the cut and been registered for this course, nine of you will leave us before the end through one of the two trapdoors I just named. The wages of sin in the Intelligence community are erasure. I know you understand this. If you did not, you would not have reached this class.

But there is one other pitfall rarely acknowledged in our field, and it is the one to which I have already alluded: the risk of obsession with the pieces on the board. To put this in comprehensible literary terms: you are in danger of becoming transfixed by Paris and Helen, those idiots, who care nothing for either Greece or Troy, for Hector or Achilles, for the Trojan Horse or all the brilliant engines of war. They go on making love while the battle rages, and you may become obsessed with wanting to make them pay.

This can lead to serious errors in judgment.

Or you can become deranged by Shadrach, Meshach, and Abednego; or by Daniel, by Lions'-Den Daniel, stubborn stupid Daniel in the den. You become obsessed with the ones who cannot be broken or bent.

Watch for this.

Such an obsession will precipitate fatal errors in judgment.

Such an obsession will disqualify you permanently.

Even your code name will be expunged.

And then, finally, there is the perennial day-by-day challenge of your counterpart on the other side, the zealot whose energy you seek to harness, the rogue agent who can match you ruse for ruse, who can out-double-agent you, double-double-cross you, who can lead you into an ever-more-frenzied dance of death. Outwitting him is the secret addiction that will bind you to this career, that will obsess you to the exclusion of everything else in your life. It is he who will destroy you unless you kill him first, but you dare not kill him until he has served the purpose for which you first caught hold of his tiger's mane and embarked on the wild ride with him.

We are gamblers, ladies and gentlemen, in a high-stakes game. Timing is everything.

One further reminder: should we meet, or should you meet one another, in social circumstances, social names will be used.

Within this course, within any sphere of our professional endeavor, only code names are permissible. Never use other than a code name in writing. If any evidence is ever found that links a code name with an identifiable name, you will be expunged.

In the world of shadows you have now entered, you will call me Salamander.

3.

I want you to stop the dreams, Dr. Reuben.

I want the children removed from my dreams.

You see that one, the little one with the dark hair and solemn eyes? His breath is a sweet concoction of curried food, fear, and something resembling cardamom. "What's your name?" I ask him, and he says, "Agit," and I promise him, "Everything's going to be all right, Agit." That was my promise to the little face that filled the screen of my monitor. The way I tell it, the way I feel it, the way the keeping of my promise feels true to me, is the moment when I set him (so to speak) on the escape slide, which is to say when one of Sirocco's thuggish crew gave him a push and he slid into Germany.

But he does not grow up into gratitude.

Would it have been better then, back then, to let him stay with his mother on the plane? That is the question. Would it have been better to let him slip across that line that all must cross in the end? Would it have been better then, back then, instead of thirteen years later, the way it happened, had to happen, as required? This is a grave moral question. Such dreadful accidents are the things I have been called upon to arrange.

No more, I said.

I refuse. Arrangements for Agit Shankara will not be made.

But what difference does it make when there are always others who will handle these matters?

Nevertheless, I refused. I know the price I will pay.

I am racked by what has been required. *I am in blood stepped in so far,* and Macbeth too started out with ordinary clean ambition and extraordinary zeal and simply got out of his depth, because one does not notice it happening, that is the trouble, until the day one takes a step too far and suddenly one is sloshing through blood and there is blood on one's hands and blood on the ceiling and walls and blood in one's breath and in one's thinking and one recognizes Operation Macbeth, or Operation Blood, and yes, yes, *I am stepped in so far, that, should I wade no more, Returning were as tedious as go o'er.*

There is nothing new under the sun, Dr. Reuben.

You see the little girl in the blue coat? I have picked her up a thousand times in my mind. "Don't be afraid," I murmur, because I am in fact a very gentle man, especially and invariably with children. I slide her coat off her shoulders because it will be easier for her that way, and I stroke her cheek when I set her down at the top of the chute. Her cotton dress catches on something, a metal edge, the lever of the escape hatch, and how frantically I work to unhook her clothing and let her slide free (there is so very little time available), and I am left with a swatch of cloth between my fingers. It is white, sprinkled with forget-me-nots, and there is a fragment of smocking at one end: a few ruchings of cotton, some white thread, a smocked rosebud. On the monitor, I watched one of Sirocco's thugs put it in his pocket, and I keep it in a pocket in my mind. It is there at all times.

She, sweet little bird, flies down to the tarmac, unharmed.

And now look. What can it mean, that such innocence should be so harsh and vengeful? She has the face of an angel. Her wings are silken and they glide like languid blue kites, fantastically beautiful, but the tips of the wings are barbed.

I cry back into the dream: *You don't understand. You do not know what riding a tiger is like. If it had not been for me, not one of you would have been saved, not one. Not one single child would have been led off that plane, if not for me.*

But no one hears.

4.

Tocade. I suppose I became as obsessed with him as my daughter did and as Sirocco did and as the woman whose code name is Geneva did, and you can imagine how that particular collision interested us. When two separate people whom we have under surveillance make connection, we assume our suspicions were correct.

You can see that, can't you, Dr. Reuben?

You can understand that the compound unit becomes an object of the most intense scrutiny, and in this case, in their case, the Tocade-Geneva case, there was the additional factor, the X factor, the goad. We—my colleagues in the profession and I—are fascinated by those objects of surveillance who are not suggestible, who have a zero suggestibility index, as we say, who do not succumb to inducement, who do not crack under pressure, who often do not even understand the exceptional nature of their own stubbornness, which may be sheer stupidity, I often think that, or may be a certain kind of obtuseness of comic-book dimensions, like the coyote in the roadrunner cartoons, for example, with his lunatic inability to understand when he has been utterly expunged and flattened and wiped out, and it is precisely his insane thickheadedness which paradoxically makes him impossible to kill. You will understand that is why Tocade and Geneva became an obsession with me, and hence with Sirocco.

With us.

We are as attracted to people like that as we are deeply wary of them. We keep them under close observation. They are dangerous. If they do not already work for someone else, we want them to work for us, and not only because their line of work would make them such ideal covers for our purposes. We are, perhaps, not unlike vampires—I can say this sort of thing to you, Dr. Reuben, because the dark corners of human behavior would be no surprise, would they?—we are not so unlike vampires, I admit it. We have lost our own souls and so we seek out people whose vibrancy reminds us painfully of what we once were, because in this career we all began as idealists, that is our tragedy. We began because we believed—most passionately we believed—in the idea of a free society. We believed that our way of life had to be preserved. We believed that our forms of government must, at all costs, be upheld.

Aye, there's the rub: at all costs. That is where the slide begins. . . .

We slip, we make one small, compromising—yet absolutely necessary—decision, an expedient decision, a complex and difficult and informed choice between the lesser of two evils, and this decision leads, in one month or ten, or in a year, to another slippery but essential decision, and then we find ourselves on loose scree, slipping and sliding and falling and falling and falling. . . .

I often find myself pondering the meteoric descent of Icarus, wondering what he thought of on the way down.

And what about his father, watching? What was going through his father's mind?

And Isabella's, when the plane exploded, what was she thinking? But no, I never think about that, I never think about Isabella, my second wife, whom I believed I had saved. I never think about Icarus or Isabella or any of those doomed fliers—

What . . . ?

Oh.

Tocade and Geneva. Certainly I think about *them,* because I'm drawn to people who—, we all are in this profession, it's a fatal attraction. We lust after them, we feed on them, we want to pass on the kiss of living death. You see, we want to say: you are just like us after all, corruptible. You can be bought; or if you cannot be bought, you can be broken. You can be brought to acknowledge that multiple compromises—even shady ones, even ones that in ordinary circumstances you would find abhorrent—are the *sine qua non* of a nation's good.

You want me to recall the moment when I would say this obsession began? Let me see . . . with a photograph, I suppose, a photograph of the man and my daughter in a bistro because of course I had to keep them under surveillance for my daughter's own protection as well as mine, and for the good of the nation. For global peace, in fact, because you understand, I'm sure, that Françoise and her mother were flashpoints, Achilles' heels—you see the risk?—they could be used for blackmail, they never fully understood, I believe, the extent to which I worried about them. . . .

So I showed her the photograph and Françoise said, "You can't have him, Papa. I won't let you. He's mine."

"Where did you find him?"

"I'm not going to tell you," she said. "I'm not going to tell you anything about him. I want you to leave us alone."

"My dear," I said, stroking her hand. I was very, very fond of her, very proud of her beauty. "You know how futile that is. I already know his place and date of birth, his military service record, his reading habits, and his medical record, for which reason let me strongly advise you to take proper protection during sex."

"I hate you, Papa," she said.

She didn't hate me, of course. Not then. Not until after I saved her life, after which she *knew.* . . . But earlier, before all that, she didn't hate me. For one thing, she cared too much about her allowance and her little *atelier* in the seventh, but because she was in love in that desperate intemperate way—that way in which one is only in love once in a lifetime—because of this, I decided to sound him out myself.

"Monsieur Charron," I said, presenting my card at the Paris Book Fair. "Mather Hawkins of Trident Books, a small literary press. We share—"

What?

Oh. Yes, you make an interesting point, Dr. Reuben. Something there is that doesn't love erasure. There's some core of identity that insists on declaring itself, even when aliases and codes are a way of life. So. Yes. Mather Hawkins.

"Mather Hawkins," I said. "We share an interest in African and East European writers."

"Yes?" he said, studying my card. "I haven't heard of you."

"We're a high-literary-end operation, very small, and we work out of New Haven, not New York." He was a nobody himself then, a mere peon at one of the big houses, but someone to watch, people said, *une affaire à suivre,* tough and brilliant, *un stratège ténébreux,* a voracious and encyclopedic reader, and an attentive one, with a knack for spotting future literary success. This was long before the creation of his own small but brilliant publishing house, Editions du Double, but already that was what people in the book trade were saying. He had a lean and hungry look that excited me. I can use people who have that look.

"I thought we might be of use to each other," I said. We were speaking in French, you understand. His English is so-so; I made my French sound merely adequate, my accent deliberately poor.

He raised one eyebrow. "Really?" he said, and I asked him, "May I buy you a drink?" and he said, "Why not?" And then over scotch-and-soda at the Brasserie de Cluny, he asked bluntly, "Who's on your publishing list?"

"Drozic, for one," I said, removing an elegant little poetry collection from my briefcase. "As you know, Gallimard publishes him here." I watched him leaf through the book. I was very proud of that production, which I'd had some old Yale classmates put together. I had them do the translation and design a chapbook. My classmates are bibliophiles who keep a hand-set press, a genuine antique, and I had them do a print run of ten copies.

"Beautiful cover," he said appreciatively.

"I've heard that the book as artefact matters to you."

"Where'd you hear that?"

"Oh, on the grapevine. It matters to us too, but to fewer and fewer in the trade, as we both know to our sorrow."

"How big is your print run?" he wanted to know.

"Very small," I said. "Five hundred copies."

"How can you afford paper like this?" he asked, fingering it.

"We have a private backer," I said. "Patron of the arts. This sort of thing is his hobby. And here," I added, taking from my briefcase a novella, an exquisite little thing with matte silk covers, "the Algerian writer Virginie Khalid. Gallimard does her too, as you know."

I remember the way he turned the pages, the way he touched them. He is a man for whom books—books themselves, you understand, the physical objects—are items of erotic interest as well as being repositories of ideas and occasions for stylistic bravura. It pleased me to watch him, it pleased me that my daughter had found him. She has inherited my good taste, I thought. I watched the way Charron caressed the pages with his fingers as he spoke, and I understood why my daughter desired him.

"I'm surprised to learn these writers have English-language publishers," he said. "Even in France, they don't sell. They have very few readers. The cognoscenti, the literati, that's all. And American publishers are notoriously—"

"To our dishonor," I agreed. "But at Trident, we have a small yet distinguished readership, by subscription only." I leaned across the table. "At present, our only conduit to writers such as these is via the French translations. As you know"—and I lifted my eyebrows ruefully—"it's difficult for Americans to get access to certain countries and certain books. We're looking for a contact in Paris who can go to

Prague, for example, or to Budapest, more easily than we can. We want someone French-speaking—"

"You speak French fluently enough," he said, and he was the kind of man whose eyes hold yours and challenge them, he never lowers his gaze, and nor do we, of course, it is the very essence of our training, so I eyeballed him back and I said, "But I'm unmistakably an American speaking French," and he laughed at that.

"You are," he said.

"So you can see," I pointed out, "how this restricts my mobility in Algeria, say, or French Cameroon. You can see how it puts certain areas and contacts off limits. What I want is a scout who can make direct connection with writers in Belgrade or Casablanca or Djibouti, especially with those writers who have to stay . . . in the shadows, shall we say? Even within their own countries."

"We're talking about Muslim writers."

"Well," I said, shrugging. "If that's your mode of categorization. I'd call them African and East European. Does this interest you?"

"I'm listening," he said, and then I produced my little list. "These are writers who've attracted our attention," I told him. "Some are published in French, but none are in English yet."

I remember he turned that X-ray gaze on me again and went straight for the flaw in my pitch. "If your only access is via French translations, how do you know about the ones not yet published in French?" he asked, but I was just as fast, I was equal to him, and I told him that we'd heard about them through scholarly contacts, through specialists in the literatures of Eastern Europe and Africa. Trident's editorial board members were all academics, I told him.

He studied the names for a long time and then he looked at me. "Given what I know about American publishing," he said, "this is a curious list." I raised my eyebrows and waited. "No American publisher would touch these books," he said, and I rushed in with a preemptive comment where angels might well have taken pause.

"Because the writers are political activists, you mean?"

"Of the sort not approved by your State Department," he said.

Well, I thought. So. I've got you on my line, little fish. You know a lot about these writers, it would seem. I leaned across the table, close to him, and spoke low. "You are political, monsieur."

"No," he said impatiently. "I'm not. Or not in any sense that you would mean. Nevertheless, I'm fully aware that no American publisher would touch these writers. They're too prickly. Dissidents within the Communist Bloc, yes, and against socialist African regimes. But they are noted intellectuals who are also critical of the U.S."

"That's our point, you see," I said. "No American publisher would touch them except a small one like ourselves, with private backing."

"And with subscription readers."

"We understand each other," I said.

"Which means," he said with a strange little smile, "that there'll be no trace of your existence in the trade journals. Should I doubt your claims, I mean."

He met my eyes directly, at high voltage, and I eyeballed him back.

"Our subscribers are people like you," I said. "They care about literary style, not politics. They're bibliophiles. They have a passion for the book as objet d'art, and they're willing to pay for rice paper and a hand-set press. We could do business, you and I." And then I baited my hook. "Both our patron and our subscribers are very wealthy indeed. Your expenses would be covered, it goes without saying. But beyond that, remuneration would be generous. Extremely generous, I believe you will find."

"I've been getting the impression," he said, "that you'd be offering substantial inducement. What exactly do you want me to do?"

"Make contact with these authors, write reports on them, get their manuscripts to us. You could scoop Gallimard for the ones who aren't published in France yet. You'd get French rights." My gaze was just as intense as his, and just as focused, because this is where I become excited with the chase, this is when the real thrill of recruiting kicks in. It's an art form, really, and a science. Once I know I've hooked him, I give my prospect some slack, I play him on the line, I pull him toward me, I let him run loose, I feign indifference, I hold the line taut, I reel him in.

Minutes passed, I think, and neither of us broke eye contact by more than a blink because I cannot bear to miss a second at this stage, I have always loved to watch from close up that interval of teetering on the brink—*what's the catch?* the prospect is asking himself; *is this too good to be true? what's going to be demanded of me?*—before capitulation comes. And so I waited patiently for my daughter's lover, the ambitious young publisher, to swallow bait and hook and line and sinker. We can keep this all in the family, I thought.

And then, without lowering his eyes from mine, without blinking, he began to tear my list into little pieces and to drop the confetti in his scotch. "Do you think I'm stupid?" he asked, rising. He poured the scotch over my head.

From that moment, I feared for my daughter and for myself. "*J'ai une tocade pour lui, Papa,*" she had told me, and I could see it. She was crazy about him. And for myself, I felt a nerve fluttering violently behind one eye which I knew to be the warning tic of obsession and should have heeded, but already it was too late.

"If I lost him, Papa," my daughter said, "I'd want to die."

No one dies for love, I assured her, and I did not add—or not, at least, for her ears—but one *can* die from knowing too much and people do die from presuming to think that they can't be broken or bought. I promised myself as I reached for a napkin and brushed the scotch and sodden confetti from my suit: *You will come to regret this, Mr. Charron. You will pay for this.*

I put him down for surveillance, code name Tocade.

He may already work for them, I wrote. *Watch him closely.*

I also gave all the relevant information to Sirocco. *Know him?* I asked. *Does he work for your crowd?*

But Sirocco, as I realized far too late, answered all questions both ways, and he followed Tocade more assiduously than I could have imagined.

5.

Lecture notes: Technology of Modern Warfare and Intelligence Gathering:

Chemical Warfare

The organo-phosphate nerve agents were developed as a more or less accidental offshoot of insecticide research, and our arsenal of superior chemical weaponry has an important deterrent impact. The fear factor alone is a potent negotiating tool. Classical symptoms of nerve agent poisoning are as follows: difficulty in breathing, drooling and excessive sweating, violent vomiting, involuntary defecation and urination, twitching, jerking, staggering, cramps, headache, disorientation, dimness of vision, convulsions, and finally paralysis and death from asphyxiation, generally within minutes after inhalation.

The aim of this lecture on Chemical Warfare is not to outline drills and procedures for survival in a CW environment, nor to rehearse strategies for deployment of such agents, all of which will be dealt with later, but rather to familiarize you with the chemical and physical processes involved in toxicity, detection, and decontamination.

Physical and chemical properties

1. Vapor Pressure. The more volatile a liquid, the more readily will molecules move from the liquid to the gaseous phase, at which point they can enter the body by inhalation and can attack the eyes. Hence, the more volatile a liquid, the more likely a lethal dose can be achieved. The measure of volatility is the vapor pressure, which, for any given substance, increases with temperature.

2. Toxicity. The measure of toxicity expresses the interrelationship of the concentration of vapor with time (i.e., with the duration of exposure to the nerve agent). The same effect can be achieved by short exposure to high concentrations as by longer exposure to lower concentrations.

3. Physiological Action. Agents can be classified by the different effects they achieve: choking agents, nerve agents, blood agents, blister agents, vomiting agents, and tear agents. Agents with relatively mild effects (e.g., blistering, vomiting, temporary blinding) can be used for crowd control and riot control. Agents with stronger effects (incapacitating, lethal) can be deployed in search-and-destroy operations or to render occupied territory safe.

Desirable Features of Chemical Agents for Use in Warfare

1. Toxicity. Agents should be as toxic as required to achieve the desired effect.

2. Stability. Agents must be stable or capable of being stabilized between the time of production and use.

3. Precursors. Agents must be able to be produced from raw materials readily available in the theater of operations, or from precursors (e.g., the innovative use by the U.S. since 1987 of the sarin artillery projectile, in which two precursors of sarin, both nontoxic, are stored in separate canisters and can be transported separately and safely. At the site of operations, when both canisters are inserted into the projectile and fired, the chemicals mix to form the deadly and volatile sarin).

4. Dissemination. Agents must be able to be weaponized for dissemination in concentrations capable of producing the effects desired (e.g., by loading into projectiles or missile warheads for dispersal as vapor cloud, or by spraying from crop dusters).

5. Producibility. If possible, agents should be able to be produced quickly in existing commercial plants (e.g., fertilizer factories).

6. Corrosiveness. Agents should not be corrosive to their storage containers (barrels, shells, missile projectiles).

7. Action Against Protective Systems. If possible, agents should be capable of minimizing the effectiveness of protective equipment worn by the target population.

How Nerve Agents Work

The nervous system coordinates all the functions of the human body. Impulses from the brain are conveyed through the spine and major ganglia (central nervous system) to a network of sensory and activator nerves (peripheral nervous system).

The brain initiates commands via the *sympathetic nerve chain*, which produces epinephrine (adrenaline), and this in turn initiates enzyme action and muscle/tissue movement. The *parasympathetic* nerves work in tandem with the *sympathetic* nerves in a complex machinery of checks and balances. Thus the sympathetic nervous system will accelerate heartbeat when the brain senses danger, and the parasympathetic nervous system will slow it down again when the brain senses that the threat has passed and that increased blood flow is no longer required.

Nerve cells are not directly connected with one another, but they meet at junction points called *synapses*, the body's spark plugs, so to speak, which function as neurotransmitters. Electrochemical impulses leap back and forth from cell to cell.

What nerve agents do, to put it succinctly, is sabotage the neurotransmitter system. The body's infrastructure is destroyed. All messages from brain to body are scrambled.

To put it even more bluntly: the functioning of your body is fucked up.

All codes become unreadable at this point, and meaning vaporizes, and even the meaning of questions grows faint, like a radio signal at the edge of being lost, or like a battery emitting the weak sonic cries that foretell its extinction, and *what are we . . . ? what is it that we . . . ? we hold which truths to be self-evident . . . ?*

. . . and what is this mechanism of which we are part, and which we have enshrined in National Security, as *most likely to effect our safety and happiness?*

Carthage

To Carthage then we come . . .

. . . because all histories of conflict and of espionage return to Carthage. They return to the terrible Roman siege of the ancient city and its most dreadful destruction in 146 BC, over which even the conquering general Scipio wept. He wept for the butchered babies and the elderly hurled into the flames. He turned faint at the slaughter and leaned against his chariot in a swoon and lost the thread of his purpose, so the bards report. He pondered the fall of cities and of empires, he recalled the lamentations of the poets on the fate of Troy and on the demise of the Assyrian and Medean and Persian empires, and the words that Homer gave to Hector came as a cry of anguish from his lips: *The day shall come in which our sacred Troy, and Priam, and the people over whom spear-bearing Priam rules, shall perish all,* and he could not hold back the sobbing that came in gusts from his lips.

And Polybius, beside him, was astonished. *We have won a magnificent victory, O mighty Scipio,* he cried. *We have razed the city of the Barbarian, the city of Hannibal, he who has so ferociously tormented and mocked Eternal Rome these many years. What ails thee? What can these strange words mean? This is a great and glorious moment, Scipio Victor.*

And Scipio seized Polybius by the hand. *This is supposed to be a great and glorious moment, Polybius; and yet I am heavy with foreboding that someday the same fate will befall my own country, my own beloved city of Rome.*

And so I too, Salamander—like Scipio—came by degrees to Carthage, burning, burning, burning . . . and to the true intentions of Sirocco, and to the knowledge of our own stockpiles of nerve agents where the codes became scrambled and all the meanings grew faint, you see, and things became more and more difficult to . . .

and what are we . . . ?

and what is it that we defend at any cost . . . ?

and which truths, exactly, do we hold to be . . . ?

and night after night from the middle of the furnace of Carthage and of Flight 64, Scipio turns to me and he cries: O Salamander, how do we tell a glorious victory from horror?

And he weeps, Dr. Reuben. He weeps.

6.

There are nights when Salamander's need for Anna overwhelms us. I twitch inside the cage of him, I drink scotch to lull his nerves, but all that these delaying tactics achieve is an explosive moment when I am driven to explain in a rush to my wife that I have to meet someone, an urgent matter, a matter pertaining to national security (and this is true; oh, this is absolutely true), but I am not at liberty to say where. My breathing will be ragged. Elizabeth has already schooled herself to show neither sorrow nor surprise—I note this with helpless regret; it is one more thing for which atonement must be made—but she turns on me her large watchful eyes and observes me gravely and simply nods.

"Don't wait up," I say gruffly, to mask his panic (Salamander's panic), and as soon as we have turned the corner, he will call Anna on my cell phone from the car, but the lovely Anna, dark lady, delights in cruelty. She has other clients, she will say. Aziz. Saleem. She uses these names to seduce and to alarm, perhaps she invents them, but it is true, of course, that she is a desirable taker-in and giver-out of information. (What does she pass on about Salamander? Whom does she tell?) I cannot see you for another two hours, she may say. Or she may say three, and in the second before he hears the imperious click and the high-pitched burr of disengagement, Salamander considers whether it might be possible to explain the delicate equilibrium involved, whether this would move her, whether the imminent loss of a regular source of income would matter to her, because it is only by paying in installments that he can keep the larger penalty at bay. He dials her number again and speaks so rapidly that he is scarcely intelligible. If you could understand, Anna, how critical, he says. In three hours, I might not even be still alive—but she hangs up and takes her phone off the hook, and so for two hours, or three, we are in torment and at terrible risk.

Sometimes we handle this fear with arcane gambling rituals. We park on a dark street east of the Capitol, on the border between safety and danger, and close our eyes and count: ten, twenty, one hundred. The rules vary. When we open our eyes, if the first car we see is a white one, it means our own people will get to us before anyone else; if a black car passes, Sirocco's suicide zealots will; if the car is colored, we will never know who or how. Suddenness. That is what we pray for; and the odds are with us there.

It could come from anywhere, from anyone, any day now, or any night. It could come from Anna herself. Salamander thinks that *he* has found *her,* but it could be the other way around.

If the first car that appears before our eyes is a stretch limousine or a hearse, Salamander says to the face in the rearview mirror: *So. It will be you.*

And the face accuses back: *You are the one who's cracking up, Salamander. It will be you, and no one will weep for your going, least of all me.*

Mostly we handle the fear by driving. We drive around the labyrinth of the city and cross its bridges, moving like a falling arrow toward Arlington Cemetery which waits for us like a temptation. So far, we have been able to resist this exit because there are things we must attend to first, there are reparations (pathetic and inadequate though they may be) that must be made to Isabella and to Lowell, to Françoise, to Elizabeth, and to the survivors of Flight 64, and so we turn resolutely south and then swing east and circle the Pentagon and drive back across the Potomac and north and east into the dangerous sections of potholed roads and broken streetlights, the car doors locked because at every red light someone might try the door handle, might smash a window, might push a gun into our face. This fear—specific and manageable—eases our anguish slightly, eases Salamander's frenzy, but it is Anna he needs. When she stands over him in black leather and chains, when she cracks her whip, he tastes, very briefly, absolution.

Of course we are followed. We know we are followed. We understand the risk we have become.

> *For God's sake, let us sit upon the ground*
> *And tell sad stories of the death of kings:*
> *How some have been deposed, some slain in war,*
> *Some haunted by the ghosts they have deposed:*
> *Some poisoned by their wives, some sleeping killed;*
> *All murdered . . .*

Once, in the presence of King Fahd, Salamander had to fight back an almost overpowering urge to recite those lines. He could feel them bubbling up in his throat because the king was telling a raucous sexual joke that involved faithless queens and poisons and bloody rites of accession to certain thrones. Salamander was not alone in the royal presence, needless to say. He was posing as a minor functionary, there to hear and not to be heard, but the Royal House of Saud has a superstitious fear of the murder of kings. They practice various forms of sympathetic magic to forestall fate—public floggings, amputations—but they never feel safe.

"Next to the Jews," Sirocco told Salamander, "King Fahd hates the Palestinians most. I have this direct from his closest advisors."

"And you?" Salamander asked. "Do you hate the Palestinians too?"

"Me?" Sirocco laughed in disdain. "The Jews, the Palestinians, what do I care? I am for myself. Enlightened self-interest, I would say. Those are my politics."

Sirocco accepts large sums of money from assorted close advisors to those in power—I am speaking of power in assorted countries and of assorted political stripes—advisors who entrust him with certain offices and certain tasks. Sirocco demands, in return for this knowledge, even larger sums of money from us.

"King Fahd hates the Palestinians," Sirocco said, "and he fears them, because what they've got is contagious. What they've got is a taste for democracy, for your decadent Western ways"—here Sirocco permitted himself an ironic smile—"and he's afraid the plebs of his kingdom will catch it and then he's done for." He made a slitting motion with his index finger against his throat. "The House of Saud is a pack of cards waiting to collapse, and everyone knows it except the three thousand princes of the House of Saud."

"And you?" Salamander needled. "How will you be affected? You're a Saudi yourself."

"Am I?" Sirocco asked. "Possibly. Not every Saudi is in love with the House of Saud." Then he leaned close and whispered in Salamander's ear: "Of course the three thousand princes also know they are doomed, deep down, but they prefer opulent denial, the king and Crown Prince Abdullah most of all. Which is why they keep a very active finger in the Palestinian pie and why they add Wahhabi pepper once a week."

Salamander has amassed thick dossiers on the Wahhabis, the most extreme of Islamic sects, the most rigidly fundamentalist of all. The members of the Royal House of Saud are Wahhabis, though many exemptions to the stringent Wahhabi code, many behavioral exemptions, and many dispensations, apparently are made for royal blood.

As Sirocco spoke, he let the tip of his index finger draw a line from Salamander's earlobe to his neck. It was like a caress, and a shiver walked across Salamander's grave. "But you can't do a thing with this knowledge, except pay me to exploit it, can you?" Sirocco murmured. He was so close that their cheeks were touching, and he smiled, and for a stunned and disconcerting moment Salamander thought Sirocco was going to kiss him on the lips. "Oil runs the world, and oil most certainly runs Washington, and the Royal House of Saud runs oil,"

Sirocco murmured. His Oxford cadence was always more marked when he talked to Americans. He liked to look down from a high place. He liked to mock. "So, QED, the House of Saud runs Washington." Sirocco laughed softly. "It is a constant source of amusement to me to see how much Washington can be made to take without triggering so much as an official reprimand." And then, bizarrely, he did kiss Salamander, but on the cheek. "So no one in Washington wants to hear your sad stories, do they? No one wants to listen to your inside information predicting the death of kings unless the Saudis do this, or do that. Your people don't want to know about unless."

Well before Salamander's time, before I was shackled to him, back when I was at Yale, we did *Richard II* and I played Bushy, a minor role, but one that now seems to me curiously prophetic, as though our fate is hard-wired into us and the body senses it from the start. Someone just walked over my grave, we used to say, a child's joke to ward off dread when an involuntary shudder passed through us. But I remember, night after night, how I shivered when the guards dragged me onstage with Green, and Bolingbroke thundered: *Bushy and Green, I will not vex your souls, since presently your souls must part your bodies . . .* though perhaps it was a different sort of prescience since the classmate who played Bolingbroke, son of a Long Island banker, moved on to wealth and embezzlement and jail, and now that I think about it, there was something about him, that faint aura of the frat-boy sociopath, that air of well-bred ruthlessness, that reminds me of Sirocco. And I remember that night after night, when Bushy's lines would speak me: *More welcome is the stroke of death to me, than Bolingbroke to England. Lords farewell,* I would feel unaccountably maudlin, tears would well up in my eyes (the New Haven reviewer mentioned this favorably), because there was something in Bushy that cleaved stubbornly to the old order—the oath of loyalty, the idea of an anointed king, fealty to Richard—when he could easily have jumped ship and sailed smoothly into *Henry IV, Part I,* but he would not do it, he could not, he was a true believer, and more welcome was the stroke of death to Bushy . . .

Like Richard, he knew it was on its way.

It is on its way. We can feel it coming the way you can feel winter coming.

It grows like a tumor, this certainty of the end barreling toward us, and I find myself wondering if murder always telegraphs its coming to the nerve systems far in advance of its arrival. I don't think this is too fanciful. The Cree, for example, know when a major storm is coming many days before the meteorologists know. Native Americans, Dr. Reuben, are an esoteric security specialty of mine, and my expertise dates from those earlier times of unrest—how tranquil they seem, how innocent—the days of indigenous sit-ins and peaceful protests, so harmless in retrospect, though at the time we certainly kept our eye on the rise of the radical AIM. What I learned from those tribal elders and young rebel warriors was this: that there are ways of knowing that can fly in low, beneath the radar of rationality. I have a healthy respect for intuition.

You think I'm paranoid, of course, but then you have no idea, not the slightest idea, of how much Salamander knew about you before I called you, and if I were to tell you how much he knew, you would not sleep. A history could be written, should be written, of those who don't sleep. Insomniacs International: a roster of the late and the great and the prescient. Napoleon would get the first chapter. He could not sleep, or would not sleep, or hardly ever, but when he did, he needed only four hours a night, no more, so the history books reveal, implying glandular dysfunction of some sort. I know better. I'm convinced he didn't dare to stop watching. I'm convinced he *knew*. Even when he was a schoolchild in France, an uncouth Corsican, an outcast with his hick accent and his wretched French, even then, he knew that the inevitable fate of the outsider was lodged in the marrow of his bones. In every battlefield triumph, under the pungent smell of cannon smoke and singed horseflesh, he could smell St. Helena on its way. *My thoughts dwell on death,* he wrote in his diary when he was twelve years old—he was a desolate child in the Military Academy in Brienne—*no doubt because I see no place for myself in this world*.

And yet *there* was a man who dared his own fate and grabbed it by the lapels and stared it full in the face and defied it.

And how did he (both of him: the emperor and the one who always knew he was doomed) how did he try to keep an ignominious death at bay?

By recourse to the same old fool's gold we all so stupidly bank on. Foreknowledge. Spies. Informers. He had an intelligence system to die for, the most intricate ever evolved by a ruling clique. Fouché, the head of his secret police, used to boast in the taverns that no one could speak two words without Napoleon hearing, not at table, not in bed, not in salon or brothel, not in my lady's chamber nor in the arms of a man's own wife. If you break gas in your privy, Fouché said, one of my men will be stationed downwind and will smell it.

And that's what undid Napoleon in the end: his own intelligence network and the distrust it bred.

Here's a conundrum: the better you train a secret agent, the less he will trust his peers; hence, as a logical consequence, the less able he is to work in tandem with anyone else, and the more likely he is—unintentionally—to sabotage the entire intricate project of the desperate need to know all.

And then there's this: knowing too much can get you killed.

I could try to paint the scene when I understood all this at a visceral level, Dr. Reuben. I could describe the dinner where the moment of unraveling began. Salamander and Sirocco were to meet in a restaurant in Paris, and this was to signal *go* for Operation Black Death. What a triumph Black Death was going to be. That's what we thought. The planning, the undercover work, the funding, there's nothing I can fault. It was going to be a major Intelligence coup. I expected to make a dozen arrests, key figures, Sirocco had smoked them all out, we'd paid him a fortune, we'd given him enough arms and nerve gas to kill half the Soviets in Afghanistan (because he was a mercenary, basically; he had a finger in plenty of pies), and then, on the very eve of the operation, on my way to the restaurant, I received news from my own intelligence network, which was every bit as fine as Napoleon's, and the message was this: *Double-cross. Abort Black Death.*

I had my own man, under cover, on Sirocco's team, and he was the one who sent word. He paid a high price. The code name of my undercover man was Khalid. Before I even got to the restaurant, a second message reached me. Khalid's throat had been cut.

Of course, I secretly taped our meeting in the restaurant. No doubt Sirocco did too. Here's my own transcription and commentary.

"You lied," Salamander says to Sirocco. He says it quietly and civilly (though his voice is intense) because they are in one of the most elegant restaurants in Paris. Waiters hover around them, discreet. "You were planning to double-cross me," Salamander says. "I have proof. Operation Black Death is aborted. I'm calling it off."

Sirocco smiles and signals the sommelier. "I'm afraid you're too late," he says. "Preparations are under way as we speak. I've moved Black Death forward."

Salamander presses a button on the radio transmitter in his pocket. "We had an agreement," he says, his voice low. "A sting operation. Let me remind you of the terms of our deal. No passenger deaths. You lure the entire Paris cell into the operation, we get them, or our sharpshooters do. Those that live, we keep for interrogation. We let you escape. And absolutely no passenger deaths, that was agreed."

"Monsieur," Sirocco says to the wine steward, though without shifting his gaze from Salamander. "Another bottle, if you please. My business partner and I are celebrating a new level of understanding of our deal."

"Information has come to me," Salamander says, and in spite of a lifetime of practiced disassociation, his voice trembles. "I have irrefutable information that you have other intentions. You are planning to double-cross me. Therefore the operation is now aborted. Charles de Gaulle Airport and the French police have been put on high security alert. You will contact your hirelings immediately, or I regret to tell you that the French police will suddenly become aware of the counterfeit nature of your *carte de séjour*. You will be arrested before midnight."

"Ah, thank you, monsieur," Sirocco says to the sommelier, though he takes the bottle from the wine steward's hands and pours wine for Salamander and himself. "I think you have not fully understood our situation, my friend." He touches Salamander's glass with his own. "Certain people with whom we are both working (indirectly, in your case, but your partners nevertheless) would like to see a lot of Americans, especially American Jews, die all at once, and they are willing to pay a great deal of money to make this happen."

"Willing to pay this money to you, for example," Salamander snaps.

"Of course to me. How else can I gather the intelligence you want?"

"You want me to outbid them. You are auctioning lives."

"I'm not asking you to outbid them. I am trying to explain realpolitik. I had to select a certain kind of flight, with a certain kind of passenger list. There's no other way to lure the people you want into your trap. It's true, you said the passengers must not die, but our partners whom we shall not name say they must. Why? Because that is the point of the exercise, as far as our partners are concerned. Not because they care much one way or the other about individual Jews, you understand, but because they want to goad Israel past endurance. This is their strategy: to push Israel to retaliate violently, and of course we know that Israel will oblige. If not this time, then next time, after a little escalation. It's a very simple equation. You know it and I know it. All our governments know it. So please spare me your righteous surprise."

Salamander is breathing rapidly. "At least," he says coldly, "it is now clear where your priorities lie."

"Please," Sirocco says. "Can we skip the sanctimonious hypocrisy? The simplistic nature of American thinking is too tedious for words.

And let's not be disingenuous about the advantages to your government of a little redrafting of the plans. Believe me, martyrs are an ace up any sleeve."

"A contract means nothing to you."

"The desert wind bloweth where it listeth." Sirocco smiles. "Incidents distressing to many of your countrymen (though not to all), and to Israel, will happen many times in the months and years ahead, whether or not you are leaning over the shoulders of the perpetrators permitting this, permitting that, saying, 'That is enough; stop here.'

"You knew this perfectly well, whatever you wish to pretend with your hand held over your heart. Our agreement was to *channel* the obsession of the true believers, to reveal to you the names, the faces, the modus operandi of what you call a terrorist cell. How you catch them is strictly your affair.

"And please, spare me the complaining. We do the dirty work and take all the risks while you sit back in your armchair and watch on surveillance monitors, free to tut-tut and wring your hands if things go wrong. I've even written your speech for you, Salamander. *These barbaric acts will not go unpunished . . . !*"

Sirocco laughs and pours himself more wine. "You can't ride a whirlwind," he says. "It's not so easy. You can't order it to stop just like that." He snaps his fingers. "No more than I can. I use the energy of the zealots, but I don't control them. I can't. They are the jokers in the pack. You understand?"

"I understand I have been betrayed."

"Betrayed!" Sirocco seems genuinely amused. "That is wonderful. That you should speak of betrayal."

"It is almost interesting," Salamander says coldly, "in an anthropological way, to observe a monster close up."

Sirocco leans across the table and whispers, "It's too late to stop. Weapons are already being loaded. The baggage handlers, the maintenance crew are our men. The target flight will be hijacked whether

I am arrested or not." He smiles. "I won't tell you which flight. I don't want to spoil the surprise. But if I'm not able to be on the plane myself, as planned, I cannot vouch for the relatively moderate outcome I would seek."

"I already know what outcome you intend. It is not moderate."

"Imperfect intelligence, my friend. *Relatively* moderate, I said. I wonder if even you understand how ugly things could get if I'm not there. There are fast deaths and slow deaths, there are deaths by ritual mutilation, there are others that linger much longer in the minds of those who are left behind."

That was when Salamander knew that he was dealing with evil, but even then, Dr. Reuben, even then I could not have predicted the degree to which Sirocco took pleasure from personal revenge. I would not have believed the extent of the trouble he went to to give me pain. To give Salamander pain.

Salamander was a babe in the woods. But to return to the transcript.

"Within an hour," Salamander says curtly, "the French police will have photographs, documents—"

"Please. Don't agitate yourself." Sirocco smiles. He has a way of smiling that makes Salamander think of Eichmann and of Goebbels. "I know you know that I have been living with your daughter," Sirocco says, "when I am not otherwise engaged." He spreads his open palms toward Salamander and smiles. "What can I say? Women throw themselves at me. They are willing to do anything I ask, no matter how painful or bizarre." He takes a photograph from his wallet and shows it. Salamander covers his eyes and turns away. "What you don't know, perhaps—because I'm aware that there is some friction between you; I'm aware your daughter does not always take you into her confidence; I'm aware that she doesn't appreciate your protective surveillance—

so perhaps you don't know that your daughter has a ticket for the very flight that I've chosen to win our private little lottery. I bought it for her myself."

There is a bodily sensation that can only be equated with going down on an elevator whose cables have snapped. The freefall leaves Salamander faint. Sirocco leans across the table. "But perhaps if I'm not arrested," he says, "she could be persuaded not to get on the plane."

Check. But not checkmate.

Salamander steadies himself against the table. There is a smell of sulphur and of failure in the air. They will put me out to pasture, he knows.

"Monsieur." Sirocco signals a waiter, smiling. "I think perhaps we had a faulty glass. My companion has had a small accident."

Salamander stares at the flood of red wine on the white linen cloth and at the blood in his palm. He still holds the snapped stem of the wineglass in his hand. "All right," he says. "I concede this round. And you may pass on the assurance that we will agree to a further increase in the price of oil, but no deaths."

"This I am not at liberty to guarantee," Sirocco says, "but you may call your daughter and tell her to cancel her flight." He smiles. "Honor among thieves, as you might say."

"If there are deaths," Salamander promises, "I will disable you. I will reveal who is bankrolling you."

"But *you* are bankrolling me. The sarin canisters and the protective clothing are stamped USAF."

"For use against the Russians in Afghanistan. That route will get you nowhere, you will find."

"Get us nowhere?" Sirocco smiles. "No questions in Congress? No investigations into why you rob Peter to pay Paul?"

"Documentation will be found," Salamander promises, "to show you are biting the hand that has fed you. You'll be finished in Washington."

"How naive you are," Sirocco says. "I must say, it's been greater than I expected, the pleasure of working with you. The personal aspect, I mean. I've enjoyed making this personal. You'll see how I've worked at that aspect of the whole operation, and I do promise to keep you informed. I've set up a box seat for you, as it were, and I assure you, you'll have a grandstand view of what's going on."

"If there are any deaths, you'll be finished. I swear to you, so help me God."

"I'm assuming I will not be arrested today"—Sirocco smiles—"and, interesting though this discussion is, I'm afraid I must go. Some people are waiting for me." At the door, he turns and comes back to the table and says casually, loudly enough for several other tables to hear, "Oh, I forgot to tell you. I collect on forfeits. Always. Every time." He is smiling as he leaves.

The only words that would come to me were: *Lords farewell.*

And then I called Françoise and left a message on her answering machine. "Françoise? It's Papa. I'm in Europe. I'm not at liberty to say where."

I counted two beats. I was unnerved by the thought of her expression as she played back the tape. "I know you have a ticket for New York. On no account, Françoise, must you board that flight. This is a matter of life and death, do you understand? Don't board that flight."

I hung up, and then I called the French police. I urged extra precaution, especially for all flights to New York. Screen the baggage handlers, I said. Screen the maintenance crews. I was confident I could shut the operation down. I did what I could—every passenger was security-checked and all luggage was closely scrutinized—but Sirocco outmaneuvered me. Airport Security itself was in his pocket. The ground crew and the loading crew, and even two of the airport police, had been replaced by Sirocco's men. All this I learned months later, from an internal security report. The results of the report—*in the interests of national security*—were never made public.

Salamander did what he could.

He was too late. He was out-double-crossed.

He lost his daughter. After the hijacking, he knew she knew and he knew the knowledge broke her. She would not speak to him again. She disappeared.

Even so, I played my trump card and saved the children. Later, I fought for the hostages and lost, but I refused to destroy the evidence of that struggle. I handed over the videotapes, as ordered, but I made secret copies of those tapes, and I hid them in burglar-proof ways, and I have made arrangements to send them forward through time.

I am surrendering my life, in the end, to preserve the tapes.

I know that what will be required is my life.

This is what Salamander and I would like our tombstone to say, Dr. Reuben:

In extremity, we yet achieved two good things: we saved the children; and we saved the tapes.

7.

Lecture Notes: Decontamination and Individual Protective Equipment (IPE) in Chemical Warfare

Respiratory Protection

You are breathing and you think nothing of it.

Now, close your eyes. Breathe. Think about it.

The act of breathing transfers oxygen from the atmosphere into red blood cells. At the same time, carbon dioxide is expelled from your blood. Most of the time, your breathing is regulated by the CO_2 level in your arteries, and oxygen only becomes a regulatory factor when it is missing: that is, when its concentration in your breathing environment plummets.

Normal breathing consists of an active inhalation followed by a passive exhalation. Any system requiring forced exhalation will rapidly produce discomfort and fatigue. Consequently any device giving respiratory protection against chemical agents must minimize the difficulty of breathing out.

The typical gas mask consists of a hood that contains fiber screens and charcoal filters, an exhalation valve, and eye goggles. The filter pouches are in the cheeks of the mask. When the wearer inhales, air is drawn through the filters and thus is stripped of contaminators, but oxygen is not added to the air. If extra oxygen becomes essential (as it does with prolonged exposure to contaminated air), the hood must be connected to a portable oxygen tank.

Although it is possible to design filters that will neutralize almost any toxic agent, it is impossible to combine in one mask protection against *all* toxic substances. Gas masks, it should hardly be necessary to say, are effective only against agents that are vapors or true gases. Mustard gas, for example, which is dispersed as a liquid, attacks via the skin, and consequently protective clothing must be worn in addition to masks.

The C4 mask is a NATO standard. It has a bromobutyl rubber face piece and the goggles provide good vision and are scratch-resistant. Air flow is designed to minimize fogging. There is also a drinking tube and speech transmitters, though the distortions to speech, hearing, and peripheral vision can rapidly cause acute emotional distress.

This distress is significant.

This distress is a secondary weapon and its combat potential—with implications for both aggression and defense—should not be overlooked. Those with vivid imaginations are at greatest and most immediate risk. Conversely, with proper training, this same proclivity of the imagination to conjure up airy nothings can be the most potent indicator of those who will survive.

Protection of Skin

Evaporation causes cooling. The body is cooled by the evaporation of sweat, but if moisture on the skin cannot evaporate, the body will respond by increasing the rate of sweating. Typically, while wearing IPE, an individual can lose from one to two quarts per hour. This results in sodden clothing next to the body and a net fluid loss. Consequently, personnel wearing IPE must drink at regular intervals.

The standard protective coverall is designed to provide protection for twenty-four hours in a toxic environment. In the absence of liquid contaminants, it may be used for up to twenty-one days against vapor hazards, though heavy sweating can reduce this time.

Protective gloves keep toxic agents from entering body via hands for twenty-four hours though they limit dexterity. If possible, gloves should be removed (in a protected environment) for thirty minutes every eight hours to allow dissipation of moisture. The gloves are made of butyl rubber.

Protective overboots are made of neoprene rubber with fabric on the inside and are designed for wear over combat boots. They give protection for twenty-four hours.

Subsidiary Problems Related to Wearing of IPE

1. Thermal Stress.

Energy generated by activity must be dissipated from the body or the body temperature will rise. Such dissipation is normally achieved by the evaporation of sweat. The face accounts for twenty percent of body heat loss. The hands account for a further fifteen percent. The impact of wearing gas mask and protective gloves on the body's heat budget can now be seen. Body temperatures skyrocket; endurance levels fall.

Personnel engaged in strenuous physical activity will experience fainting spells and unconsciousness after an average of 5.2 hours in combat clothing; 5 hours if wearing IPE but not gas mask; and after 4.1 hours if wearing full IPE and mask.

2. Psychological.

Many wearers—especially civilians during emergency situations—experience such acute claustrophobia inside a gas mask that involuntary vomiting occurs. Unless the vomit is instantly removed (by rapid change of mask, or by rapid removal of vomit using scooping movement of the hand), asphyxiation will result.

Other implications of wearing IPE are more subtle, and the

degree of psychological distress will depend on the individual. The sense of isolation can be profound and disorienting. Everyone looks the same; wearers cannot detect the gender or race of other wearers; a child cannot tell his father from his mother; and this absence of standard signifiers eventually causes dizziness, confusion of mental processes, and inability to concentrate. Communication is difficult and is distorted. Peripheral vision is lost. Performance of bodily functions (eating, drinking, urination, defecation) is problematic and this has a major impact on the wearer's ability to sustain resistance to the toxic environment.

It should be clear that if personnel are *at risk* in an environment where CW agents have been deployed, survival times are short unless the area can be decontaminated within twenty-four hours, or unless weather conditions result in dispersal of toxic elements. (CW agents are extremely meteorologically sensitive.) Proper training and drills in psychological survival techniques will be paramount.

When personnel are involved in the *deployment* of CW agents, it is obviously advantageous to use both gaseous and liquid agents (thus requiring target population to wear full IPE clothing) and to maintain their presence in the atmosphere for more than twenty-four hours. Psychological attrition of the target population will augment the biochemical count.

Instructions for Use of Personalized Survival Weapon (Classified)

Each of you has been issued a personalized survival weapon, top secret, to be deployed at the limits of IPE protection in CW zones. Please prepare yourselves for the most crucial piece of classified information you will ever receive: instructions for use. Be attentive.

Please tattoo the routines on your memory.

Code name: Operation Shadrach.

Chemical-physiological principle: the body can be fooled by the mind.

Do with this secret what you will. When *in extremis,* close eyes, open mind, step out into the uncharted abysses of your own memory and imagination, open parachute, create a floating world, explore its tunnels and byways, stay there until All Clear signal sounds.

Prisoners have evolved rarefied forms of this weapon. Some have survived solitary confinement—years of it; more than was once believed possible—by mentally walking from New York to Los Angeles on B roads; or by retracing a Himalayan climb, rock by rock and rappel by rappel; or by re-visioning every house and every garden on their childhood block; or by restaging every Shakespearean play they ever saw. A man trapped under a steel girder, his arm severed, endured pain and blood loss until rescue by recalling the perfumes of every girl he had taken to bed.

To be recent and specific as this relates to terrorism: French journalist Jean-Paul Kauffmann, captured by Islamic zealots in Beirut, survived three years of solitary confinement, in blindfold and chains, by mentally recalling the aromas of Bordeaux wines. He smelled and tasted each one. He recalled the restaurant, the year, the dinner, the menu, the woman across the table from himself.

Daniel was thrown to lions. Millennia before digital editing, he saw them as pups; golden retrievers, perhaps; or Labradors—this is my belief; this is what his rabbinic training with its rigors of thought made possible—and the lions licked his hand and did no harm. Shadrach, Meshach, and Abednego, whom I have mentioned in my lectures before, smoothed the flames of Nebuchadnezzar's furnace like soothing ointment on their skins. The Buddha gentled a stampeding elephant by thinking Nirvana. Christ walked on water, which is not necessarily a miracle, but is rather a function of the well-trained mind, since Holy Men in India continue to stroll on hot coals and their bare feet are not so much as singed.

Oh, certainly, my fellow upholders of the principles we hold most dear, certainly there are more things in heaven and earth than are dreamed of in your average understanding of what a man or a woman can survive, and in this career that you have chosen, in this career which has chosen you, it is your mandate and your duty to survive; to survive not only the horrors to which the course of duty may subject you, but the horrors you may be called upon to inflict.

To return to the subject in hand: in situations of chemical warfare that outlast the protective equipment, I can assure you (by historical precedent, by the abiding principles of literature and art, and by personal experience in the field) that statistics signify nothing.

Consider Boccaccio.

In 1348, as he tells us, the plague came to Florence and killed off one-third of the populace in months. *Between March and the following July,* Boccaccio wrote, *what with the virulence of that pestiferous sickness and the number of sick folk ill-tended or forsaken in their need . . . it is believed for certain that upward of a hundred thousand human beings perished within the walls of the city. . . .*

At night, corpses were thrown from the windows and the death carts bore them to mass graves. Boccaccio, thirty-five years old, lost his father, his stepmother, and a host of peers and friends. *Reflecting on so many miseries makes me melancholy,* he wrote, and therefore he curled up into himself and took refuge from despair, and it came to pass, in the venerable church of Santa Maria Novella, he overheard Pampinea as she spoke to her circle of close friends: "*My dear ladies,*" she said, "*each of us is in fear for her life. If we go forth from here, we see the dead and the dying in the streets. Therefore what are we doing here? What are we waiting for? What are we dreaming about? Let us flee the city and take refuge in the country and build a safe house of stories in which to hide and shelter ourselves,*" and they all gave inner and urgent assent, and so ten young aristocrats (plus the eavesdropping Giovanni Boccaccio, the father creator, the voyeur, the devoutly penitent purveyor of bawdy tales), all eleven left the horror of the city behind them and traveled up into the high places of the imagination where Boccaccio wrote the *Decameron* and lived to tell the history of surviving the plague.

Plagues come and they go. They mutate and return in different form. Camus, covertly publishing for the Resistance and running interference with Nazi blight, knew this. He might not have specifically foreseen hijackings, sarin, and mustard gas, but he knew the rodents and their toxins would reappear. And, like his narrator, Dr. Rieux, *he knew that the tale he had to tell could not be one of a final victory. It could be only the record of what had had to be done, and what assuredly would have to be done again in the never-ending fight against terror . . . by all who, while unable to be saints but refusing to bow down to pestilences, strive their utmost to be healers. He knew . . . that the plague bacillus never dies or disappears for good; that it can lie dormant for years and years. . . .*

But it *will* return, my fellow keepers of the public safety. It will return.

Are you surprised that I expect you to know Boccaccio and Camus in this class? That I expect you to familiarize yourself with their work? That I expect you to *memorize* them? Let me tell you something: in the course of this career, you will remember many things you wish you could forget. You will find immeasurable comfort in reciting the words of other men in the effort to crowd unwanted words offstage.

Let me explain one further thing.

Do you think it was the plague—the plague itself—that Boccaccio, Defoe, and Camus all sought, with such frantic scribbling, to keep at bay? Were their stories to ward off the buboes, the excruciating swellings of the lymphic nodes, the bright ring of anthrax scabs that so many medieval and seventeenth century parish registers describe?

No. I can attest to this: no.

What is the brief agony of the body that comes with its own anesthetic of shock? It is nothing. Believe me, Boccaccio, Defoe, and Camus were haunted by their own nightmares, by their own betrayals, and by their dead. Like the Ancient Mariner, they were condemned to tell the stories of those who haunted them as an act of propitiation, to keep their Furies at bay.

The dead never stop telling us stories.

Those whom we have betrayed, no matter how pure our intent, how scrupulous our reasons, they tell their tales to us night after night, which is why some of you will lose all capacity to sleep.

8.

There is not much time left, Dr. Reuben. I know that.

I have selected you as the midwife, so to speak, to deliver something to my son. This is not because I trust you. It is not because I *don't* trust you, I hasten to add, but I know what I'm up against. I know you are watched and followed. I know your files on me will probably disappear. This is not without precedent in recent political history, is it? the theft of psychiatric files. For this reason, even to you, I cannot speak frankly, but I must speak passionately.

I have only this one thing of value to leave behind—the truth.

All my planning, including my offering myself up to you as a patient, is geared toward this single end: the preservation of what I am leaving behind.

Truth will out, I believe that, even though not one living person can be trusted as its bearer. You will think my lack of trust is part of my condition, and it *is* part of my condition, of course, but my condition is not one that is listed in your *Dictionary of Mental Disorders*. I see by the twitch of a nerve at the edge of your mouth that you are convinced otherwise. I let that go. I can't trust you. Nevertheless, I believe you will be sufficiently constrained by professional and ethical requirements to carry out my last will and testament to the letter.

I want you to hand-deliver to my son the key to a locker. This locker will contain a certain package.

I do not have much time.

Tonight, I will need to see Anna, and then—

Have you any conception, Dr. Reuben, of the physical pain of moral torment?

It needs leeches, Dr. Reuben. It needs to be bled. It needs flogging. . . .

I'm sorry, what was I . . . ?

There are certain things, Dr. Reuben, that once seen. . . .

Scipio wept at Carthage, did you know?

I can put my finger, now, on the moment where I should have . . . on the crucial moment. But the trouble is, we don't recognize that moment until it is past. I should have stood there with Nimrod. That should have been the turning point. *Here I stand,* I should have said, *against unacceptable risks, against unconscionable collateral damage.* But if I had said that then, I'd be where Nimrod is now.

Would we have achieved anything?

Could anyone have stopped Sirocco? Can anyone stop him?

And then there is the major problem of the evidence that cannot be put in code for its own protection. How can I keep the videotapes safe? I've been obsessed with this question. We do not yet know how to code such things. We know how to interfere with transmission, how to scramble signals . . . but we don't know how to preserve them. We don't know how to damage-proof a tape.

The originals I had to surrender thirteen years ago, but the copies that I made, the illegal copies. . . .

What a poor frail vessel nylon tape is, magnetic tape, when what I need is a Rosetta Stone to go through time.

Let me ask you something, Dr. Reuben.

Have you ever worn . . . ? No, of course not. Of course you have not. But I make the recruits wear the masks and decontamination suits for six hours straight while they unload heavy equipment, not that six hours will give us any reliable gauge of anything much, but that's the maximum permitted in training routine. Wipes out half of them, and I'm speaking of the cream of the crop, perfect physical and mental specimens. Hallucinations, drowning in their own sweat and vomit. It's like being wrapped alive in your shroud.

It's a . . . it's not a fate that. . . .

Needs to be bled. Needs flogging.

I will need to see Anna tonight.

Are you taping me, Dr. Reuben? If you're taping me, I want to say this for the record: Sirocco is not the worst of it. The worst is *seeing* and not intervening to *stop*. The worst is that this happened under hi-tech surveillance. The worst is those who watched and monitored and voted: *acceptable collateral damage.*

After certain kinds of knowledge, it is not possible to. . . .

Will you give me your word?

I don't know how to impress on you the *importance,* given that I am automatically tongue-tied, given that certain words, if I were merely to say them, would damage the chances of the evidence being preserved. If there is a single word that I wish I could chisel into stone, it is *hostages,* but I dare not say it. I dare not risk saying it.

I think, Dr. Reuben, that this will be the last time I see you.

I'm too big a risk now, and I have to be erased. I know the rules, and I've always played by them until now.

I know I don't have much time.

I want to give you this key. Will you give me your word and your hand in return?

Book VI

IN THE MARSH

The name of the slough was Despond.

—JOHN BUNYAN, **PILGRIM'S PROGRESS**

For what is water . . . but a liquid form of Nothing? And what are the Fens . . . but a landscape which, of all landscapes, most approximates to Nothing? . . . Every Fenman suffers now and then the illusion that the land he walks over is not there. . . .

—GRAHAM SWIFT, **WATERLAND**

1.

On the dock of the Saltmarsh Motel, under cover of dark, Samantha and Lowell half push, half pull the boat through sea grass and mud. "We'll pay cash," Samantha says. "That way, we leave no trail."

"Have we got enough?"

Between them, they have fifty-seven dollars.

"Should be plenty," Sam says, "for off-season. There won't be anyone else here."

"Forty-nine ninety-five," the proprietor says. "Cash on the barrel, half price, and no questions asked. Never get no one this time of year."

"We got lost in the marsh," Sam says. "Staying up the bay from here."

The proprietor is an old leather-faced fisherman who hires himself out to guests as an oystering guide in the season. "Marsh is tricky," he admits. "You can't go messin' around with 'er, you gotta know 'er."

"I figure we'll find our way out of the channels by daylight," Sam says. "Do you have a room with a VCR?"

"All our rooms got VCRs. And digital. Got our own video library over there." He jerks his thumb at two rows of shelves beneath the window. "You seen *Air Force One*? No? Seen it six times, my personal pick. Extra two bucks to rent."

"Thanks. We'll take your recommendation." Sam hands him the extra two dollars and takes *Air Force One* from the video rack.

The proprietor gives her a key attached to a plastic card. "Room 8," he says. "To the left when you go out the door."

In Room 8, they draw the curtains. Lowell slides the backpack from his shoulders and Sam sees that the drawstring bag inside it is made from an old pillowcase, a child's pillowcase, sprinkled with castles and knights-in-armor and maidens with long tresses who watch from towers.

There are six tapes, numbered in black felt marker from one through six. When they open Cassette Number One, they find a thick letter inside it, instead of a tape.

"That's my father's handwriting," Lowell says.

2.

The Confessions of Salamander

> *In the middle of the journey of my life,*
> *I came to myself in a dark wood,*
> *Where the straight way was wholly lost and gone.*

Like Dante, I have traveled down to a terrible place, the pit of nightmare, but my guide was not Virgil. I had no guide. The wood is blacker than dark, and more dense. It is impenetrable. Worse than that: no footstep is safe because the ground is soft and gives way. Funnels of quicksand wait like wet-lipped mouths.

There was—there is—no way out.

All I can do is hold up a dim lantern to show you where I have been. In all fairness I should also caution you not to look. I should urge you to draw back from this dread quagmire. Sucking foulness will cling to you. This is the worst journey you will take.

I am condemned to be your tour guide. We will travel down through the circles of Sirocco's inferno as he choreographed them. Choreographed? Choreographed and recorded. That is the sort of sick thing Sirocco does. He is a gifted designer of the custom-made hell and he enjoys a visual record of his power. I do not doubt that he watches and rewatches his own tapes. He likes to imagine us watching.

No one should underestimate the devious intelligence of Sirocco. I am, from time to time, momentarily flattered that he went to such lengths, to such extraordinarily *personal* lengths, in maneuvering certain people onto his chosen flight and into the hostage bunker: my wife, my daughter, the man my daughter loved (a man whom Sirocco saw, inevitably, as a sexual rival; a man, therefore, whom it gave him great pleasure to smash).

Did I too not fantasize about punishing my wife Isabella?

Did I not wish to make Charron pay for his stubborn defiance and pride?

Did I not seek to control—lest she be in danger; lest she be a flashpoint of risk—the life of my resentful and prickly daughter who, at the eleventh hour, was saved for breakdown and psychic collapse?

Did I not place all three under surveillance?

I plead guilty.

Such is the malevolent brilliance of Sirocco, who knows how to add guilt and complicity to grief. He could flay a human being alive with the utmost gentleness and finesse. *Today I saw a man flayed,* you might say. *You would not believe how it altered his appearance for the worse,* and yet he reported to his superiors, he filed his reports, he ate lunch and dinner and went to bed and slept and rose and went to his office for many years and married again and kept fearful watch over his son whom he was terrified of losing and filed his reports and kept his secrets and adhered to the code he was sworn to, but he was no longer among the living and he had no skin.

He passed his days and nights in perpetual terror that his son and his saved-but-lost daughter and his young third wife would come to harm. To protect them, he withdrew from them. He withdrew, even, from inside the shell of himself; from me, that is to say, and I from him. We strove to keep our thoughts separate and private. I see him now, beside me, not looking at me: Salamander, encased in ice.

Which of us is writing this confession, I do not know.

Which of us Sirocco most enjoyed playing with, as cat plays with bird, I do not know; but his single-minded dedication to tormenting both of us—his split-twin counterpart in covert operations—sometimes gives comfort for minutes at a time. It surely counts as a credential of sorts, or so I try to convince myself. It confers—it seems to confer—the distinction of hand-to-hand combat with evil. It therefore makes me dare to hope that I am, after all—that perhaps I am—the knight who wears the white plume, and it buttresses my vow to preserve the damning evidence through time. These tapes, I dare to hope, are my Rosetta Stone and my Dead Sea Scrolls.

I cannot ever re-create the horrible effect of receiving Sirocco's transmissions live, but three of the tapes (those labeled #4, #5, #6) preserve the interminable descent to the seventh circle in real time: for future historians; for those who can bear to watch.

Cassette #1 holds this document.

Cassette #2 is a collage of public footage of newsreel tapes.

Cassette #3, the crucial one, is my edited version of the raw primary evidence. It contains the Last Words. From this tape I have excised the agonies that will not bear watching, I have cut and spliced, I have kept the Illuminations, I have inserted subtitles and I have memorialized the dead. I call it the Decameron tape, and it is my act of propitiation, my rite of mourning, my wailing wall, my monument to those who perished so terribly, my *Kyrie eleison,* my prayer.

It is also my indictment. (The leaden weight of my sins pulls me down. *Oh, I'd leap up to my God,* but no forgiveness is possible. There is no way out.)

Making the Decameron tape is the most important thing I have ever done; preserving it, the most dangerous.

Transmissions came in live from AF 64, and then from the bunker in Iraq. Sirocco had brilliant minds at his disposal, trained to the highest pitch (by us, of course) in information technology, biochemical warfare, and explosives.

Transmissions came in live, and I was by no means the sole monitor.

The first transmission, made available to global news services, was broadcast in a dozen countries, including ours, without censorship. Why has this footage disappeared? It has not, in fact, disappeared; it has been *elided* by subsequent editorial construction and slant. Its impact has been diluted. It is history lost; or rather, temporarily mislaid, as history so frequently is. For this reason, I include an exact transcript of Sirocco's ultimatum, though it is readily available (both visually and in transcript) in public archival footage.

Throughout the twenty-four hours in the bunker, desperate negotiations were being carried on. I record below the transcripts of telephone conversations that took place between myself and those higher in the decision-making process than I.

Transcripts

Transcript of Sirocco's ultimatum

(Transmitted as audiovisual on September 13, 1987; monitored by Salamander; patched on to, and viewed by, unknown number of unknown individuals in higher levels of command; also broadcast globally on CNN and national newscasts on September 14, 1987; subsequently—with all due and deliberate intention to deceive—construed as hoax.)

Voice of Sirocco:

> You have seen what has happened to Flight Black Death, formerly Air France 64. Before the plane was blown up, we removed ten hostages. They are safe.
>
> By refusing us landing rights in Paris, by ignoring our ultimatum on the imminent fate of the passengers, you treated our demands lightly. Now you know that we are not to be trifled with. We therefore give you this one final chance.

The hostages are in an underground bunker which has been sealed. Sarin and mustard gas have been piped in, but the hostages are unharmed. They have been issued with gas masks and protective suits which will shield them for up to twenty-four hours (though some may succumb earlier than this).

We have named ten freedom fighters who languish unjustly in Israeli, French, and American jails. Release them by midnight, and the hostages will be freed. Release one of ours, we release one of yours. You have twenty-four hours at most. If our terms are not met, the hostages will go the way of the plane, though not before they have suffered agonies.

Transcript of telephone conversation (September 14, 1987)

Salamander:

Sirocco has the bunker wired and I'm patching you in. He's a sicko. He wants us to see the death struggles live. This has to go all the way up. Let me know when you've got them patched in.

Responding Voice:

Receiving visuals. We haven't decided how far up this should go. We're monitoring.

Salamander:

This has to go all the way up. I know Sirocco. He's posturing. He can always be bought. Hostages-for-prisoners is window dressing for the benefit of his thugs. He's playing both sides against the middle, and he has to keep those zealots on a leash. He'll cut a deal, but it involves oil rights, not just cash, and it'll take two calls from the top: one from us and one from the Saudis. I can stall him.

Responding Voice:

Yes, stall him. That's your directive.

Salamander:

I will, but there isn't much time. This whole horror shop can be shut down fast with a call to King Fahd or Prince Abdullah. It has to come from the top, though, you understand? Find out where the bunker is. Precisely, I mean. It's close to Tikrit, twenty miles from the airport or less. There hasn't been time to go further. We have a contact in Tikrit.

Responding Voice:

We no longer have a contact in Tikrit. Saddam destroyed our CIA base a year ago, September '86. With his Unit 999.

Salamander:

You think I don't know that? He did it with the nerve gas we gave him.

Responding Voice:

That was when we needed him against Iran. He was supposed to use that against Iran. We couldn't have predicted what a double-crossing swine—

Salamander:

Right. Wiped out a swath of his own Kurds simultaneously. Just the same, I'm telling you I still have a contact in Tikrit. And there are people I can buy.

Responding Voice:

We're taking this under advisement. Your directive is to stall.

Salamander:

The Saudis know he's getting money from us, so that won't faze them. They think he's *their* double agent, but this guy would sell his mother four times over. You've got to show them he's in the pay of groups plotting to bring down the king. Make sure they understand that at the top.

Responding Voice:

We're receiving you. Incoming visual data is excellent. God, they're barbarians, aren't they? This is diabolic stuff, but we have to proceed with caution. The word from upstairs is: we can't afford to rock any Saudi boats.

Salamander:

This isn't rocking boats. It's saving their bacon.

Responding Voice:

We don't think they'll see it that way. Sirocco's a Saudi.

Salamander:

He also carries two other passports that we know of. He's shipped his family to Algeria so his wife can teach and his daughters can go to school. The word is, his oldest daughter wants to be a doctor and he wants to get her into the Sorbonne. The Saudis can claim he's Algerian or Libyan if it suits them. Won't be the first time. But for God's sake, get them to *act*.

Responding Voice:

But the point is, he *is* a Saudi, and the princes do not appreciate unpleasant hints. They do not appreciate any suggestion that they have ties to terrorist acts. Stall him as best you can.

Salamander:

We've got twenty-four hours. No, we've got less than that now. You've got to arrange the call to King Fahd or Prince Abdullah. Do you have any idea of how horrible these deaths will be?

Responding Voice:

We'll do what we can. Response just in from the spokesman for the House of Saud. The princes have no knowledge whatsoever of Sirocco.

Salamander:

Oh, for shit's sake, what else would you expect a palace spokesman to say? I can give you photographs of Sirocco with the princes. They know him personally, he's got their ear. I've got tapes, video with audio, of social events—

Responding Voice:

That's exactly our point. The Saudis won't appreciate it, and we are not to rock boats. It would not be in the best interests of national security at this time.

Salamander:

The bulk of the funding for this hijacking came from the Saudis (and the rest from us, of course, before we knew we'd been double-crossed).

Responding Voice:

We are fully aware of this, Salamander, but it would not be in the best interests—

Salamander:

And the weapons are ours, remember, in case some journalist gets hold of this, and so are the gas canisters, so you'd better damn well argue that it damn well *is* in the interests of national security. . . . For the Saudis too, if their funding connection comes to light. You've got to make the president understand the long-term consequences of this, and he's got to make the king understand.

Responding Voice:

Your recommendations are noted, Salamander. We'll do what we can. But I've been asked to pass down from the highest levels that they know you have a highly personal stake in the hostage issue and there is a consensus that this is clouding your judgment. I would urge restraint, Salamander. Issues of national security do override personal concerns.

I knew then, instinctively, that nothing would be done, that there would be a cover-up, that all evidence would be destroyed. I knew, as I replaced the receiver in its cradle, that my own days were numbered from that moment.

It was not long after this that my telephone contact with my own superiors ceased altogether. My calls were not answered. I have never known, of course, what level of the administration my pleas and proposals reached, though I have made hypotheses based on after-effect, and based on the insistence that the tapes be surrendered and destroyed. I have been aware of repeated attempts to search for any possible illegal copy I might have made.

At about the same time that I lost contact with our own people, I also lost contact with Sirocco. The break was abrupt. Both visual and sound transmissions were cut. Perhaps that was ordered and controlled from our end, perhaps from his. I do not know. I do know that the silence of the devil is more alarming than the silence of God because we ask ourselves fearfully: what is the Evil One planning, beyond the range of our ability to listen and observe?

Under some distant and future administration, when different treaties and alliances prevail, we will perhaps learn finally of the whereabouts of the bunker that is somewhere in Iraq, and we will recover the remains of those who perished there.

Did everyone die?

Almost certainly. And yet we cannot know, since contact was lost before the end. Even a sealed bunker is porous and subject to draft, and there is a chance, a slim chance. . . .

I find myself hoping.

This, you will be quick to accuse, is wishful thinking. I know it is. Even so, until conclusive evidence is obtained. . . .

As for Sirocco, he was considered too useful, too essential to our Intelligence needs in Afghanistan—against the Russians—to be eliminated or exposed. He has been receiving arms shipments, support, and various payments in kind as our double agent throughout the nineties. When the rogue agent is all we have, the rogue agent is what we use, balancing hazardous odds and short-term gain.

Once it was clear that sucking doubt was pulling me under, my own access to official Intelligence information was at first gradually, then rapidly, curtailed. I was reduced to training recruits. I was subsequently relieved of this duty and charged with "lack of academic neutrality" and "inappropriate and overly emotional lectures." Nevertheless, my own unofficial sources are my own unofficial sources, an agent's contacts remain his contacts, and I do have reliable information that at the time of my compilation of this edited tape, in the summer of 2000, Sirocco moves between Kabul and Peshawar and is considered useful to our national purposes.

That which I have done—though I can never atone for its outcome—I continue to believe was that which was required at a time of complex risk to our nation and to international equilibrium and world peace. I believed I could lure all the members of an elite terrorist cell into one confined space and neutralize them.

Things went wrong.

If I could pinpoint the sole moment when I acted improperly, it would be the moment when Nimrod urged that Operation Black Death be aborted and I declined to support him. Hubris: I still believed I could pull Sirocco into line. Also: I did not wish to pay the price that Nimrod paid.

I know that price will fall due.

Against my terrible (though unintended) crimes, I post these small achievements: the children were released from the plane; I saved the life of my daughter Françoise; through contacts with French Intelligence and the French police, I have made it impossible (or as close to impossible as such things can be) for Sirocco ever to reenter France.

The rest is silence.

How, then, can I begin to recreate the effect of Sirocco's live transmission from the bunker?

Imagine this:

The screen is almost, but not quite, dark. Strangely shaped shadow-beings, with grotesque heads, move about in a slow ballet, and if it were not for the dread fact that we know all too well what we are watching, we might think we were in the first circle of Dante's hell.

The light is murky, somewhere between the color of muddy water and of twilight in thick industrial smog. Hooded shapes, stumbling about like the damned—they *are* the damned—reach out and grope at each other. They feel the walls, they stretch their padded arms against it, reaching up, reaching down, describing large arcs in many directions, measuring the dimensions of their cage like blind men who have been told that somewhere on the walls is an Open Sesame switch. They have twenty-four hours to find it. Their hands are rounded and fingerless, like lepers' stumps. Their body shapes resemble prehistoric insects; they have puffy segmented bodies and bug eyes. The stage set seems to be a room, or a bunker, about twelve feet square. There is no furniture. There are only the ten padded shapes which sometimes curl up on the ground, immobile, and sometimes bump into one another. When collision occurs, sometimes the bodies embrace and cling. At other times, they start apart like similarly charged magnetic poles repelling each other. High in one corner, where two walls and the ceiling meet, there is an eye of infrared light.

The camera was set up by Sirocco, who wanted me, in particular, to watch, and who wanted the world to watch. See how calmly torture can be inflicted, he wanted to say. I am setting up shop in your nightmares. I live under your pillow and under your skin. You will never sleep peacefully again.

Sirocco's scheme was a long time in the planning. It was meticulous. It held just one small flaw. The decision makers not only achieved total blackout, they unmade Sirocco. They shifted him into the realm of the bogeyman, the hoax, the figment of nightmare. They deconstructed hell.

And they were right to do so. They were right to puncture Sirocco's fantasy of global scope and mythic power. They turned him into a shadow-play on a wall.

I have no quarrel with that.

It was the failure to save the passengers and the hostages that appalls. Their deaths were avoidable, though "not without unacceptable risk to the national good." (I quote those who decide our fates.) Even this I could possibly accept: that in times of crisis, triage may be necessary. Some must perish for the greater good of all.

But if so, I pleaded, the many owe homage to the few. The record of their sacrifice should not be expunged. It is our side, our own side, which has obliterated the hostages more absolutely than Sirocco did. It is we who have denied them due rites and obsequies.

This is blasphemy, I argued. It is a moral stain on the national conscience.

I was sternly rebuked.

"Though collateral damage was regrettably high," I was instructed, "Operation Black Death was a success. A qualified success, perhaps—we would have preferred to save the passengers—but nevertheless a success. A terrorist cell was neutralized, its remnants scattered. (From remote caves in Afghanistan, where they now must hide, what possible harm can they do, except to Russia?) Beyond and above this, a benchmark for strategy, we did not buckle under to blackmail. No unacceptable precedent has been established. This is a mark of our strength. When dealing with terrorists, this is triumph."

And so I came to Carthage and to Scipio. I began to ask the troubling question Scipio asked: *How can we tell triumph from horror?*

In my chosen career path, this line of questioning is fatal. It signals the beginning of the end.

I was ordered to hand over the tapes and I did so, and in the interests of national security—so I was told—the tapes were destroyed. Before I surrendered the originals, however, I made secret copies. When you watch my Decameron tape, you are watching the same screen that I was watching live, knowing, as I watched, that I was being watched. Consider that it is entirely possible that you too are being watched as you watch.

On the tape, shadow-figures move and grope, watched by an infrared eye. By the paisley swirls of their motion, though not by the speed, the wraiths suggest a colony of ants in organized search of a mate. The mittened hands of one on the padded shoulders of another, two by two, they meditate, goggle to goggle, snout to snout. Then, often, they will embrace like fat clowns. They stand coupled; for ten seconds, thirty, one full minute, but then some knowledge, or some sense of dismay, must pass by osmosis. Each seems to sense error. The two will part, bowing with regret like Sumo wrestlers, to continue a dream minuet.

As the partners change, then change again, and then again, you, the watcher, will find yourself wondering if the unchanging partner that each shadow seeks is Death Himself.

Even out of atrocity, one is stirred to make art. *Especially* out of atrocity. One feels impelled to transform it. *They* felt so impelled. The Decameron tape is my own act of creative transformation and my act of atonement.

What I am preserving are stories fashioned in hell.

What we learn in a time of pestilence, wrote Albert Camus, *is that there are more things to admire in men than to despise.*

3.

Lowell lies full length on the carpet, face down, his forehead cradled on his arms. "*My son whom I am terrified of losing,*" he murmurs to the floor. He rocks his head the way people with migraines do.

Declassified fragments and seventy-six blacked-out spaces tramp through Samantha's head, left right left right, with a hundred and one half-lines close behind: *Salamander in charge of operations . . . XXXXXXXXXXXXXXXXXX loose cannon, Salamander warns, but as rogue agents go, we can use XXXXXXXXXX backstairs contacts in the Saudi palaces and has usable information . . . XXXXXX payments and arms supplies to be arranged XXXXXXXXX Salamander to meet with Sirocco. . . .*

Boom, boom, boom, beats the drum of indictments. Boom: the stroke of the censor's pen. Boom, boom, faster and faster, Samantha's noisy blood keeps time. It pounds at her temples. She feels a surge of incapacitating rage and pain. She wants to pound on the walls with her fists. How could you not have known? she wants to ask Lowell. She wants to scream.

I would have known, she believes. If my father had crimes on his head, I would have known. I would have confronted him, I would have argued, I would have raged.

If necessary, I would grab his ghost by the lapels.

"He lived in perpetual terror that his son would come to harm," Lowell says. He recites the words like a child memorizing a catechism or a magic charm. He begins to move around the room like a sleepwalker, stumbling against the bed, bumping into the dresser and chair, butting the wall with his head. "My father was Salamander," he says. The room seems to tilt and spin. His voice drops to a whisper. "My God, my God. My father was Salamander."

Sam slides the number 2 cassette into place. She presses the POWER button on the remote. She clicks to VCR mode. She presses PAUSE.

"Say something," Lowell demands.

"I don't know what to say."

"Say something, damn it. You made Salamander your north star. You've been steering your life by my father. You had fantasies of making him pay."

"He seems to have paid," Sam says with difficulty. (But did he pay *enough*? she asks herself. Is he *paid up*? How do we get due reparations for and from the dead?) She says in a flat quiet voice, "Your father couldn't have killed my Jacob. Your father was already dead. Someone else was pulling Salamander's strings."

"He was *afraid* for me. I thought he watched me like a hawk because he expected me to fuck up. I thought he was ashamed, and all the time. . . ."

Samantha goes to the window and parts the heavy drapes. A single floodlight puddles gold on the only car in the lot: the proprietor's van. The small motel office is lit; the rest is darkness. On the other side of the room, the windows look onto the marsh. Sam lifts the drape and looks out. The expanse of water and sweetgrass is eerily beautiful in the moonlight. Nothing stirs except the grasses and the night birds, the slow-gliding seabirds of the night.

"Lowell?" Sam touches him on the shoulder. "The other cassettes . . . ?"

"I don't know if I can," he says.

"It's what he asked of you."

"I'm afraid."

"So am I. We have reason to be."

"I'm afraid of disappointing him yet again. I'm afraid of not measuring up. I've already lost the ring binders."

"You saved the tapes."

"If you'd seen my apartment after they ransacked. . . . How am I going to keep these safe?"

"You've kept them safe. They're here."

"Sam. Samantha. How are we going to stay alive?"

Sam considers peering between the drapes again, but is afraid to. "We'll figure that one out later," she says. "Don't think about it. First we have to watch the tapes."

"I'm afraid of what he wants us to see."

"So am I."

Lowell checks the chain on the door. "What if I was followed?"

"We'll sit in the dark."

"The psychiatrist," Lowell says. "He knows I've got them. Someone's bound to have been tailing him. They could be at the boathouse by now. They could be at the motel office." He peers between the drapes. The parking lot is still quiet as death. "You're right," he says urgently. "We have to watch these before—" He takes the remote. "We have to watch while we can. Where's the—?"

"I've already put it in the VCR," Sam whispers. "Keep the sound low."

Lowell presses PLAY. Sam turns out the lamp and they sit in the dark, side by side on the double bed, propped against pillows and headboard, their faces ghostly in the flickering light from the screen.

CBS Anchorman:

We bring you the latest breaking news on the hijacking of Air France 64, which took off from Paris on September eighth, six days ago. After twenty-two children were safely disembarked in Germany, the plane was permitted to refuel.

The hijackers then flew to Libya, where gas canisters were brought on board and protective masks and clothing were distributed to passengers. Permission to land in Paris was demanded by the hijackers.

The hijackers' claim to have released sarin in the plane, and the limited protection-time offered by the gas masks, were used as blackmail to secure landing rights. The hijackers also declared that flammable gases had been released, and that any attempt at rescue by sharpshooters would cause the plane to explode. The hijackers demanded that ten named terrorists, currently in prison, be released and allowed to board the plane at Charles de Gaulle Airport.

Intelligence sources could not confirm the release of gases and experts believed this unlikely. Permission to land in Paris was refused.

Yesterday, September thirteenth, on the Tikrit airstrip in northern Iraq, the plane was blown up, and it was believed that all remaining lives were lost.

Visual of explosion of plane
Screen shows an airstrip with plane in distance.
There is a blinding flash.
A sun appears to be rising at the edge of the airstrip.

CBS Anchorman:

Today, CBS received a copy of a tape from an Iraqi television station. It appears that ten passengers from Flight 64 are still alive and are being held as hostages until certain demands of the hijackers are met. At this point, CBS has been unable to verify the authenticity of the tape. You are about to see the tape as we received it.

Visuals:

A figure in black clothing and a gas mask appears against a stark white ground. He holds a machine gun. He is backlit by harsh bright light so that a shimmer appears at his edges. On the white wall behind him, three words are written in blood (or perhaps they are crudely brush-stroked in red paint): **OPERATION BLACK DEATH.**

Voice of Man in Black:

You have seen what has happened to Flight Black Death, formerly Air France 64. Before the plane was blown up, we removed ten hostages. They are safe.

By refusing us landing rights in Paris, by ignoring our ultimatum on the imminent fate of the passengers, you treated our demands lightly. Now you know that we are not to be trifled with. We therefore give you this one final chance.

The hostages are in an underground bunker which has been sealed. Sarin and mustard gas have been piped in, but the hostages are unharmed. They have been issued with gas masks and protective suits which will shield them for up to twenty-four hours (though some may succumb earlier than this).

We have named ten freedom fighters who languish unjustly in French prisons. Many others are in Israeli and American jails. Release any ten Islamic freedom fighters by midnight, and the hostages will be freed. Release one of ours, we release one of yours. You have twenty-four hours at most. If our terms are not met, the hostages will go the way of the plane, though not before they have suffered agonies.

Visuals:

A man against the backdrop of the Capitol.
Subtitled lettering on-screen:
SPOKESPERSON FOR STATE DEPARTMENT.

Spokesperson for State Department:

We will make no deals with barbarians. We have been given no proof that there are *any hostages. We believe this to be the desperate and pathetic ruse of terrorists who have already played their last trump card and done their worst.*

ABC Anchorman:

Intelligence sources have revealed that the so-called hostage demand was a hoax. The tape received yesterday from an Iraqi television station, and distributed to global news organizations, has been analyzed by forensic experts. "This footage has been very cleverly put together," one expert claimed on condition of anonymity, "but it is, without a shadow of doubt, fraudulent."

The ultimatum that convicted terrorists be released in exchange for the hostages' lives is believed to be a desperate plan by a peripheral cell of the terrorist network. Our sources indicate that this group was not even involved in the hijacking, and their film footage has been obtained secondhand and spliced into the so-called Operation Black Death ultimatum. Reliable evidence indicates the hijackers were suicide zealots, all of whom perished when they blew up the plane two days ago.

"We would not, in any case, have cut a deal with barbarians," an official of the State Department said. "But in this instance, we were deeply suspicious from the moment the demands were received. Apart from the children, whom our negotiations succeeded in liberating from the plane, we can say categorically that there were no survivors from Flight 64, and no hostages. UN observers have been permitted on Iraqi soil, and the charred remains of the plane have been examined. All the hijackers are accounted for. Our evidence is that they were part of a highly trained terrorist cell of Islamic fundamentalists based in Paris, but made up of a diverse group of Algerians with French citizenship, Palestinians, and Pakistanis. All due steps will be taken to demand reparations from the governments of those involved.

"Although the toll in American lives has been horrific," the State Department said, "we do at least know that the dangerous Parisian cell has been eliminated."

Visual of explosion of airplane

Voiceover:

This is Salamander. The tape you are about to see was sent to CNN and to the major television news networks by an Iraqi television station, but at the request of the State Department was never broadcast. As requested, the networks surrendered their copies to the State Department.

Visuals:

Head of a man in black wearing gas mask and carrying machine gun.

He rips at the velcro collar and pulls the gas mask from his head.

Underneath, he wears a black ski mask.

Voice of Man in Black Mask:

(He speaks impeccable English and has the accent of an Oxford don)

People of America, we have given your journalists the names of ten Muslim heroes who are prisoners in Western jails. Your government, by bringing pressure to bear on its allies and puppet states, can ensure their release. Now we give you the names of ten hostages. If our demands are not met, they will die.

(Sound of a muffled gong)

Number one. Isabella Hawthorne, American. Wife of American spy.

Visuals:

A woman's face. She is beautiful. Her hair is shoulder-length and brunette and it wisps at her cheeks. She is smiling.

(The gong reverberates again like a death bell tolling.)

Voice of Man in Mask:

Number two. Avi Levinstein, American Jew.

Visuals:

A brooding face. The man has a violin under his chin, the bow half drawn across the strings. A dark curl falls over his forehead.

(Gong.)

Voice of Man in Mask:

Number three. Jonathan Raleigh, American.

Sam grabs for the remote and hits PAUSE.

She is stunned by the sight of her father, by the way he gives off energy even in a still photograph. The energy hits her like a hard rubber ball and bounces back. On PAUSE, the image wavers and blurs, so she rewinds a little and sees him clear for a second and then hits the PAUSE button again. Her hands shake because she knows the photograph, and it is part of a whole. It is a detail from a framed family portrait that she keeps on her desk. Her father stands to the right of a swing on which she herself sits. Sam is three years old in the photograph. Her mother stands behind her, her mother's hands are on the ropes. Her mother has paused in the act of pushing the swing and is turning slightly to smile at her father. Her father is wearing jeans and an Atlanta Braves sweatshirt, and his right arm is raised because his hand closes over his wife's hand on the rope.

In the still image on the screen, Sam's father wears jeans and an Atlanta Braves shirt. His right arm is raised, but the edge of the screen slices his arm at the elbow. One cannot see the rope, nor the swing, nor her father's hand, nor any hint of the presence of Sam herself.

She rewinds again and her father smiles for three seconds, and she smells his warm father smell and takes his hand. There is a fleshy imperfection that grows like a bud on his thumb. Her fingertips play with it.

As far as Sam knows, there is only one other copy of the photograph on her desk. It is in Lou's photograph album. Sam's mother must have sent it to her sister. Lou must have taken it to France.

"I don't understand," Sam says. "I don't understand how they got that."

Lowell reaches for the remote and presses PLAY.

The gong tolls and tolls, and the voice intones,
and faces hover on the screen for five seconds.

Voice of Man in Mask:

Number four. Tristan Charron, French publisher of books critical of Islam.

Number five. Genevieve Teague, Australian smuggler of subversive material to Islamic countries.

Number six. Yasmina Shankara, Hindu film actress from Bombay, involved in immoral films that corrupt Muslim women in India.

Number seven. Victoria Goldberg, American. Married to American Jew.

Number eight. Daniel Schulz. Polish Israeli. Yiddish writer.

Number nine. William Jenkins, American college student.

Number ten. Homer Longchamp, American.

Visual:

Man in black ski mask.

Voice:

America, you have twenty-four hours.
Release our prisoners if you want the hostages to live.

(Lute music; Middle Eastern music)

Visual:

A mosaic composed of the ten faces of the hostages.

Book VII

THE DECAMERON TAPE

Wherefore . . . I think it would be excellently well done that we depart this place . . . and betake ourselves quietly to other places in our thought . . . and there take such diversion as we may.

—GIOVANNI BOCCACCIO, **DECAMERON**

From now on it can be said that plague was the concern of all of us. . . . Once the town gates were shut, every one of us realized that all, the narrator included, were, so to speak, in the same boat, and each would have to adapt himself to the new conditions of life.

—ALBERT CAMUS, **THE PLAGUE**

Captivity is above all a smell, an incommunicable odor of humiliation. . . . For imprisonment is a form of erosion. The captive devours himself trying to understand his abandonment.

—JEAN-PAUL KAUFFMANN, **THE BLACK ROOM OF LONGWOOD**

1.

The screen is shadowy. Some young director of *film noir*, it would seem, has dispensed with the notion of lighting, and the watcher is tricked into enclosed space and then trapped. In order to get out alive, the watcher must find the sealed opening in the wall.

You are the watcher.

You must navigate between dread shapes in the red-flushed dark. (Or you must turn on all the lights and smash the television set, and even so. . . .) Even so, from high in the cube of your dream, where two walls and the ceiling meet, a red light watches. The effect is surreal and dire. This live ember, you know instantly, is the ringmaster's eye: *Let the circus begin.*

The watcher performs as required.

You clutch at bedding, a handful of sheet in your fist. Vertigo strikes. Your breathing turns ragged. You sweat. You have the certainty that you are being watched. You are monitored not only by the all-seeing light—red devil's eye, or eye of God—that catalogues your every reaction from deep inside the television set; but you sense some further invisible and overarching presence that hovers and has you under surveillance. And then there are the bug-eyed creatures, monstrously shaped, who peer at you as they grope at the walls and at each other. They snuffle through their filters. They sniff at you with their sensitive snouts. Hog people, you think. Truffle hunters. They huddle and point. They gesture desperately. *Step into our box,* they plead. *We know you can see us. Do not leave us here. Let us out, let us out, let us out.*

Some beat against the membrane that separates them from you. They pummel the screen with padded fists. (You can feel this. You can feel it in the thudding of your heart.) Others sit, propped against the walls. They hunch into themselves like question marks. One is standing beneath the red light, arms lifted in worship, or possibly in supplication or in prayer. One figure is prostrate on the floor.

Enough, you say. This—the waiting—is intolerable. Let the circus begin.

Sam studies the brown wraiths with awful fascination. Which one is her father? She believes she can tell, though the shadow-beings are without distinguishing shape. What she recognizes is her father's intensity. The others drift, becalmed, but her father moves rapidly, thinking escape. He pounds on the wall with gloved fists. He swims through the murk in circles, as though tracking sharks. Seaweedy arms reach for him, then drift aside. He is generating currents, generating energy as he moves, generating a whirlpool of which he is the pulsating core.

Sam remembers that. She remembers the way of that transfer of energy: her hand in his as they wait to cross a busy city street. Her father is pins-and-needles on her skin and a surge of omnipotence passes through her. People give way to her father. Things give way. He steps into the street and raises one hand. *It is my intention to cross,* the hand announces, and a path opens up through the swirl of buses and cars and taxis and trucks. The Red Sea parts. Harm cannot touch her father. His life is charmed.

Before the red eye of God, he raises both arms. This is no act of meekness. *If there was a way in, there is a way out,* his body says. *You will let us go.*

Now his nine companions have fallen back, and some mysterious consensus is at work. Dreamlike fatigue overcomes them. One by one, they sink to the floor until only Sam's father stands. Sam's father, Odysseus, stares down the red eye of Circe, and thunder answers.

Voice of Red Eye:

(It is enraged, though it speaks with a polished aristocratic accent)

Dogs! I am Sirocco, the desert wind that scorches where it blows. For me, circus dogs, you will perform. For me, you will beg and grovel before you die. For me, dogs, you will dance. Faster, I will say, and you will dance faster. Die, I will say. And you will die.

You have been sacrificed by your own countries and your death will be as bird bones in the mouth of a bear. Your governments have been trifling with us, stalling for time, using up the minutes of your lives.

You have six hours before the filters in your masks become useless. Long before that, you will lose the power of speech. Your bunker is sealed. Your deaths by asphyxiation will be slow and painful.

Or your deaths could be fast. You know this. You have seen fast deaths on the plane. You may choose.

If you choose the fast exit, while you yet have the power of speech, you may send a last message to your loved ones. The eye of the camera is recording. The world is watching. When you take off your mask to speak, you will have five minutes, perhaps ten. Use your time well.

An intimation passes from goggled head to goggled head and the viewer can mark the jet stream of its passage. *We are down among the dead men,* the message says. There is a wilting and buckling of padded forms. They fold themselves up like used clothing. They sink to the floor. In the twilight, they stack themselves loosely, messily, in despair.

Sam's father alone is standing. His hands grapple with the Velcro fastening at his neck. Samantha is not surprised to see her father defy his fate, she is thrilled by his raw determination, and somehow, somehow (though she knows how this story ends), somehow she believes the red eye will blink and look away. She believes the sarin and mustard gas will part, she believes a nontoxic channel will open itself up for him and he will cross over and emerge from the lost years of her life and take her hand.

The Velcro collar gives way.

He pulls the thick clumsy mitts from his hands and a ripple of excitement and dread passes visibly through the other padded shades. His hands reach for the mask. It is off, and a cascade of long dark hair spills over the padded suit.

Sam stares in shocked disbelief.

How can . . . ?

This is not her father.

Yasmina Shankara, the Bombay movie star, smiles mournfully and rakes her fingers through her hair.

2.

"Isn't it strange?" Yasmina asks her companions. The flash of her eyes above her ugly suit and the movement of her slender wrists suggest someone whom shock and oxygen deprivation have removed to a different world. "Isn't it strange what we think we fear absolutely, only to find at the last that it gives us wings? And isn't it strange what we think we could never understand? My father used to say, 'Yasmina, anyone who wears a watch does not understand time.'

" 'Daddy,' I used to say, 'you are so old-fashioned, you should live inside the temple compound all night instead of only by day.' " She laughs and her laughter is light and silvery and full of tranquil resignation, like the strands of small bells around a temple elephant's neck. " 'Even in Bombay, Daddy, modern times have come,' I used to tell him. 'Gucci watches have come. Even in Bombay, time moves on, time flies, but you have been left behind with oxcarts and rickshaw wallahs.'

" 'Time is air, Yasmina,' he would tell me. 'Time is ocean. Does the air we breathe move on? Does the ocean have beginning or end? All of time and all of matter is a blink in Shiva's red eye.'

"I thought it was old-fashioned Hindu gobbledygook, not modern at all. Isn't it strange, now that I have no time left, that I understand what my father meant?" She is facing the eye of the camera, gesturing to her companions, inviting them to ponder this curious fact. "Suddenly I know it is so. Now. Here." She looks around the cramped twilit space. "And where is here? We are underground, yes? In a cave? In a cellar? What country are we in? We do not know. What use are maps or watches to us now? We are nowhere. We are outside time."

She looks her watcher in his dark bloodshot eye. She raises her cupped hands as though releasing a dove toward the light. "Agit, my son, my dear little boy, I am sending the cloud messenger."

Her breathing turns ragged. She begins to cough. "My eyes, my eyes," she murmurs. "There is salt in my eyes.

"Agit!" she calls urgently. She gasps. Her padded chest heaves, she doubles over, but she raises her cupped hands above her head. She offers the chalice of her curved fingers to her son. "Agit!" she calls. "Here is time. Here is my father on the steps of the temple tank where he died; and here is the moment of your birth, Agit; and here is the beggar girl who lives at our gates, and here are the tinsel dreams I dreamed in Bollywood, and here *we* are, all of us in this strange place, bound together for a reason we do not yet know, with no time and all time in our hands.

"And now I have no fear and no grief, because, do you see?"—and she is speaking in a singsong lilt, in ancestral patterns of Sanskrit chant as sages speak from stone steps by temple pools—"our story will go through time as Kālidāsa's poetry passes through time, as his Cloud Messenger passes through fifteen hundred years and still settles in the minds of all exiles and of those who will die far from home."

She gives way to a spasm of coughing. "I am burning," she murmurs. "I am drowning in my suit." She sways. She closes her eyes.

"Here is time, Agit. Here is Bombay.

"When I was a child in Bombay, poverty frightened me. Once I struck a beggar child with my riding whip because he touched me.

"Here is my father at sixty. He wants to give away his wealth and live like Gandhi. He wants to sit by the temple pool all day, he wants only to meditate on the thousand names of the Lord. But as for me, I want to put many, many layers of wealth between me and the children who die in the street. Inside the high wall around our house are lawns and fountains and peacocks and those who serve us. Outside is contamination. I leave our garden as rarely as possible, only seated in the back of our car.

"Our driver gets out and opens the gates, and drives through, and gets out and closes them again. And there is the beggar girl who sits outside our gates, and always, day after day, she taps at my window and stares in and I open the window a crack and toss her a coin. I cannot bear to touch her or put the coin in her hand. She is covered with sores."

Yasmina begins to scratch the backs of her hands. She begins to cough again. She talks faster.

"Year after year, day after day, I toss her a coin, and one day she is not there.

" 'Where is the beggar girl?' I ask.

" 'She died,' says our driver. 'The porter found her body this morning.'

" 'What did she die of?'

" 'Of hunger,' he says.

"At night, in my bedroom, her eyes float in the dark like bloodshot moons, and I have fled from her, but like her I am hungry. I am famished. For years and years, I am hungry for wealth, for fame, for more wealth and more fame, for more houses in Paris and Majorca and New York. But now"—she turns to the red eye high above her in the room—"see how she has found me with her bloodshot eye? See how she has waited for me to recognize myself?"

Yasmina is coughing badly. She presses her hands to her face, and the skin of her cheeks blisters and breaks. She rubs her padded arms and blinks rapidly with her bloodshot eyes. She talks faster and faster.

"Now I die her death, covered in sores, but I must tell you this story, Agit, before I leave you. I must pass on Kālidāsa's great and beloved Sanskrit poem which has been told before and will be told again, over and over, and you in your turn must retell it and pass it on.

"A year ago, Bollywood made a movie of Kālidāsa's *Meghaduta,* and this is the story of *The Cloud Messenger*: a *yaksha* is sent into exile from the Himalayan paradise and banished to the end of the world. He is sent to the farthest point of the idea of South, where the monsoon coast of Kerala slides up against the edge of the earth. The *yaksha* is dying of lovesickness for his mountains of snow and for his lady. He summons a cloud. Go, sweet cloud, he says, and tell my love. . . . He gives the cloud directions for the long journey north.

"In the film—do you see me, Agit?—I am in the marketplace buying strands of jasmine for my hair—" she lets her hair fall forward over her face and braids it with imaginary flowers—"and the first wet cloud of the monsoon floats by, and in that fog I stumble and fall across a beggar child, and I draw back with horror, because it is *she,* it is the girl again, the girl who sat at the gates of my childhood, but the cloud . . ."—she makes motions of bathing herself in the toxic air that surrounds her—"the cloud envelopes me with the smells of my homeland, curries cooking, cinnamon, incense, the smell of my father and my mother, the sweet smell of my son, my Agit, and the beggar girl says to me, 'Everything returns. Nothing can ever be lost.' "

Yasmina coughs. She bats her hands at the toxic mist. "Go, sweet cloud. . . ."

And then she begins to struggle for air, and to writhe. "Tell my son," she gasps, "tell Agit—"

Her voice is stretched out, racked, in a long rising siren of agony, unbearable—

The scene is cut.

Blank screen on which only the lettering of a name appears.

Yasmina Shankara

Born Bombay, 1952

There is the sound of a flute.

3.

Nine shadow-beings converge. They have become, it would seem, one organism, multicelled, and an atavistic decree has gone forth: due ritual is required; due obsequies must be performed. The message passes as it must pass through an ant colony or a swarm of bees. The shadow-beings kneel in a circle. The tangled body-knot of Yasmina Shankara is their sun. A murmuring is heard, a sense of chant, though all sounds through the speaker tubes of the gas masks are weirdly distorted. But yes, there is choral mourning, a keening in nine-part harmony, each being, no doubt, conferring such rites as his or her own tradition suggests.

Another swarm-message seems to pass from each to each. One by one, with bowed head, each padded wraith kneels by the body and touches it with the "forehead" of the mask. And then, nine pallbearers, they carry Yasmina to the corner beneath the red eye.

Silence.

Stillness.

A sound like muffled hoofbeats approaching from a great distance off.

One of the shadows is clapping his thick-mittened hands. The sound swells in a long crescendo—swarm knowledge again—and each wraith is making galloping sounds, glove thumping glove.

Then he who began the drumming pulls off his gloves and rips at his Velcro collar, and Daniel Shulz, the Yiddish writer, tosses and catches his headpiece as though it were a ball. Soccer ball. He bounces it off his knee, kicks it neatly backward off his ankle, catches it, bounces it off his head. He tosses the ball to someone else, and the catcher passes it on, and then everyone is catching and passing, tossing the ball, and tiny Daniel Shulz, aged seventy, with his creased face and silver hair, vibrant in the murky reddish light, throws back his head and lifts his arms to the watching devil's eye and throws a goal.

He takes a long deep breath. He bows. He gives the impression of someone who has just been awarded the Nobel prize of untrammeled speech. He makes a thunder of hoofbeats again by slapping his hands against his arms.

"Riddle," he says. "What is this sound that never stops?"

Clippety-clop, clippety-clop, go his hands.

"Answer: the horsemen of Death," he says. "Still they gallop and still they fail utterly to extinguish wonder."

Clippety-clop, clippety-clop, he drums and drums, but now he beats dance time, ragtime, now he is tapping his feet. His accent is thick, and even though he speaks English, one hears Yiddish.

"I must share with you, my friends, this huge joke. Before the masked horsemen of Death boarded our plane, I was going to the Festival of Yiddish Literature in New York. But before even I am flying to Paris, in Tel Aviv, a journalist wishes to interview me. He is from the *Jerusalem Post.* Why do you write in Yiddish? he wants to know. He is ambitious, a young intellectual, the belligerent kind who have all answers before they ask questions. It is a fossil, this Yiddish, he says. It is the yoke of our bondage, the sign of linguistic subjugation. Why do you cling to our chains?

"We must still tell stories, I say, because the Horsemen of Death still gallop.

"But now we stop them with tanks, he tells me. Not with tales of magic, but with tanks. What use are the rabbis who fly and the golems as big as the world? You write stories for those who retreat from the world and for children.

"It is true that I write for children, I say. I write for my great-grandson, David.

"And it is so.

"David, I am telling this story for you. I want you to laugh.

"Once upon a time, in the days of the Baal Shem Tov, first of the zaddiks, when pogroms rained upon the face of the earth, and when Death, in his black suit and his black gas mask, galloped through the towns on his great black horse, in those days, the Baal Shem Tov told stories *because there was no escape,* and the followers of the Baal Shem Tov lived in the land of *even so.*

"Our villages are plundered, he told them, our houses are burned, but *even so,* the spark of the divine cannot be quenched, and where the spark of the divine touches, there is dancing and play."

Daniel Shulz picks up his gas mask again and tosses it to someone else, who passes it on. "This is my last will and testament, little David," Daniel says, as the game of catch proceeds. "This is my gift to you: that you live long in the land of *even so.*

"Ahh, ahh . . ." Daniel misses a catch. He wrings his hands and rubs his bloodshot eyes. "Ahhh. My eyes! My eyes! I cannot see!" He vomits mucus and blood. "Even so," he gasps. "Even here. Hold my hands . . . let us dance in Death's waiting room."

And a circle forms, mittened hand in mittened hand. It is a slow dance, very slow, though Daniel Shulz speaks faster and faster.

"It is told of the Baal Shem Tov that during the feast of Simhat Torah . . . disciples dancing . . . such abandon, such wildness . . . ring of blue fire above their heads . . ."

Daniel Schulz, dancing slowly, blinded now, draws his breath raggedly and shakes his fist at the red light above his head. He speaks with difficulty. "What . . . can you take? . . . Cannot take dance.

"David, David . . . your great-grandfather's blessing. . . . Dance!"

He falls. "Even so," he whispers, and the circle breaks and hovers around him, and his dance, horizontal, intensifies in a last writhing, convulsive—

CUT

Lettering on black screen:

Daniel Schulz

born in Warsaw, 1917

Survived Auschwitz

A bugle plays taps.

4.

"Mom, Joe will tell you. I tried to get home for your birthday, but it looks like I'm not going to make it. I'm sorry, Mom." The young man pounds on the floor with his gas mask as though he is smashing someone's skull. He stands and addresses himself directly to the red eye. "Billy Jenkins here." He bows melodramatically, then clowns a little, making rabbit ears with his fingers, making goggles with his hands and peering through them. He wiggles his hands, adjusting an imaginary focus. "Hey, that's better. Happy birthday, Mom. You know what's weird? I camped at Paris airport all night to make standby for this flight. Slept in my sleeping bag, and it was worth it. I was the last standby, the last one let on. I was so happy, I called Joe from the gate. They were boarding already. I said: Joe, surprise, surprise, I'll be there! Don't let Mom know, it'll be a surprise.

"Got that one right, didn't I?

"Not the kind of surprise I meant.

"It's so weird that it's gotta mean something, but I sure can't figure out what. I mean, what am I doing here with all these Martians? I don't come from the same planet as these guys, and I sure don't buy this marshmallow shit about death. Peace and light, dancing? Forget it? I'm madder than a hornet in a jar. I'm twenty-two years old, I just graduated, I don't want to die, and I damn well won't. I may be late for your birthday, Mom, but I'll get there, okay?

"What the hell is the matter with you wimps?" He swings around to address the alien Martians, his back to the red camera eye. He flails his arms like a preacher. "What is this? Obedience training? The man says *Die,* so you lie down like good little doggies? Get off your padded asses, you losers"—he has moved to the wall and is running his bare palms across its surface—"and start feeling for fissures and for cracks, because that's how—oh shit, my eyes . . . !"

He shields his face with his arms and leans his back against the wall and rocks himself. "Jesus H. Christ, that's the mustard gas," he says. "Attacks the eyes first. I just got a B.S., I'm a chemistry student, right? Okay, so this is what you all need to know, listen up." He looks like Oedipus, blinded, his eyes puffy and closed, his arms lifted, his pronouncements oracular. "We got sarin and mustard gas here. Mustard gas's never lethal, okay? You got that? Temporary blindness, then blindness, but it can't kill us off.

"The sarin can, in minutes, lungs and blood and sputum, that's what—" He draws in deep shuddering breaths. "Oh shit, clogging up my lungs already. That's what got 'em. Asphyxiation." He jerks his head to the bodies beneath the red lamp of Death. "Oh heck, oh heck, my eyes! This is worse than peeling a hundred pounds of onions at summer camp, which I had to do at Camp Saranac the year I was twelve. Remember that, Joe? Man, what a punishment.

"And why?

"All I did was lead a panty raid to the girls' camp.

"Weird thing, though—it's freaking me out, the stuff I'm remembering—next day, the day after the onions, was Girls' Camp Visit, and I've got a face like the Pillsbury Doughboy, all puffy and red, my eyes bloodshot. No way I want any girl to see me, so I go crawling off into the woods, feeling sorry for myself and hard done by, and I'm climbing over this humongous fallen tree that came down in a storm, and I bump into—well, I thought she was a goddess, she was that gorgeous, long blond hair down to her bum. She's wearing tight jeans and a halter top, and get this, she's got bloodshot eyes and tears running down her cheeks.

"So I say: 'Did you get onion duty too?'

"She just stares at me like I'm holding a gun at her head. She stares and stares and she doesn't move and doesn't say a word. And I stare back because she's so damn beautiful, the sort of girl who can give you wet dreams for years when you're twelve years old. I'm scared to speak, you know, in case she's not real, in case she disappears, and because I'm nervous, this stupid thing comes out of my mouth. 'You dumb, or something?'

"And then she gets up and just walks away. Two nights I dream about her. Two days I'm figuring how I can get to see her again, I've *got* to see her, I've got to see her now my swelling's gone down and I'm back to my good-looking self.

"Then the third day, at breakfast, we get this announcement. Her body's been found in the lake. Her picture's on the *Saranac Times,* front page.

"I haven't thought of her for ages, but it's come back to me because of my eyes. This mustard gas's worse than onions even, so look, so look, I'm losing track of things here. . . .

"So look, to get back to serious business, we've each got max, about eight minutes, right? We've gotta work like a team, like a relay, make good use of our time, eight of us by eight minutes, that's an hour to find a way out. Hopeless with the gloves, so we each take our turn with bare hands, right?"

He is reading the walls with his fingertips as though they were braille. "What *is* this stuff? It's not brick, it's not stone, well, it feels like stone, but there aren't any joins, it's not cement. . . ." He moves faster and faster, reading surfaces, working his way through the library of the walls. He scratches it with his fingernails. "I think it's chalk. I think it's some sort of chalk, no, limestone, maybe. Hard chalk. But that's porous, you get it?" There's excitement in his voice. He's moving faster and faster, feeling higher up the wall. "Can somebody lift me?" And two of his fellow prisoners do, making a saddle with their arms. "Higher," he commands. "Higher. I can't feel the ceiling yet. Lift me up to the red light, that's where we should—"

He starts gasping, his breath rattling and bubbling through mucus-thick lungs. "Put me djow . . . djow . . . *down,*" he gasps, with whooping-cough sounds. "Gotta get my breath . . . right in a minute . . . listen up, now . . . this's important. . . .

"Sarin's deadly, but it's volatile. No staying power. Same for mustard gas. Low persistency rates, and they settle low to the ground, so stay high, okay? Don't lie on the floor. Now, what we have to do is find vents, leaks, cracks . . . oh shit, uhh . . . uhhh . . . can't get my . . ." He leans against the wall, exhausted. "Sweating . . . like a pig . . . hot flashes . . . funny, huh, Joe? Me . . . hot flashes." The camera picks up the gleam of moisture on his skin. Water drips from his hair. "Okay. Listen . . . lis'n up. Shit, I'm drowning in here, I'm drowning inside my friggin' suit. . . . Okay, lis'n . . . 'nother chemistry fact . . . as y'can see, high activ . . . cuts down s'vival time . . . so okay, quick re . . . cal . . . cu . . . lation"—his words slur and pile up against each other—"eight of us, sixminseach, thssstill for'y-five mins, 'nough time . . . find hairline crack. Get freshair . . . toxic's seeping out anyway . . . 'coz porous . . . walls porous . . ." He licks his finger and holds it up. "Weak draft, see? Hellhole's not airtight . . . shit's dispersing . . . not fast enough, though. . . ."

He breathes noisily, raspily, for several seconds, then taps an adrenaline riff. He throws his body and arms against the wall, making great sweeping arcs. "If they got us in, there's a way out . . . stands to reason. Why can't I remember . . . ? Ahhh, my eyes, ahhh . . . ahh . . ."

He slumps against the wall and shields his face. "Anyone remember . . . how they got us in? Trapdoor . . . ceiling? floor? A door? Anyone know?"

In slow stately fashion, bodies encumbered, his Martian cell mates sweep the walls with their gloves.

"Must have drugged us . . . bricked us in, walled us in . . . but there'd be wet mortar, we could push . . . can't find any joins . . . I don't get it.

"Must be the ceiling . . . a trapdoor . . . has to be . . . ahhh . . . ughugh!" He doubles over and shields his eyes with his arms, but as though taking up his crusade, the Martians group themselves and make arm-saddles, and others climb onto the saddles and push at the ceiling, testing for wet mortar that might give way. It's swarm activity, a hive of frenzy and hope.

"Damn thing is . . ." Billy Jenkins gasps, "same time your eyes adjusting to dark, same time you're just starting to see, you go blind. . . ."

He begins to laugh in a helpless hysterical way. "Like getting last standby seat, huh? Been there, seen God, he's a joker."

He is staggering now, admonishing himself, "Don't fall, don't fall, gases settle low, gotta stay high," but he is gasping, crumpling to his knees, until the shadow-swarm, acting as one, lifts him and raises him high above their heads. He lies there, on an elevated bier, and speaks to the red eye.

"That girl? With the onion eyes? They said accident, but rumor went around it was suicide . . . mother cancer jus' before . . . sh'didn' wanna go camp . . . father thought, good for her, good to get away . . . color photograph in camp newspaper . . . cut it out . . . still in my wallet . . .

"Mom? Dad? Joe? I don't get it. I don't get death, I just don't get it. Who th'hell thought it up? F'life, y'know. I'm for life. Love football, booze, getting laid.

"And now I won't ever—

"Larissa Barclay, that was her name. Girl with onion eyes. Picture's in my wallet.

"Uhh . . . can't . . . got fucking great wad of spunk in my throat. . . .

"Joe? Joe, you there? Do something for me? Call Mary Sue . . . tell 'er sorry about abortion . . . really sorry. Tell her . . . just realized . . . stupid moron I've been. Tell her . . . she was the one . . . only one.

"Dad? I was saving . . . surprise for y' birthday? Super Bowl, air tickets, everything. You 'n Joe 'n me. Dad . . . promise . . . you 'n Joe? Send word upstairs, eh, if Pittsburgh wins?

"Mom? I don't get it, Mom . . . last standby . . . ten min's later . . . I woonta made't'ome . . . just live instead . . . God's a joker, eh?

"Hap' birth . . . Love you, Mom."

The hum of the bee swarm rises to cover him, a sonorous chant, but as the shadows bear him aloft to the corner and lower him, he sits up suddenly, in a final access of energy, and says clearly and desperately, "Volatile . . . low persistence . . . sarin dispersing . . . find cracks."

And then he begins to convulse and moan and . . .

CUT

William Jenkins

Born Pittsburgh, Pennsylvania, 1965

5.

On screen, time has stopped. A spell has been cast and everyone is stilled in mid-action. Private assessments are being made and you yourself are required to take stock and to place your bet. You feel claustrophobic, trapped, suffocating, as though you too are sweating like a pig inside your suit. You are making urgent statements (making noise, making babble) through your speaking tube. You are engaging in earnest debate. *Listen!* you shout. *Listen to me! There is x and y to consider.* And the earnest blather of response comes shussing and rabble-rushing back. Your ears are full of the hiss and spit and white-noise bubbling of chaos. You must recalculate. There is no room for error. If Billy Jenkins is right that the volatile gases are dispersing and leaking away, then you and your fellow padded shadows should wait.

Simply that: wait.

Wait things out.

Should you? Yes, yes, obviously. But for how long?

You will die entombed in your suit when the filter gives out. Five hours left? Four? Before that, you will drown in your sweat. You will die of body fevers that climb above the upper reaches of medical records. You are placing bets on a roulette wheel. Which will come first:

Dispersal of gases? Or clogged filter? You are gambling away the chance to speak your last words. You know this.

Place your bet.

You lean against the wall, overcome by the torture of choice. You wait. You calculate and recalculate. You hedge your bet.

You are for manageable risk and survival.

You are for survival.

You make a heavy decision and hedge your bet. In this decision, you are not alone.

Someone rips off gloves, but not gas mask. The person-thing signals for a saddle to be formed. The intention is clear. He-she will read the ceiling's braille. She-he will search for the trapdoor, the opening, the fault line, the entrance that has been sealed up. But the ceiling is high and cannot be reached from the saddle. More signals. Four beings lock arms to form a square, and two others, two smaller beings, in spite of their lumbering clothing, half clamber, half vault into standing position, balancing precariously on the others' arms.

Slowly, then, very slowly, the first rampart of the pyramid bends at the knees, and the one whose gloves have been removed vaults up to the second tier and then seeks to mount the final two. Failure. The structure collapses.

Begin again.

Failure.

Begin again, slowly, carefully . . . almost . . . No. Yes. The delicate pyramid is achieved.

The being at the apex grunts in triumph. "Contact!" he-she calls, though the speech tube is an echo tunnel and sound bounces like a stone in a well, genderless and furred at the edge. The climber reads by fingertip; the supporters, below, move like a cumbersome truck. These movements are awkward and dangerous. Inch by inch, the ceiling is mapped. A muffled order is called through the speech tube, unintelligible. The base of the pyramid lurches one way, the second tier another.

The pyramid crashes.

The shadow-beings are extremely fatigued from this exertion. Big-headed, they swoon against the walls and gulp air through their breathing tubes. They are drowning inside their suits, their body temperatures are at dangerous levels. Sirens scream in their heads. They fantasize ambulance drivers, paramedics, oxygen tanks. They hallucinate air and ice.

The person-thing with no gloves rips at the Velcro collar of the mask.

"Daddy!" Samantha cries.

Without warning, a rogue breaker smashes over her. She cannot stop sobbing.

Lowell presses the STOP button and waits.

"The ceiling feels the same as the walls," Jonathan Raleigh announces. "If there's a trapdoor, it would take way too long to find it by groping in the dark. I think the rest of you should try to wait it out. If Billy was right. . . .

"And think about this. Why haven't we had any more sneering announcements from Sirocco? Because the Marines have got to him and his pals, that's why. That must be why. Sharpshooters have got them. So it's only a matter of time. . . . Uh . . . my eyes!

"Uhh . . . " He leans against the wall. "Never knew breathing could be such hard work." He breathes heavily, slowly, deeply. "Don't have much time and there are things I have to say before I go. Things I have to say."

He looks into the camera's eye. "Lou, I've wanted to say it publicly from Day One, but I've been such a coward and a jerk. I'm sorry. Pathetic word, I know. I don't expect you to forgive me, because what I did can't be forgiven, it was criminal, but I don't want to die without your knowing that I know what a coward I was."

He coughs a hacking cough and spits up phlegm.

He rubs his eyes. "Little Matthew died on the plane, and Rosalie's gone . . . but Sam's safe somewhere. She's yours now, Lou. Take care of her. Don't let her turn out like me.

"I think there'll be some survivors of this mess, and for Sam's sake, I was tempted to wait it out, but the dues I've got to pay are too steep. I thought if I could use my time to find an opening, help the others, it might atone. . . .

"Anyway, tell your parents. They have a right to know. . . .

"If it helps, tell mine too, even though it'll break their hearts. My fault. I've disgraced my ancestors, who have plenty of sins on their heads, but cowardice was never one of them. I'm sure you and Rosalie got sick to death of hearing *seven generations, blah blah,* all the Raleigh movers and shakers, Revolutionary War, Civil War, all the medals, and how we never backed down, *blah blah blah,* always got our own way, mansions in Charleston, plantations, state legislature in our pockets, great slaveholders, and charm on top of all that, the Raleigh charm."

He sinks to his knees, coughing and spitting phlegm. "Jesus," he moans. "My eyes." He turns his blind face to the watching eye.

"Only two other times in my life, Lou . . . felt helpless like this. . . .

"You know about one.

"Other one's about my father and I've never told. . . .

"Three years ago in my office . . . eighteenth floor . . . fabulous view of Atlanta . . . secretary says, 'You'vegotappointment . . .' " His words slur. He gasps, breathing raspily, then goes on with a rush: "Very sexy young black woman walks in, gorgeous.

" 'Penelope Lukins,' she says.

"Doesn't ring any bells.

" 'Remember Arabella Lukins?' she asks me.

" 'Good God, yes, housekeeper, like a mother to me.' I go weak at the knees, Lou. Fresh-baked biscuits, peach cobbler, smells of childhood, I'm weak at the knees.

" 'I'm her daughter,' she says.

" 'Good grief. Little Penny Lukins, used to hang around the kitchen door?'

" 'That's the one,' she says. 'You used to put junebugs in my hair to make me scream.' "

Jonathan Raleigh laughs, and the laughter turns into a desperate coughing fit. He gasps and makes whooping sounds, struggling for breath. "Oh shit, my eyes." He stumbles about, pounding on the wall with his fists, and manages to draw new breath from the stone.

" 'Used to be a scrawny duckling,' I tell her, 'and look at you. Wha . . . doing now?'

" 'Law degree,' she says.

"Could've knocked me over with a feather. 'Could your mother,' I say, 'ever imagine . . . ?'

" 'Yes,' she says."

Another paroxysm of coughing rattles him, but memory pushes up through it, forceful and clear. " 'Matterovfact,' Penny Lukins says to me, 'My mama always say: If that pea-brained little delinquent Jonathan Raleigh can get into college, then so can you.' "

Jonathan Raleigh is laughing and coughing and choking. His eyes are streaming red tears. "I tell her, 'Sweetarabella never talk like that in her life.'

" 'Didn't talk like that to white folks, is all,' she says. 'I do.'

" 'So,' I say. 'What can I do . . . ?'

"She says, 'Nothing for me, but for my little boy Damien . . .' And I take my checkbook and say, 'Sure, and I might have known this would be about a handout, and how much do you . . . ?' And she says, 'Damien's your nephew, I'm your half-sister.'

" 'Bullshit,' I say.

" 'Part of my mama's regular duties,' she says, 'being screwed by your father Wednesday nights when your mother played bridge. Give you a blood sample,' she says, 'DNA tests. Damien's got sickle-cell anemia,' she says, 'and I've got no medical insurance. Pay you back after I get my law degree.'

"Opens her damn briefcase, formal loan agreement all made out with repayment terms. 'You decide the interest rate,' she says.

"I'm staring at her. 'Did you go to my father?' I ask.

"Uh, uh, uh . . ." Jonathan Raleigh gasps. "My eyes . . . oh God, look at this . . . my hands."

Where Jonathan Raleigh's hands rub against each other, the skin comes off.

"Ahhhh . . . Penny!" he calls. "Penny, call them off. Call your dogs off."

He tips his head back and the red eye of God glares. "Where was I?" he asks. "Oh yes, Penny.

" 'No,' Penny says to me. 'No, I didn't go to your father.'

" 'Why not?' I want to know.

" 'Two reasons,' she says. 'Despise your father, too much to speak to him. And two: curious to find out if you're a self-righteous and fraudulent shit just like him.'

" 'Get out,' I say.

" 'I will,' she says. 'But 'cause of Damien, I'll be filing a paternity suit for medical support . . . and I'm sure your gracious mother will deal with the publicity with all her usual—'

" 'Manipulative bitch,' I say.

" 'Must be the family gene pool,' she says.

"So I wrote the checks for Damien's treatments, Lou, but I never met him. I never saw Penny Lukins again, but she paid back her loan. Never told my father.

"Had the shakes after she left.

"It was, like, free fall. . . .

"My father . . . pillar of the church . . . good Republican . . . couldn't get my mind around it . . . fraudulent shit just like him. . . ."

He's gasping now. His eyes are swollen shut. He tries to speak and he can't. He's red in the face, but his will—a tornado—barrels through.

"Lou," he says, "got no right to ask anything . . . but if you could find Penny and Damien . . . my oral will. Leave everything to Sam . . .

but twenty thousand dollars a year to Penny and Damien . . . should stand up in a court of law."

He is speaking faster and faster. He is coughing up phlegm. "Lou . . . unless you told her, Ros never knew. Tell Sam . . . apple of my eye. Tell her . . . she's her mother's daughter . . . no pretense . . . the real thing."

CUT

Jonathan Marion Raleigh

Born Charleston, South Carolina, 1956

6.

Four bodies lie beneath the red eye, laid neatly, their shoulders touching. Six shadow-beings kneel and touch the bodies with the foreheads of their masks.

One stands. He removes his headpiece as though he were a priest removing vestments. His motions are full of dignity and grace.

The hair of Avi Levinstein, violinist, is sodden with sweat. It drips rain on his face.

"I am a secular Jew," he says to the red eye. He explains this earnestly. He speaks as though taking thoughtful part in a discussion, after dinner, say, or over sherry. "I don't have a religious bone in my body—at least, that is what I have always believed. I have always said that my only religions are music and love."

"Avi, wait!"

The embrace of Avi Levinstein and Isabella Hawthorne is long and passionate, or seems long, though in fact it lasts for less than half a minute. Avi presses Isabella to himself, his hand on the back of her head, her cheek on his shoulder.

"I discover, after all," Avi Levinstein says, "and very much to my own surprise, that I am a religious Jew. I see now, I understand, that the religious impulse begins in awe, and awe begins at death.

"It's very strange. My father was a devout man and he often exasperated me and I argued with him and rejected everything he stood for, but I see I was wrong. I feel the need, the compulsion, for *ceremony*. I want to say something for these four—for us ten. I want to say something formal. I need to. We are joined in such an extraordinary bond. . . ."

He steps closer to the red eye. "You think you have forged this bond, Sirocco, but it no longer has anything to do with you. You are nothing. Do you understand?

"Something is happening here and I need ritual to contain the feeling.

"Words of my father are welling up in me, words I had no idea that I remembered." He lifts his arms to the invisible opening above him and sings in Hebrew, then in English:

> *"All flesh is grass . . .*
> *surely the people is grass.*
> *The grass withereth, the flower fadeth:*
> *but the word of our God shall stand . . ."*

"Avi, Avi." Isabella is pressing her fingers around the sockets of her eyes. Her breathing is labored. "There are things I have to say. Be quick, Avi—"

"The word shall stand," Avi sings. *"For ever, amen."*

"My eyes!" Isabella says. "You must speak to Jacob, Avi. Be quick."

"My message to Jacob is music. You speak."

"Lowell," Isabella says, but she cannot get her breath. She presses her right hand against her breastbone as though trying to dislodge something—mucus, a blood clot—and Avi Levinstein begins to play his violin. He moves his imaginary bow across the strings, his fingering is intricate, he sings the melody with his body and with his lungs.

"Lowell," Isabella says again, offering her cupped hands to the camera and the red eye. "Here are white doves. Do you remember that bedtime story? When you were little, you used to ask me to tell it over and over again. Here are white doves, Lowell."

Avi Levinstein hums, and the slow movement of the Bach Violin Concerto in A Minor rises lushly around Isabella.

"There was a dove . . ." she says, and her voice rattles unevenly, "there was a dove who was kept in a cage with a black cloth over it. In the house where the cage was kept lived the father and the mother and little Boy Blue.

"Boy Blue watched doves from his window and he heard their soft calling. 'Why doesn't our dove sing?' he asked his mother.

" 'Our dove is sad,' his mother said. 'Because of the cage and the black cloth.'

" 'Why do we keep our dove in a cage? And why do we cover her?'

" 'The cage is to keep her safe,' his father said. 'And the black cloth is so no one will see her and wish to steal.'

"But the cage and the black cloth saddened Boy Blue. Secretly, when his father was at work, he removed the cloth and opened the door of the cage. 'Fly away,' he whispered. 'You are free.'

"But his dove cooed sadly from her perch. 'It has been too long. My wings have grown weak. I can't fly.'

"Day after day, Boy Blue removed the cloth and opened the door of the cage, and his dove's silence and stillness broke his heart. He grieved for her. He grew thin and sad and his Boy Blue wing feathers drooped. The child and his dove both languished and grew ill.

"And then, out of the blue, one unnoticed day, another dove settled on the windowsill and called. Boy Blue's dove fluttered and fell from her perch.

"She picked herself up and flew clumsily to the sill.

"She steadied herself . . .

". . . and the two doves flew off into the sky."

Avi Levinstein has laid down his imaginary bow to hold his hands over his eyes, but the strains of the slow movement continue. The music has a life of its own. Sometimes there is a break in a phrase. Sometimes there is coughing.

"Jacob," Avi Levinstein says. He is gasping now. "Here is something your grandfather told me. This is the way to say Torah. *You must be nothing but an ear which hears what the universe says.* Hold on to my violin, Jacob, because my violin is my way of saying Torah."

"Lowell," Isabella says, "here are doves," and she lofts them into the air. "Mather, forgive me. I send my blessing to you both."

Even when the convulsions start, Avi and Isabella hold each other, and fragments of the A Minor seem to drift through the room.

CUT

Isabella Hawthorne, née Taylor

Born Boston, 1942

Avi Levinstein

Born New York, 1940

7.

Victoria Goldberg inverts her gas mask and offers it like a chalice to the dead.

"I too will speak in music," she says. "In memory of my beloved Izak, who died on the plane, and to my darling child Cass, who was saved, and to my parents, and to the memory of Avi Levinstein, with whom I have so often made music, and to Isabella, who brought him such great happiness in these last few months, I offer a song which Izak and Avi and I have often performed together.

"In fact, just last week, we performed this trio in Paris in a concert in La Sainte Chapelle.

"The music is by Orlando Gibbons, court composer, to Elizabeth I."

Victoria Goldberg begins to sing and brightness falls from the air. You listen. You are transformed. The air in the bunker turns green and gold. You step into the cramped space of the dream and you offer Victoria Goldberg your hand and the wall opens and she takes you away.

The silver swan, who living had no note,
When death approached unlocked her silent throat,
Leaning her breast against the reedy shore,
Thus sung her first and last, and sung no more:
Farewell all joys, O death come close mine eyes,
More geese than swans now live, more fools than wise.

She begins to sing the short ballad a second time, and then a third, folding her wings over her streaming eyes until her voice falters and chokes—

CUT

Victoria Goldberg, née Angelino
Born Chicago, 1940

8.

"The seventh one sang herself to death and then there were three," Homer Longchamp says. He busies himself with making a small cairn of the seven discarded gas masks and adding his own to the top. "The mind astonishes me," he says. "What a search engine. Two completely disparate associations come fizzing along the synapses, the way they only do in dreams or during the flow of the creative act—or facing death, I suppose—and you realize, yes, there's a meaningful link between the two: between a Mother Goose jingle about Ten Little Niggers and Pol Pot's small mountains of skulls in Cambodia.

"Of course, it's easy to trace the lines of association in this instance. If anyone is going to get mass deaths and nursery rhymes tangled up, it's going to be the only nigger in the room. But how did one dazed nigger from New Orleans get himself into the middle of this?"

He shakes his head at the red eye and at his two companions in genuine bafflement, as though they are sitting in a seminar room, as though not one of them has noticed that the class has gone an hour overtime because they are held spellbound by the intellectual conundrum pulled like a rabbit from a gas mask.

"To whom are we speaking?" he asks his two companions. (They have moved together and stand holding each other. They hold each other, but their bug-eyed heads are turned to the speaker.) "To whom are we speaking?" He raises his outstretched arms, palms up, in a gesture that implies an unanswerable question. "Who is watching? Who is listening? Are we speaking to the world on television? Are we speaking to Intelligence agencies? " He gestures at the red eye. "We know that God, if He's there, and if He watches and listens, never answers. He's turned a deaf ear and a blind eye to suffering for millennia. But at least we've always had the devil to talk to, to rail against or cozen up with. And now nothing. Why has the devil fallen silent? We've learned to manage without God, but how can we deal with the death of Satan?

"To whom are we speaking?

"Sirocco? Are you there? No. If you were, you wouldn't be able to resist cutting in. Nobody's there.

"The plain truth is: we are talking to ourselves, which is where all arguments begin and end. Life is a monologue that we tweak and edit every day. We take in the big questions"—he feeds a question from his cupped hand into his mouth—"and we chew them like cud. And here's one worth chewing: how can we account for this spontaneous outbreak of ritual, *religious* ritual—this reverence for death itself, and for life itself, and this grief for the death of strangers—how can we account for this arising from the death of Satan and the silence of God?

"I don't know," he says, puzzling at it, absorbed, "which of the three great mysteries can be considered the most impenetrable. Life. Or death. Or randomness. But I think randomness, the maddening neatness of randomness. Yes, I think the geography of chance is the ultimate teaser, intellectually and morally, because of the sheer enormity of divergence that results from a micro-change here and a micro-change there. It's almost a commonplace now, with mathematicians: the Lorenz discovery—an accidental finding in itself—that minute changes in weather systems can have catastrophic results.

"So the precise geometry of chance gets my vote, because here's the thing: if the fluke event which led to my being on Air France 64 had not happened, and instead I had ten more years to live out, say, or twenty, teaching in this university or that, arguing with colleagues and graduate students, would I have gotten any closer to a solution of the patterning of thought processes in creativity? Could I ever have set up a thought experiment that would concentrate the mind as intensely as this one does?

"Consider the puzzle of my own existence: Homer Longchamp, born in New Orleans, descendant of slaves on one side, and of a seventeenth century French plantation family of stupendous wealth and great classical scholarship on the other; heir, therefore, of ancient Greece, Europe, Africa and the New World. I grew up in New Orleans, I consider jazz a religion and a passion, I spent two years in jail in Mississippi in the turbulent years, and now I live in New York. I teach philosophy at Columbia, though my research and my doctorate are in psychology. I sometimes think of myself as a philosopher of psychology and sometimes as a psychologist of comparative philosophies or of comparative systems of cohesion. I play jazz saxophone. This year, I'm a visiting professor at the Sorbonne, but I really come to Paris for the jazz.

"The randomness of my life and the tangential changes in direction never cease to astound me. They're my primary research field, although of course I have been taking into account the information that Billy Jenkins gave us: the volatility of the gases, their settling low. . . .

"I noted less eye inflammation, less skin corrosion in the last two deaths. The secret may lie in breathing only the upper levels of air—good to be tall—but the risk will shift to oxygen deprivation." He licks his index finger and holds it up. "Faint current of air from somewhere. . . ."

He is pacing the room. He has forgotten the red eye, his two companions, the dead hostages.

"I have a confession to make to myself: my dominant emotion at this moment is intense curiosity; my secondary emotion, very close in intensity to the first, is an oceanic sense of love and connectedness to the nine people with me in this room. This second feeling is so intense that it is intellectually suspect; it seems hysterical, pathological, related to the shortage of air, the shortage of time, and the murk in which I can now distinguish at least twenty shades of brown. If I have another lifetime—and perhaps I will; I have come to take the unexpected turn of events for granted—I will devote it to understanding the psychology of fusion and its biological links to swarm and herd behavior: the sort of thing that happens in football stadiums, or that happened at Hitler rallies, and that happens in black gospel revival meetings, and that has been happening here. There can be good fusion and bad fusion; revival fervor, Hitler fervor.

"What sets it off?

"What set of chances drew the ten of us together?

"Have we bonded *because* we don't know each other? Because we won't ever meet again?

"The mathematical philosophers have decoded chance for us: a series of seemingly nonsequential events within a deterministic universe.

"A butterfly fluttering its wings in the Amazon rain forest can cause a tornado in Texas. *And may not imagination trace the noble dust of Alexander till he find it stopping a bunghole?* And might not a boy whose father hauls garbage in New Orleans turn into a thinker? This is how it happens: the garbage man takes his son with him on a certain day when the father's route includes the federal courthouse. The boy climbs on a ledge and looks through a window. He doesn't know he's looking into the judge's chambers, but he sees a room that fills him with awe: oriental carpet, mahogany desk, books stacked to the ceiling. The man at the desk has a book in his hands, but he is not reading. He stares into the middle distance and thinks.

" 'I want a room like that,' the boy decides. 'I want books. I want to sit at a desk and *think*.' The wish has the force of a vow.

"Pure chance, and it brings me here instead of driving trucks in the Big Easy and hauling garbage.

"And here's another puzzle.

"Yesterday in Paris—yesterday? four days ago? five?—in a restaurant in Paris, I'm watching two men at a nearby table. They're not close enough for me to overhear, but body language fascinates me. Analyzing it is one of the games with which I amuse myself: I note how revealing it is, but also how subject to misinterpretation. If we get the translation wrong, the Lorenz effect kicks in: small errors, big consequences.

"One of the men is stocky and Egyptian-looking, but I can tell they are both speaking English. An acute observer can deduce any language from the movement of lips and cheeks. The other man is American. (No prizes for that guess. In Europe, Americans stick out like sore thumbs. You spot them by clothing, by the way they walk, the way they sit, what they order for a drink, and the way they drink it.)

"The American is fifty or so, the Egyptian man younger, forty perhaps. I'll call them Mr. A and Mr. B. Mr. A is fiercely angry, but his anger is kept tightly under control. His wineglass and his silverware obey strict geometrical rules. Mr. B is also a control freak, but he is enjoying himself. He is greatly amused. It is clear to me that whatever their quiet but intense argument is about, Mr. B is holding an ace up his sleeve and is savoring the moment when he will play it.

"What holds my attention in particular is this: Mr. A, though intensely involved in discussion, is keeping the room under surveillance. His glance is covert and quick, but he takes note of each entry and exit, each movement. Mr. B, on the other, seems oblivious to the room. His laser focus on Mr. A is intense. When a sommelier passing close to their table stumbles a little, causing a wineglass to teeter dangerously on his tray, Mr. A starts and leaps to his feet and saves the glass. Mr. B, around whose lips a slight smirk plays continually, seems unaware of the passing waiter, though his eyes follow Mr. A's reach for the tray. He watches Mr. A with the concentration of cat observing a bird.

"And then, suddenly, Mr. A becomes noticeably agitated, so agitated that the stem of his wineglass snaps and there is red wine all over the linen cloth and blood on Mr. A's hand. Mr. B smiles serenely and signals the sommelier, though his focus never wavers from Mr. A.

Their intense discussion is resumed for a few minutes and then Mr. B leaves the table nonchalantly, pauses at the door, returns to the table, and this time I hear what he says: 'Oh, I forgot to tell you. I collect on forfeits. Always. Every time.'

"It is Mr. B's obliviousness to everything except Mr. A that engrosses me, because in his concentrated predatory gaze I recognize one of the telltale signs of the psychopath.

"How could I not yield to a research temptation like that?

"I followed him.

"I followed him, eventually (it took several hours) into a Moroccan coffeehouse in the eighteenth arrondissement, the Arab quarter of Paris. It was the kind of crowded smoky place where a non-Arab is instantly conspicuous and is instantly aware of a cloud of suspicion and hostility, hardly an unfamiliar experience for an African-American.

"I have a little Arabic, not much, but enough to order my coffee. A murmur spread like a breeze through the room. I ignored it. I did not look at Mr. B. I took *Le Monde* from my jacket pocket, unfolded it, and began to read.

"Mr. B came to my table and sat down.

"I ignored him. I did not look up. It was discount psychology. It was like taking candy from a baby, because people like Mr. B cannot tolerate being ignored. They are magnets and they take this for granted. They are white-hot bulbs who make sport of collecting moths. They are irresistibly aroused by those who fail to respond to their charm.

" 'Where are you from?' he asked me in excellent French.

"I replied in French, without looking up, 'Is that any of your business, monsieur?'

"He waited. I went on reading *Le Monde*. It was a contest of wills.

"I finished my coffee—it was an espresso, Moroccan-style, a thimbleful blacker than tar—and folded my newspaper, tucked it under my arm, and left. I knew he would follow me. In fact, I did not get as far as the door.

" 'I have a proposition for you,' he said. 'Are you looking for a woman or drugs?'

"I did not answer.

" 'Perhaps you would like something a little stronger than coffee?' he suggested. 'I have an office behind the shop and some very good scotch.'

"I said, 'I thought the Prophet forbade alcohol.'

" 'I am not a good Muslim,' he said. 'Can we talk business?'

" 'Okay,' I said.

"And in the small room at the back, he asked me, 'You are Haitian? Or from Guadeloupe?'

" 'I'm American,' I said in English.

"He raised his eyebrows, then switched to an English joke: 'Ahh. So, you are CIA.'

"I laughed. 'Close,' I said. 'I'm on their blacklist. Spent two years in jail in Mississippi.' I could see the electrical zap of interest on his part. 'I'm a jazz musician,' I said, 'trying to make ends meet. Funny how I can't get gigs in New York or New Orleans, but I can play in any club on the Left Bank.'

"He leaned forward. 'Do you have a *carte de séjour?*'

" 'Good grief, no,' I said. 'Strictly illegal moonlighting. I play for cash.'

" 'I could get you a *carte de séjour,*' he said.

" 'Really? And how much would that cost?'

" 'We could make an arrangement,' he said. 'You could do something for me.'

" 'And what would that be?'

" 'I need someone to take a package to New York,' he said. 'A friend was going to take it tomorrow, but at the last minute, he finds he is unable to go.' He reached into an inner pocket of his jacket and pulled out a travel folder. 'I have a round-trip ticket. If you take the package for me, when you come back, I will have a *carte de séjour* waiting for you. Are you interested, monsieur?'

"The ticket was for an Air France flight, Paris–New York, Flight Number 64, leaving the next day, September eighth. The name on the airline ticket was Khalid Waburi. 'I'm not going to be permitted on the plane with a ticket that doesn't match my ID,' I pointed out.

" 'I have a passport that matches the ticket,' he said. 'Of course, we'll need to insert your photograph, but that's easily done.'

"He lifted his arm and signaled to someone unseen and then there was a flash and my picture was taken.

" 'I don't think I look like a Khalid Waburi,' I said.

" 'If there's any question, you can say you are a Black Muslim.'

"I laughed. 'You think that would get me smooth passage?'

" 'You will say your father was a refugee from Idi Amin, and you were born in the USA.'

" 'I see. Then I am assuming that the package you wish me to deliver is something I may have trouble getting through customs?'

" 'Not at all, my friend. It is a letter that I need hand-delivered.' He gave it to me. There was no address. 'There is another envelope inside this one,' he said, 'which you will open in New York. Of course, I will need a photocopy of your American passport, in order to have the details for the *carte de séjour*. We will make it when I meet you at the airport. Tomorrow.'

"And here I am, another tangent, another coincidence, and a question of minor interest to me is: had he already decided on revenge because I ignored him in the coffee shop? Was his threshold for sensing insult so low? Or was he intending to make use of me until he ran a check on my name? Did he decide the jail time in Mississippi was not sufficient to vouch for me as a renegade? Did he put together the Sorbonne and my French and my Arabic and wrongly conclude: CIA after all?

"It doesn't matter.

"It would seem that the tangent must be significant, and the meaning tantalizes but eludes me because what hovers as of equal significance is another random moment from the day of the flight, a street musician I heard in the Place des Vosges. I had my ticket and my fake passport, I was filling in time before the two o'clock Roissybus from Place de l'Opéra, and I heard the unmistakable sounds of New Orleans jazz. Someone was playing Duke Ellington's 'Caravan' on a tenor sax, and I can't begin to explain to you the effect, the excitment, the extraordinary coincidence. The night before I'd left New York to fly here, to the Sorbonne, I mean, I'd gone to a concert of a new young trumpeter from my home town: Wynton Marsalis. He played 'Caravan'—well, every jazz musician who's ever lived has played 'Caravan'—but this bracketing of my flights with the song filled me with an intense and obscure excitement. I had an inner conviction, entirely irrational, that something profound would come of this. The feeling was just as intense as the one that flooded me at the New Orleans courthouse thirty years earlier. *This will come to pass,* I knew then.

"*This flight will have profound significance for me,* I knew as I listened to 'Caravan.'

"The musician was black. We made eye contact and never lost it. At the end of his set, he asked me, 'Where you from, man?' And when I said 'New Orleans,' he began to laugh and said, 'Me too, bro. Got a riddle for you. When two niggers from Nawlins meet in Paris, what's the first thing they ask one another?'

" 'Don't know,' I said. 'Tell me.'

"And he said, 'Where can I get me some grits and where can I get me some good blues?' And we laughed and shook hands and I said no, sorry, I couldn't stay for a drink because I had a flight to New York.

"But I can't stop thinking about him. I have 'Caravan' running through my head, and I am also noticing that though my eyes are stinging and my vision is blurred, and my lungs feel as though they are stuffed with wet towels, the gases are clearly dispersing because here I am still talking and you two have just come to the same conclusion and it is time to find the way out."

CUT

Editorial Voiceover:

This is Salamander. Homer Longchamp was accurate. I did observe everyone in the restaurant. I noted Longchamp's presence, for example, even as I bargained for the lives of the passengers with Sirocco. I noticed that Longchamp was reading *Le Monde*. I noticed that he addressed the waiters in French. I noted that French was not his first language; his facial muscles did not have the shape of a French-speaking face.

Khalid Waburi was one of our agents. He successfully infiltrated an Islamic fundamentalist cell and was selected for the crew of Black Death. It was he who gave me the information that Sirocco had other plans and that the stinger was to be stung. Waburi paid a steep price.

CUT

9.

"Symmetry." Tristan speaks to his gas mask as though it were Yorick's skull. "Symmetry keeps cropping up like a dandelion, but it doesn't make any—"

". . . there at the same time as you, listening to 'Caravan.' I'm Genevieve Teague. At exactly the same time, in Place des Vosges. Isn't that weird?"

". . . in the end, some vast symmetry, and everything tends there the way water runs downhill, even though that defies—"

"You heard my friend on the tenor sax?"

"Playing 'Caravan.' "

"Three of us there, and three of us here," Tristan says. "It defies all odds."

"It's so bizarre it has to mean something."

"We want it to mean something," Homer says.

"But it couldn't, because no conspiracy could be so—"

"Forget conspiracy," Homer says. "There's something awesome about the patterns of chance, something mysterious, and we need that mystery. Especially now."

"At least it makes our deaths interesting," Tristan says. "Stupid and horrible, but interesting. These seven grotesque deaths . . ."

They are all talking at once in little rushes of sound, and touching one another, holding one another, stroking one another in a manic kind of way as though the sarin will return if they slacken or if they let the heat of connection drop for one heartbeat. And then—click. On the stroke of *grotesque deaths,* a switch is thrown, or so it seems. It is as though one group-brain is governing them, the change is so uniform and sudden. They fall silent and still, three solitudes. Their hands and arms, which were flashing about, droop, then twitch, then hang slack.

This lasts for three seconds.

"There's air," Homer says. "A small current."

"Has to come from the opening." Tristan pulls off his gloves and rakes the walls with the palms of his hands. "Door. Trapdoor. Whatever they sealed up. There must be a crack."

The unseen puppeteer picks up their strings again, but the three marionette figures move strangely. They flicker. The movie they are in—an old black-and-white reel, nicked and grainy—seems to be on fast forward. The actors bend, stretch, reach, in double-quick time. They are reading the walls with their hands. They hold up index fingers, they rest cheeks against cracks in the wall. They gravitate toward one corner and then suddenly the movie slows down.

"It's here," Genevieve says. "Feel it? There's a definite draft."

Homer leans against the wall. "Something's strange. I feel as though I've been doped."

"What if it's gas?"

"I'll be the canary." Homer tilts his face into the crevice where two walls meet and breathes deeply.

"I think we're not going to die"—Genevieve flinches and raises her arms defensively in an odd motion, as though the idea has swooped by her like a bat—"the same way they did. My muscles feel strange."

"I don't think it's gas," Homer says. "My lungs are okay. I just feel weak."

"I think oxygen deprivation's our problem now," Tristan says.

"My eyes are really giving me hell all of a sudden. My vision's going cloudy."

"Can you two lift me up? Let me feel around the light?" Genevieve asks.

Homer says, "I can't see you. Arms won't do what I tell them. Give me time . . . to get air . . . my lungs . . . "

"The stench," Tristan says. "*C'est insupportable.*"

"It's getting hotter. Why's it getting hotter? I'm boiling in this wretched suit."

"The bodies are starting to decompose."

"Ugh. . . ."

"Oh my God"

The marionettes stagger. They are buffeted by unseen waves.

"Got to move . . . other side of the room," Homer gasps. "Need to sit . . . conserve strength."

"Not sit," Tristan warns. "Gases settle low. Lean on the wall."

"Can't," Homer says. "Too weak."

"People are negotiating," Genevieve says, "at the highest levels. For us. You know they are. Must be."

"Doubt it. The line's cut and the devil's dead."

"*Someone's* watching us," Genevieve insists. "We're Sirocco's last bargaining chip. He can't let us die."

"Don't count on that," Homer says. "Curious thing . . . about psychopaths . . . notably deficient . . . in capacity to anticipate consequences."

"If he were watching," Tristan says, "he couldn't resist taunting us again. I'm sure you were right about that."

"The red light's still on," Genevieve says. "The camera's still watching, so someone somewhere is still watching us."

"Sharpshooters must have got Sirocco," Tristan says. "Only explanation for the silence."

"If sharpshooters got him, rescue's close," Genevieve says.

"Hell of a case study, Sirocco . . . subject of my next book. Definitely." Homer, slumped low against the wall, begins playing, with great lassitude, an imaginary tenor sax. *Wa-wa-wa-waa,* he quavers. His fingers move like sleepwalkers on the keys. His voice, in startling saxophone mimicry, sounds like an old 78 version of "Caravan" played slow. "Heard Duke Ellington and Charlie Mingus together?" he pauses to ask. "The gold standard. But that Wynton . . . ! Inside my head . . . angel music, man. Gabriel's horn." His voice slides into a Marsalis rendition. "I need drums," he says drowsily. And Tristan joins him as drummer, thumping his hands against the wall, adagio version, the tape speed slow. . . .

"*Swing low,*" Homer croons, switching mood, "*sweet chariot. . . .*"

"Gonna get me some grits," Homer smiles. He sings again, slow, molasses-slow: "*When I get to heav'n, gonna play my blues, gonna play all over God's heav'n. . . .*"

"Homer, you're letting go. Don't let go."

"*Wa-wa-wa-waaaaa,*" Homer quavers. He has his sax propped against his knees. "*Wa-wa-wa-waaa . . . wa-wa-wa-waaa. . . .*"

CUT

Homer Delaware Longchamp

Born New Orleans, 1949

10.

"Génie?"

"Unh?"

"How are your eyes?"

"Could be worse. Yours?"

"Bad. *Mais la puanteur!*"

"Yes," she murmurs, drugged, as though the stench has indeed stunned her. "Worst thing."

"Got to find the opening."

"Must be here where the draft is."

"Crack's nearly one centimeter wide."

"I know. If we could wedge something in . . . pry it open. . . . Fingernails all we've got."

"My belt buckle!" Tristan fumbles with the drawstring at the neck of his padded suit. "Help me get this damned straitjacket—"

"Not sure I can. No energy. Ugh . . . uh . . . this smell . . . I think I'm going to be sick."

"Can you pull—?"

"Wait." Génie goes to the far corner of the room and stoops over, leaning her head against the wall. "Oh, I feel ghastly." Her body heaves violently. She is sick. "Don't come near me, okay?" She wards him off.

Minutes pass.

"Can I—?"

"No," Génie says. "I just want to crawl off like a cat and die in private."

"I won't let you."

"Okay, okay," she moans.

As though she would collapse without the walls, she marks her slow route at arm's length, leaning in, tilting against her wrist and her open palm. She resembles a blind woman groping.

"See?" She tries to make a fist to show Tristan how the muscles in her fingers have gone slack. "See what's happened?"

Nevertheless, working clumsily together, struggling, panting, grunting, they free Tristan's arms from his suit. Génie tugs back the quilted top and begins to laugh helplessly. "You look like a half-peeled banana." Laughter hangs as loose as oversized clothing from her shoulders. It folds itself round her. It floats and lifts. It climbs into baggy hysteria. It is infectious. The two of them reel about like drunken clowns. "Half-peeled banana," she splutters. "Floating in sweat. You're soaked."

"*Je suis la soupe du jour.*"

"*Soupe de banane.*"

"I've been swimming in here."

"Go diving," she commands, her eyes streaming, "for your belt."

"Uh . . . uh . . ." He gropes beneath the waistline of his suit and pulls the belt out like a water snake. "Moisture burning my eyes," he says. "It's like nettles."

"Mine too. Stinging like crazy. Push your buckle into the crack."

"Trying to. . . . Can't see properly."

"You got it. It's in."

The laughter and weakness leave them abruptly then, like a weather system blown out to sea. They are intent and somber. They jiggle the metal back and forth.

"Open sesame," Genie says, but nothing moves.

"There's space behind here."

"See if you can feed the belt in."

"It's going."

They thread leather through the eye of the crack and the slit in the wall eats the belt.

"First hole," Génie says, measuring off distance with her fingers. "Second hole, third hole, fourth. . . . We're going places." Half of the belt has disappeared. "If we were paper-thin, we could follow it."

"Going to try something." Tristan pulls suddenly and the buckle wedges itself, locks itself, on the far side of the crack. "Got it," he says, jubilant. "Now we can pry the lid off this box."

They hold the leather—soft lever—taut and close. They work like galley slaves, pushing, pulling, forward, back, forward, back. They strain at the oars. They are racing for freedom, fast, faster, frenzied, a futile paroxysm of hope.

"Stop," Tristan says, gasping. "This is stupid. We're using up oxygen. Sweat in my eyes . . . like razor blades . . . "

"No, no, don't stop. I can feel the wall giving way."

"It's not the wall, it's me. It's me giving way."

Tristan slackens, breath raspy, but Génie rows faster and faster, delirious, a comic-book blur, until she gives a sharp cry of pain and presses both hands to her chest.

"Uh . . . !"

"Lean on the wall."

"Pain's killing me."

"Is it your heart?"

"I think so. Must be."

"Breathe slowly."

"My eyes!"

"Mine too. Stay by the draft. It helps."

"We've got . . . air . . . at least," Génie says. They are both taking short rapid breaths.

"Rest. Don't talk. Don't try to talk."

"I feel dizzy." Genevieve is crumpling. "I'm going to black out."

"No, you're not. I won't let you. Don't sit on the floor."

"Have to."

"No. Here." Tristan props her up in the corner by the thin wisp of air. He holds her there with his own body, pressing against her, kissing her lips. "Kiss of death," he jokes. "That's symmetry for you. Remember the first . . . ?"

"Never forget."

"I backed you up against the Quai d'Anjou."

"Seine didn't smell so great either."

"Better than this."

"That's for sure."

Their speech is slow and fading, like old vinyl being played at half speed.

"Thought . . . I was having . . . a heart attack."

"Think of something happy," Tristan urges. "Think of Quai d'Anjou."

"Mmm."

"Left the party early, remember? My own party."

"Your own author. Very bad taste . . . on the publisher's part."

"*Au contraire*. Good taste. . . . I wanted to eat you."

"Mooring ring left a scar on my back." Génie's back is against the wall. Her eyes are closed. Only Tristan's body holds her upright.

"Had to put my mark on you," he says.

"Very primitive."

"*Je suis l'homme.*"

"*L'homme français*." Génie smiles. "Notorious subcategory of species. Distinguishing markings: possessiveness; jealousy."

"No virtues, *c'est ça*?"

"Some."

"*Femme australienne,*" Tristan retaliates. "*Espèce férocement indépendante*. Very prickly. Dangerous to get close. Refuses to let man carry suitcase."

"Never let anyone carry my suitcase. Too much contraband."

"Génie?"

"Hmm?"

"Tell me now, *finalement*. You work in Intelligence?"

"You're joking. Me? Never."

"No covert operations?"

"Letters . . . I smuggle letters, that's all."

"Pains of the heart."

"They're not so bad now. Feel like jelly, though. I could sleep standing up."

"Days since we slept."

"Days since we ate."

"Don't think about that. What do you mean, you smuggle letters? What kind of letters?"

"Personal ones, not political. Like you and your manuscripts." Génie takes long shaky breaths, and her breaths rattle like rice grains in a shaker. "Knew you were doing . . . something shady. . . . You never told me."

"Couldn't. Have to protect the writers. Have to publish them under pseudonyms."

"No wonder you've been under surveillance. Ever . . . get caught?"

"A few times. Hungary once. Romania. Prague, just last week. I was lucky. Don't know what happened to the authors. Not as lucky, I fear. You ever been caught?"

"Spent a night in a cell . . . in Slovakia. Very scary. They didn't find the letters, though. . . . All that matters."

"You alone in the cell?"

"Yes. Horrible."

"Nightmares?"

"Constant."

"Same thing happens to me. It's not knowing what's going to happen, that's the killer."

"Had a horrible dream and woke up screaming. There was a guard with a machine gun watching . . . leering at me." She takes Tristan's hand and pressses it against her cheek. "He was enjoying himself . . . like a kid at the circus. . . ."

"The waiting gets to you."

"Having no idea how long it will be."

"Or what they might do."

"Your mind . . . starts chewing on itself."

"This could be a long wait, Génie."

"Hope not. . . . Feel as though I'm floating away. . . ."

"How long since we've eaten?"

"Can't remember. Too weak to feel hungry."

"Remember that village near Etampes where we stayed in the gîte?"

"Remember the mushrooms? We picked a basketful and then we sauteed them."

"Don't."

"Remember the map?"

"The flea market map? What a bargain. Ten francs, and it's probably worth a few thousand."

"*Région d'Etampes.* And we tried to find a village that existed in 1681."

"I know it's still there," Tristan says. "It's just not on a road anymore."

"If we find it, we'll live there, okay?"

"When we find the opening."

"We'll crawl through . . . hitch a ride to Etampes."

"Ugh . . . stink's getting worse."

"Once upon a time," Génie says, "in a faraway land, a troll hid a priceless treasure at the bottom of a pit of stinking sewage . . . It's your turn. Finish the story."

"And a knight on a white horse came galloping up with an enormous vacuum cleaner and sucked up every molecule of filth, schlurp schlurp, and the air smelled sweet as springtime, and the knight rode into the pit and seized the treasure and took it back to the king's daughter—"

"And they lived happily ever after—"

"In a village near Etampes—"

"Which is no longer on maps—"

"And is therefore accessible at any time—"

"And also unfindable, so no one could put them under surveillance ever again."

"That was good. I forgot about the smell for three seconds."

"I forgot I can't even make a fist."

"Tell me another story, quick."

"I'll tell you the story of Tristan and Iseult."

"Don't like the way that one ends. Tell me a different story."

"Can't think of one."

"Think of one. Here's the first line: *Though the sky was blue, the prisoners could see only the bars on the window, until all of a sudden . . .*

"All I can think of," Tristan says drowsily, "is Paul Verlaine. *Le ciel est, pardessus le toit, Si bleu, si calme . . .*"

"Sky above the roof." Genevieve's voice drifts, translating from the middle of a dream. "I want to see sky again."

"Oxygen," Tristan says, his voice faint. "Oxygen's going. . . ."

(*Stay awake*, you want to shout at them. *Fight!*

(You want to scrabble from the outside of the nightmare with bare hands, because they are moving like sleep-swimmers now, drifting deep underwater. Tristan turns to Génie and kisses her in slow motion, mouth against mouth, and you are floating with them through green fluid space. You see starfish, seaweed streamers, antlers of coral.)

"*Un grand sommeil noir,*" Tristan murmurs, "*tombe sur ma vie . . .*"

(You hear the words like wavelets against your gills, but you thrash against that long dark sleep, you will not let it close over their lives or yours, you refuse to let them sink gracefully, you stir up the waters, you make Leviathan rise from his dark cave. . . .)

"Did you hear that?" Tristan asks.

"What?"

"I don't know. I thought I heard something."

"Can't hear anything," Genevieve mumbles, her voice slurred.

"Something shifted. There are people out there. The crack's getting bigger."

"Tris . . . ?"

STATIC. SEA OF WHITE NOISE. VISUAL BLIZZARD.

The screen goes dark.

Book VIII

AFTERMATH

In this respect our townsfolk were like everybody else, wrapped up in themselves; in other words, they were humanists; they disbelieved in pestilences. A pestilence isn't a thing made to man's measure; therefore we tell ourselves that pestilence is a mere bogey of the mind, a bad dream that will pass away. But it doesn't always pass away and, from one bad dream to another, it is men who pass away, and the humanists first of all, because they haven't taken their precautions.

—ALBERT CAMUS, THE PLAGUE

1.

In the darkened room at the Saltmarsh Motel, Lowell and Sam sit in silence.

Lowell smells western Massachusetts in the fall. He smells pine resin. He smells the thirteenth of September, 1987. He remembers what he did the day the plane blew up on the national news. He remembers that he left the school's common room blindly and drunkenly. Other boys made way for him, he vaguely remembers that, though he told no one his mother had been on the flight. He stumbled down the hall to the only pay telephone in his dorm.

He dialed Washington.

"Your father's still away, Lowell," the secretary said. "He hasn't called in since the hijacking. What message should I give him when he calls?"

"I don't know," Lowell said. He hung up.

He walked out through the school grounds and found himself on the highway heading east. It was dark. He passed a green billboard that announced in phosphorescent letters: BOSTON 90. He realized he must have walked for several hours. Cars passed him. Trucks passed. He decided to hitch a ride. It was only minutes before a pick-up stopped.

"Where you headed, kid?" the driver asked. He wore a plaid shirt and a Red Sox baseball cap.

"I don't know," Lowell said.

"Are you from the school? You look like a prep school kid."

Lowell felt he should know the answer to this question, but he could not think of it.

"You running away?" the driver asked.

"I don't know," Lowell said.

The driver frowned. "Are you *on* something? Like, are you . . . ?"

"No," Lowell said firmly.

"Rumor is that school's a running river of drugs."

"I'm not on anything," Lowell said. This certainty felt like an anchor, like the one thing, for the time being, that he knew to be unquestionably true.

The driver scratched his head. "How about I buy you a hamburger?" he said. "There's a pit stop about ten miles on. Hop in."

Lowell climbed in. There was a tool kit on the passenger seat, the kind that carpenters wear like an apron. The driver pushed it onto the floor. "Put your feet on it," he said cheerfully. "Nothing you can hurt." A pine-scented air freshener in the shape of a Christmas tree dangled from the rearview mirror. The cabin smelled of dog. "Name's Joel," the driver said. "What's yours?"

"Lowell."

"You in trouble, Lowell?"

"I guess so," Lowell said.

"Boy kind?" Joel asked. "Girlfriend left you? Got her knocked up?"

Lowell said nothing.

"Feels like the end of the world?" the driver asked sympathetically.

"Yes," Lowell said.

"It ain't," the driver assured him cheerfully. "I know it feels like it, but it ain't. Hell, I still remember the night I found out my high school sweetheart was cheating on me. I got blind stinking drunk and I borrowed my dad's car and drove it about one hundred miles an hour. I actually thought about smashing myself into a tree. Make her sorry, you know? Talk about stupid. What I did was hit something on the shoulder, spun out of control, got the fright of my life. Boy, did I suddenly find out how much I wanted to stay alive!

"I was lucky. Now, correct me if I'm wrong, but you just lost someone, right?"

"Yes," Lowell said.

"You want to talk about it?"

"No," Lowell said.

"Okay. That's fine. You go with your gut, kid. You want to tell me her name?"

"My mother," Lowell said.

"Your mother?"

"She just died."

"Oh." Joel had no contribution to make on this subject. "Shit. Well, shit. That's heavy stuff."

They drove in silence until the glow of a Shell station came over the highway like a sunrise. "Bathroom," Joel said. "Meet you in the restaurant."

"Sure. Thanks."

But the pines of the state forest rose like a wall just fifty feet from the gas pumps and as soon as Joel disappeared into the men's room, Lowell walked into the pines. He kept walking. It was cold and he wished he had a warmer jacket. He walked until he was too weary to walk any further, then he made a nest for himself in the spongy pine-straw and curled into it. He slept and dreamed that he was alone in a rowboat without any oars. There were rocks. There was a lighthouse somewhere. There was fog. He could see debris floating past his boat: lost luggage; his father's books; the Dead Sea Scrolls; a birdcage with doves.

Shipwreck, he realized.

He realized other boats were drifting nearby in the dark.

He could hear his mother calling for help. "Lowell!" she called all night. "Lowell!"

But he had no oars and no light. He could not find her. There was nothing he could do.

He woke to find himself sobbing, his mouth full of spiky needles and earth.

When they found him, he was huddled at the base of a tree, numb with cold. He spent a week in the school infirmary with pneumonia.

All that night, he thinks now—thirteen years and four months later—all that night when she called and called, she was still alive in that black place, sending me doves.

2.

Sam can hear the suck of sea-water through the marsh grasses, but she is not really thinking at all. She feels blank, she is floating, she is seeing hairline cracks and trapdoors in the ceiling of time, jigsaw pieces, images like cirrus clouds scudding across Charleston Harbor. They have no sequence or logic. Visual moments arrive entire, they hover, they shimmer, they go.

Daddy, she thinks. The sensation of her hand in his is intense. She can feel the slight callus on his index finger. She wants to hang on to him and pull him back. She feels him resist. She feels obscurely angry with him. She is not sure why.

Here she is pulling him along the seafront wall in Charleston. . . .

Here is the harbor and Battery Park . . . the screaming gulls, the live oaks, the trailing boas of Spanish moss. Here is the house of Grandpa and Grandma Raleigh with its wide verandas and silent black servants offering tea. Here are the sago palms in the courtyard where breakfast is served.

A conversation over toast and coffee comes back to Sam like a riddle she never quite worked out. It seems to have detached itself from her father's flickering resurrection in the Saltmarsh Motel because he is buttering toast and Grandma Raleigh is saying: Out of the question, John. Samantha can't visit there alone. Your sister-in-law's out of the question.

Just for a week, her father says, and he is explaining something about Rosalie needing a break, and Grandma Raleigh is protesting that Rosalie's loyalty she can understand but John is under no such obligation, and besides, that woman is *louche,* she is *louche,* and her father is laughing and conceding.

Okay, Mother, you win, he says. Lou *is* a bit disreputable. It's true.

And then Arabella is bringing hot biscuits on a tray and saying, Now what mischief you gettin' into, l'il miz Sam?

And Grandpa Raleigh says: What kind of a question is that, Arabella? No grandchild of mine . . . , and Arabella laughs her high Arabella-laugh and says, Yes, sir, that is the truth. No one strays from the straight and narrow when Mr. Raleigh in charge.

And Samantha's daddy asks: And how is Penny doing these days, Arabella?

And Arabella says: She doing jus' fine, Mr. Jonathan, jus' fine.

Cirrus clouds . . . hurricane clouds . . . high winds. . . .

Here are Grandpa and Grandma Hamilton in *their* Charleston house with lawns like velvet and a widow's walk from which you can see Fort Sumter. You see? Grandpa Hamilton says, adjusting his telescope for Sam. First shots in the two great wars: Revolutionary War and the War between the States. They both began here. He hangs his yellow flag, his DON'T TREAD ON ME rattlesnake flag, from the live-oak tree by the gate. And on the veranda in the white wicker swing, Grandma Hamilton says to Sam's mother, You're such a blessing to us, Rosalie, especially since your sister broke our hearts.

And here is the gymnasium somewhere in Germany, here are the cots where the children are wetting their beds, where all the children are dreaming bad dreams by night, and playing with matches or crash-diving their camp cots by day, here are the relatives arriving, here is Lou—Aunt Lou—who holds Sam and smothers her and sobs until Sam hits her because she can't breathe, and here are Grandpa and Grandma Raleigh also, and here is Grandma Raleigh pulling Sam out of Lou's arms . . . and here is the courtroom and here are the custody battles . . . and here are the schools where Sam is always in trouble, and here is the boarding school where she is sent "to get straightened out," and here she is running away to Lou and screaming at Lou and throwing things, and here she is not knowing why, and running away again, and here are the police, and here is the courtroom, and here are the Hamiltons and the Raleighs who don't speak to each other any more, and here is the boarding school library and the teacher who shows Sam the newspaper articles, *terrorists . . . Flight 64* . . . and here she is wolfing down history and getting obsessed with finding answers instead of getting into trouble . . . and here she is filing access-to-previously-classified-information briefs related to Operation Black Death. . . .

And here she is. . . .

Here she is in bigger trouble than ever before in her life.

3.

"I have to call my children," Lowell says urgently, reaching for the phone. "I have to tell them where I am."

Sam stares at him. "Lowell, it's nearly midnight."

Lowell starts dialing. "They'll know, the way I did. Kids know. They'll know I'm in trouble."

"But they'll be asleep."

"They'll be having nightmares," he says. "They need to know I'm okay." He hangs up abruptly. "I'm *not* okay. My God, what am I thinking of? By now, Rowena's phone's probably tapped."

Samantha goes to the television set and pushes EJECT. She puts the videotape back into its plastic cassette and snaps it shut. She hands it to Lowell.

"What are we going to do with these?" he wants to know. "My God, what are we going to do?"

"I don't know," Sam says. "I feel as though—" She casts about for a metaphor equal to her state of numb disequilibrium. "I feel like a tornado survivor."

"It's still twisting," Lowell says. "It got my father. It's going to get us."

"No," Sam says. She makes a fist and thumps the top of the television set. "It won't get us. It won't. We have to get the tapes out of the country."

"How?"

"I don't know, but I'll think of something."

Lowell goes nervously to the window that looks toward the main office. He parts the drapes a fraction of an inch and peers out. "Shit!" he says. "This is it, this is it. We've had it."

"What? What is it?"

"There's another car outside the office. That guy's called someone."

"Don't panic. We need to stay calm." Sam joins him at the narrow slit between the drapes. "Probably just someone else checking in—"

"It's a *police* car!" Lowell says. "Oh shit. We're not even going to get out of here alive."

"There's no movement," Sam whispers. "No one's coming this way."

"What am I going to do with these?" Lowell is stuffing the tapes into the pillowcase of his childhood, then pushing the knights on chargers frantically into the backpack, prodding at boxy shapes that sprawl and slip. The zipper jams. A loop of pillowcase is caught in its metal teeth. Lowell is sweating. He slides his arms through the straps and holds the backpack like a fevered baby over his heart. He tugs at the zipper to no avail. He wraps his arms around the gaping lips of the bag like someone with a slashed abdomen trying to hold internal organs in place.

"They're coming out of the office," Sam whispers. "They're standing under the floodlight. They're looking in this direction. We have to get out the back way."

"There's no door that side. There's only one way out."

"There's the window."

"It doesn't open."

"The ventilators," Sam says. A large fixed window of double-glazed glass faces the marsh, but beneath it are two sliding panes with removable screens. The sliders are small. Fully open, they leave a space measuring just eighteen inches high and two feet long. Sam unhooks the screen and lets it drop. She puts her right leg through and wriggles out. "Lucky we're on ground level," she says. "Give me the bag."

Lowell hesitates. The bundle feels like an extension of his body.

"For heaven's sake," Sam hisses. "You want to save it or not?"

"You have to hold it closed," he says, anxious. "Don't let anything fall out." He passes it over with some reluctance, and Sam slips her arms through the straps.

"Got it. Be quick."

"I don't know if I—"

"Yes, you can. Suck yourself in."

Lowell gets stuck at the hips.

"Wriggle around," Sam hisses. "Push yourself out."

"I can't."

"You can."

And he does catapult out like an overweight baby from a narrow birth canal.

"Let's go."

There's enough moonlight to see their way to the dock.

"No time to stay dry," Lowell says.

"You're right."

They wade into sucking mud and freezing water, pulling the boat as they go. As soon as it floats, they clamber in.

"Quick. Over there. Pull, pull, *pull,*" and the oars bring them mercifully to a clump of rushes standing five feet high above the tide line. They push their way in between the canes, using the oar like a pole.

"Just in time," Lowell breathes.

From between the canes, they see the light in their motel room go on.

"Now we're in for it," Lowell says. "They'll call for floodlights and dogs."

"Maybe not. But we need to push further in. We'll have to stay here. I wouldn't dare try to find the boathouse in the dark."

They are now so deep inside a clicking forest of canes that they can see no lights at all from the motel.

"To be rational about this," Sam says, "the proprietor probably thought it was fishy that we didn't have a car. Probably afraid of theft. That's probably why he called the police."

"I don't believe you," Lowell says. "If you'd seen my apartment—"

"There's no way anyone could trace us to here. There's just no way."

"Even if that were true," Lowell says, "once that officer calls in a report. . . ."

"If they're watching for you," Sam says.

"We *know* they're watching for me."

"Yes, you're right."

"Once that cop calls in, they'll have our ID. They'll have our last known whereabouts. They'll get your car registration and put out a trace. We won't get past the first gas station."

"I'm sure they already have my car registration and plates. I'm sure they've had that for months."

"You *see*?" Lowell says. "So we could have been followed to the boathouse. We could have been traced to the motel."

"I suppose."

"We'll never make it out of here," Lowell says lugubriously. "We'll be reported as a boating accident."

"Okay." Sam makes a decision. "That's it. We're going to try to get to the boathouse in the dark."

"Give me the tapes," Lowell says. He manages to get the zipper unstuck and then closed. He wears the tapes where he can feel his heart beat against them.

"We've got to keep pushing," Sam says, "till we get to a channel on the other side of this clump. You better hope and pray there *is* a channel."

Exertion calms them. The canes click softly as they pass.

"Listen!" Lowell says.

They rest their oars.

"I thought I heard dogs."

"Wouldn't help them. They couldn't follow our scent over water."

"I think I see blackness ahead, instead of canes."

"Good sign."

"Channel!" Lowell says. "We made it."

"Okay. The boathouse is in this general direction." Sam points. "We have to hope the tide's still high. We have to hope the channels take us there."

The soft slap of the oars is comforting. The marsh is noisy with creatures and birds. Overhead is nothing but stars and the occasional slow flapping of black wings. In the dark, Sam almost misses the boathouse. It looms sudden as a great rock and she gives a small cry and then guides the boat between the rotting boards.

"Shh," she warns, and they sit for some minutes rocking gently in the slip, but they hear no sounds from overhead.

Sam's car is still where she left it.

"I'm going to drive without lights till we get to the highway," she says. "Then it's high speed straight back to Washington."

"I don't know," Lowell says. "If a call is put out for your car. . . . All it takes is one officer spotting you."

"What do you suggest?"

"We should switch cars." Sam stares at him. "Abandon this one," he explains.

"I hope you're not suggesting *steal*," she says. "Just what we need. A felony on our records."

"Greyhound," he says. "I mean Greyhound. That's what I had to do."

"Okay," she concedes. "But for that we've got to get to Washington first. There's no Greyhound stop closer than that." She is thinking fast as she drives. "I don't want to leave my car in the Greyhound terminal like a public announcement."

"Leave it in a supermarket lot."

"A twenty-four-hour market, yes. Okay. They never tow at those, so it'll take them longer to notice a car that never leaves."

"And there'll be an ATM. We can get more cash."

"That'll leave a trail that's very easy to follow."

"No choice," Lowell says.

"I guess you're right. We'll leave the car, get cash, and take a cab to the Greyhound terminal. Brilliant thinking, Lowell."

"Then what?"

"Good question," Sam says. "Well, we could go Greyhound to Canada."

"They'll be watching the borders. We'd never get through."

"You're probably right. Think of something."

"I'm thinking. I'm trying to think of something."

They are slipping through darkness, the car like a soft-purring feline on the hunt. From time to time, the lights of a farmhouse wink and shimmer. There is a dusting of snow on the road, and trees lean toward them and toss in the chill January wind. The stars are like bits of ice.

"I know!" Sam says. "Lou! My aunt Lou. I'll call her before we leave Washington. *She* can fly to Paris with the tapes, because no one will be watching her. Not yet, anyway."

"You hope," Lowell says.

4.

Lou is waiting at the Port Authority terminal, watching for the Washington bus. She waits at bay number 5. She is bracing herself, preparing herself, in case Samantha is not, after all, on board. This would not be a new script.

The bus arrives. She cannot see in through the dark-tinted glass. She has to wait. Most of the passengers are black: mothers with sleepy children in their arms, old women struggling with bulging soft-sided bags, young men with shaven heads and jeans so loose it seems a minor miracle that the pants stay up.

And then Samantha appears at the top of the steps and Lou feels vertigo. She feels stuck in the zoom lens of a camera that is fixated on a white-faced child at the top of a chute. The child turns back to look inside the plane. She does not want to leave. Somebody pushes her. Helter-skelter, limbs cartwheeling, she hurtles toward Lou.

"Lou," Sam says, hugging her. "Why are you crying?"

"I'm just—I'm not," Lou protests. "I'm just happy you're here."

"Lou, this is Lowell. Lowell, this is my aunt."

Lowell is carrying what Lou at first takes to be a baby in a blue canvas sling. He wears the sling low, against his heart, and cradles the infant with his arms.

"Do you have your car?" Sam asks.

"No. You told me not to."

"Right," Sam says. "Right. I forgot I said that. It's good you don't have it. But we need to get out of sight as quickly as possible. Can we take a cab direct to your place?"

"Sure," Lou says, slightly dazed. "By the way, someone called and asked for you today."

Lowell and Sam look at each other.

"Uh-oh," Sam says. "Who called?"

"Well, I don't know. They didn't leave a message."

"How did they ask? What did you tell them?"

"It was a man. Very pleasant. He said—let me think now . . . I'll try to get this exact . . . He said, 'I'm trying to get in touch with Samantha Raleigh and I understand that you're her aunt.'

"And I said, 'Yes, I am. But she doesn't live in New York.' "

"Then what?"

"Then he said, 'I know that, but she isn't answering at her Washington number. I'm a close friend and I need to reach her urgently. Do you happen to know where she is?'

"I said, 'No, I'm afraid I don't. Would you like to leave a message?'

"And then he hung up."

"On second thought," Sam says, "we won't go to your place." She takes a deep breath. "Let's get coffee here in the concourse."

As soon as they are installed at a bistro table, Sam excuses herself. "Phone book," she says. "Won't be long." She finds a Bell booth and a telephone directory and flips to the yellow pages. She makes a call.

"Okay," she says, back at the table. "I've reserved a room at some nothing little motel near JFK. Lou, can I ask a very big favor?"

Lou purses her lips, half affectionate, half amused. "Is this a new trend? Asking permission to ask big favors?"

"Would you be able to fly to Paris today?"

Lou blinks. "That's a . . . whew! Well. That certainly sets a new benchmark. Your visits are never humdrum, Sam."

"Just for a couple of days," Sam says.

"Oh well," Lou says. "Piece of cake."

"We've got some videotapes we have to get out of the country. Lowell's father was murdered for them."

Lou makes a helpless gesture with her hand. "When you put it like that," she says dryly, "how can I refuse? Let me think. Let me think. . . . I'd have to call the college and the gallery. Make arrangements. I suppose I could do it."

"Could you make the calls after you get to Paris?"

"Sam, honestly."

"I'm serious. In case your phone's tapped. Or can I make them after you're gone?"

"It's not the sort of thing that a call from a stranger can arrange, Sam. But I suppose I could call from Paris, or e-mail the department. Claim emergency."

"I love you," Sam says. "Take a cab to your apartment, pick up your passport and toothbrush, and then meet us at the Flyaway Motel near JFK. I can explain everything now, or later at the motel, whichever you'd prefer."

"I think you'd better explain now," Lou says.

"Okay. Then we'll need another round of cappuccinos."

5.

At security, Lou shakes Lowell's hand.

"I won't sleep till you call us from Paris," he says.

"Forget Paris," Lou says. "I won't *breathe* till I clear security here. Till I'm on the plane with the tapes."

They have all agreed that in spite of the risks—which are considerable—the tapes should travel in Lou's carry-on bag.

"Checked baggage can end up *anywhere,*" Lowell says.

Sam is scribbling a number on a piece of paper. "Here it is. Call as soon as you get to your gate."

"First time I've ever seen the point of those things," Lou says. She has just bought a Nokia at an airport boutique and given it to Sam. "My nerves will probably transmit signals to it."

"Call when you get to Paris too," Sam says.

"I will."

"Look after yourself, Lou."

"That's supposed to be my line," Lou says.

"This time I'll be the one waiting and chewing my nails. Bit of a switch, huh?"

"Might do you good."

"As soon as you can," Sam says in a low voice, "hole up with a

VCR and watch the tapes. As soon as you can do it safely, I mean." She frowns, and her hands move about, searching for words—adequate words—in the air. "By safely, I don't just mean . . . I'm not only talking about the tapes themselves. You need to . . . you have to prepare yourself, Lou. It's rough going."

"Got you," Lou says.

"I think you'll need some hi-tech help too. I think the VCR system is different in Europe. I don't think you can watch our tapes there."

"I've got friends from art-school days," Lou says. "Someone's bound to be in electronics."

"Maybe someone will have media contacts. If you can get the word out in the French newspapers—"

"I'll play it by ear."

"And Françoise should see them. You'll know why when you read the stuff in the first cassette case."

"Okay."

" 'Bye, then."

" 'Bye."

Lou turns back to wave from the entrance to International Departures. The automatic doors close behind her.

She puts her bag on the scanner belt. She walks through the metal-detector archway and submits her body, passive, with outstretched arms, to the attendant's wand, and goes to retrieve her bag.

"Ma'am, I'll need to check through that, if you don't mind."

"No problem," Lou says. She wants to sound nonchalant, but her voice cracks. She sounds as though she has a chest cold.

The attendant unzips the bag and pulls out, one by one, a plastic sack full of toiletries, a hair dryer, underwear, panty hose, two skirts, two sweaters, six videocassettes.

"You raiding Blockbuster?" he asks, eyeing her sharply.

"Family videos." Lou's laugh sounds fake in her own ears. "Visiting relatives for the weekend." She warms to the risky thrill of invention and knows the secret of brilliant lying is in the details. "Found a cheap flight on Orbitz," she says.

The attendant frowns. "Relatives in Paris?"

"My sister and brother-in-law are there for a year," Lou says. This, she thinks, is a kind of displaced truth; moved on thirteen and a half years and turned back to front.

The attendant opens each cassette box. "What's this?" he asks, frowning, lifting the folded wad of paper from cassette case number one.

"It's a . . ." Blizzards of words, none of them helpful, pass through Lou's mind: *documents, holograph will, shopping list, film commentary* . . . "It's . . . uh . . . family letters," she says desperately. "To preserve them, we—"

"We'll have to run all these through the scanner again, ma'am. Something magnetic caught our eye on the first run through."

Lou holds her breath as the tapes, one by one, are fed into the black machine.

Nothing happens. No bells ring. No warning light flashes.

"Okay, ma'am," the attendant says. "Sorry for the delay, but better sure than sorry, eh? We've had plastic explosives hidden in videotapes."

Lou realizes that her heart has been beating very loudly and fast. She walks to her gate. Twice, en route, she bumps into people. At the gate, she finds a pay phone at the extreme edge of the waiting area. She dials the cell-phone number. "I'm through," she says. "I've still got them with me."

On the plane, she remembers Christmas Day and desolation. She remembers danger and Virgil Jefferson, cab driver, and a small gleam of hope. *This is your year. I got the gift of reading signs, and I know it.*

Françoise will be waiting at Charles de Gaulle Airport.

Sam will be waiting for Lou's call.

6.

Amy has the puck and Lowell holds his goalie-padded legs close together. Jason slides toward Amy with blithe disregard for risk to bones. He tackles his sister and both tumble and their skate blades screech against the ice. Jason skids into his father and the puck crosses an imaginary line.

"Goal!" Jason calls triumphantly. "Daddy, I got a goal!"

"Hey, Wayne Gretzky!" Lowell says, scooping his son into his arms. They spin in a victory circle and Lowell's skates shoot off from underneath him and they fall in a snowsuit-padded heap on top of Amy. They all laugh and pick themselves up.

The skating rink is in Rowena's backyard and Lowell himself has just made it. He is proud of this. He has followed the Home Depot instructions (*Make Your Own Ice Rink*) to the letter. The temperature is five degrees below freezing and so the crucial ingredient is a given. Apart from that: simple as ABC. Lowell has constructed the outline with vinyl edging and the children have contributed the flooding of the enclosure with the garden hose. Nature has done the rest.

"Lowell!" Rowena calls from the back porch. "Telephone! Long distance."

"Be back in a minute, kids," Lowell calls. He runs to the house.

The receiver feels clammy to the touch. Lowell thinks, irrationally, of dead people holding it.

"Yes?" he says, tense.

"Lowell, it's me. Sam."

"Anything new?"

"Yes," Sam says, excited. "Françoise knows someone who writes columns for *Libération* and she knows someone at Radio France. Lou is meeting with the *Libération* guy as we speak."

"When will we know?"

"As soon as she does. In a couple of hours, I hope. I told her: I don't care what time of day or night it is, call me. She's pretty confident. And Françoise says once there's something in *Libération, Le Monde* will be onto it in a flash. And then Reuters and AP will pick it up, and you'll be reading about it in the *New York Times*."

"I don't know," Lowell says. "It sounds too easy. You shouldn't even be saying this on the phone until we're sure."

"You're underestimating a French reporter on the trail of an irresistible story: corruption in American Intelligence. Blind spots. Incompetence. Cover-up."

"I hope you're right."

"Did you go back to your apartment yet?"

"Not yet. Haven't been able to bring myself to see it again."

"So where—?"

"Rowena lets me sleep on the couch in the basement."

"Is that a good sign?"

"It's good to be with my kids. Other than that, it's not an anything sign, really. I have to find my own place, and it sure won't be that ransacked apartment. Think I'll even send Rowena to get my stuff. Bad vibes there."

"If Lou and Françoise pull this off . . . ," Sam says. "And don't forget, Lowell. They may have torn your apartment to shreds, but you saved the tapes. You got them out of the country. You did that, Lowell. And Françoise will set them loose on the world."

The children of Salamander, Lowell thinks with amazement. The guardians of the family's Rosetta Stone. The successful keepers of the Dead Sea Scrolls.

"I want to meet Françoise," he says. "I want to take my children to Paris to see their aunt."

"*I'm* going to Paris," Sam tells him. "Remember I told you I'd applied for a research fellowship? Well, I got it. I'm going."

"When?" Lowell asks in dismay.

"As soon as Lou gets back. Lou says I can stay with Françoise."

Lowell closes his eyes. People leave, he reminds himself. That is what people do. They leave and they never come back. They are never around.

"How long will you be gone?"

"I guess I'll play it by ear, but I think I'll stay all spring and summer. I want to get as far as possible from Washington for a while. And I haven't been back. . . ." She takes a long shuddering breath. "I haven't been in Paris since I was six. I've got ghosts to lay."

Me too, Lowell thinks.

"Maybe I'll see you there," he says. "Maybe I'll visit with the kids."

"I'd like to meet your children," Sam says.

"I'd like my children to meet you."

Into the silence that hovers, Sam says cautiously, "I'll miss you, Lowell."

Through the window, Lowell sees the sun glint off his ice rink. His radiant children skate through a pool of light. "I'll miss you too," he says.

"I hope you *do* visit. I hope you do bring your children to Paris."

"I will."

"I'll call as soon as I get word we've hit the press."

"I'll be waiting," Lowell says. "Samantha?"

"Hmm?"

"I'm glad you were such a pain in the neck all last summer."

Sam laughs. "I'm very good at being a pain in the neck. Lifelong specialty."

"You just never quit," he says.

"Plain stubborn, I guess. Willful, my Grandfather Raleigh used to say. Pigheaded."

"That's what got us into this and out of it again."

"Cross your fingers on the getting-out-of-it bit."

Lowell hears the *thonk* of feet still wearing skates on the back porch. "Got to go," he says. "Playing hockey with my kids."

"Take care then," Sam says. "See you soon."

"I hope it *will* be soon," Lowell says to the hallway as he hangs up.

"Hope what will be soon?" Rowena asks.

Lowell takes a deep breath. "Rowena, this weekend I'd like to take the kids to Washington to see their grandfather's grave."

"That wouldn't be a good idea," Rowena says.

"I'm not asking you, I'm informing you," Lowell says. "I have legal visiting rights, remember."

They stare at each other like duelists, and Rowena's glare gradually softens. "Take good care of them then," she says.

"We'll call as often as you want."

Rowena smiles and shakes her head in wonder. "Whoever tore your room apart did you a favor," she says. "For years you've been like my third child. You wore me out. And now you're Amy and Jason's father."

"If you want to come with us . . ." he says.

She shakes her head. "You'll be fine with them, Lowell. I know you'll be just fine."

7.

Samantha's taxi is stuck in traffic on Broadway between the Federal Plaza and City Hall Park. She is heading south toward the Staten Island ferry. Her cab has not moved for five minutes and the cacophony of car horns, so incessant, so futile, makes her think anxiously of camp cots that buckle in panic and give off screams, but all this desperate energy, all this noise, fails to distance them by so much as an inch from starkness that falls like ash. Sam begins to have a harrowing certainty that she will never move, never escape, she is gridlocked forever inside the gymnasium, in the rows upon rows of stalled cots.

She presses her damp forehead to the window of the cab and stares at a billboard, corner of Broadway and Reade. Her hands shake. The August heat comes off the black surface of lower Manhattan like an outbreak of plague: dampness leaks from her skin. The clamminess of the taxi's fake-leather upholstery disgusts her. The seat belt prickles like a rash. The pavement burns. The billboard at the corner of Broadway and Reade is made of vertical shutters that rotate: now she sees paradise: BORA BORA FOR $1500 ROUND-TRIP, THREE NIGHTS, INCLUDES CRUISE ON LAGOON AND CORAL REEF; blink; now she sees lacy nothings: VICTORIA'S SECRET: LESS IS MORE IF YOU WANT TO DRIVE

HIM WILD; blink; now she sees sky, cloud, Icarus: a hang glider, free as a bird, drifting over Manhattan: SPREAD YOUR WINGS, STRETCH YOUR LIMITS, SUMMER COURSES AT NYU; blink; now she sees hell: a car wreckage, twisted metal, two stretchers, bodies covered in white sheets, distraught child in policeman's arms: WHEN TRAGEDY STRIKES, ARE YOUR LOVED ONES PROTECTED? CALL METROPOLITAN LIFE. Flip, flip, flip, flip, paradise, sex, flight, hell; paradise, Jacob, Icarus, hell; boathouse, motel, Black Death, hell, and are her loved ones protected? Are they safe? The billboard is stuck at hell, Sam's mind is stuck, her shirt is stuck to her wet skin.

The traffic comes unstuck for a minute or so. Sam's cab crawls forward.

This is what it is like: She is in a taxi on an ordinary day in lower Manhattan, late in the summer of the year 2001. She has come direct from JFK Airport but has no luggage in the trunk of the cab. Her luggage is where? Who knows? She has filled in the necessary form. Her bag will be on the next flight, she is assured. Probably. Her suitcase will be delivered to her door.

"My aunt's door," she said.

Lou said, "Here's the address. The phone number's on my card."

"We'll call," the attendant said, "if your bag can't be traced."

Sam feels like an astronaut undergoing reentry shock. She has that homecoming feeling and she feels alien. Both.

"Where you coming from?" the cab driver asks. His name on the license displayed on the Plexiglas divider is Ibram Siddiqi.

"Paris," Sam says.

"First time America?" he asks.

"I'm American," Sam says.

The cab driver raises his eyebrows. "Sound foreign," he assures her in heavily accented English.

Lou tells him, "She's been in France for the last seven months."

It does feel like a lifetime, Sam thinks. She is somebody else in French.

Manhattan looks beautiful and strange.

The trees are in full leaf, flower vendors bloom gloriously on every corner, she smells pretzels, roasted hickory nuts, falafel, she sees poodles on leashes and the lovely half-clad bodies of the rollerblading young. The sun is shining, and the day, though humid, is otherwise perfect and flawless, but she cannot shut out the blink blink blink of the billboard and that is what it is like, she wants to explain.

Manhattan feels dangerous.

Blink, and paradise can flip you into hell, she knows this can happen any second, she knows this could happen when the traffic lights change. She has lapses. She has bouts of regression. When she has lapses, she is unable to believe in equilibrium as anything more than a balancing act on the tip of a steeple, the steeple of St. Paul's Chapel, for instance, which looms just ahead on the right. The steeple is small and graceful, exquisitely proportioned, and this is what Sam's life is like sometimes: one foot on the pinnacle of St. Paul's, the other dangling over nothing. The city unfurls southward down Broadway like a carpet, but flipflipflip, at any moment the carpet could be yanked from beneath her, the road could subside, the whole of lower Manhattan could drop into a sinkhole, the tall canyons of real estate could roar into flames.

Sam's heart is pounding, her taxi is gridlocked again at Broadway and Vesey, a shower of small black meteors is blurring her eyes, the road undulates, the buildings sway, she cannot breathe. She recognizes the warning signs of a full-scale panic attack.

Ibram Siddiqi is watching her in the rearview mirror. Is he putting the doors on central locking? The cab feels like a sealed bunker.

"Lou," she gasps, choking. "I'm sorry, I can't—I have to get out—"

She wrenches open the door and hurls herself free. She is in a jungle and she finds herself sobbing. Drivers shout, drivers give her the finger, she hears a jazz medley of horns, brakes screech, she is dodging, weaving, running, breathless, she has reached the sidewalk, she collides with pedestrians, she ricochets, she is making for a small green park with a sycamore tree.

She collapses onto a bench in the tranquil little space behind St. Paul's and waits for the shaking to stop. Her bench is a grave. She is sitting under the spreading boughs of a massive tree and she leans her head gratefully against the angel's stone rivers of hair. MARY ELIZABETH SHARROD, 1762–1770. She closes her eyes and listens to her heart prepare for landing, wing flaps down, engines in reverse, fierce windrush, speed dropping, slowing, brakes, stillness, calm.

When she opens her eyes, her aunt is sitting on the neighboring tomb.

"Sorry, Lou," she says, embarrassed. "I haven't had one of those since Jacob—not since Lowell and I first saw the tape."

"It's okay, Sam. It happens. Take your time."

"I don't know what set it off. I suppose it's being back in New York. Back in the country."

"Let's just sit here for a while," Lou says. "It's so peaceful. We don't have to go anywhere."

"Always gets worse near anniversary time." Sam rubs her hands in the grass to get rid of the jangled self that she is smeared with. She takes deep breaths. "I actually thought I'd be okay this year."

"Because the tapes are safe."

"Because we've let jack out of the box. I thought everything would be different."

"The indifference upsets you."

"Yes. No. I mean, I knew it would be discounted. Anything coming out of France can be ignored here, but it *is* out there now, it's on the Web."

"Articles in *Libération* and *Le Monde*," Lou reminds.

"And the British Press too. The *Guardian*. The *Independent*. It's *something*. I knew there wasn't going to be an announcement on national television. *We apologize for the terrible suffering*. . . ."

"But you still hoped."

"I thought at least *Harper's* and the *New York Times*. I suppose I thought at least there'd be serious questions raised in Congress."

"And instead, it's just another crackpot conspiracy thing like the 'hostage hoax.' "

"I thought I was braced for it. I was much more afraid the website would be blocked."

"Ignoring it's more effective. There's such an overload of information on the Web. No one knows what matters and what doesn't."

"But the lies and the cover-up . . . why isn't there outrage? And those horrible deaths. . . ."

"Horror doesn't reach people anymore. Horror's TV. Horror's special effects."

"Well, at least we've kept evidence alive. That's something," Sam says. "I should feel great about it. I do feel great about it. I do."

"Let it go, Sam." Lou moves over to sit beside her niece on Mary Elizabeth's grave. "You're alive. Lowell's alive. You've got years to make up for."

Sam smiles. "You should have seen Amy and Jason feeding the pigeons in the Luxembourg Gardens. Jason'd talk to them in French like the other little kids. Aren't children amazing?"

"You like being with them."

"I do. I miss them. For some stupid reason, I don't fly up to Boston till next week."

"I have a surprise for you," Lou says. "I'm not supposed to tell, but I can't resist. Lowell and the children will be here tomorrow."

Sam closes her eyes and smiles. "We're like war vets," she says. "Lowell and me. We've been through the trenches together." Her hands clench into fists. "We've visited hell. Even though no one believes in it."

"Let it go, Sam. The past leaves indelible traces. Trust them."

"Trust," Sam says. "We have a big problem with trust."

"The past leaves its own mark. Do you know that we're sitting on landfill? This used to be the bed of the harbor. Feel that vibration?"

"Subway."

"Right. When they laid this line, somewhere around 1900, construction workers found pieces of a Dutch ship that sank in 1613.

You can see bits of the ship in the city museum, that's how I know. But you see what I mean? The past leaves traces that eventually come to light. No one can stop them."

"Oh, that's a great comfort. So one of these years, when they find the bones in a bunker somewhere in Iraq and do DNA tests, our great-great-grandchildren—"

"Does it help to torment yourself?"

"It's not as though I want to. It's not something I work at. It's something that eats at me."

"I've found it's possible to live with grief and still tap into . . ."—Lou casts about for a word—"not happiness; I wouldn't call it that; but I suppose I'd call it a state of acceptance. A state of being at peace."

"I didn't freak out like this the whole time in France," Sam tells her. "Not even at Charles de Gaulle Airport. I've been calm all summer. Well, I mean, relatively calm. For me, calm."

She traces the coils of the angel's hair with an index finger.

"The dead never leave us, Sam," her aunt says quietly. Lou's voice is different, Sam thinks, since she saw the tape. Something has changed. *Serenity,* that is the quality. "That's what I've found," Lou says. "The dead are close to us. I suppose that's why I've come to love graveyards."

"Our dead aren't in graveyards," Sam says.

"They are close," her aunt insists. "The dead are gentle with us. It's the living who cause us pain."

"You mean Grandpa and Grandma Hamilton?"

Lou does not answer, and Sam lets the silence go on in the damp August air. Light comes down through the sycamore leaves like an unreliable blessing, flickering and on the slant. Police sirens bounce off the tombstones. A fire truck hurtles north.

"Lou?" Sam prods. "Do you mean your own parents? Or the Raleighs?"

"I didn't mean anyone in particular," Lou says.

"Françoise says the Raleighs treated you disgracefully. She says you felt about them the way she felt about Sirocco."

Lou dismisses this. "Oh, back then. We were both young and miserable back then, me and Françoise."

"We're so lucky she has good media contacts."

"Good political ones too," Lou says. "Ironic that she owes those to her father."

"Ironic that she met some of them in a psychiatric ward."

Lou sighs. "She's been through a long bad patch."

"Haven't we all?"

"But she's reborn now. Her father's tapes are a mission."

"Did you get the feeling she's been approached by French Intelligence?"

"It crossed my mind."

"She's got intimate knowledge of Sirocco. She could play the spider and lure him."

"I hope she won't try anything that dangerous," Lou says.

"I think she wants to. I think she wants to revenge her father's ghost."

"For *murder most foul,*" Lou murmurs. "But it's curious what can happen to revenge fantasies."

"What can happen?"

"They can dissolve. They can cease to matter."

"Did you have them about Grandpa and Grandma Raleigh?"

"Oh, I had them about plenty of people. I was a walking anguish-grenade for years."

"What a smarmy hypocrite that old man is. Have you told him you know about Arabella and Penny Lukins?"

"Good heavens, no."

"Were you shocked?"

"I wasn't shocked and I wasn't surprised, but I stopped caring about what they thought of me years ago. It doesn't matter much to Penny Lukins either. She hopes you'll make contact, by the way."

"I will," Sam says. "I will. It's just— I have trouble, Lou. . . . I'm jealous of people who knew my parents better than I did. I'm drawn to them, I'm jealous of them, and I stay away from them. I get too upset."

"Funny thing, jealousy." Lou traces the dates on Mary Sharrod's grave. "People died so young back then," she murmurs.

"Did you realize that's what made me so furious with you all the time? Not that I realized it myself."

Lou smiles. "I thought it might be because we're too much alike," she says. "A bit on the wild side."

Sam laughs. "Remember that time—I guess I was twelve—and a policeman brought me home at two in the morning?"

"I remember it vividly," Lou says.

"I was such a pain in the ass," Sam says. "I don't know why you put up with me."

"I was pretty tempestuous myself at that age."

"Lou?"

"Hmm?"

"There's something I want to know, but I'm afraid to ask."

The sun slants down through the sycamore and touches MARY ELIZABETH SHARROD, dead at the age of eight. Did she know she was dying? Sam wonders. *Let sleeping dogs lie,* Jacob warns. Sam's heartbeat skips and falters and beats double and misses a stroke and revs for takeoff. She is having breathing trouble again. "Lou? Aren't you going to ask me what I'm afraid to ask?"

"You'll ask when you're ready, Sam."

"What did my father mean? What did he do? He said he was a jerk and a coward. What did he mean?" Sam turns away from Lou and looks Mary Elizabeth's angel in the eye. The eyes of the angel are untroubled. Sam takes hold of the top of the tombstone with both hands. Her hands are trembling. "Tell me quick," she says. "I don't want him to have done something bad."

Lou leans her cheek against Sam's back and puts her arms around Sam's waist. "It wasn't so terrible, Sam, it really wasn't. If he was a coward, he was a very ordinary sort of one, the kind most people are—though you and I, in fact, aren't, and never would be." Lou ponders this as though just struck by the revelation. Surprised by it. "Probably because we're both too stubborn," she says, puzzled. "Too mulish. We won't say things to please or placate.

"There was a party," Lou says. "An engagement party for your parents at someone's house on the Isle of Palms, only Rosalie got sick and had to go home early. I wouldn't go home with her, I was having too good a time. It was a hot summer night and couples were wandering off along the beach and lying in the dunes and things got a bit wild. . . .

"I was young and giddy and going off to college in the fall. I thought, you know, that I had the world in my pocket, and I drank too much, way too much, I'd never had alcohol before. I remember kissing someone, I remember sand in my hair. . . ."

Two months later, Lou says, she knew she was pregnant and she ran away to New York. She wrote to her parents from there. *I cannot tell you who the father is,* she wrote, *because I was very drunk, and I never even knew his name. He was from somewhere up north, and it wasn't his fault. I was very willing. I was intoxicated, but I did know what I was doing. I am so sorry for causing you all such pain and embarrassment, especially just before Rosalie's wedding.*

Apart from that, Lou told her family, she was fine. She was living in a home for unwed mothers, and then, afterward, she would stay in New York and get a job.

"My mother," Lou says, "was so distraught, she had to be hospitalized. A daughter in disgrace, a wedding in jeopardy. What would people say if I didn't show up at my sister's wedding? And what would they say if I *did*? I'd be showing by then."

As for the man who had taken advantage of Lou, what else could you expect of a Yankee?

"Poor Lou," Sam murmurs. "Poor Lou. Did you . . . ?"

"I had my baby and I gave her up for adoption."

"When you said you went to Paris to get over someone . . . ?"

"I meant my baby. I was bleeding grief and I thought I'd die. I wanted to die. The only person I ever told was Françoise. On New

Year's Eve, we were drunk and depressed and we made a pact. You have to leave your violent boyfriend, I told her, before he kills you. You have to find your baby, she said. *Ton bébé*. She wrote it on my mirror with lipstick: *Il faut trouver ton BB*."

"And then you got stuck with a brat like me. What a lousy consolation prize I was."

Lou moves away, studying gravestones. Sam follows.

"So somewhere in the world I've got a cousin," she says, awed by the thought. She thinks about it. "We must have been born about the same time, because I've calculated that I was conceived—"

"About the same time, yes. The difference was, Rosalie could keep you, and I couldn't keep mine. I was insanely jealous of Rosalie." Lou pulls at long blades of grass and shreds them with a thumbnail.

"But you can find her, Lou. You can find your baby again. People do it all the time."

"Yes," Lou says. "Well, I did, in fact. But I don't want to intrude on her life. I'm waiting for her to want to find me."

"Oh, she will, she will," Sam says. "And she'll be so lucky, Lou, to have you as a—"

And then it arrives, the heavy thing Sam has been afraid to know, though she seems—quite suddenly—to have known it all her life. It rises inside her head like a plane turning into a sun. There is a crashing noise in her ears.

"Lou, are you . . . ? Am I . . . ?"

Lou nods. Sam thinks Lou nods. They are not touching, and she thinks Lou is weeping, but all she can see is fog. For a very long time, Sam traces Mary Elizabeth Sharrod's name with one finger. Tributaries of angel hair are tangled in the letters and they flow around the years of her death and of her birth.

"It was Rosalie's idea," Lou says softly. "She was such a generous person. She was a genuinely good person, Ros. She was with me when you were born."

Mary Elizabeth Sharrod, Sam's finger spells. Born 1762, Died 1770.

"They adopted you formally. They had to give up the wedding so no one would know. That's the sort of thing you had to do in Charleston in those days. In our kind of circle in Charleston. The circle the Raleighs and the Hamiltons lived in."

"So what's different?" Sam asks. "In the circles of the Hamiltons and Raleighs."

"Broke our mother's heart, everyone whispering about how Rosalie and Jonathan *had to get married* and how Lou *got herself into trouble* and how the Hamiltons *had to take care of things. . . .* But we kept you in the family, and nobody outside the family knew, and I was grateful. I thought I'd be grateful."

Lou buries her face in her hands then, but when Sam touches her, she lurches off toward the chapel. *Lou!* Sam wants to call out, but her tongue sticks in her mouth, because what name should she use? She runs clumsily, catching hold of Lou's sleeve, but Lou pulls away. "Leave me, Sam. I'll be all right. I just need to be alone for a bit."

What Sam feels is panic. She is standing at the top of a chute that drops into nothing. "No," she pleads. "Don't leave me alone, please don't."

And then Lou turns and they hold each other.

It seems to Sam that they each have one foot on the tip of a steeple, and if they let go of each other, they both will fall.

When dark comes, they are still sitting on Mary Sharrod's grave.

"We should get a cab," Lou says.

"Yes," Sam agrees, but they do not move.

The city lights blink and shimmer. The sycamore sighs.

"So my father is from somewhere up north?" Sam says. "My father's a Yankee like Lowell."

"No, Sam. Your father is your father," Lou says.

A fist of air shoves Sam like a punch and the chute tilts to vertical and she hangs onto the stone angel's hair. Knowledge rains down on her like a building collapsing. She cannot support the weight. Don't tell me anything more, she begs mutely.

"I think Ros knew," Lou says. "I think she always knew. Your father doted on you so extravagantly. I think she guessed. And I think she forgave both of us, your father and me. That's the kind of person Ros was."

A fog settles in on the churchyard, thick with presence. Sam can smell Matthew's baby powder, her father's pipe, her mother Rosalie's perfume. She smells the boathouse and the salt marsh. She smells Jacob's violin and Cassie's fear. She can feel a wave rising up within her, not happiness, she could not say that, but something rich and mellow that she could call a state of being at peace. She knows what Lou means then. She knows what her mother means. The dead are always with us; they are close; but we must cling to the living. She wants to hold Lowell and Amy and Jason and Lou, her mother Lou, in the sacristy of her mind. But this is the mystery, she thinks: how do we ready ourselves for what might happen tomorrow?

What possible preparations can be made?

DUE PREPARATIONS FOR THE PLAGUE

Janette Turner Hospital

READING GROUP GUIDE

DUE PREPARATIONS FOR THE PLAGUE

Janette Turner Hospital

READING GROUP GUIDE

AN INTERVIEW WITH THE AUTHOR

Q: Your novel has been described by some reviewers as "John le Carré meets Virginia Woolf," and one of your colleagues at the University of South Carolina said that your novel is like a spy thriller written by Henry James. Do you like these descriptions? And what do you think they mean?

A: Since I love the work of Virginia Woolf and Henry James, I'm delighted to be elevated to their company. I guess the comments are meant to indicate that I have indeed written a spy thriller, but that I'm as concerned with the nuances of the interior life as Woolf and James were.

Q: It is about terrorism, but you had been working on it for two or three years before the September 11 attack on the World Trade Center, is that right?

A: For three years before that. The idea of the novel began in 1988, and I began the actual writing in the summer of '99. I had not quite finished the first draft, however, when the September 11 attacks occurred, and that did have a bearing on the final section of the novel.

Q: What kind of a bearing?

A: Well, not the kind of bearing you might expect. In my novel, ten hostages from the hijacked plane which has been blown up are kept by the terrorists as a last negotiating card. The hostages know their chances for survival are not great, and each tells the story he or she must tell in preparation for dying. This comes late in the novel. I had blocked out the tenor and the mood of these stories in my mind, but I hadn't written them yet. The mood was stark and dark.

And then, the media began to piece together the narrative of all the final cell-phone conversations: from those with minutes to live on the hijacked planes; from those on the top floors of the World Trade Center after they realized that there was no way down. And that narrative was not at all what I would have expected. It was not stark with terror or fear. The calls seemed imbued with a kind of radiant calm. Those who were about to die wanted to tell the people they loved just that: I love you. They wanted to make peace while there was still time with any estranged family members or friends.

It rather stunned me, to tell you the truth. And it made the writing of the hostage tales in the bunker far more difficult, from a novelist's point of view. It is so much easier to write dramatic scenes full of angst and torment than it is to write tales of radiant calm. The scene in the hostage bunker was hell to write. I felt that I was walking a high wire between the risk of sentimentality and the data of authenticity: the knowledge of what people actually said in those cell-phone calls in the last minutes of their lives.

Q. So how did you first get the idea for Due Preparations*?*

A: All my novels begin with the collision of an image and an idea. There's white light, heat, fission. Kaboom: the moment of conception is like an explosion inside my head. Not just my head; my body too. I'm in a state of intellectual excitation. I'm riveted by an image; I'm obsessed by an idea, and the idea always takes the form of a burning question that I feel a compulsion to answer *for myself.* The novel is my search for an answer.

The image for this novel came from a TV documentary on World War II that I watched some time in '98. There was a short clip of people huddled together in an air-raid shelter in London during the Nazi *Blitzkreig*. There were about a dozen people in a very small dark space, and everyone was wearing a gas mask, and I was startled by the eerie sci-fi quality of the scene. You couldn't tell who was male, who was female, you could not tell what race anyone was, and you could only guess at who might be a big-built child or a small-boned adult. There was something disturbing and slightly monstrous about the figures.

Sometimes, the documentary voiceover informed me, *people had to spend a whole night like this.*

I suddenly found myself pondering this question: what would it be like to be trapped and confined for a really lengthy period of time (for 24 hours? for days?) with a small group of people, all wearing gas masks and padded suits, all knowing that death and destruction were on the rampage outside the cramped shelter, all knowing they might or might not get out of the shelter alive? How would they deal with fear? What would they do to pass the time? And if all the usual signifiers of gender and age and race were missing, what would happen to the way they talked to one another, and to the way they interacted with one another?

Because I tend always to think in literary paradigms, and because my own academic training is in medieval literature, I immediately thought of Boccaccio's *Decameron* as a parallel situation. Ten young people (seven women, three men), fleeing the plague which killed off half the population of Florence in 1348, cocooned themselves in a palatial villa in the hills outside the city. They had been shell-shocked by the nightly death carts, by the corpses in the streets, by the deaths of family and friends. Both literally and psychologically, they escaped the plague by walling themselves off from it and taking turns to tell stories to one another.

Q: So that explains the link between gas masks and the plague. And did the link between the plague and terrorism follow immediately?

A: No, it didn't follow immediately. After the dramatic and intense moment of conception of my novels—when I feel a bit like Saint Paul being blinded and stunned on the road to Damascus—there's a long slow period of gestation. Very long, really. At least a year, though all that time I'm obsessed with the image and the idea. I toy with them, I move them around in possible scenarios, I think about them, I follow mental tangents, I read widely. . . .

It was the idea of having ten people holed up somewhere, cut off from the world, that obsessed me most. That and the plague. I sort of lost track of the gas masks for a while. I guess Boccaccio just kept hanging around, looking over my shoulder. Because of him, it was ten people from the start, and that stayed at ten, though they ended up being ten hijacked hostages trapped in a bunker.

But in the beginning, the nature of the "plague" remained vague in my mind. My characters would know they would very likely die, but they would resist. They would survive psychologically by telling stories, either to themselves or to the others. At first, I thought that I would have each character narrate his or her tale silently and mentally, making wild misjudgments about the other characters which the reader would learn as he moved inside the heads of the other characters, one by one.

I wanted a sense of powerful and awful mystery: my characters would not know where they were. They would not even know what country they were in. They would be in darkness. They would not know one another. I wanted to have a kind of mythic dimension to their trauma and isolation, rather like that of King Lear on the heath in the storm. But I definitely didn't want a futuristic atmosphere or an aura of fantasy or otherworldliness. I wanted their plight to be very firmly grounded in realism and in the present time.

So I read again accounts of prisoners of the Japanese, who survived solitary confinement by retelling themselves stories, by reciting Shakespeare or the Bible, by mapping their childhood neighborhoods in their heads. I read about the hostages in Beirut in the '70s who survived beatings and solitary confinement, often in darkness, by similar means. And I kept feeling more excitement about this: Boccaccio, who himself survived the year of the Black Death in Florence, knew what he was talking about. Telling stories is essential to survival when one is imprisoned or trapped or blindfolded and kept literally in the dark.

Q: So it was the solitary confinement of the hostages in Beirut that tied The Decameron *to terrorism?*

A: I guess so. You know, the evolution of a novel is a mysterious process, even to the author. The gas masks had been there from the beginning, but they'd gone underground, so to speak. Things simmer away in the unconscious at the same time as one is pursuing another tangent at the conscious level. I followed several trails simultaneously for a long time before the novel had any clear shape in my head.

I followed the plague trail assiduously for a while. I reread Boccaccio's *Decameron*, and then I reread Daniel Defoe's 1722 novel, *A Journal of the Plague Year*, and then I reread Albert Camus' *The Plague*.

The first two writers had first-hand visceral experience of the bubonic plague: Boccaccio in Florence in 1348; and Defoe in London in 1665, the year of the Black Death. He was a child of five in that year, and all his life he remained obsessively afraid that the plague would return, and he wrote about this obsessively. He published two books and something like thirty articles and pamphlets on the subject.

Camus used the plague as a metaphor for the Nazi occupation of France; but to my surprise, I discovered not only that the town of Oran in Algeria is a real place (and not a fictional one, as I had always supposed) but also that there was a real outbreak of the bubonic plague there in Camus' lifetime.

And here is a very curious bit of Trivial Pursuit data that came to have a bearing on the novel: all three of these authors were themselves engaged in espionage at some point of their lives: Boccaccio for the City of Florence at the papal courts in both Avignon and Rome; Defoe passed information from and to Dutch merchants for William of Orange, and—here was a startling and unexpected twist, given where I now live—he acted as a sort of spy and undercover agent at the Court of King James on behalf of the dissenters in South Carolina. And Camus, of course, published an underground newspaper for the French Resistance.

Q: The title of your novel is taken from Defoe, isn't it?

A: Yes. In 1720, the plague broke out again in Marseilles. Defoe was a merchant (though a spectacularly unsuccessful one, I must say. He went bankrupt several times) and he was a politically active and involved man. He had argued forcefully for free trade with Europe and for open ports. But after the outbreak of plague in Marseilles, against his own mercantile interests, he voted to blockade English ports against European ships. He was so afraid the plague would return that he wrote two books within a couple of months in 1722. One was the well-known novel *A Journal of the Plague Year*, which is still used in university courses on the eighteenth-century novel, and so is always available in paperback. The other has been out of print for over a century. It was a nonfiction book, a how-to-survive manual, for if the plague reached English shores. It was called *Due Preparations for the Plague*. It was a kind of Red Alert of the kind now issued by the Department for Homeland Security: this is what you can do to protect yourself from terrorists: stay away from New York City; and if you're in the city, stay away from Grand Central Station and Yankee Stadium and the Statue of Liberty and Wall Street and airports and so on. . . .

And what both kinds of warning amounted to was this: no matter what precautions you take, with terrorists, as with the bubonic plague, there's ultimately not too much you can do to be safe. Both are like stealth bombers. They come in under radar, and you don't know where they will strike next.

Q: So once you had linked the plague and terrorism, how did the CIA come into it, and how did you find out so much about Intelligence operations?

A: First, I started with the idea of a hijacked plane. That seemed the most likely reason that a group of strangers would be trapped together in a small space and not know where they were. I had two actual models for my fictional hijacking: it was a blend of the 1976 hijacking of the Frankfurt-Paris flight to Entebbe, and of the 1988 hijacked flight that blew up over Lockerbie in Scotland. I read an enormous amount, especially on the Web, about those two hijackings, and this is where the idea of conspiracy and Intelligence agencies first came into the mental picture. In the Entebbe hijacking, you will remember, Mossad, the Israeli Secret Service Agency, carried out a brilliant and daring rescue of all the passengers. But what really startled me, and introduced a fresh direction to the novel, was the proliferation of Web sites about both hijackings—but especially about the Lockerbie disaster—which revealed that many relatives of those who died are convinced that American intelligence knew this was going to happen, and that diplomatic and foreign-service people were warned not to fly on certain routes within a certain time period, but that average traveling Americans were given no warning.

Now, I have no idea whether or not these conspiracy theories are true, but from a *novelist's* point of view, the idea was irresistible.

Q: And how did you find out so much about chemical warfare and the CIA?

A: Partly from research and reading; and partly from incredibly good luck. I lucked into an extraordinary source of information.

It just so happened that I met someone whose duty is to train recruits for Intelligence, and to train them in the deployment of, and in methods of defense against, biochemical warfare. He brought home for me a gas mask and the protective clothing used. I put them on, because I needed to know how it felt to be inside one of those gas masks.

It is horrible! Only the fear of death by incredible agony keeps people suited up in them. Anyone claustrophobic is done for pretty fast. There's a voice tube, but sound comes out muffled and distorted (so I knew I couldn't have my hostages telling stories with their gas masks on, as the stories would be largely unintelligible!).

I learned that even highly trained military personnel suffer severe psychological (as well as physical) problems if they have to wear masks and protective clothing for long. A lot of people vomit into the masks, and one of the drills is for what to do if this happens, because if the vomit isn't instantly scooped out, the wearer suffocates.

All of this is part of the lecture notes and part of the training, and my friend lent me his lecture notes for the course, which gave me the idea for Salamander's lecture notes.

Q: Do you always do such intense visceral and "bodily" research for your novels?

A: I do actually. And for this novel I happened to have a visceral experience of armed attack and confinement in a small cell which was terrifying at the time, but which turned out to be very good for the novel.

Q: What happened?

A: In May 1999, I was one of four Australian writers who were invited, along with our Czech-Australian translator, to participate in the Prague Literary Festival for the launch of the Czech editions of our books. From Prague, we were to travel to Budapest in Hungary to give readings at the University of Budapest.

We took the Orient Express from Prague at midnight and were to arrive at Budpest at about 7 a.m. the next morning. Unfortunately, although we were not even getting off the train when it passed through the Slovak Republic on its night ride, the guard on the train said we were supposed to have transit visas in our passports. We had heard nothing of this. The guard said he could "fix" things for us for a fee. We smelled a scam and a bribe, and refused to pay.

Big mistake. At 2 a.m., at a railway siding on the Czech-Slovak border, the doors of our sleeping compartments were kicked open by border guards with machine guns, our passports were confiscated, and we were forced off the train in the middle of nowhere. It was rather terrifying. We were all kept in a cell (the same one, fortunately, crowded though it was) for the rest of the night.

What saved us, I think, is that one of the writers had a cell phone and called the home number of the cultural attaché at the Australian Embassy in Budapest. Wheels were set in motion and in the morning we were released and put back on a train to Prague. We had to pay our own fare back; we had to pay the "fine" for not having visas; and our passports were stamped as miscreants who were henceforth "persona non grata" in Slovakia. We will not be permitted to enter that republic for the next ten years. At which point, I'm afraid we irreverent Australians burst out laughing and asked, "Is that a promise?"

Our poor translator, who had escaped from Communist Czechoslovakia under terrifying circumstances many years earlier, explained to the armed men that we were laughing because we were so grateful to them for releasing us. She told us she had to keep mistranslating our responses throughout the night for fear of further inciting the guards.

Since the novel was already forming in my head when all this was happening, even though I was scared at the time, the novelist part of me was humming with excitement: *Now I know what it's like! This will be so useful for the novel.*

Q: Is Salamander based on a real person?

A: Good grief, if he were, do you think I'd tell you? The more you learn about how Intelligence agencies operate, the more spooked you are by them. But Sirocco, the double agent for the other side, is very loosely based on an Osama bin Laden type of figure. At the time I was writing this, it was bin Laden, not Saddam Hussein, who loomed large in all our minds and in the media.

DISCUSSION QUESTIONS

1. What themes do the novel's motifs of plague and pestilence underscore?
2. *Due Preparations for the Plague* is told through a variety of perspectives. What does each narrator contribute to the larger picture presented in the novel? How does each help unravel the mysteries of Air France Flight 64?
3. Lowell and Samantha find many answers in the contents of the blue duffel bag, but what questions remain unanswered at the novel's end?
4. Guilt ravages the lives of the individuals who lost loved ones in Operation Black Death. What are the different strategies that each adopts to deal with the past?
5. How are the bonds of family recast over the course of the novel? Do their discoveries of the past strengthen or diminish the power of familial bonds for Lowell and Samantha?
6. Hypocrisy and cowardice are the vices that enable many of the cover-ups surrounding Air France Flight 64. What are the long-term repercussions of these behaviors?
7. Lowell's handling of his father's blue duffel bag might well be described as paranoid. How subtle are the boundaries between reality and delusion in the survivors' lives?
8. What might account for Françoise's attraction to Sirocco?
9. Identify the different communities to which the various characters of the novel belong. What does each community represent?
10. Of the hostages' final hours in the hands of their captors, Homer Longchamp remarks, "this reverence for death itself, and life itself, and this grief for the death of strangers—how can we account for this arising from the death of Satan and the silence of God?" Describe the emergence of spirituality in the hostages' testimonials. Does spirituality offer solace in the lives of the child survivors?
11. Through the novel, Janette Turner Hospital alludes to great works of literature from throughout the Western canon, notably Dante's *Inferno*, Defoe's *A Journal of the Plague Year*, Boccaccio's *The Decameron*, and Camus' *The Plague*. What timeless themes of morality does D*ue Preparations for the Plague* hold in common with these works?
12. List the sins of Salamander. Is he as guilty of evil-doing as Sirocco?

13. "What can be worse than not knowing?" Samantha demands when she initially approaches Lowell about the mystery of Air France Flight 64. Does knowledge really bring consolation?

Praise for *The Last Magician*

"Evocative settings, characters we care deeply about, and language that is entrancingly lyrical." —*New York Times Book Review*

"[O]ne of the most powerful and innovative writers in the English language today." —*Times Literary Supplement*

"A highwire act . . . [that holds] us with attention riveted, breath held." —*Washington Post Book World*

Praise for *Oyster*

"The mad Oyster, dead before the narrative begins, and the hate-filled mining town, dead as the last page turns, have their own bitter, brilliant reality in this impressive novel." —John Skow, *Time*

"Hospital creates her most powerful and dazzling novel to date. In sensuous prose, feverish with the cadences of mystery and doom, sometimes hallucinatory but always meticulously controlled, she spins a story eerie in its timeliness and credibility." —*Publishers Weekly*, starred review

"Echoes of Waco, Heaven's Gate, and Jonestown combine with intimations of apocalypse in a stunningly evocative story . . . recorded in luminous prose." —*Kirkus Reviews*, starred review

"A rare story and an accomplished piece of writing." —Dale Peck, *New York Times Book Review*

"One of the most powerful and innovative writers in English today." —*Times Literary Supplement*

"Hospital's finest book, a novel full of Australia's blazing, prophetic light." —Thomas Keneally

MORE NORTON BOOKS WITH READING GROUP GUIDES AVAILABLE

Diana Abu-Jaber, *Arabian Jazz*
Rabih Alameddine, *I, the Divine*
Robert Alter, *Genesis**
Christine Balint, *The Salt Letters**
Brad Barkley, *Money, Love*
Andrea Barrett, *Servants of the Map*
Ship Fever
The Voyage of the Narwhal
Charles Baxter, *Shadow Play*
Frederick Busch, *Harry and Catherine*
Abigail De Witt, *Lili*
Jared Diamond, *Guns, Germs, and Steel*
Jack Driscoll, *Lucky Man, Lucky Woman*
Paula Fox, *The Widow's Children*
Judith Freeman, *The Chinchilla Farm*
Betty Friedan, *The Feminine Mystique*
Sara Hall, *Drawn to the Rhythm*
Patricia Highsmith, *Stranger on a Train*
Suspension of Mercy
Hannah Hinchman, *A Trail Through Leaves**
Linda Hogan, *Power*
Dara Horn, *In the Image*
Janette Turner Hospital, *The Last Magician*
Erica Jong, *Fanny*
Shylock's Daughters
James Lasdun, *The Horned Man*
Don Lee, *Yellow*
Lisa Michaels, *Grand Ambition*
Lydia Minatoya, *The Strangeness of Beauty*
Patrick O'Brian, *The Yellow Admiral**
Jean Rhys, *Wide Sargasso Sea*
Josh Russell, *Yellow Jack*
Kerri Sakamoto, *The Electrical Field*
May Sarton, *Journal of a Solitude**
Frances Sherwood, *The Book of Splendor*

Gustaf Sobin, *The Fly-Truffler*
In Pursuit of a Vanishing Star
Ted Solotaroff, *Truth Comes in Blows*
Jean Christopher Spaugh, *Something Blue*
Mark Strand and Eavan Boland, *The Making of a Poem*
Barry Unsworth, *Losing Nelson*
Morality Play
Sacred Hunger
Brad Watson, *The Heaven of Mercury*

*Available only on the Norton Web site:
www.wwnorton.com/guides